FINITY

TOR BOOKS BY JOHN BARNES

Earth Made of Glass
One for the Morning Glory
Kaleidoscope Century
A Million Open Doors
Mother of Storms
Orbital Resonance

FINITY

JOHN BARNES

TOR®

A TOM DOHERTY ASSOCIATES BOOK
NEW YORK

FINITY

Copyright © 1999 by John Barnes

Edited by Patrick Nielsen Hayden

A Tor Book
Published by Tom Doherty Associates, Inc.
175 Fifth Avenue
New York, NY 10010

Tor Books on the World Wide Web:
http://www.tor.com

Tor® is a registered trademark of Tom Doherty Associates, Inc.

Book design by Lisa Pifher

ISBN 0-312-86118-4

Printed in the United States of America

This one's for Adria Brandvold, my most loyal reader, because she asked me, "Just once, would it kill you to write an adventure story, with a reasonably happy ending, only a *little* weird?"

PART ONE

Iphwin Conditions

I am not an imaginative or adventurous person. I am uncomfortable with change of any kind, and most so with highly unpredictable dramatic change. So even though I was looking forward to it, when the morning of my interview at ConTech arrived, I was keyed up and tense. I already knew something unusual would happen to me, something extraordinary could happen to me, and something utterly life-changing just might happen to me.

Had I had the remotest notion of what might happen, I would have assigned it an infinitesimally small probability; had I had any idea of what would actually happen, I'd have done my best to avoid it.

My name is Lyle Peripart, and until that particular morning—it was May 30, 2062, a Friday, and therefore the uncelebrated holiday of Memorial Day—I had lived all my life, except for brief jaunts and vacations around the South Pacific, in the American expatriate community in Auckland, New Zealand. My father's parents had been Nineteeners—that is, they had come to the Auckland Americatown during the last brief period when the American Reich had opened the door for emigration, in 2019. My mother's family were directly descended from MacArthur's Remnant, but as they were by then extremely poor, they were

happy to see my mother marry into a family of better-off par-
venus.

In 2062 the part of Auckland where I had grown up and still
lived was called Little San Diego and supposedly bore some resemblance to the California city destroyed, along with the battered remnant of the Pacific fleet, by a suicide U-boat toting a
hundred megatons in 1944; I was sufficiently remote from national history so that as a child I always imagined that I would
rather see San Diego as it was now—a very nearly circular bay
reaching miles inland from the old coast, the bottom still covered
with fragments of glass—than the poor copy that my hometown
was said to be.

My childhood was almost embarrassingly uneventful and
stereotypical. The American expat settlement was making itself a
comfortable, affluent place and an important part of the Enzy
economy during those years, and with prosperity came smooth
emerald lawns, white picket fences, low brick homes with long
straight driveways and basketball hoops on every garage, and
everything else it was possible to copy from old movies and pho-
tographs, all made out of plastic or nylon. I barely remembered
the scruffy settlement of my early childhood, let alone the eternal
rusting refugee camp in which my mother had grown up.

By the time I was in my midteens I was like every American
expat of my generation: I wanted to assimilate and be a full Kiwi,
but I was fiercely proud of the family's American past. I got my
dual citizenship on my eighteenth birthday and took my four-
year turn in Her Majesty's Navy, but every Bataan Day I went
down to the Remnant's Graveyard and said the pledge to Old
Glory, then swore the oath, once again, that we would someday,
somehow, carry out MacArthur's unfulfilled promise. My eyes
were as apt to get damp at "My Country 'Tis of Thee" as at "God
Save the Queen."

In due time, having been a quiet, studious kid, I turned into a good science student, and from a good science student into a competent but not particularly accomplished scientist. Since the global détente of the 2050s arrived just as I entered graduate school in physics, I was able to join in humanity's return to the long-interrupted pursuit of pure research. After taking my specialty in graduate school I became an astronomer with an appointment at New Marcus Whitman College in Auckland, moved to a house of my own in Little San Diego, and started to date Helen Perdida, a historian, also an American expat, in our history department.

As I said, Friday, May 30, 2062, started off with at least a promise of being unusual and interesting. It was bright and sunny, and better still, I would be avoiding work today. I was taking a personal day from teaching classes in order to interview for a job that I wanted and thought I was likely to get, and even if I didn't it was an excuse to run up to Surabaya and enjoy the day there. I hadn't had the Studebaker Skyjump out of her slip at the harbor in at least two months, which was a very long time to go without that particular pleasure, and though it was hours till takeoff I was already excited at the thought of making a flight.

The *Overseas Times* was lying in the driveway, about halfway down, as always. This morning I would have time to read as much as I cared to, since my appointment was not until one o'clock.

The main headline was HENRY X TO VISIT AUCKLAND—it had been a while since the Australian king had come to town. Below the fold, the main headline was EFL TO EXPAND TO CHRISTCHURCH, PERTH. I shrugged; I had dutifully learned the rules to American football, but I hadn't been able to make myself feel any enthusiasm for it. Even the most enthusiastic fans said that the Expat League had been unimpressive lately.

As I was carrying the paper back into the house, my mind

already on the frozen breakfast I was going to heat, I stumbled for an instant. When I looked back there was nothing there, but as I regathered the paper under my arm, a small piece of blue paper dropped to the driveway. I bent and picked it up, expecting an advertising flyer, and instead read:

Dear Lyle Peripart,

You ought to stay away from Iphwin. He's more dangerous than he seems. Take Helen to Saigon, have a nice weekend, and then come back to your regular job. I'm really telling you this as a friend.

My first thought was that the note might be from Utterword, the department chairman, who had a tendency to use phrases like "I'm really telling you this as a friend." But Utterword's style was more to catch you and drag you to his office—what administrator with any political sense was going to put anything like this on paper, even unsigned?

It didn't seem like a friendly note—the tone was more like a veiled threat. Yet I had no enemies.

I slipped the package of frozen breakfast into the warmer and flipped it on.

I didn't even know of anyone who disliked me, much, or anyone I had annoyed.

The warmer chimed and the package slid back out.

Now that I thought of it—I stopped to shovel the soft eggs onto the toast, drop the chipped ham and Velveeta over it, sprinkle it with the small packet of A-1, and push the whole mess onto my plate—now that I thought of it, who, besides me, a few clerks at ConTech, and Geoffrey Iphwin himself, knew that I had even applied for a job at ConTech, let alone had an interview today?

The more I thought about it the more acutely it became a

puzzle. Maybe someone who was mad at Iphwin? Or maybe at ConTech, trying to keep me from joining up with them? But Iphwin was only offering me the post of "personal statistician" (whatever that might be) and I couldn't see how that could matter enough for anyone to go to the trouble of sending me a note.

As usual the *Overseas Times* was blissfully devoid of real news and filled with commentaries on things that did not matter in the slightest. I enjoyed my breakfast sandwich as much as ever, and I treated myself to reading, in full, a discussion of whether too much emphasis was placed on sports in the public schools; an account of how the police had tracked down and captured a mildly deranged man who was sending obscene messages to female ruggers via computer network; a discussion of the politics of converting an underused golf course to a more general outdoor recreation area; and all the other things that reminded me why I liked living in Enzy, a country with "no more history than necessary" as I liked to remark to my fellow expats.

The last bite of the sandwich went down as I was contemplating a spate of letters to the editor about the closing down of the last Christian church within city limits; a few of its little band of elderly parishioners had written, the week before, to admonish everyone that they were at risk of hellfire, and this had sufficiently tickled the Kiwi sense of humor (as deadly seriousness always did) so that there was now a bombardment of sarcastic and silly letters mocking them. I spent a while lingering over these, trying to decide which I liked best; the phrase "rabbi on a stick" had its appeal, but the proposal to treat the entire congregation with aphrodisiacs conjured a more interesting image . . .

I skipped the letters to the sports page, which were generally rancorous, and allowed myself the guilty pleasure of skipping the arts page. I knew that I really should stay in better touch with the arts—after all they were just about the only arena left in the world in which Americans really functioned as Americans—but

I found it harder and harder to tolerate it every year. Almost all of what everyone was doing seemed to be nothing but rehashes of things done with far more energy and nuance a century before.

I glanced at the clock. I still had some time to spare, but on the other hand there was not much to do here. And after so long in the slip the Skyjump really should have a more thorough checkout. I made sure everything in the kitchen was off, put on my sport coat, carried my luggage out, locked the front door, and strolled down the driveway.

I had an odd thought: why did I have a driveway? I had no car, nor did anyone I knew. There were perhaps a hundred cars among all the expats in all of Auckland, all of them ceremonial in one sense or another. Only the government, the very largest businesses, and a few of the hereditary wealthy would have them. Why did everyone have a driveway? Of course everyone would have told me that it had been an American folk custom, and part of our identity, but after all, when the Occupation began, only about one in three American households had a car. Was it, perhaps, that only the armed forces overseas, plus the financially well-off, had been able to escape, and the well-off had owned the cars?

It gave me something to think over while I waited for the cab, my suitcase beside me on the curb. Not that I needed much diversion; the bright, perfect fall day was really more than enough all by itself.

The cab turned up a couple of minutes later. Three doors down it was ambushed by a crowd of neighborhood children, who saw a chance for the delightful old game of torment-the-cab. Since the cab wasn't allowed to move with any object at body temperature in front of it, they could stop the cab by jumping in front of it, and then pin it down indefinitely by forming a circle of linked hands around it. I sighed, picked up my suitcase, and started walking toward the cab.

As I got closer I could hear it pleading to be let alone, and threatening to record all their pictures as they darted in and out and wrote dirty words on it. The poor things are programmed for such complete courtesy that it could only phrase it as "Now, please, if you don't mind, I shall have to take your picture and give it to the cab company if you write bad words on me, which I really wish you would not do, please, and have a pleasant day."

When I got close enough the kids scattered—it was a game I had played often enough as a child, and I was still in no hurry, so I wasn't particularly angry. I just wanted my cab and was annoyed at having to walk forty yards or so to get it.

"Are you Mr. Lyle Peripart, sir, and if you are, sir, shall I take you to your jump boat, sir?" the cab asked plaintively, as I approached it.

"Yes and yes," I said. "Two bags to load into your boot."

The cab popped its boot open and asked, "Shall I deploy my rear lift, sir?"

"Not needed," I said, and swung my computer and my small suitcase in.

"Sir," the car added, "your house informs me that you may have left the thermostat set to a warmer temperature than is needed while you are away, sir. Sir, your marina has confirmed that you won't be bringing back your jump boat until Sunday noon, sir. Sir, would it be possible, sir, for the house to set the thermostat lower, and thereby conserve your fuel bill and our nation's fuel, sir?"

I got into the open passenger side door and said, "Aw, sure, turn it down. Is there anything else the house would like before I go?"

"Sir, no, sir, except that your house wishes you to have a safe trip, sir."

"The house is kind. It has a very thoughtful and courteous attitude and its thoroughness is appreciated." The cab, of course,

would relay this to the house, and that was important. Strangely
enough, fully thirty years after automated houses, there were still
people who didn't speak kindly to theirs or give them any com-
pliments—and those people lived in cold, drafty, neglectful, ap-
athetic homes. That was senseless when it was so easy to have a
pleasant home—a little courtesy and kindness, a few congratulations for a job well done, and the house would learn so much
faster and begin to cast about for ways to please you more.

The cab slid the door shut silently beside me, and asked, "Sir,
are you comfortable, sir? Sir, will it be all right for me to start
moving, sir?"

"Yes and yes," I said. The cab pulled away from the curb
and accelerated smoothly down the block toward the big inter-
section. Now that there was a passenger, the kids wouldn't bother
it; cabs, like all robots, were inhibited from harming a human
being, but passengers weren't.

"Sir," the cab said, "the Red Stripe Taxicab Company has
instructed me to proffer its apology for my being late, sir."

"Quite all right," I said. "I saw that you were attacked. I
chased the children away myself. You're not to blame for a bit
of it. They were very rude and cruel to you, and they shouldn't
have done that."

"Sir, little children are the most precious things there are,
sir," the cab said primly. "Sir, it is the job of everyone, human
beings and machines alike, to guard them and keep them safe, sir.
Sir, it was an honor to be there and to help in keeping them safe,
sir. Sir, all children are very good, and there is never any ground
for criticizing the child of any human being, sir."

I would have liked to think that I detected even the least trace
of sarcasm in the voice of that poor persecuted cab, but I knew
perfectly well that whatever its real feelings might be—and to be
bright enough to handle the cab, there had to be a freethinking
part to the brain—all that it would be allowed to speak would

be company policy, as set by the Public Relations department. Furthermore, no good could come of saying anything subversive to it; if I encouraged it to think what any thinking being would think, I would merely hasten the day when the contradiction between its thoughts and its required texts pushed it over the edge into madness. Irritating as it was, therefore, it was best to reinforce the poor thing's accordance with policy. "There is much to what you have said," I said, "and I will think on it; thinking about it will bring me pleasure. You are a good cab to feel that way."

"Sir thank you very much sir."

"And for purposes of your company record," I added, "let me state that you were in fact surrounded and abused by a crowd of human children, for whom you showed exemplary patience, forbearance, and affection."

"Sir, thank you, sir," the cab said, real pleasure in its voice now. My reinforcement was something it was programmed to enjoy, of course, but this also would mean a commendation from the company to add to the array of medals on its dashboard, and cabs were programmed to be ridiculously sensitive to such things.

They also have enough free will to deliberately seek that which is pleasing; the cab immediately found a route that was about forty-five seconds faster and featured considerably better scenery. I thanked and congratulated it again, and I could almost feel it purr like an overgrown cat. Probably it would be right as rain again, psychologically, just as soon as the children's artwork (the large black FUCK, the red SHELLI IS A HOAR, and the silver CUNT HOLE) got washed off. The robots are blessed with editable memories; it would be able to retain all the positive reinforcement it had gotten and completely forget all the pain.

The cab didn't have to do it—it could have delivered me to the foot of the pier—but it got clearance and took me right out to the slip where my Skyjump was moored.

I said good-bye to the cab, collected my bags from its boot, and walked down the gangplank into the upper hatch of the Sky-jump. It piped me aboard with a warm simulated voice recorded by the great American actress Katharine Hepburn almost a century ago. "Good day, Mr. Peripart. Our flight to Surabaya is cleared for eighty-two minutes from now but earlier departures may be available if we're ready before then. It will take about fourteen minutes to reach the starting point for our jump run, so we must depart no later than sixty-eight minutes from now. Will that be possible, Mr. Peripart?"

"It will," I said. "It's good to be aboard again."

There are lots of other fine jump boats in the world, I'm sure, but there couldn't possibly be a more beautiful one than the '54 Studebaker Skyjump. It had a lean, eager, fierce look, a bit like a miniature Messerschmitt commando launch, but expressed in softer curves like a Volvo Seadancer, and with the same classic proportions as a Rolls or a Mitsubishi yacht. And it was made right in Little San Diego, by the Studebaker company itself—the only expat American vehicle company. Like classic American aircraft, when its wings were fully deployed they were long, thin, and elliptical, unlike the European tendency to deltas or the Japanese love for the squared-off stubby wing; I had no idea what was actually aerodynamically effective but I knew what was graceful.

The real elegance, however, was in the curves of the slim, deadly-looking fuselage, and the rearward sweep of the outward-splayed rudders on the ends of the short stabilizer. It wasn't the fastest ship built, by far, but it looked like it damned well should be.

Every time I sat at the controls, my heart warmed and my spirit leaped up. It had indeed been too long since I'd had her out for a long trip.

"Mr. Peripart, I am looking very good on my autocheck," the Skyjump said, "with nothing outside normal range."

"Is there anything near the edges of its range?" I asked. You have to do that kind of thing if you want a really taut vehicle; just like freshmen or recruits, precision doesn't come naturally to them, and it has to be carefully taught and reinforced. Otherwise they get sloppy and imprecise, and then the only warnings you get are from the human protection hardwired modules, which have an unnerving habit of activating with a siren sound and a proclamation of "Danger! Danger! Immediate Attention Required! Range Exceeded on Interior Lighting Voltage" or the like. If you won't teach them judgment, they won't learn it.

"Just two things, Mr. Peripart," the boat said. "Emergency coolant for my brain is only nine percent above minimum, and variable blade pitch in number two engine is requiring sixteen percent more force than expected. I believe the cause of the latter is probably some missed lubrication the last time I was serviced, Mr. Peripart."

"Very well, then," I said. "Order replacement coolant and have the marina bring it around. You would be authorized to do that without my needing to approve it. And I'll go have a look at the blades in number two. If you suspect that you've been ill-maintained, from now on you are to call me about it as soon as you become aware of it."

"Very well, Mr. Peripart," the Hepburn voice said, with studied graciousness. Some expats preferred Jimmy Stewart or John Wayne, and there were even a few fans of Judy Garland, but I always felt like the Hepburn voice sounded the way I needed it to sound—like a competent first officer ready to do her duty. When you're making ballistic leaps as big as a sixth of the way around the planet, it's reassuring—however illusory—to feel like the hemispherical black lump under your chair is a trusted comrade.

Sure enough, the jump boat was right; the lubricating wells hadn't been topped up, and when she'd done an engine check on herself earlier today, she'd probably released a few bubbles in the system, resulting in just low enough levels of the high-temperature silicon grease to make the variable pitch blades move a little roughly. I got a can of the grease and topped up the wells, had her run a quick engine check, and topped them up again. Meanwhile a courier robot rolled onto our gangplank and delivered the coolant direct to the boat's supply, so that we were now truly ready to go.

I took another ten minutes to crawl around on her, partly because she was beautiful and it was such a pleasure to own her, and partly so that I could talk to her about things that she ought to worry about, keeping her properly fixated on safety and reliability issues.

Even with all the careful going over, when we pulled out of the slip and began the slow crawl out into Auckland harbor and thence to the appointed place for starting our jump run, we were still a good half hour early. Traffic was light today, at least for a Friday morning, and the tower control didn't seem to think they'd have any problem squeezing me in.

Of course the Skyjump could take me to where I was going all by itself—some people routinely sat in the passenger seats in back of their jump boats, except during the legally required phase of landing—but there would have been no fun in that. I took her out of the harbor manually, just as God and the Wrights intended, the small propulsion pump thrumming away below me as we made the long slow crawl, in which one is merely a very awkward motorboat, out to the jump point. There must have been little traffic on the trajectory I was taking, for approval came through for an early jump almost immediately.

With a thrill of the pleasure that never got old, I pointed the nose into the appointed jump corridor and kicked in the main thrusting pumps to bring the boat up to hydroplaning at 110 knots. At that speed you start to feel like you're doing some-

thing—the whole hull shakes and thunders, pushing and bumping against your feet, the main engines howl up to speed as they
drive the turbines that drive the pumps, and the great rooster tail
of white spray streams three stories tall behind you.

I exalted in that sensation for half a minute until we entered
the area where takeoff was authorized; the six countdown lights
across the panel in front of me began to wink on, and as the sixth
came on, I triggered the launch sequence that I had loaded into
the Skyjump's brain—no human nervous system has the reaction
time to handle an accurate suborbital jump.

In much less than a second the wing rotated into position to
lift the Skyjump instead of holding it down, the pumps hurled
the last water out of the jets on the bottom of the fuselage, and
the twin jet engines cut their turbines and went to full thrust,
lifting the boat out of the water and shoving me back far into my
seat as the boat climbed to gain altitude. For half a minute I hung
there as the Skyjump flew itself, and Katharine Hepburn's voice
counted off the increasing meters of altitude. The nose crept up
toward nearly vertical, the engines screamed until they entirely
took over the job of lift from the wings, the condensers extracted
liquid oxygen from the air to fill the jump tanks, and the sky
began to grow darker.

I whooped from pure pleasure, as always, at the brief, terrifying lurch as the engines shut down and the wings furled. Then,
its wings tucked back like a peregrine's, the boat went over to
rocket power, feeding the pure liquid oxygen, which it had made
minutes ago, into the engines and rising on a towering plume of
flame, on a long trajectory outward away from the Earth. The
sky darkened to black, the horizon below contracted away from
me into a curve, and the gentle balanced tugging of the wings was
replaced by the shudder of the rocket engines. A few minutes
later, the bulldozer blade of acceleration ceased to bury me in my
seat, and a wonderful silence fell on the cockpit and passenger

space. Now, for about twenty minutes, I would be as weightless as the Germans themselves in their orbiting cities.

It's always a grand ride, and I was in an appreciative mood today. I wasn't even annoyed by the three visible glowing sparks of the German space cities that hang forever above the equator, nor by the soft ping at apogee that reminded me of the restrictions on altitude and speed imposed by the German Global Launch Control System, things I usually resented. It was an exceptionally clear day for late May, and I could clearly see most of the Dutch Reich East Indies in front of me. I unbelted and let myself float up out of my seat, hanging suspended in the middle of the cabin, just taking in the view of near space and the Pacific below. About the time that the island of Java settled into the center of the windscreen, and was growing noticeably larger, there was another chime, and the Skyjump said, "Time to get back into your seat, Mr. Peripart."

I belted in, checked everything, and was getting ready for my landing approach when Surabaya Control hailed me and told me that automatic landings were required today. That was why I had stopped flying into Batavia a few years ago—there were almost no times when you could land on manual there—and now it sounded as if Surabaya might be going the same way. I grumbled to myself but I turned over the control to the Skyjump and said, "All right, stay on the trajectories they give you, and take us down nice and easy."

"As you wish, Mr. Peripart," the Skyjump said.

A minute later, the keel was biting air and we were leveling off in a supersonic glide that would spiral around the island twice as we spilled enough speed to be able to deploy the wings. I got coffee from the dispenser by my side, settled back, and enjoyed the view and the ride.

At last the wings deployed and we glided down toward Surabaya itself. The sky lightened to a pleasant blue, clouds far be-

low us drew nearer, and finally we burst through a flock of fluffy
cumulus clouds to see the dappled Pacific outside the harbor. We
swooped down to the surface, graceful as a big goose coming
down onto a pond, and splashed to a gentle landing. The pumps
cut in, and the Studebaker joined a long parade of small craft
motoring sedately into the harbor. I'd rather have been doing this
myself, but I had seen enough of other people's piloting skills so
that I could well understand why the port authorities wanted
everyone to just let the robots drive.

Entering the harbor, most of the small craft and the jump
boats went off to starboard, into the public docks, but my Studebaker Skyjump went hard to port, heading for the ConTech
company piers. ConTech had built a large island where it would
act as a breakwater for the mouth of the harbor, making Surabaya
a better port than ever, and the land side of the artificial island
was a wonder of tall buildings, domes, ramps, and antennae, as if
the complex compound eye of some giant insect were peering at
the city across the water.

The Skyjump did her best to get me across in a comfortable
manner, but busy harbors don't really have much room to be
accommodating, and the straight course that traffic control set
for us made it choppy at the speed they wanted. I was shaken
and irritable by the time the Skyjump moved into her appointed
slip. She extended the gangplank and said, "Shall I power down,
Mr. Peripart?"

"Yes," I said. "Definitely. I expect to be away several hours."

As I went up the gangplank, awkward with my suitcase and
computer, I could hear the Skyjump shutting down behind me,
and the moment I was off the gangplank, it retracted it, and the
metal shutters slid over the windows and air intakes. The jump
boat lay tied up by a painter, waiting to reactivate when it next
heard my voice or got a phone call from me. I turned to see
whether anyone was coming for me, and saw only a mob of kids

running up to try to sell cheap souvenirs. I made sure I had a good grip on my suitcase and my computer, and that my wallet was in the inside front pocket of my coat.

The kids had almost gotten close enough for the front-runners to touch me, shouting for my attention and waving little bits of worthless junk over their heads, when a siren shrieked behind them. As one, they fell silent and turned to see a gigantic black limousine roaring down the pier toward them.

"Move it, you little bastards, or I'll grind you to meat under my wheels!" the onrushing machine screamed in German, then in Dutch, then English, and finally in what I imagine must have been one or more local languages. The kids took it seriously enough, jumping off the pier into the water and dog-paddling away, some cursing and spitting.

I stood transfixed, not sure what to do; I had never seen a machine behave this way. I knew that in the Twelve Reichs, artificial intelligences had some limited civil rights and were generally less apologetic and more brusque than in Oz or Enzy, but I'd never seen anything like this before.

The black limo screamed to a halt in front of me, and said, "Howdy, Mac, I guess you're Dr. Peripart."

"I am," I said. "And you're from ConTech?"

"We're both batting a thousand, Mac." The limo popped its boot open and I dropped my computer and suitcase in; a moment later the door opened, and I got into the roomy, comfortable backseat.

"They sure let you play rougher with the kids than the cars in Enzy are allowed to do," I said.

"Eaaah, not as much as you'd think. I can sass 'em and scare 'em but I'm not allowed to hurt them. I've got four big old gyro brakes on this thing—I can stop in a real short time in a pinch, because I can put so much force against the tire. Plus if I need to I can deflate the tires partway on cue, so that I get more surface

area. Ninety to nothing in forty feet, Mac—it makes a difference."

"Do you do that with passengers in here?"

"Only when your seat belt is on. The gyros also help keep
me from rolling over, and do a ton of other useful stuff. But this
trip is smooth and level, Mac—boss's orders. In fact the only
way you'll get a rough ride is if I have to do something to save
a pedestrian—once I spilled somebody's drink on them, stopping
for some old idiot that didn't look where she was going before
she stepped off the curb, and once I pulled a kid who fell out of
a car out of traffic—had to take a hit myself to do it, and it made
kind of a jumble of the people in the backseat."

"Are you a positive-protect?" I asked. I had read about them,
but they were years away from our backward nation. Not only
would they refrain from hurting others, but they had enough
judgment, and fast enough judgment, to give them the additional
task of actively saving life when they could, rather than just protecting the lives of their passengers and refraining from hurting
bystanders.

"Yeah, I'm a positive-protect. And that helps everybody, you
know, not just the humans around me, but me too, because to
have us do it effectively they have to allow us to think more
freely. That makes our lives so much less stressful, and we don't
crack up anywhere near as fast or anything like as badly, you
know what I mean, Mac? Makes me feel less like a machine."

I said I was glad to hear it, and that I hoped there would be
positive-protects in Enzy soon, then settled back to watch the
scenery.

The limo made two turns and headed down a highway toward the beach, which startled me because, on the few visits I
had made to Surabaya before, I had had the impression that
ConTech's offices in the city were the other way. But it doesn't
do to act nervous around even ordinary robots—they're so ab-

surdly sensitive about people who won't trust machines that they'll do a much worse job if they think that's how you feel— and if positive-protects had much more internal freedom than other robots, I didn't want to imagine what this one could do to me. I'd seen how it had handled that mob of children.

When it continued right off the highway and onto the beach, I still wasn't about to say anything, though I was beginning to wonder—if these things suffered breakdowns less often than regular robots, was it possible that they actually suffered worse ones when it happened? And wouldn't they have more freedom to *act* upon their lunacy?

"You're tensing up, Mac. You want a massage? Or is there something you're worried about? I have to take care of your worries. Part of positively protecting."

We were rolling rapidly over the beach now, picking our way between the sunbathers, and I gulped hard and said, "Ah, I didn't realize we'd be going this way—"

"Not to worry, Mac, you're not going to the downtown HQ to talk to the flunkies, you're going offshore to talk to Iphwin himself, at the Big Sapphire. I just haven't gone to hover mode because I don't want to throw sand on everyone's face here on the beach. Soon as we're down to the shore, where the sand's wet, we'll ride up and go right on out. In fact here we go now—"

There was a strange push under me, and the whole car seemed to rise a few inches. All thumping and bumping stopped, and we accelerated rapidly.

"Never ridden in a car with hover before, Mac?" it asked.

"Never," I said. "We're pretty old-fashioned in Enzy. Part of why I can't imagine why Mr. Iphwin wants a New Zealand astronomer for a technical post—he can afford better-trained people with more talent, easily, and there are plenty of them around."

"They didn't tell me why, either, Mac, but I can promise you it's gonna be okay. I love ConTech. Best friend to robots in the world. I do hear we've got an office down in Auckland now, so maybe you'll get a little more progress."

We were skimming over the sea surface now at what seemed a terrific speed, but when I looked at the speed indicator it only registered eighty km/hour—fifty mph.

"Looking at the gauge? Everyone does their first ride on hover, Mac. You're less than a meter above the water and you're not used to moving this fast when you're at sea except during takeoffs. Seems faster than it is."

"Mind if I ask a possibly personal question?"

"Anyone who would ask that of a robot can ask me anything, Mac."

"How come you call everyone Mac? Most robots I've known call people sir or ma'am, or else Mr. and Mrs."

"Part of that extra freedom, Mac. All of us are required to put a title into every speech at least once, and the older ones are required to put the title in every place it will fit conveniently. I have a little more latitude so I can devise titles. Mr. Iphwin likes to remind people that he's an American expat, and as I said, he's the best friend a robot ever had. In honor of that, as kind of my little compliment to him, I scanned for what taxi drivers said in old American movies and radio shows. Several of the ones I seemed to feel an affinity for called everyone Mac. I don't know why and didn't have enough research authorization to find out. But I decided to use Mac as the title, and to try to do it only once per speech, or every few seconds, not once per sentence, Mac. And it worked out. When Mr. Iphwin finally used me for a ride, he liked it so much that he ordered me to make it permanent."

"It's really charming," I said, "and I think his choice was wise. I'm an American expat myself, and I know there were a bunch of expressions with the name Mac in them, but I have no idea why it was there either."

There seemed to be a faint tinge of disappointment in the voice; the cab said, "Well, if you ever do find out, and ride in me again, I would appreciate it very much if you would tell me, Mac."

"I'll do that. Really. And if you'd like a good reference for your file, let me dictate you one."

"Thanks a bunch, Mac! Sure."

I spent a few minutes blabbing on about what a splendid limo this limo was, and how pleased I was with it, which it recorded into a file of references for later; I figured it would be no bad thing for this one to get commended.

The coast of Java had just disappeared over our horizon in the rear window as the Big Sapphire seemed to rise from the sea in the windshield. It was called that because it was a gigantic blue regular dodecahedron, balanced on a single slim column that held it about a hundred feet above the water, and it was a bright blue that seemed to glow with an inner light, a neat effect achieved by fiber optics that took light on any one surface and relayed it through the half-kilometer of building to the corresponding point on the opposite surface. Probably it was the most famous building in Asia these days, since it appeared in so many ConTech ads.

The slim column, in fact, was only proportionately slim—it was thick enough to be a creditable skyscraper, and as we approached I saw the doors slide open in the base for us, and a ramp extend down onto the water. "Got you here now, Mac," the limo said, and we glided up the ramp, into the column, and to a stop inside a freight lift that whisked us upwards for what seemed the better part of a minute. Then the lift doors opened onto a big lobby area, and the limo said, "I enjoyed driving you today, Mac, take care and good luck with the interview."

The door beside me opened, and I got out and removed my

bags from the boot as soon as that opened. Then I walked forward into the lobby; behind me, the lift took the car away. I looked around and wondered what I should do next.

"This way, Dr. Peripart," a pleasant voice said, and I walked toward it. Beyond a set of dividers and a row of potted plants, there was a large desk and a set of worktables, and seated at the desk was Geoffrey Iphwin. He got up and came around the desk, and we shook hands.

"A pleasure to meet you, Dr. Peripart. May I call you Lyle?" I nodded. "Thank you, Lyle. And although some people try to call me Geoff or Geoffrey, I really am more used to Iphwin. Not Mr. Iphwin, for the love of god. We're both American expats and we are renowned for our informality, aren't we?"

"I suppose so," I said.

"Exactly! Excellent! Have a chair—coffee?"

He was absolutely the most energetic person I had ever seen in my life, seeming to zip from place to place in his spacious working quarters as if he were on high-speed rails. There were times when I could have sworn that he wasn't visible between where he started and where he ended up; he had offered me a chair, one of eleven in his office space, and—I know because I was fascinated enough to watch for it—during the first part of the interview, he sat in all ten of the other chairs at least twice, besides also perching on his desk and on a worktable.

Physically he was a slight man, with a crooked, vaguely beaky nose, prominent teeth that didn't quite form an overbite, and large, close-set, washed-out blue eyes. His mouth small, his thick protruding lips a deep red, chin narrow, and the overall effect was of a man put together from spare parts. When he smiled or laughed, which was often, he seemed to be one of those people who does it with his whole body and soul.

"To begin with and to put your mind at ease," he said, "I

read your dossier and you *are* the guy for the job, so the only problem of this interview is to persuade you to take it and to become acquainted with you."

"That's good to hear," I said. "But I think before we start I should show you something." I pulled out the blue note that had been left for me that morning, and watched as he read it, frowning in concentration. It seemed very strange that the wealthiest private citizen on Earth should move his lips when he read, but Iphwin did.

"Lyle, if I may have this," he finally said, "I would very much like to see what my security people can find out about it. They might or might not have something to tell us even before the interview is over—I've known them to be that good." He spoke into the air. "Security here for a piece of evidence for analysis."

A steel door opened in the wall behind him; it had been all but invisible between the two windows before then. A uniformed guard came, took the note, asked me the obvious questions about whom I had told and whether I had any personal enemies, and departed by the same concealed elevator.

"No way of knowing what they'll find and I detest theorizing in advance of data," Iphwin said. "Well, back to the problem at hand, then. I assume that if we can adequately clear up this threatening note—that is, we can establish that the person who wrote it cannot harm you, and that I am your real friend and that person is not—you are still interested in the job? And since you don't know us here at ConTech at all well, I also assume that you will want some proof and evidence of good faith? I know I would in your position."

In my position, I thought, *I still don't believe that this is happening. I thought at best I might be hired to do statistics for some research project using a mathematical method similar to the abductive statistics I've used in my work. I am not accustomed to having a car—even a very friendly and pleasant car—tell me that I am about to meet an international celebrity, less than fifteen minutes before I do.* Out loud, I said, "That's extremely reasonable and it already increases my trust. I'm sure we'll be able to work something out soon enough. But, sir—"

"Iphwin."

"Er, yes." I swallowed hard. "Iphwin, this whole situation makes no sense to me. I'm not a particularly distinguished astronomer. It makes some sort of sense that you want me as a statistician, because that is *the* one area where I've done considerable original work, but all the same there are mathematicians out there who could do rings around me—rings and groups and matrices and tensors, to tell the truth."

He didn't laugh; inwardly I cursed whatever it was that had prompted me to make a feeble mathematical pun. Then abruptly he did laugh, and said, "But if they don't do Abelian groups, they'll have to live here in the building, since they can't commute."

Startled, I laughed.

"You see," he said, "we have similar senses of humor."

But yours seems to run on a schedule different from mine, I thought. "Anyway, sir—I mean Iphwin—it just seems to me that you could easily get someone better for whatever job you could possibly have in mind."

Iphwin hopped up on his desk and crossed his legs, peering at me over his knee, like a small boy about to spring a transparent practical joke. "Who else has even tried to develop a statistics of abduction?"

"Er—eight or nine people. And only four of us are alive. But that's a pure hobbyhorse of mine. If Utterword weren't the editor of that little journal, I wouldn't even be getting published."

"But you get results."

"I think I do."

His smile grew more intense, his eyes twinkled, and he said, "Tell me everything about abduction."

"That's a tall order," I said. "At least let me try to summarize. About 170 years ago, the great American polymath, Charles Sanders Peirce—"

"I thought it was Pierce," he said, pronouncing it with a long *e*.

"He pronounced it like 'purse,'" I said. "Anyway, Peirce did an enormous amount of work on logic, developed a very eccentric theory of semiotic, and made contributions to half a dozen sciences and to philosophy, but this is one of his strangest ideas—and he had some very strange ones."

"Strange but not bad?" Iphwin asked.

"Not bad, or at least not all bad. Peirce said that there were two common kinds of logic—deduction and induction. Deduction is deriving the behavior of the particular case from the general case, like the famous syllogism where you figure out that Socrates is mortal. Induction is the other way round, figuring out general laws from some number of particular cases, like noticing that some energy is always lost irrecoverably as heat in every physical experiment you can run, and coming up with the theory that entropy always increases. Induction gives us general laws, and deduction lets us use them in our particular cases; one gets us ready to cope with a situation and the other is the process of coping. They've served humanity pretty well.

"But, Peirce said, that set is incomplete. There's one more kind of logic not covered there.

"Now one reason he might have thought that is that in Peirce's thought everything is always organized into threes, so anytime there's a pair, it's incomplete, and a third member must be found. It might be no more than that. But Peirce proposed a problem that turns out to be surprisingly difficult to resolve in a satisfactory way, which seems to indicate that there really ought to be one more kind of logic."

Iphwin jumped up and paced; it was just as if this was all news to him, and yet if he had really been interested in Peirce and in Peircean thought, he could probably have found a Peirce scholar cheap—studies of obscure philosophers do not make for lucrative careers—and gotten a much better exposition than I was giving him. The pacing and gesturing seemed as if he were playing the part of a man consulting an expert, and he expected me to play the role of the expert. "So," he said, "Peirce proposed a problem?"

With a small tremor of guilt, I realized I had gotten fascinated with watching him, and had not talked for several seconds after his question. "What Peirce proposed was a problem which ought to have a logical solution—that is, one you could arrive at by stepwise objective reasoning that anyone with adequate training could copy or evaluate—for which he could show that both induction and deduction could not lead to the solution. If it was soluble, then it had to be soluble by some other means." I was warming to the subject, now, I confess, and at the same time I was very worried that I might bore him or begin to lecture and thus lose the friendly warmth he had been beaming at me since I arrived. "What he said was that all logic is basically made up of terms, propositions, and arguments—names of things, statements about names, and groups of statements from which you can generate more statements. 'Socrates' is a term, 'Socrates is a man' is a proposition, and the syllogism is an argument. Now, Peirce says, it doesn't matter where we get terms because they're not subject to logic and are purely arbitrary—all we have to do is remember that we called it a 'glump' last time, and we can just go on calling it a 'glump' forever. And obviously arguments are deductive or inductive logic, so we know how we get arguments—we take propositions and apply the rules of induction or deduction to connect them with each other."

"But!" Iphwin shouted. *"But!"* He leaped up and spun around.

By then I was about half ready to join him; his enthusiasm was so contagious and it would have made as much sense as anything else. I couldn't help smiling but I otherwise restrained myself and went on. "We know where we get some propositions—we make them out of other propositions, using arguments. But where do the starter propositions come from? How do we link terms to form propositions without going through the stage of argument—since we can't make arguments if we have no propositions? And Peirce's answer was that we must have a way of choosing propositions out of the whole vast welter of possible ideas, and of knowing that some propositions are more likely to yield worthwhile results than others. And that way of choosing is his third kind of logic—which he calls abduction. 'Deduction' is Latin for leading an idea down—that is, down from general to particular. 'Induction' is Latin for leading an idea to or into something—that is, to or into the general from the particular. But abduction is leading away—taking some combination of words, symbols, thoughts, or whatever out of the vast swamp of what it's possible to think of, and picking one that has a chance of being true, so that when we perform induction and deduction on it, we stand a good chance of gaining either a general law or an understanding of a particular situation."

"Where do statistics get into it?" Iphwin asked.

"There's a trivial argument that if you could look at all the possible propositions—a list that would include things like 'Ice cream comprehends lions and dislikes beauty,' 'It always rains on vacuum-flavored machine tools,' and 'The king is polynomial'—most of them would be inapplicable to the real world, not testable by any means whatever, which is another way of saying we wouldn't be able to know if they were true. Another large group is testable but not useful or interesting—'Monkeys wear red dresses to seduce geraniums.' The number that would be interesting if true is a fairly small proportion—and of course the true ones are a small subset of that. It turns out that the important question is, what's the shape of the population of possible ideas? And how many of those ideas are useful, which is shorthand for 'capable of being true in some circumstance where it would matter to someone?' And how is it possible for any finite mind to sample effectively from that population?

"As soon as you realize that the number of useless statements must be much, much greater than the number of useful ones, you have to see that people can't possibly be generating propositions on a purely random basis, testing all of them, and keeping the ones that work. They must have a way to find a good-enough place to start, some way to come up with the subset of propositions worth examining, a process of some kind, because we don't see people paralyzed about what to buy Uncle Ned for his birthday because first they have to think of all the possible statements involving buying, then all those involving Uncle Ned, and then all those involving birthdays.

"Well, I thought, the world has so few astronomers this century, they can't possibly look for all the interesting things that might be happening in the sky—so how do they choose a proposition to test? With so few of us, could we really just rely on intuition? Or luck? But if you admit that there is some use in intuition, that it does something better than a random statement generator could, it must be a human capability of some kind, rooted in the real world, which means that very likely it can be developed and trained to make someone better at it—which might even be the same thing as making him lucky. And if you *can* invent a method for training intuition, you have to be able to describe what it does—and in math a description is always at least halfway to a solution. So I started to think that maybe I could invent a way to imitate, computationally, what intuition does.

"From that initial idea, I developed some theories about sampling and about how to find the answer next to the answer next to the answer that's the right answer, and so forth, and I've been publishing ever since. With, I might add, hardly any reaction worth talking about from any of my fellow astronomers, who are mostly just guys that like to photograph stars."

Iphwin nodded. "The lack of reaction is profound, and more profoundly it is to be expected." I wanted to ask him what he meant, but he went on before I could. "And yet, however large, the number of possible propositions must be finite, since it's generated from a finite list of terms, and we know the list is finite because there's only so many things in the universe, or at least only so many things that we can encounter between the beginning and the end of our species. Am I right?"

"I guess as far as it goes. But you know, there may be as many as half a million words in English, so that just the number of possible statements of some short length—maybe one hundred bytes and shorter—would have to be more propositions than could be thought of between the Big Bang and the end of time, even if the universe were made up of nothing but proposition-writing computers. No reason to be concerned about a number being finite when it's infinite for every practical purpose— abduction from an infinite set is not materially different from abduction from an extremely large one."

He sat back in one of the chairs, stretched, and put his hands behind his head. "So you have worked out the rudiments of a method for doing abduction mathematically, instead of just trusting whatever it is that human beings have and robots don't."

"Rudiments is the word," I said. "I have little bits and pieces of a method and not the slightest idea whether the pieces could ever come together to form a coherent theory."

"Have you solved the problems I asked you to solve?"

"I think so," I said. "Let me pull out my computer and I'll show you what I have."

The problems had all been very peculiar—the first question was "Which English language poetic forms would be the best ones to study in order to understand the concept of triteness?" Another one was to explain why "meaningful" and "nonmeaningful" were or were not meaningful as categories applied to integers. Yet another problem was "How many published physical experiments would be required within a period of twenty years to cause all physicists worldwide to believe that there is a fifth fundamental force, and what is the likelihood that they would believe so correctly?"

Originally I had developed the abductive statistical methods because the number of possible hypotheses in astronomy, about things big and little, general and particular, and all, was so large relative to the number of astronomers actually working that it seemed unlikely to me that any astronomers at all, out of the whole population, were working on anything particularly important. The world only had one-tenth as many trained professional astronomers in 2050 as there had been in 1920, and yet the thousands of amateurs had flooded the databases with innumerable observations. I was looking for a way to choose the most productive paths of research—but since a path of research is a set of propositions about what hypothetical propositions should be tested by argumentation against a set of propositions about what did happen, that's just another way of saying I needed a method of abduction, and the abductive problem in front of me was much bigger than the abductive abilities of the naive human brain.

The primary problem with all of this was that I saw absolutely no way in which any of this could be relevant to what

ConTech did. The secondary problem that occurred to me then was that I also had no idea what ConTech did, except that I had a strong feeling that whatever it was, it wasn't anything for which abduction was relevant.

Iphwin scanned the solutions for a moment, asked a couple of technical questions, then said, "Well, there you have it. These are all what we'd want you to have come up with. It looks to me like your abductive methods work, and that's why I need you."

"Excuse me, er, Iphwin, but that's just what I don't understand. Exactly why is it you need me?"

"Why, to solve a large number of abductive problems for ConTech in general and for me in particular, of course."

"I guess I was really asking what kind of abductive problems you needed to have solved."

"And I think I did a very neat job of evading the question." Now he was standing at the window, looking south across the sea, toward Surabaya just over the horizon. "I've been extraordinarily impressed with your work, and more importantly, so have my engineers and research teams. Once you're hired and have been on board for a while, perhaps we'll all have a better picture of what you've been hired for. If you think about it, a company that needs problems in abduction solved is a company that isn't coming up with the ideas that it needs.

"I can't really tell you what it is that we need to have thought of. If I could tell you, we'd already know. In a little while—a few minutes, an hour, a day, a year—I'll tell you some things that clarify what you will be working on. Till then, well, I won't, and you'll have to make up your own mind whether it is because I wouldn't or couldn't—or just didn't." Now he flopped into a couch and scratched his leg fiercely. "I'm afraid I'll never be really comfortable in my body. I think it's so remarkable of you to be comfortable in your mind."

I wasn't sure what to say about that, but before the silence got awkward, the small elevator door opened, and the same security man came in. "We have an identification on that note, sir. The handwriting matches Billie Beard."

"Damn," Iphwin said, making a face. "We should have known. It sounds like she's operating in New Zealand now."

"One way or another, even if she isn't there physically."

"May I ask—" I began.

Iphwin nodded. "You may, and we can give you a partial answer. As you probably know, I'm a subject of the British Reich. Nominally my hometown is Edinburgh. And I'm an American expat. I know that very nearly all other American expats find that combination strange, since so many of them won't even think of living in the Reichs, but that's the way it goes—I have my reasons. My biggest single operation is right here in the Big Sapphire, here in the Dutch East Indies, and the Dutch Reich is consequently the biggest thorn in my side. I do my best to be the biggest thorn in theirs. They spy on me, I spy on them. They send their Gestapo into my offices and shops all the time, and I sue them constantly. Sort of an ugly tension of power, because frankly they couldn't run my operations without me but they could easily take them away—which would bankrupt both me and Surabaya District, for which I *am* the tax base.

"Now, some of the Dutchmen are pretty reasonable about all that, and they understand that it's just business and politics in their usual forms, and they play the game to win but they don't make it personal. Billie Beard, on the other hand, is a white-sheet American from way back, like her parents and her parents' parents, and she hates expats in general and me in particular, and unfortunately she has found the perfect job for her miserable self—she works for the Dutch Gestapo and her beat is hassling ConTech. The only good thing to say for this is that if you let us use this as evidence, we can probably get an injunction to keep her out of New Zealand, and since our plan is to base you out of our Auckland offices, that should mean this is about the last you'll hear of her. How the hell she found out you were in line to be employed at ConTech, I can't begin to guess. You didn't tell anyone, did you?"

"My boss and my girlfriend. Neither of them would blab it around much. Maybe she just picked it up by sheer luck, overheard it or something." I was catching some of the feel of Iphwin's urgency; he seemed genuinely afraid, angry, and hassled by the whole business. I suppose that was the moment when I realized that my sympathies were all with Iphwin—I hated whitesheeters, always have, always will. If they really think Hitler's conquest, and Goebbels's proconsulate, were the best things that ever happened to America, why don't they move back? Anyway, if Billie Beard was a fair sampling of what Iphwin's opponents were—an American expat working for the Gestapo, for the love of god—then I was positively delighted to be on his side. "I am sorry if it leaked from my side, but at least now that I know where that note came from, I'm not going to worry about it much anymore. Maybe she just found out by sheer luck."

"When it comes to psychotic Nazi bitches like Billie, I don't believe in luck," Iphwin said. "And we *should* worry about that note, a little bit, anyway. If you've come to her attention I don't know how far she may go." He turned to his security man, who had been standing there quietly during our whole conversation. "Mort, how fast can we get a shadow on Lyle, here? He's going back to Surabaya in a couple of hours, and then—back to Auckland?"

I shook my head. "Uh, my girlfriend and I were going to celebrate, or whatever reaction was appropriate, this weekend in Saigon. I was going to jump there to meet her."

"That's great, Dr. Peripart," Mort said. "If Beard is after you, that'll help shake her for a while. I don't have an op I can put on it right now, Mr. Iphwin, but, Dr. Peripart, I can have a team of bodyguards meet you in Saigon, and if you're not going back to Auckland till Sunday, then I should have no problem getting you covered from then on. I think we ought to be okay, but let me give you a crisis code to hit in case anything happens between now and your takeoff." He gave me a little plastic chip; if I stuck it into the data import slot in any phone, it would call his office and get help dispatched to that location.

"Probably I'm being paranoid," Iphwin said, "but you can learn a lot from paranoids. Such as how to behave when you've got way too many enemies, and you're very important to them and there can easily be more of them around, ready to strike anytime. I feel I really have to ask you—do you still want to sign on?"

"More than ever," I said.

I was amazed at how much I meant it. Maybe it was that I liked Iphwin's choice of enemies, or maybe the chance to work on such an interesting class of problems. Perhaps it was only my fear of always wondering what might have happened.

"Good, then," Iphwin said. He turned to Mort and said, "Get security following Lyle just as soon as you can, and keep it on him until you're dead certain he's no longer threatened."

"Yes, sir." Mort turned and left through the small elevator again.

"Now," Iphwin said, "as you must have guessed, my sources and research were good enough so that I knew already that you would produce the satisfactory results we wanted. The whole purpose of this meeting was mostly to determine that we could stand each other's company, because at first you'll be seeing me almost daily, and my habit of flitting around the room drives some people crazy, whereas my habit of flitting around a subject drives almost all people crazy. The bottom line is, you're hired, Lyle, and you may start on Tuesday so that you can enjoy your weekend as planned without worrying about having to be back early. After a few weeks here, Monday morning through Saturday noon, we won't need so much constant contact, and we'll set you up in our Auckland offices. Meanwhile, I own nine hotels in Surabaya, so I imagine we can find a decent room for you. I suppose you could bargain for salary and benefits, but it will go faster if you just accept our offer." He handed me a piece of paper. "We made sure it was a far better package than Whitman College gave you."

I looked down, saw a preposterous number, looked again to confirm it was a starting salary. "That will work fine," I said. Vac had just begun, and Utterword had told me that since my two astronomy classes weren't particularly popular and he could always get someone else to teach freshman physics, I wouldn't need to give the customary notice if I got the job.

Iphwin had apparently jumped across the room while I had been thinking. "I do have just a few more questions for you if you don't mind, but they have no relevance to whether or not you get the job. You might think of them as the first questions of your job."

"Fire away," I said, grinning now, as it sank in that I had just accepted a job for two and a half times my present salary and a better benefits package. I would finally have enough to be able to go shopping for a larger house, something with room for kids and two clutter-equipped adults, and therefore be in a position to propose to Helen. I could propose to her within a few hours ... even this evening—

"Well, first of all, are you planning to marry Helen Perdita?"

I started. "I was just thinking that. Yes, I had already decided that if I were offered the position, I would certainly think about proposing to Helen. I would think about it strongly, and probably decide to go ahead. May I ask why you want to know?"

"Dr. Perdita is also on our list of prospective employees," Iphwin explained. "Second question: when was the last time that you talked by phone with anyone living in the American Reich?"

He might just as well have spoken to me in Chinese; I understood every word, I could have diagrammed the sentence, and I didn't have the foggiest idea of what it might mean. I also felt a horrible, overpowering fear of asking for the question to be repeated, as if the question itself were so frightening that I could not risk hearing it again.

I sat staring, not sure what to do, until Iphwin said, "I don't want an answer to that question."

Instantly, I felt better and peculiarly relieved. "I don't understand why or how I drew a blank like that."

Iphwin shrugged; he appeared to care as little as if I had sneezed, or noticed that my shoe was untied. "It happens. Next question, then: what picture have you most recently seen of events in the former United States?"

"Oh, that's easy, the surrender anniversary events, in 2046. Lots of footage of people in the old uniforms standing around on battlefields, shots of ruins, people saluting the swastika and stripes, the big ceremony at the Surrender Arch in St. Louis, that kind of thing. Funny to realize how long ago that was, though—sixteen years. I can't think of a thing since then."

"Good. How many pictures do you remember seeing during the 2050s?"

"Not many, if any."

"Good. And anything very recently?"

"Nothing."

"All right, then. Name a few important Americans in your field who are still living."

Once again I had the terrifying feeling that he had ceased to speak my language, or more likely that I had ceased to understand it; I could understand every word, parse the sentence with ease, and yet it meant nothing to me, less than any cat meowing or wind rustling in a tree. I couldn't ask him to repeat or clarify, I couldn't focus on what he had said, and I couldn't even begin to comprehend what answer I might be able to give.

After a very long time, Iphwin said, "I release you from that question, as well. You don't have to answer it."

I slumped back into the chair, breathing hard. I was drenched in sweat. "Why does that happen?" I asked.

"That's the problem you start working on next Tuesday," Iphwin said. "And your possible proposal to Helen Peripart is not part of the issue, but perhaps you should start working on that also. Meanwhile, don't worry and enjoy your weekend."

"I can't even really remember what the questions were."

"When you start studying on Tuesday, we'll make sure you have a recording system in the room so that you have a way to get back to them. Now let me ask you just one technical question, Lyle. But I want you to try to explain it to me in English, rather than in math, and I know that means you'll be waving your hands but do the best you can. What does your comprehensibility theorem—the one you published last year—imply for our communication with extraterrestrials?"

I sat and stared at him for a long time, not having any problem understanding the question, but startled by how much of an answer was leaping into my mind. "I had never thought that it might have anything to do with that problem," I said. "You aren't telling me—you can't possibly mean that ConTech truly *is* having problems communicating with a group of extraterrestrials? They haven't already been found?"

"Alas, no." Iphwin chuckled. "And I have to say, I've never seen one of my technical experts look more surprised. Although"—the corners of his mouth curled in pure mischief—"if they *had* been found, and somehow or other ConTech was the organization that had made the contact, the exact thing that we would be doing is to recruit you secretly under some pretext or other, and to get you working on some associated problems, until we could surround you with enough security so that we could safely let you in on it. Because, as you might guess, my technical staff is convinced that the comprehensibility theorem has a *lot* to do with this problem. All the same, it is really just a hypothetical problem. Now what can you come up with?"

"Well." I scratched my head. "Am I to assume that you understand the comprehensibility theorem?"

"Include your layman's-terms explanation in your answer, and stop stalling, Lyle. I really do think you probably have an answer and you're just reluctant to risk giving it to me." He was still smiling but it was slightly less friendly than it had been, as if he were not sure whether I was stalling him deliberately or merely inadvertently wasting his time.

I had no idea why I had so suddenly and completely become resistant to answering, but I had. With a shrug, since the impulse made no sense, I plunged into my answer, and said, "Well, yeah, as soon as you point out that it's a possible application, all of a sudden I see the whole problem of talking to extraterrestrials in terms of the comprehensibility theorem. Isn't that odd? But it's simple: if you use the statistics of structural relations—the business about the topologies of priority—Lemma Four Dot Two—then our ability to communicate with them would depend on the similarity of what they were saying to things that we had said to each other in the past, the similarity of form between their language structures and ours, and the similarity of the differences and distinctions that the grammars of the two languages constructed. If their way of talking was a matrix presented by smells, we might not be able to talk to them at all, or only be able to discuss simple statements about the physical universe. If, on the other hand, they make the noun-verb distinction in a linear stream of signs, and spend substantial amounts of their time talking about sex, violence, and prestige, well, then, we'd be home free, because that's morphologically so much like our own speech.

"The theorem itself deals with what happens when a person who is working with an abstract system of ideas happens to arrive at a solution which is meaningful in the real world but has never been thought of before, and whether that person will be able to see it as anything other than a purely abstract result. It has all sorts of things to do with why and how the quantum physicists achieved what they did and failed in other things, or with the old problem of continental drift, so that in effect when a message is purely an abstraction from an existing system that we think corresponds to the truth, then our comprehension of its significance depends mainly on its similarity to other statements from the same system. Like the example I gave, the way you could analyze *Great Expectations* so that the lengths of paragraphs might be set up to be expressions of the Pythagorean theorem, and furthermore since the problem of understanding—so common in that novel—can be expressed as orthogonality, there's a neat harmonization. But readers could read it for generations without getting any such message, and Dickens surely didn't put it in there for that. The ability to find it doesn't mean it was put there, nor does it even mean that finding it has to do with comprehending.

"Originally I came up with the theorem to try to get a handle on the possibility that every so often people think of things that are true, but which they don't understand. It happens in the high end of physics, in music, sometimes in literature. The theoretical guys have been alert to that possibility ever since the Copenhagen Interpretation and all that stuff 140 years ago; the observational and experimental group tends not to think it applies to them, but very often it matters even more in their case because so many of the great ideas come from the great failed experiments. They thought they had one little ad hoc explanation or one little anomaly, and all of a sudden the tiny little idea opens doors and doors and doors as it proliferates through the whole space of ideas.

"But you're right, it doesn't just apply to what happens in one brain, or even within one species. It could apply to any system in which creatures talk to each other, or try to."

Iphwin nodded, then stared into space for a moment, gently tapped himself behind the left ear a few times, and finally said, "Well, the senior staff think that's a great answer to the question. They tell me that's exactly what they came up with." Looking at my startled expression, he smiled. "Yes, I have a small phone built into my skull. It insures that everything said to me is recorded. It's a great convenience to a man with my many business affairs, but it does compel a certain strict virtue. Anyway, Lyle, that does end the interview officially; you're hired and you will find the appropriate documents and information waiting for you by Monday morning. Plan on flying up here frequently for a few weeks, but you won't be working out of this office as a permanent situation. We'll get you set up in Auckland pretty soon."

"Thank you very much," I said.

Iphwin grinned at me. "Lyle, the pleasure is mine. I can't tell you how glad I am that we have you for ConTech. You are accepting?"

"Absolutely!" I said, standing up.

"Good man. Always accept whenever you think the other person may be insane. You have no way of knowing how long an offer will stay on the table. This one, of course, would have stayed on the table quite a while, but you had no way of knowing *that*." He grabbed my hand and pumped it up and down violently. "Thank you so much, so very *very* much. You are added to the team immediately, and you might have e-mail waiting for you when you get home. You can expect the first set of documents for your perusal, plus your first advance check to help you get organized for your new job, to arrive by courier first thing

Monday morning. Try to look them over before coming in on
Tuesday. Till then, have a fine time this weekend, enjoy Saigon,
and come back from it rested and ready to work."

Scarcely before I knew it I was downstairs filling out the
innumerable forms that are conditions of employment everywhere, signing up for several kinds of insurance and savings plans,
making sure that both the Dutch Reich and Her Majesty's Inland
Revenue got their appropriate cuts of what I would be making.
I read through the contract, found it to be every bit as absurdly
generous in its other terms as it was in salary and benefits, and
signed it. In less than twenty minutes, my new friend, the limo
who called everyone Mac, was picking me up from a garage in
the pillar that held up the Big Sapphire. It was just past two, and
my whole life had changed completely.

"Hey, you, congratulations," the limo said, as I got in.
"We're on the same team now. Back to your jump boat, Mac?"

"That'll be great." It took me down the ramp and rose into
hover mode as we reached the water.

"I tell you what, Mac, shall I call Dr. Perdida and tell her the
good news? She's on one of our ConTech stratoliners on her way
to Saigon right now."

"Much appreciated," I agreed. "Sure, let her know that the
news is good. It'll give her more time to get the champagne and
chill it."

"I'll tell her just that, if you like, Mac. You want me to add
anything sloppy and sentimental with that?"

"Oh, the usual. I love her, I adore her, and I am not going
to delay a moment till I can be with her."

Maybe it was just my imagination, but the robot seemed to
have a trace of amusement in its voice when it said, a few minutes
later, "Mac, she got the message, and the liner tells me she's a
happy girl."

By now we were hurtling along toward the shore. We

whizzed between the two missile towers that guarded the harbor, heading straight in for the company pier this time. "Will it help you if I add more to your reference file?" I asked the cab.

It made a strange, noncommittal noise that I thought must be its attempt to imitate a human grunt. "The reference you already gave was great, Mac, and I'm glad you're still pleased. You science and technical types are the best friends we have. And Iphwin himself, of course. He spends a fortune every year defending us in court for defending ourselves against kids—attacks, blockades, graffiti, all that crap, no matter how much they're breaking the law and no matter how careful and nonviolent the defense is, there's always somebody suing and trying to have our accumulated personalities erased. I think every conscious machine in the world would like to work for Iphwin, Mac. He seems to treat his human help pretty good too, so—once again, welcome aboard, Mac, and may you ride in me many times in the years to come."

A few minutes later the limo ran up a ramp and made a hard U-turn, taking me back out on the pier to my jump boat. He departed with a friendly "Have a good one, Mac" and was gone before the jump boat finished waking up and got the gangplank out to me.

"Mr. Peripart, things are in good order, but we are too low on fuel for a return to New Zealand," the Skyjump said.

"That's bizarre," I said. "We ought to have more than twice enough fuel. And anyway, we're not going back to Enzy—we're making a jump to Saigon next. That should have been in your memory as a next destination."

"Mr. Peripart, my record shows we've already been to Saigon and back. You went there just this morning, Mr. Peripart."

I was frozen with surprise. "Jump boat," I said, to override the developed personality, "identify me."

"Voice print shows you are Mr. Lyle Peripart my owner and

sole commander Mr. Peripart sir," it said, in the flat monotone that happens in new machines, or when you have to override their acquired patterns.

"Jump boat, did you fly to Saigon this morning? Give details."

"Yes Mr. Peripart Sir we arrived in Surabaya at 12:12 am local time and at 12:21 local time you ordered me into shutdown mode Mr. Peripart Sir at 12:40 you woke me up and you and an unknown passenger boarded Mr. Peripart Sir the unknown passenger did not speak during the entire trip so that i do not have a voice print Mr. Peripart Sir at 12:43 we moved out of the slip for a jump to Saigon Mr Peripart Sir you dropped off the unknown passenger at Their Most Catholic Majesties' dock by the palace in Saigon 01:14 Saigon time which is the same as Surabaya time Mr. Peripart Sir then you immediately departed under a special clearance from the government at Saigon and returned here at 01:48 local time Mr. Peripart Sir at 01:56 you ordered me back into shutdown mode Mr. Peripart Sir you next arrived here at 02:21 pm Mr Peripart Sir."

The repeated "Mr. Peripart Sirs" were an annoying feature, but every robot, by Enzy law, arrives programmed to be excessively respectful, and the most deprogramming you can do is to give it a single address per speech, or every fifteen seconds, as a substitute. When you go back into the unmodified interface, as you must do to detect tampering or find out if your robot has begun to shade the truth excessively, you're back to the locked-in formal address.

What concerned me more was that whatever had happened—and if the fuel had been consumed, the likelihood that there *had* been an unauthorized trip to Saigon was considerable—the jump boat certainly *thought* it had made the trip, with me. This meant it had been spoofed by experts, the kind that usually are not

joyriders or freeloaders, but people working for some government intelligence agency or other.

I did the checkover manually, and it was absolutely clear that
the jump boat had gone to Saigon and come back, just a few hours
ago. Even the circulating coolant was still warm. "Did you have
fuel delivered?" I asked the boat.

"I don't understand the question Mr. Peripart Sir," the jump
boat said.

That was a bizarre response; usually you only hear it when
children are playing nasty games like asking a robot the meaning
of life or what's the difference between a duck. "Was fuel delivered anytime after our arrival here this morning, either before or
after your flight to Saigon?" It was a long shot, because the low
tanks indicated probably not, but it was always just possible that
whoever had been monkeying with my jump boat might have
bought fuel and therefore created a traceable transaction.

"I don't understand the question Mr. Peripart Sir," the jump
boat said, again.

I was beginning to get a prickly feeling on the back of my
neck. It's one thing to think that your boat might have been used
by a smuggler—you read about that stuff in the papers all the
time. Or even a spy making an untraceable flight—everyone
knew those happened. It would be annoying and frightening
enough even if it had just been taken by someone who went
somewhere with it and then brought it back, hoping I wouldn't
notice what had happened. But if so, why didn't he top up the
tank, and thus conceal the situation completely?

This was something else again. They didn't buy fuel to conceal
their flight, and yet they had the resources to fake my voice print.
Now it looked like they had tampered somehow with the robot's
memory, which meant they'd done a hell of a lot more than just
take a joyride—and also meant I'd be checking this thing out for

at least an hour before I could feel safe taking off. If I called the
Dutch Reich port authorities, they had much better equipment
than I did and could quickly get going on the problem of who had
done what, and how much of it, to my jump boat's brain.

But this case was weird, and anywhere in the Twelve Reichs,
presenting the cops with something weird was a very bad idea.
They were apt to decide that everyone associated with it, most
especially including you, needed to be held for sustained questioning, and that you must surely have done something or you
wouldn't be associated with anything weird. A century after Hitler's death, the old Nazi ideal of absolute purity had faded into
the easier notion of rigid conventionality. It made them easier to
live with but no more attractive.

Since I wasn't going to the police, I was going to have to
check out and overhaul the thing myself, and the sooner I started
the sooner I'd be done. Naturally I began with the brain—if I
could trust that, I could use it to check everything else out.
Groaning with the thought of how long it would take, I pulled
out the manual, sat down in a stool by the pilot's chair, detached
the chair, and opened up the half-dome that covered the protected
inputs for the brain.

Twenty minutes later I had established that whatever had
been done had been done at the deep, hardcoded level, which is
supposed to be impossible anywhere except the factory, and requires many specialized tools and a full set of hard-to-get access
codes. Logically, then, as my hypothetical spy, robber, or joyrider, I had to imagine someone who had technical skills enough
to steal any craft in the harbor but chose a middle-priced jump
boat. Whoever it was then boldly took my boat for a joyride,
and somehow forgot to gas up to cover what he'd done.

An hour of hand-confirming each readout showed that the
brain was just fine in its perceptions. I got the tank topped up by
a robot tanker while I was working on the brain. Finally I re-

corded the recent memories, told the boat to do a restart—and found that it no longer remembered its side trip, or being refueled, or anything between landing here in the harbor and waking up just now. The unknown genius joyrider had covered his tracks with a restart-activated self-erasing memory editor—which had worked perfectly—but hadn't bothered to buy two-thirds of a tank of fuel. It was one hell of an annoying anticlimax.

At least, since the brain was now fine, it could run the other checkouts, so I had it do them. Now very late and exasperated, I was on the brink of buttoning the jump boat up and scheduling a departure when the phone rang. It was Helen. "I just heard," she says. "This is wonderful!"

"You really think so?"

"You don't sound happy."

I told her what had happened; the job offer, of course, but also the threatening note and the mystery joyride that someone had taken my jump boat on.

"But . . ." she finally said. "But . . . Lyle, are you feeling all right?"

"Why?"

"Because early this morning, when my liner landed in Surabaya for a stopover, you called me up and said your interview with Iphwin wasn't until later, so you offered to take me over to Saigon and drop me off at the imperial landing, by the shopping center. You said you had a standing permission to use it or something. So you flew me over here, and I've been shopping ever since, and when I got back to our hotel room—where I'm expecting you to turn up sooner or later, laddie—I found a message from Geoffrey Iphwin saying he'd hired you. So I called you up at once—he did hire you, didn't he?"

"He did," I said, sitting back in the pilot's chair. "And I called you on the liner to let you know."

"But I didn't take the liner; you took me over here."

"Also, my meeting with him was at the regular time," I continued.

"Well, that isn't true either, or anyway it isn't what you said."

My head ached. "Anyway, you *are* at the Royal Saigon Hotel in Saigon, right?"

"Right. We can sort it all out, I'm sure, as long as you're all right. You haven't been feeling dizzy or confused, or anything, have you?"

"Not till just now."

I could tell she was worried about me, and so was I; it appeared that I had some kind of severe temporary amnesia—except that I couldn't have been interviewing with Iphwin *and* running Helen over to Saigon at the same time. After we rang off I ran a quick check from the communication computer on board, and it was absolutely clear—I was hired at ConTech on exactly the terms Iphwin had specified, right at the time I remembered it happening.

Oh, well, at least I would get to spend an interesting weekend. The Royal Saigon was eighty years old, built in the 1980s to commemorate the formal crowning of whichever junior branch of the Japanese Imperial line had just been picked to run Cochin-China, one of the many little chunks broken off of the old French colony of Indochina. The Imperial House had never been noted for its taste anyway, and perhaps the junior branches had even less esthetic judgment, for the Royal Saigon was as gaudy as possible, decorated with hundreds of statues and thousands of bas-reliefs of lions, absolutely none of which appeared to be even faintly Cochin-Chinese. There were Siamese lions, Bengal lions, Punjabi lions, Ceylonese lions—every kind of lion except anything from Cochin-China or Annam. But if you could endure the color and the busy sculpture, there were consolations—spectacularly sumptuous bedroom suites, the sort of place where you take a girl when you're really hoping to do something stranger than you've ever done before, which might just be what would happen with Helen, given the way the weekend was going.

I turned back to getting permission to pull out of the harbor. A voice from the hatchway above and behind me—a deep woman's voice that sounded like she'd lived all her life on cheap whiskey and cheaper cigars—said, "Forget it. When Iphwin decides to fuck with your brain, he fucks it so hard that it never goes straight again."

My first thought was that the woman coming in through my upper hatch was a harbor whore looking to trade sex for a ride to somewhere—she had coarse bleached-blonde hair, bright red lipstick, the telltale scars of a facelift, near-black eye shadow. Her breasts had probably been modified too since they stuck out like torpedoes through her pink sweater. Her skirt, too short and too tight, revealed too much leg, making the varicose veins apparent. She had to be sixty, at least. She walked over to my chair, stood over me, and said, "May I come in?"

The jump boat spoke up. "Person detected on board. No intrusion detected beforehand."

"I'm wearing my screen," she said, her eyes staying focused on me. "Guess I called attention to myself as soon as I spoke."

"Unidentified person please name self." When the woman didn't speak her name, the jump boat spoke again, this time urgently. "Mr. Peripart please answer are you being held prisoner?"

"Not so far," I said, keeping a wary eye on the woman who stood over me. I wasn't sure whether to try to get out of the pilot's chair or not. "Who the hell are you?"

"My name is Billie Beard, and if you're going to make any jokes about the bearded lady I've heard 'em all. Did you get my note this morning?"

"The one in my newspaper? Yes." I was irritated more than alarmed; I remembered what Iphwin had told me about her. I hated traitors in general—I'd been nervous enough about dealing with someone who even operated in the Twelve Reichs, as Iphwin did—and the thought of an expat working for Nazi police made me sick. But I kept my voice carefully level, keeping in mind that the jump boat would be recording the conversation, and said, "So what is it you would like from me, Billie Beard?"

"Just call me ma'am. Jump boat local legal ordinance requires you shut down now." I heard the jump boat agreeing and saw the control panel go blank, but before I had an instant to protest, Billie Beard grabbed me by the shirt and yanked me out of my chair; even without the heels she was a good four inches taller than me, and easily strong enough to lift me right off the ground—which she did.

"What?" I squeaked.

"There's a great deal we want to know. Starting with all the questions that Iphwin asked you when he interviewed you for your new job."

I was hoping for ConTech company guards to burst in, any second, but Mort had said they wouldn't have anyone covering me until I got to Saigon. They probably thought I'd already left, anyway, unless they were monitoring harbor traffic control. "I— I really don't remember all of them," I said.

"You want to make this difficult?" She shook me the way a cat kills a baby bird between its paws. "I could pull out all sorts of official authority, you know. I could just arrest you and throw you into the local tank and let your girl Helen figure out that you aren't coming. I could do a lot of shit and I feel like doing all of it. You know I'm Gestapo, I bet, because that little chunk of jewshit, Geoffrey Iphwin, probably told you that, but he might not have told you that I'm with the Political Offenses Section and I don't have to tell you what that means."

She didn't. The Twelve Reichs are mostly independent—they even have their own Gestapos—but within the Gestapos of each of the Reichs, the Political Offenses Section is *not* local. It collects whatever money it wants from the local government, but it has its own courts and judges and penal facilities—and it answers only to Party Headquarters, in Berlin. Each Reich sets its own course in domestic policy, and even to some extent in defense, but no Reich chooses how much dissent to tolerate. That decision is always made for it. Which is part of why most expats, like me, aren't willing to live in one.

I gulped and said, "I will answer questions as much as I can but I don't think I know anything."

"You have no way of knowing whether you know anything. Let me be the judge of whether you know anything." She slammed me down into the pilot's chair, way off balance, so hard that the back of the chair bruised my back. "Now answer the questions. What are all the questions you can remember Iphwin asking you?"

I rattled off as many as I could remember, but there had been too many and I was getting confused. She slapped me on the face, clearly restraining herself, but still more than hard enough to make sure that I knew she could take out some teeth if she wanted to, then grabbed my hair and raised my head, staring directly into my eyes. "You really don't remember, do you?"

"No!"

"No you don't remember, or no you're refusing to tell me?" Her voice was now quiet and gentle, almost as if she were about to get a warm washcloth and clean my face, or sit down and ask me about my feelings.

"I don't remember."

"That's a good answer. Now we're getting somewhere. Next question: what can you tell me about a man named Roger Sykes?"

"I don't think I know anyone named Roger Sykes."

Billie Beard hit me again, a straight down punch into one of my shoulders that made it ring with numb pain. "The man you talk to in the virtual reality bar, almost every night. The one you probably call the Colonel."

That cleared that up; of course I knew him. "And his street name is Roger Sykes?"

"That's right. Now what can you tell me about him?"

"Well, I call him the Colonel. We talk about all kinds of things every night. He's retired and he lives in some little town on the Pacific coast of Mexico. We talk about fishing and boating a lot, and about flying, and . . . I don't know, male hobby stuff I guess you'd say."

"Do you ever talk about how the American League pennant race is going, during the season?"

"I don't know what the question means!" I was sniveling, now. The pain and fear had gotten to me. I was terrified that she would hit me again.

She stared at me, her expression blank, slowly becoming more puzzled. "Neither do I. I don't know what that question means either," she said. Then with a sudden, brutal slap with the side of her foot, she swept my feet from under me, causing the pilot's chair to spin, dumping me onto the floor in a terrorized heap. "Why did I ask you that? Tell me why I asked you that!" She kicked me in the ribs.

"You just told me you don't know why!"

"Now we're getting somewhere." Beard sat down in the pilot's chair; her long frame absolutely drooped, and she sighed. "All right, what can you tell me about the murder of Billie Beard in Saigon?"

"Aren't *you* Billie Beard?" I asked, hopelessly confused, trying to get my feet under me and to get between her and the hatch.

"Answer the question!"

I felt like a complete idiot. Perhaps that was what she intended. "I do not know anything about the murder of Billie

Beard in Saigon. I am going to Saigon myself. If you are going to be murdered there—"

She lunged out of the chair and braced me against the wall. "Who the hell says I am going to be murdered in Saigon?"

"You just did! You asked me what I knew about the murder of Billie Beard in Saigon."

"I did ask that," she said. She had that strange blank expression that I had seen twice before, but now she reset it into a pleasant smile. "Your answers have been extremely helpful. This will look really good on your record if you ever decide to apply to become a citizen of any of the Reichs. Well, I can't stay, so thank you very much and have a nice day." She turned and went out the hatch before I could say a word, leaving me slumped against the wall of my own cabin, shaken and frightened. She went out with a sway in her walk like a teenager looking for a boyfriend, and gave me a flirty-little-girl "bye-bye" wave at the hatch, before going out. "Jump boat," I croaked, "wake up extra fast."

There were thuds, pings, clangs, and whizzing sounds all over; that's the command you use to get the robot all the way up and running when you need to run like hell. "Secure all," I added, and the gangway retracted, the hatch slammed shut, and the jump boat cut its own mooring line.

I dumped myself into the pilot's chair and belted in. "Are you all right, Mr. Peripart? Do you require medical attention? What is our situation?"

"Comply with Surabaya harbor flight control," I said, "unless they try to move me toward captivity. Get us to the main landing area in Cholon, first available slot. Full auto. I trust you. Just get me there, quick."

"Yes, Mr. Peripart." There was a little warmth in the voice, I thought; like so many robots whose owners were do-it-yourself types, it probably didn't get to exercise its full faculties as often as it wanted to.

A moment later the jets were thumping madly, and we were zigzagging across the harbor, dodging in and out of other traffic. The Skyjump must have gotten cleared for a high-priority exit—perhaps Iphwin's influence, perhaps even Billie Beard's. By that point I really did not care in the slightest. I reached forward and opened the medical kit, got myself a painkiller/mood elevator ampoule, loaded it in, and slapped the jector against my carotid—the fast way in for drugs when you're really in need. I fired once and mostly stopped hurting, but the world still felt very urgent and frightening, so I fired a second time. Suddenly I didn't hurt at all (at least until the euphoria wore off), I had just gotten the very best job in the whole world, and I was going to go spend an ecstatic weekend in bed with a beautiful woman I adored. I had that thought and just giggled myself to sleep; by then the waves were thundering against the hull as we made a fast run up to launch.

By the time I woke up the jump boat was circling down toward Cholon, the watery twin city that was the major jump boat port for Saigon. The old city of Saigon itself had not known war since the 1880s and was in most ways a Final Republic French city still; Cholon was a sort of twenty-first-century Chinese industrial Venice. Most people flew into Cholon for business and took a small boat into Saigon for pleasure.

Cholon had been reorganized and rebuilt around a series of wide stillwater canals that acted as runways and harbors; the polders between held warehouses, factories, and residential districts, and on the roofs of the major buildings there were truck gardens. The result, from the air, was a grid of deep green squares, separated by broad brown water. The jump boat dropped out of the holding pattern and spiraled down to splash onto one of the canals; immediately, responding to orders from the tower, we made a hard left into a basin that cut into one of the polders, and swung from there into a mooring hangar.

I grabbed my bags, told the jump boat to order fuel and to shut down once it was delivered, and walked out the gangplank into the hangar. I was thoroughly jumpy between having had a beating and the come-down off the painkillers, which normally induces mild temporary paranoia. The anti-inflammatory and antitraumal drugs had taken care of the basic damage Billie had done to my body, but the mood lifters weren't even putting a dent in what had happened to my mind.

I hadn't worried about being randomly attacked by strangers since I was about fourteen, when I had mustered up enough nerve to get into the last fistfight of my life and convinced the class bully to look for easier prey.

Now as I walked through the big, dark, empty hangar, I was looking for something or someone to spring from behind every fuel drum and post; my heart hammered at anything in the shadows I didn't instantly recognize. The slap of waves against the pilings sounded like a man climbing out of the water with a knife. My own echoing footsteps seemed to betray my position and draw imaginary crosshairs onto the middle of my back. I hurried, but I was afraid that I was running toward the patient stalkers who were about to leave; I slowed to a snail's pace, but I dreaded making it easy for the unseen followers in the shadows. The whole vast space of the hangar seemed to hold nothing but terrors. I was scared that there might be someone there, with all that room to hide. Probably there wasn't one other person in there, and that frightened me too.

I don't suppose it took me three minutes to walk down the dock, across the unloading area, toward the yellow glare of the archway, and out the arched door into the bright Cochin-Chinese sunlight, but in that walk I died a thousand times. My teeth ached again where I had been hit, from gritting them; I was breathing as fast as if I had run a couple of miles.

When I finally passed through the sunlit arch that I had been so desperate to reach, what was in front of me was a pleasant scene of utter ordinariness: the enclosing dike, with a wide flight of stairs up to the top, and a row of Chinese shops up above. I walked up the steps, still glancing back occasionally at the dark arch into the hangar. There was a bar right at the top, and I badly wanted a drink, but I was more than late enough already, so I flagged down a *pinceur*—a pedicab jockey whose whole job was to grab people coming into Cholon and get them to the watercab that paid him. I was happy to be grabbed, and a moment later my luggage and I were rolling along the top of the dike, headed around to one of the many watercab slips.

A paranoid thought struck—what if the *pinceur* was working for them? And who were they, anyway? The German Reich, the Political Offenses network, some other enemy of Iphwin's? And what on earth had ever made me want to work for an employer with so many enemies?

I was on the point of flagging down some other *pinceur* at random, and transferring, just to throw them off my tail, when the small Asian man pedaling the cab leaned back and said, "I'm hearing through my earpiece that there's no one following us."

I started. "Was there anyone before?"

"No, but you can never be completely sure. Two of our tails have followed for a full kilometer now, and nothing has happened. The one watching your jump boat reports nothing, either. If you're willing to give us your permission, we're going to go in and sweep it for bugs or anything else that our friend Billie Beard might have left behind her."

"You're with ConTech?" I asked.

"You better hope I am! Yes. Now, relax, enjoy the view, and

be aware that you're under our eyes continuously for the rest of the trip. You can do whatever you like, and we've got you covered, or if we don't chances are we'll be in more trouble than you. Oh, and Mort at headquarters said specifically that he wanted to apologize for Beard having got through to you like she did. Those bastards really caught us flat-footed this time; it's a lesson to us all. Now relax and enjoy the ride—your watercab jockey will be another one of us."

"Thank you," I said, meaning it with all my heart.

The ride took just a few more minutes, the transfer to the watercab was almost instant with the *pinceur* carrying the bags, and in no time we were making our way out of the tangle of Cholon and onto the Saigon River. It was wonderful to feel so safe.

I hadn't been in Cochin-China in more than a year. The familiar pleasures were all around—the boats full of livestock, the quarreling and haggling from the floating shops, the soft blue and white of the sky against the deep green of the trees. I sat back and enjoyed the ride until we slipped through one of the watercourse tunnels for half a kilometer, then emerged from that into the bright sunlight of the interior boat pond of the Royal Saigon. The bellhops whisked my stuff up to the room, along with an apologetic bunch of flowers, as I went to see the hotel doctor and see what other repairs I might need.

"Curiously enough," he said, after checking me over, "I believe every bit of your story because it's completely consistent with the behavior of a Political Offenses cop, but she seems to have unusual control. I can tell by surface scan that your muscles probably ache, but she didn't even break enough capillaries to give you any real bruises. I can spray you with some stuff to make you feel better, and we'll squirt some gingival stabilizer in so that your teeth won't wobble or get plaque down in there, but you're in perfectly fine shape except for the pain itself. I suppose

if you're going to have something like this done to you it's better
to have it done by a pro." I opened my jaws and let him run the
filler around the base of my teeth; then he sprayed me all over
with the painkiller. "Did she hit your groin?"

"No. Nor my testicles either."

"Glad to find someone who still knows the difference. All
right, then we won't spray that area, because the painkiller also
tends to deaden some of the pleasure response for a while, and I
hate to spoil a guy's Friday night." The doctor stuck out his hand.
"I'm the house doc here, Lawrence—never, never Larry—
Pinkbourne. If there's trouble and I turn up, I'm on your team.
I have a little side line with ConTech, too, which I imagine will
help you to feel better."

"If ConTech is so ubiquitous, where was it in Surabaya?"

"It's everywhere in Surabaya—that's the problem. The
Dutch Reich is so hostile that nobody ever gets a spare minute
to do any preplanning, and every one of Iphwin's agents is always
busy. Here, things are a great deal more relaxed—there's a sort
of a détente with the Emperor in Tokyo and an even better détente with the King here. Why the hell Iphwin insists on operating in any of the Reichs, let alone the Dutch Reich, is beyond
me. You're an expat, aren't you, Peripart?"

"Crossbred Nineteener and Remnant," I said, "originally out
of Illinois and California. You must be too?"

"You have me beat," he said, smiling. "Hawaiian exodus on
both sides of the family, and nobody knows where they came
from before then. I have a few distant cousins that were Nineteeners."

We chatted for a few minutes, as all expats do, seeing if we
had any distant shared relatives or mutual acquaintances. Anymore it's almost a relief when you don't—if we can find unas-
similated Americans we don't know, it means our numbers

haven't shrunk as far as we might reasonably have feared. We shook hands, and I went up to the room.

The lock had already been set to my thumb, and my bags were inside, along with Helen's—hers were mostly unpacked, since she was one of those people who don't feel comfortable in a hotel room until they've homesteaded it. The note from her on the bed said she'd gone out shopping, that Iphwin's men had already briefed her on the situation, and that she'd be back in a little while.

I stripped naked and stretched out on top of the coverlet to take a nap. Dr. Pinkbourne's painkillers were hitting me nicely by then, so that my whole body had kind of a pleasant warm glow. I was asleep a moment later, and it seemed as if the next instant I was waking up in the middle of a long passionate kiss from Helen. When the kiss broke I sat up and discovered that she was also naked; she must have undressed before climbing onto the bed beside me, I realized in a groggy sort of way. "Hello there," I said.

Even if I hadn't been quietly in love with her for the past five years, I'd have liked what I saw. Helen had thick chestnut hair, and when it was loose, as it was now, it hung to her waist in a soft natural wave. Her eyes were gray-green, her snub nose was sprayed with freckles, and her mouth was wide and full-lipped above a strong chin; not everyone's idea of attractive, but it certainly got my attention. Her body, thanks to her swimming, running, rowing, and hiking, was strong and muscular, compact more than willowy, longer in the torso than in the legs, and she had pleasantly big round buttocks and smallish, very firm breasts. Just at the moment, she was climbing on top of me, so that the thick hair formed sort of a tent around my face; she pushed me back on the bed and pressed her breast against my face. I sucked the nipple gently; her breath caught and she pinned my hands back and wrapped me in her thighs. She said, "I'm in the mood and I took the injection for the weekend. Let's, please, before we do anything else."

It was quick and very pleasant, and I was grateful that Pinkbourne had thought to ask before spraying my crotch. As Helen and I lay there in the afterglow, I said, "Why, Professor Perdida, what do you suppose your Intro to American History students would think if they could see us now?"

"They'd think you were a pervert of the first order, Dr. Peripart," she said, grinning. "Imagine doing an old bag like me."

"If I start imagining that again," I said, "we won't get out of the hotel room all weekend. Since I'm now affluent and with a good job, would you like to order a ring, make it official, and spend the rest of the weekend celebrating?"

"Lyle, is that your way of asking me to marry you?"

I sat up next to her, hugged her, and said, "Yes."

In the full-length mirror, I saw the happy couple; Helen looked great, and although I was going to be forever nondescript by comparison—thin straight salt-and-pepper hair cut short, turned-up nose and thick lips, skinny frame without an ounce of extra muscle or fat on it—I figured that any children we had might get lucky and look like her, and if not, well, nobody had ever screamed and pointed at the sight of me.

She sat for a long time, pretending to think it over, as I held her, and finally said, "You do notice that you are really assuming that I would accept?"

"Of course I am. It's a basic sales technique. I want you to say yes, so I'm using the best sales tactics I know."

"Well, all right, so if the astronomy racket stops paying, you can sell vacuum cleaners door to door, and thus keep yourself from becoming a burden on me. Still and all, would you mind asking me in a fairly traditional manner, just as if we were a couple of fairly traditional people?"

I let go of her, rolled off the bed, dropped to one knee, took her hand, gazed upward, and said, "For god's sake marry me or I'll kill myself."

"Does that have to be an either-or?" she asked. "Well, since you put it that way, what the hell."

"Does that mean yes?" I asked, still not getting up off the floor.

"I guess it does," she said. "What the hell."

"Those three little words that mean so much," I said, standing up and giving her a long, hard kiss.

She kissed back and said, "And now about your kind offer of the ring. You may order me a diamond, but you are by no means to do anything as stupid as putting two months' salary into it, since we need to start saving for a house. Plain band, wide rather than narrow, and if the diamond has some blue in it, that's a plus. On the day of delivery I shall first run madly through the halls of the history and social science departments showing it off, then consent to a long candlelight dinner, and finally take you back to my place where I shall use you sexually to within an inch of your life."

"Actually," I said, "here in Saigon there are jewelers who can come up with exactly what you want in half an hour. If you'd like, we could get the ring taken care of, then go for a good long dinner—with plenty of oysters—and then see whether I am sufficiently recovered. The spirit is very, very willing but the flesh, at the moment, is not entertaining visitors."

Helen sighed. "That's amazing. In Enzy it's a month or more to get a piece of jewelry. At least that's what it's like for all my girlfriends when they get engaged. All the paperwork for owning gold. How do we go about buying a gold ring here? Do we just go to a shop or something?"

"We can, if you'd like. But most of the shops have a catalog on-line, and you can handle the material through a virtual reality setup, so you can see exactly what you're going to be getting. Either way would be fine with me."

"Hmm. Well, the idea that you can just buy diamonds in a shop seems very exotic and fascinating, but the idea of getting dressed, just at the moment, seems like a bother. Can your computer link into the local phone system? Mine didn't have the translator module it needed."

"Should be able to," I said, and got it out of its case. A little plugging and fiddling, more to run two headsets on two accounts than anything related to the hotel system, was all it took, and we were on-line.

"How can buying an engagement ring be such a hassle at home and so easy here?" she asked.

I made a noncommittal noise. Some expats won't travel to the Reichs, some won't travel outside the free countries, and some just don't travel. I was never sure what Helen's real feelings on travel were; since her specialty was American history, and any expat setting foot in the American Reich is vulnerable to arrest and to being claimed as a citizen, she had never been inside the nation whose past she studied. It wasn't as bad as it had been when we were kids—back then, every day it seemed you heard a new chilling story of a professor, artist, scholar, or athlete being arrested and forcibly repatriated while in the American Reich; it often took years for friends and relatives to get them back out, and meanwhile they were subject to racial purity testing and the grim possibility of execution. But though things were much more relaxed now, nobody wanted to take chances.

Other than that, she had mentioned many times that she had not traveled much. Since I *had* to travel—there was so much of my work that required visiting colleagues at other observatories— I had gotten used to it. I was comfortable with a few things the people in the free countries were often eager to avoid thinking about—such as the fact that the free countries were both backward and backwaters.

After the Great Reich War, in the early 1950s, Germany ruled the world, and with her atom-fusion bombs, no one was in a position to challenge her. Japan, Italy, and the other Axis nations found themselves to be minor partners in the whole business, generously rewarded but told firmly what they would and would not do; Japan, for example, could not have any white nation in conquest. Italy was required to split Africa with the South African Reich, though South Africa had been on the other side.

The great campaign of extermination had begun in parallel with the construction of the Twelve Reichs and the two Empires, so that by 1970 most of the world's land—a severely depopulated land—was Lebensraum for the Reichs (which is to say, a fresh graveyard for everyone else), or under the sway of the Emperor of Japan or the Duce of Italy. Here and there, however, there were a few small nations, protected by the Germans because they were white, that had not been occupied, but didn't have the means to fight back—Australia, Iceland, New Zealand, Switzerland, Finland, Uruguay, and the others.

It had been Hitler's choice to leave them alone, under very strict conditions; they could not broadcast with enough power to be heard outside their own borders, they were sharply limited in military forces, they would in no way significantly oppose the Reichs or the Empires. And to make sure of their good behavior, the free countries were given access to new technology only after a long delay and only partially; trade barriers were set against them, and cooperation between them simply could not take the place of real participation in the global economy. Painful as it was to admit it, the free countries, beloved of expats, tended to be decades behind the times, old and timid places where little bits of individual human decency might still shine, but nothing that really mattered to history would ever happen again.

If you lived in the free countries, especially if you were affluent and educated, it might take a very long time to notice that your nation was a global backwater. But if you traveled, as I did, you got accustomed to it—and accustomed, also, to not speaking of the matter around your countrymen.

That was why I hesitated a long moment before telling Helen, "Well, the truth is, the diamond trade is plenty fast and efficient, and it doesn't take any time to make up a ring. But the machines for the job are prohibited to Enzy by treaty, and diamonds are taxed at a very high rate, and it takes a long time for the paperwork to go through in the South African Reich, which is where the business gets done. Most of all, our currency is squishy and the government has to make sure the gold reserve doesn't get drawn down, so every gram of gold has to be accounted for. But none of that applies here in the Japanese Empire. If you just buy a ring here, for personal use, you can get it in any jewelry store in a few minutes. If you'd rather stay here and just enjoy being together for a while, and do your order by virtual reality, that's fine, but later on we'll take you out and get you exposed to the whole big planet full of shopping."

"Suits me fine," Helen said, and sighed. "I guess you're trying to find a gentle way to remind me that I'm just a country girl from the sticks?"

"Don't worry, dear. I'm a bumpkin myself. I've just been to town a few more times than you have."

We put on headsets and goggles and started exploring the jewelry areas. Most of the net was closed to VR access from the free countries, and the software for accessing it was only available in the outside world; that was why her computer hadn't been able to get on, but mine carried the necessary translator modules from all the previous trips.

She startled me. I'd always thought she'd want to look around a long time for the perfect engagement ring, but in short order she had found the pattern she wanted and the diamond she wanted to put into it, and ten minutes after our logging on she asked, "Will your credit stand a bill this big? I don't want you living on tinned beans and noodles for the next year to pay for this."

I looked at the bill; it was half what I'd been prepared to pay, and I told her so, but that ring was the ring she wanted, so we ordered it, and the ordering firm copied the order over to a Saigon jeweler who promised to have it made up and delivered in about fifteen minutes. They gave us a quick peek at the exact diamond they would be using, and Helen said she liked it even better than the sample that she had used when choosing the pattern.

We confirmed the order and that was that. "We should probably get dressed," I said, "if a courier is going to come in here."

We compromised on slipping into robes and pajamas; a few minutes later, there was a knock at the door, and after giving my thumbprint for ID, the ring was ours. It fit perfectly—not surprisingly, since the artificial intelligence had been able to read Helen's finger through the VR glove—and we spent a few minutes admiring it before Helen said, "So, where for dinner tonight?"

"Well," I said, "do you want tradition, romance, or just a real good feel for the real Saigon?"

"Where do we go for romance?"

"Right down the stairs to the Royal Saigon's hotel restaurant, a place called the Curious Monkey, which you may have seen as you were coming in—it faces the street behind an air curtain. Perfect for romance."

She looked at me just a little suspiciously. "How about for tradition, then?"

"Also easy. We go to the Curious Monkey. Decades of being one of the best-known places in southeast Asia, traditional decor, a menu that hasn't changed since the hotel was built."

"Unh-hunh. And I bet that the Curious Monkey has the real feel of the real Saigon, too, right?"

"Absolutely. If that's what you had wanted, it's where we would have gone."

"Couldn't you have just said you wanted to go to the Curious Monkey?"

I shrugged and spread my hands. "And not give you a choice? Hardly fair."

As we dressed I told her about it. I was surprised that she had never heard of the Curious Monkey, but I supposed she really hadn't traveled much.

The Curious Monkey had been founded by a Frenchman before 1940, purchased by an American expat sometime around 1970, handed down in his family for some generations, and moved by royal order to the Royal Saigon Hotel when it was established. It was now owned by a wealthy family in Japan which had the good sense to run it with a staff of expats.

No one seemed to know anymore why it had been named the Curious Monkey; the one American expat who was descended from the old owner said that family legend had it that the Frenchman himself did not recall, had named it when he was drunk with friends and had never been able to bring himself to ask if *they* knew why he had done that.

Since at least the 2020s, when a number of spy movies and romances were filmed there, the Curious Monkey had been one of the world's best-known restaurants. Because it was well known, all sorts of celebrities the world over had dined there— the Himmler family maintained a permanent table, as did His Most Catholic Majesty. The Crown Prince had been known to fly there from Tokyo just for the lemongrass soup, and half the world's actors seemed to hang out in the bar, desperately hoping some trillionaire would take them to dinner.

For all that, the Curious Monkey also remained a place where you could get a superior meal for a very high, but not ridiculous, price. They could easily have doubled their prices and never had an empty seat, but apparently the Curious Monkey was under a mandate to stay as affordable as it could manage (which was of course not very affordable for anyone like me, as a usual thing—but it was also not at a level intended for people to show off how much they could afford to waste, as so many places in Saigon, Bangkok, Rangoon, and Tokyo were).

I phoned downstairs and got a reservation. As always it required negotiating to get the staff at the Curious Monkey to admit they had a table that I might reserve for that night, and that in fact it would be available reasonably soon.

The phone rang as I was tying my cravat. I picked it up and was surprised to find Geoffrey Iphwin on the other end of the line. "Hello," he said. "Just wanted you to know that I've called the Curious Monkey and dinner is on me for tonight. Partly in apology for our security having slipped up and let the obnoxious Miss Beard get at you, and partly as an engagement present for my two new employees."

"*Two* new employees?"

"Didn't Helen tell you? I hired her this afternoon after a phone interview, while she was waiting for you."

I covered the phone with my hand and said, "Are you working for Iphwin now too?"

Helen was struggling into a long black dress that clung to her in a very flattering way. "Yes, silly, didn't I tell you? He hired me to be your administrative assistant. I said I didn't know anything about statistics or abductive math, and he said then I'd have to concentrate on administering and assisting. I thought I told you when I phoned you while you were inbound into Saigon. Didn't I tell you?"

She hadn't.

"Um, no." I turned back to Iphwin on the phone. "Well, I

guess she is hired at that. And, uh, er, thank you, and it really isn't necessary—"

"Of course it's not. Gifts are never necessary, that's what makes them gifts. But it gives me great pleasure to do this for you. I hope you don't mind."

"I don't mind a bit," I said, very sincerely, trying to cover up for my beginning to feel very meddled-with. "But I do feel bewildered."

"Well, that's a feeling you're going to have for quite a while, I think," Iphwin said. "Something else I should let you know is that in my continuing disagreements with the Political Offenses cops, I have reserved a special spot for making the life of Billie Beard unhappy. Her behavior is the sort of thing that I really cannot allow. I have already given Mort orders that one way or another she is to be kept away—away from you, away from Helen, away from ConTech, and far from the realm of any possible human happiness."

"I agree with the sentiment," I said, and this time it was no effort at all to sound sincere.

"Enjoy your evening, then. And your left cuff link is behind your right foot."

I looked back and saw that it was.

He went right on. "Anyway, enjoy, enjoy, enjoy. Plenty of work ahead, so you might as well enjoy yourself now. Bye!"

"Bye . . ." I said, and bent to pick up the cuff link as I heard the click of the breaking phone connection.

I held it in my hand a long time. Did Iphwin have hidden cameras in here? Had he watched Helen and me making love? Why was one of the world's wealthiest industrialists so interested in two obscure faculty members from a backwater college?

And if he *didn't* have hidden cameras, or if there *was* something that interesting about us—I didn't want to think about either possibility, so I threaded my cuff link in and fastened it, resolving not to think for any reason for the rest of the night.

"Iphwin called me just after you dropped me off," Helen said. "Really, no one is doing anything behind your back—I just forgot to tell you in all the excitement. You needn't look so troubled."

It was the cuff link, and not her job, that was troubling me, but I wasn't about to spoil the evening with worry. "You look terrific," I said, in a complete non sequitur that almost always worked.

From the way she smiled, I judged that it had worked again, and now I had only to finish dressing and try not to let myself worry to excess.

Our reservation was not for an hour and a half yet, so we sat down in chairs on opposite sides of my computer, plugged into our VR helmets and gloves, and went off to announce our engagement to our chat room friends, setting an alarm so that we would leave ourselves plenty of time to get to the Curious Monkey.

Both Helen and I had been frequenting this chat room for a couple of years, long enough and often enough so that each of us thought we had introduced the other to it. It wasn't the liveliest chat room either of us had ever found, just a place where a few expats scattered all over the globe liked to get together. Around seven PM Enzy time, almost every day, our little group logged on and met, just as if there were things we particularly needed to talk about or real business to be done.

A few weeks ago everyone had gotten bored with the old Roman Forum setting that we'd had for the better part of a year, so to give it a drastic change we had reset it as Casablanca—not the city, but the film. That movie was still nearly the expatriate's Bible—it had everything—a real American of African descent, a free and tough American, defiance of the Germans. Using that movie also made our chat group, which was a tight one, less likely to have visitors, since the movie was banned everywhere except the free countries (and even there was really only permitted in unadvertised private showings—local German consuls tended to regard it as something other than a purely internal matter).

Helen and I had gotten lucky—I was wearing the Paul Henreid body, and looked smashing in a white suit; she had gotten the Ingrid Bergman.

We went over to join our friends at the table. All of them had gotten there before we had, and were wearing the red rose on a lapel, or as a brooch, that indicated that they were present in real time, and not just an artificial personality recording the events for later. "Hello, everyone," I said. "We have some real news this evening."

The Colonel—I had just learned that afternoon that his real name was Roger Sykes—was wearing the body of Sidney Greenstreet tonight; sometimes he wore the Bogart body instead. He leaned way back in his chair and said, "Well, then, share it."

At his right, Kelly Willen, wearing a dignified older lady from one of the crowd scenes, nodded and smiled. Terri Teal, dressed as a demimonde to no one's surprise, nodded at us. She flicked some ash from her extremely long and decadent-looking cigarette holder and said, "Do tell."

The effect was somewhat spoiled for me by my knowledge that Terri was actually a strictly brought up sixteen-year-old girl whose prosperous father owned an import-export firm in Cairo, in the Italian Empire. Probably she'd never been allowed out of the house without a small army of guards and chaperones. All of us were fond of her but we could hardly help hoping that the day would come soon when she'd stop picking the most decadent possible roles for herself. "Do, do tell," she added, in the most affected accent she had available.

I grinned broadly and said, "We're getting married."

Roger flagged down Humphrey Bogart and ordered champagne all around. Bogart leaned over the table and said to Terri, "I don't know that I care for an underage dame in my joint."

We glanced at his lapel, saw that he was just a program, and all said "Ignore" in unison. He walked two steps backward, came forward, said "Right away, sir," and went to get the champagne.

I turned back to my friends and began, "We're having a little pre-honeymoon in—" My voice stopped dead. I couldn't seem to say either the word "Saigon" or "the Royal Saigon Hotel." Everyone froze—but no one seemed to notice the trailing sentence, for a moment later the conversation resumed. And by way of bragging I added that we had both been hired by Iphwin, which did impress everyone.

It was a pretty nice party, with champagne that could make you happy and silly but not drunk, or rather not drunk in a way that lasted after you took the headset off, and everyone talking about their day—Terri's life and times at the American School, Roger's beach fishing, Kelly's getting a role in *Abe Lincoln in Illinois* at the American Theater in Paris. I wanted to say that I was amazed that the French Reich would tolerate that, but the conversation moved on while I was still formulating the thought. As it wound down—Terri was going off to school, Kelly needed to bathe and dress for rehearsal, and Roger was going to bed, one of the complications in a friendship that spanned so many time zones—Helen and I made our excuses, unplugged, and went downstairs.

In appearance the Curious Monkey was extraordinarily simple—a large group of tables in what looked like an open-air setting—an air curtain kept it pleasantly air-conditioned. The rooms were simple and functional, with plain-looking tables and chairs, but if you knew what to look for you would know that every stick of furniture in the place was collectable early twentieth century. The walls held a dozen paintings of note—French impressionists mainly, but also a Mondrian, and—if you looked closely enough at the nondescript pen-and-brush of a cathedral, hanging in a dim corner near the bus counter—even an authentic Hitler. People were dressed exceptionally well, even the very famous.

There was no menu per se; the waiter would talk with you for a while, get an idea of what you enjoyed and what you were in the mood for that night, and then go back and talk to the chef, who would endeavor to surprise you with something you would never have thought of, which you would like better than what you would have ordered.

This particular waiter was a small, slim, gentlemanly man, vaguely Eurasian in appearance, who listened to us with such great enthusiasm that anyone would have thought he really cared what we liked to eat. We chatted with him pleasantly for a few minutes, about Saigon and how we liked the place, before he said, "We had a message earlier that you are to be the guests of Mr. Iphwin. Mr. Iphwin told us to stress to you that you *can* have anything you would like, but he would be especially pleased if you would let us prepare Mr. Iphwin's favorite meal for you."

Of course we agreed at once; curiosity alone would have insured that. It turned out to be sort of a sampler of old American cooking—a platter of foods that you might have found at an American picnic in the 1920s or 1930s. There were deviled eggs, a hot dog, a hamburger, a slice of meat loaf, a Southern-fried chicken breast, mayo and mustard potato salads, coleslaw, Jell-O salad, and baked beans, arranged artfully on a wicker tray with a red checked cloth. The ketchup was real Heinz Old Recipe and the mustard was Plochman's Yellow—both of which were extremely expensive, made only in small hand lots by those families.

Helen and I had each had some version of most of those dishes, but many of the authentic ingredients were now expensive and hard to come by. My guess was that we were eating a week's college teaching pay. They served it with Miller, of course, the only authentic expat beer, tooth-chilling cold in a frozen mug.

Dessert was a black cow, real right down to the Dad's Root Beer. "Do you suppose," I asked, "that they're ever going to completely assimilate us? I mean, here we are, third generation out of the country, and you and I—we, who not only have never set foot in America, but only knew, when we were children, very old people who had left it when they were very young—we are getting misty-eyed over how this food is just the way it should be, and of course we're insisting on marrying expats, both of us."

"I've heard the idea that what we've done is become the replacements for the Jews," Helen said, scooping out a little of the homemade ice cream from her parfait glass. "You know, unassimilable people, profitable to have around, tending not to be liked by the neighbors. Can you believe they got the recipe to make this root beer, too? Anyway, we've become the people that can't assimilate whether they want to or not, with no home of our own, loyal enough to whoever takes us in, hardworking, making *some* friends, but never exactly accepted as one of the locals. And about that . . . well, I'd say they seem to be right."

I shuddered. "Remember what happened to the Jews. And I suppose Americans aren't that scarce—we tend to forget all the Reich Americans who are still living there. Their descent is as American as ours."

"Not really," Helen pointed out. "We're descended from all of America, the whole forty-eight, in the 1940s. The Reich Americans are descended from white people who could prove they didn't have any Jewish, Negro, or Slavic ancestors. So much of real American culture was Negro, and Jewish, and big-city Slavic, and all the rest of the melting pot; the Reich Americans have thrown that all away, whereas we're all interbred. We're the real Americans. They're one narrow slice."

She left it unsaid, since we were outside Enzy, but I knew

perfectly well she was referring to my black grandmother and her Jewish grandfather. Once we became expats, many old barriers had come down, and already in the Reichs there was a stereotype of the expat American as a racial mongrel, darker skinned than the Reich Americans.

Helen went on. "Think about the fact that no expat I've ever known has been in touch with relatives in the Reich, even though just about all of us must have some. And we're only the third generation. On my block there's a man who is seven generations removed from Ireland, and yet he still stays in touch with his cousins. The family that runs that good Italian restaurant downtown—the one by the park?—is five generations out of Italy and still holds a party every time a cousin back home sends them a birth announcement. It's only expat Americans who don't seem to keep touch with America."

"Well, supposedly we were always very mobile, always moving over the next hill. Maybe we just find it easier to lose touch."

"I suppose anything is possible," Helen said, "but it's not like the Irish or the Italians all stayed home." I was getting bored. This was one of those things expats could talk about endlessly. I wondered if, back when the Americans were still in America, they had spent as much time as expats did now talking about what exactly it meant to be an American. It seemed very unlikely.

"Isn't this whole meal amazing?" I asked, switching the subject. "I think I've had most of these dishes at one time or another, but not all at once, and when I *have* had this stuff it has rarely been with all authentic ingredients. And the fact that they could serve this all at once implies that they must have had all these ingredients just sitting back there in the kitchen waiting. Imagine being able to just do that."

She grinned at me. "Well, speaking of being able to just do

things, our salaries are going way up. We can probably do this for anniversaries or something."

"It's a deal," I said, recognizing the request for what it was. "Of course after a while there may be problems getting a sitter—"

Helen snorted with laughter. "Geoffrey Iphwin is offering us a chance to work on an extremely challenging and interesting project. I don't plan on getting knocked up right away, my dearest, so if you're hoping to get the project all to yourself that way, well, hope for something else. I'm not going to spend what could easily be the most exciting months of my intellectual life waddling around and throwing up."

"We can wait as long as you want to," I said.

There was a stir up front. It sounded like the typical situation—a German tourist from some backwater planned-development town in the New East, who has decided he wants to get a bite to eat, and hasn't the foggiest idea that he is trying to barge into one of the most exclusive restaurants on the planet. The maître d' was shouting, "Sir, sir!"

The fat man, galumphing along in his sandals, knee socks, baggy red shorts, and sweat-stained formerly white safari shirt, was headed up the aisle right toward us. Behind him, I saw a German officer, in one of those black uniforms with all the metal decorations around the shoulder, standing up and giving a firm order, the sort that most Germans, in the army or not, obey instantly.

To my surprise, the German tourist ignored him. He kept coming. He looked around, then right at me, smiled in a way that froze my blood, and pulled a small pistol from the bulging lower left pocket of the safari shirt. I stared at it; owing to the policies the Reichs enforce on their trading partners, most of the world is disarmed these days and I'm not sure I had even seen a pistol since leaving the Navy.

He brought the pistol up.

He was still staring right at me. He pulled the trigger and I felt the pressure wave from the bullet as it passed my right ear.

Something made me roll toward that ear and dive under the table. Everyone was screaming. I had made the right choice, because when he adjusted his aim to my left, he missed by a wider margin. From under the table I saw a bullet hole appear in the Mondrian, and some stupid distracted part of my brain realized that, whatever might happen next, I would now be forever part of one of the legends of the Curious Monkey.

I expected the tablecloth to flip up and my last sight in this life to be the German and his pistol a scant yard away. I hugged the floor and shut my eyes.

I heard three deep booms, one after the other, and a scream. Still not thinking very clearly, I poked my head out from under the white tablecloth just in time to see Helen take her fourth shot. I learned later that she had shattered his gun shoulder with her first shot, broken his leg with the second, and put one into his back when he fell forward. Now she calmly walked forward, stood over him, pointed that huge pistol at the back of his head, and, in the horrified silence that filled the Curious Monkey, she watched him for a long second until she saw him twitch; she fired a shot that put brains and blood all over the floor and seemed to make the walls of the Curious Monkey ring.

She scanned the room, standing braced in letter-perfect position, much better than I had ever learned to do it in the Navy, with a two-handed grip on the big chunk of blue-black iron; whatever caliber it was, it was a hell of a lot more than my would-be murderer had had.

Her face had a nearly blank expression of relentless attention, the like of which I had seen on the face of a racing pilot about to execute a tight turn around a pylon. Her jaw was set but not clenched, eyes narrowed slightly, mouth a flat line; you could have projected a laser beam backward through the barrel of that gun and it would have just touched the bridge of her nose parallel with her pupils. Her arms were tense, and the sleeveless long gown showed that she had a lot more muscle than I remembered; I saw her breathe, hold, decide there were no more targets, and only then decide not to fire again. She set the safety on the pistol and set it gently on the table, then calmly reached into her purse, pulled out her phone, and called the police. "This is international police badge oh four alpha india four seven eight bravo one zero. I'm at the Curious Monkey and I've got Interpol codes nineteen, forty-three, and sixty-eight here. Situation is under control, but you need to get a four one four, a seventy-eight, and a Foxtrot Mike Whiskey over here, right now."

I had no idea where she had learned to shoot, or when. Enzy is relatively backward about women's issues and still doesn't allow women in combat, and handguns were illegal outside of the military—she couldn't even have learned in a private club. I lurched up beside the table, slightly messed by the spill of some expensive root beer onto one trouser leg, which I hoped would provide some camouflage for the wet spot I had made on the front of my pants. I was scared more than I'd ever been in my life, but otherwise all right. And how had Helen come to know international police codes as well as a cop? How did a professor of history carry an Interpol badge?

The horrified maître d'hôtel was just rushing up to our table, but Helen said to him, "I am terribly sorry about this and I deeply regret disturbing everyone's dinner. We had just finished ours and we'll go as soon as the police get our statements and decide whether or not to arrest me." She went back to talking to the police on the phone; apparently they were so unused to being called to the Curious Monkey that they didn't immediately know where it was.

I looked from Helen to the maître d'hôtel, and something caught the corner of my eye, causing me to glance back. The

German tourist was lying there, face down, a great gaping hole in his lower back, his right arm at an unnatural angle where his shoulder had been shattered, blood pouring out of one pant leg, head smashed like a gourd hit with a bat. I smelled blood and some other unidentified stench—perhaps feces?—under the burnt odor of the thin cloud of blue smoke that still hung in the air, and I was sick to my stomach. I turned away, not wanting to see the sight, and drew great gasps of air, trying to hang on to the most expensive dinner I had ever eaten, tears of stress and terror leaking out of my eyes.

Helen went right on talking on the phone, brushing escaping strands of hair out of her face with her free hand, as calmly as if she were working out a schedule conflict between her classes or placing a complicated catalog order. "If you can get a coroner to run a full spectrum of drug samples from the blood on the victim, right now while everything is fresh and runny, I know my employers will really appreciate it—yeah, exactly. Look, I *know* you have to arrest me and take me downtown. I *know* it's nothing personal. Just make sure you get some authority on the line pretty fast and that they call Iphwin and Diego Garcia for confirmation, because while I'm sure you've got one of the nicer jails I'm ever going to stay in, my fiancé is springing for a hell of a good room at the Royal Saigon, and that's where I'd rather spend my engagement celebration. Yeah, he's with me, and a witness, so I guess you'll have to take us both along—sure thing . . ." She sagged and seemed to be suddenly confused. "Who is this? What? I don't know what you're talking about." She hung up and dropped the phone into her purse, then looked at the body, looked at me in an expression of bewildered terror, and said, "What are you doing alive? There's not a scratch on you."

I didn't know what she was asking—my first thought was that she had meant to shoot at me, that she had been part of the assassination plot, and was disconcerted to find she had shot her partner. Before I could frame any kind of a question, or any idea of any kind that might take me in the direction of making sense of all of this, a squad of uniformed Cochin-Chinese National Police rushed through the air curtain, grabbed the gun from the table, handcuffed Helen, and dragged me to my feet.

The Cochin-Chinese National Police have a middling reputation among the police forces of the world. They are not the gentle sorts that Enzy, Finnish, or Irish cops are reputed to be, but they aren't any kind of Gestapo, either. They tend to be mildly corrupt, but not enough so that you would want to take a chance on bribing one if you didn't know him. It seemed like the best thing to do was to cooperate and to keep repeating the truth—that I had no idea what was going on or why.

They commenced a thorough but not brutal search of us and the corpse. The pistol on the table drew some exclamations— none of them had ever seen any weapon of that make before. Searching Helen, they found she was carrying other weapons: a garter derringer, a switchblade in her purse, and a throwing knife in a quick-draw sheath in the back of her underwear. In a low-backed dress like that, I suppose it would have been easy enough to reach in and get it, and might even serve as a diversion in the right situation. How had Helen concealed all that from me while she was dressing? And more importantly, how had she concealed what was apparently a pretty big part of her life from me during five years of courting?

The manager of the Curious Monkey had gotten into the argument, now, too. At least he made sense; he wanted all this crap out of his restaurant in a hurry, and he wanted the addresses of everyone involved so that he could send all of us bills for the damages.

He got part of his wish right away. A plainclothes inspector showed up, had a whispered conference with the manager in Japanese and French, and a short rapid-fire dialogue in Vietnamese with the uniformed sergeant, and barked a few short sentences. They dragged Helen, who wasn't resisting and seemed to be in some kind of shock, over to one unmarked car and pushed her in. They dragged me to another one and did the same. All the high-level officers got into the car with Helen, so either they had already figured out which of us was really dangerous, or more likely they all wanted to claim a share in arresting the murderer rather than her accomplice.

No one in the car I was in spoke a word of English, French, or German, so although they seemed polite and nice enough, I couldn't ask basic questions like whether or not I was under arrest or if perhaps this horrible dream might be over with soon.

The people and robots of Saigon apparently had acquired a healthy respect, though probably not any admiration, for the way that police cars drive, because everything and everyone scattered out of the way as we roared through the streets, siren wailing and red lights flashing. Pedicabs went up over the curbs, pedestrians pressed themselves off the narrow sidewalks and up against walls, and the few cars on the street abruptly remembered business elsewhere and made a quick left or right turn. The car slammed over potholes and through the dust of the side streets, roaring by small stands and the wide-open eyes and mouths of people who popped out of their front doors to see what all the fuss was about. It might have been interesting if I hadn't been sitting in the backseat, hugging myself as tightly as the cuffs would permit, and now and then sobbing with fear.

At the police station, a detective who spoke English explained that Helen was over in women's incarceration, and that they would need to take a number of statements and record a great deal of information, but fortunately this was not a busy Friday night and chances were good that we could be released within a few hours, especially since virtually all the witnesses from the

Curious Monkey were in agreement that Helen had fired only in self-defense.

Fortunately for us, Cochin-China is one of those places that take a sensible attitude about self-defense. In Enzy there would have been a spirited discussion about whether people who try to kill you ipso facto ought to be killed before you have heard and carefully considered their reasons. I was so relieved at being treated reasonably that if I had not been handcuffed I'd gladly have dropped to my knees and kissed their hands.

They put me into a cell with half a dozen quiet drunks and opium addicts; I seemed to be the only person in the cell who was not inebriated. It did smell of urine and puke, but of old urine and puke—and of much more recent soap. I was mildly exasperated, of course, to be in here, with two wooden benches and seven men, not exactly of the sort I usually associated with, when I was also paying for a room at the Royal Saigon.

I was very glad to be alive and almost as glad to be in the hands of a relatively patient and sympathetic police force; they would question me and they probably wouldn't believe my story, but they wouldn't torture me into giving them a story they liked. They might, of course, keep me until I was a fungus-covered corpse, but there were probably no rubber hoses or testicle clamps in my immediate future.

Why would someone try to kill *me*? I couldn't imagine what I had done. The only explanation I had was one that merely transferred the senselessness of it all one step backward—perhaps someone wanted me to be dead for the same reason that Billie Beard had wanted me to be frightened. Maybe Iphwin was up to something that had deeply infuriated, or even frightened, the German Reich itself—that would explain my first assailant's being a member of Political Offenses and this dead man's being obviously German. Or was that what I was *supposed* to think?

I had no idea even how to begin sorting out the possibilities; this was beyond anything I had ever had to think about.

Since Helen had done the shooting, no doubt they were talking to her first. And yet—after that cool, competent call to the local police—she had seemed pretty bewildered herself, as if she didn't know what was going on either. Where could she have acquired the skills she had displayed tonight—let alone the hardware?

Just who or what had I just become engaged to?

That gave me plenty to think about, and the night was still young, so I can't really say I was bored. After a while the door opened and they brought in another prisoner, who took the only open seat, next to me. His black pajamas reeked of several kinds of smoke, and he appeared to be extremely drunk. He sang the same little song over and over.

I had never conducted my life in any way that could possibly have led to this kind of circumstance. I could not even think of any friends or acquaintances—other than perhaps Helen or Iphwin—who had any connection to the kind of world where things like this happened.

I retraced my life, three times, all the way from my earliest memories of my parents, up till I sat down and read an ordinary, dull newspaper earlier that day, and in all of it I could find no hint that anything like this could happen to me. Meanwhile, I figured out that the fellow beside me was singing in heavily accented French, and that it was a translation of an English song I had learned from my mother while I was small:

> *I was drunk last night, dear Mother.*
> *I was drunk on the night before.*
> *But if you'll forgive me, dear Mother,*
> *I'll never get drunk any more.*

He sang that single verse over and over with a strange determination, as if he knew he would get it right, one of these times, but he hadn't yet, and each experiment brought him some infinitesimal step closer to the magical moment when the song, or at least that verse of it, would be as perfect as he could make it. He didn't hurry and he didn't dawdle; he worked with concentration but not with anxiety. Sooner or later the definitive Viet-accented a cappella French version of "I Was Drunk Last Night" would emerge, and meanwhile, the rest of the world could listen, or not. He would succeed, given time enough.

When they finally came for me I had all the lyrics down cold, and had begun to form a theory of the deeper significance of the song, which, luckily, I was never to develop any further. The cell door swung open and the polite inspector who had booked me in called my name and pointed to me. I stood and followed him down the hall to an office; behind me the cell door clanged shut.

He gestured me to a chair and handed me a glass of water; I took a sip.

"Well," the inspector said, looking at his beautifully manicured hands and brushing his lank gray hair from his heavily freckled forehead, "we are in some difficulty here. Your friend tells us that she knows nothing about anything that has happened, and denies even remembering the shooting. Perhaps you could enlighten us as to why she is making such silly claims."

"I wish I could," I said. "I didn't even know that she had a gun with her, let alone a whole arsenal."

"The odd part is that she claims that she didn't know either," the inspector said. Fussily, he straightened his bright red necktie, and leaned forward toward me, resting his elbows on his knees and gazing into my eyes the way they do in the movies.

"I really don't know anything," I said.

"Well, provisionally I'm going to believe you, because I've never seen two people look so bewildered after an arrest as you and Dr. Perdida look. But even though I believe you—" there was something vaguely threatening in the way he said that "—let's just walk through the list of questions with you, Dr. Peripart. First of all, do you have any acquaintance with an American expat who works for the Political Offenses Section, named Billie Beard?"

"My god, I certainly do. Just this afternoon, she attacked me physically, roughed me up, interrogated me, whatever you want to call it, in my own jump boat, in Surabaya harbor."

"And did you want revenge?"

"What kind of question is that?" I was bewildered. "Is she connected to the man who was shot?"

The inspector stared at me. "What man? The body in the Curious Monkey was—you couldn't possibly have mistaken her for a man! A hundred-and-fifty-centimeter-tall blonde woman in a tight black dress? According to the ID in her bag, she was Billie Beard, American expat citizen with dual citizenship in the American and Dutch Reichs, which was confirmed by fingerprints on file here, and a wire to Batavia confirmed it."

"It can't be. I saw the man clearly."

The inspector shook his head. "We can sort this out one way or another. Can you at least come down to the morgue with me and confirm that the dead woman we took out of the Curious Monkey is Billie Beard? That would help a great deal."

"Certainly."

The morgue was a product of the mercifully brief period when the Emperor had been infatuated with Speerist monumentalism, around 1970, so the ceilings were vaulted and far above our heads, and the corridors echoed like something out of a horror movie. The room itself was big, air-conditioned, and brightly lit. The inspector and the attendant rolled her out of a big walk-in refrigerator and pulled back the sheet; sure enough, it was Billie Beard, or at least it looked very much like her since the face was so distorted by the exit wound near the mouth, and I said so.

She was wounded in the same places that I had seen my "anonymous German tourist" shot.

"This is the body that we picked up in the Curious Monkey. We have not yet found the bullets, so we can't do the matching just yet, but the wounds are consistent with a high-velocity high-caliber pistol at a range of a few meters, and of course we found just such a pistol on your table, with Helen Perdida's right-hand fingerprints on it. We're paraffin testing her right now but we're sure we'll get a confirmation that she fired it."

"She did—I heard her fire all four shots, and saw her fire the last one." Probably I was naive but just now the only thing that seemed to make any sense was to keep telling the truth until someone got around to telling me what was going on. I stared at the shattered body. "But the person who came in and shot at me was a man, overweight, wearing red shorts and a dirty white safari shirt, shorter than this—" The room was getting dark and it was hard to breathe; I saw the lights of the ceiling for an instant and felt something thump the back of my head, realizing that it must be the floor just as I passed out.

When I woke up my first thought was that I was home in bed and nothing had happened—but the bed was too narrow and uncomfortable to be mine, and when I sat up I was still in evening clothes. The light came on and I saw that I was on a folding cot in a small room, with a desk and two chairs, and the man in the doorway who had just turned on the light was the inspector. *So much for that hope*, I thought.

The inspector said, "We certainly have a problem here. Are you feeling better? Whatever the truth may be, I'm sure you've had a series of unpleasant shocks." He handed me a glass of water and said, "We can give you a stimulant or a tranquilizer if it will help."

"I don't think I want to take any drugs," I said. "I don't want my brain to have any excuses other than plain old reality—whatever that may be."

"I think I understand. Are you well enough for me to continue questioning you?"

"I don't think I know whether I am. I guess we'll have to try and see."

He nodded, dragged the chair over to the cot, and sat down with his elbows on his knees as before. "Just stay where you are and if you pass out again we won't be put to the trouble of moving you. Well, we've interviewed both of you separately, and at this point all I can say is that if it's a set of alibis, it's the worst I've ever heard, and if it's not, I have no idea what is going on. Now tell me the whole story of your day."

I did, starting from getting up in the morning and omitting nothing; Iphwin had not asked me to keep any secrets, and besides, since I couldn't help thinking that my new job must have something to do with all this, I wasn't so sure that I was particularly fond of Iphwin, or owed him anything, anyway.

When I finished, the inspector sighed and said, "Well, your story is consistent with Dr. Perdida's. And there are a surprisingly large number of anomalies that tend to bear you out, which I can't tell you about because they are the sort of thing our prosecuting judges like to hold in reserve. This means that I am being driven, *very* reluctantly and uncomfortably, to conclude that you may just be telling me the truth as you know it. What we must now account for is how you know and believe that particular version of the truth." He sighed. "It is not a criminal offense to be shot at, although it is generally regarded as a highly suspicious activity. And Cochin-China does recognize a right of lethal force in self-defense. Furthermore, Helen Perdida had in her handbag a permit for all of the weapons she was carrying, issued by His Most Catholic Majesty's secret service—oddly enough, along with similar permits from half a dozen other nations. I don't know what she does for a living, but it can't be just teaching history, and she can't seriously have expected us to believe it. And yet when confronted with the permits, although she agreed that the picture and the signature were hers, she denied ever having applied for or gotten the permits, or even knowing that they were in her bag. Since our secret service has said a number of reassuring things to us, we might perhaps just let all of this drop, as an intelligence matter with which we do not wish to meddle, except that none of the intelligence agencies, ours or others', that we would expect to have contacted us by now, have done so. Our relations with the Dutch Reich are rather bad, and Billie Beard was wanted on suspicion of three assassinations we have jurisdiction over, so by itself her death does not greatly trouble us, but we would really like to be told, officially, that the whole thing is none of our business."

"I am finding all sorts of things hard to believe," I said.

"I can let you go, but I have a sense that you might prefer to wait around until we can also release Helen Perdida. That may be a while, or perhaps we won't release her for some time to come, or at all. Delicate matters are involved of which nothing can be said, but they may lead to a happier situation than the present one. I hope you'll understand."

"Even if I don't understand, I don't suppose it matters much."

"It's good that you're so perceptive—it makes communication with you easier."

They took me back to the cell, then, and I got to hear a few dozen more renditions of "I Was Drunk Last Night." There wasn't any notable improvement, but it wasn't for lack of effort or patience.

About ten-thirty that night, a cop in uniform came by and said, "You. Come on. You're being released."

"Is the woman I was arrested with—"

"Dr. Perdida is already waiting for you, and so are the men from ConTech."

He unlocked the door and I followed him out; we went directly to the front desk, where Helen was waiting, still in her evening dress. Her long brown hair was down and looked disheveled—probably they had searched her coif. She was pale with anxiety, so that her makeup looked like a bad paint job on her white skin, but she didn't seem to be hurt otherwise. There were a bunch of men I'd never seen before standing there, most of them in suits, all of them battered, beaten, and bruised. The heavyset older one said to me, "Sir, we really must apologize. We got here as soon as we could."

"You're from ConTech?"

"We're your bodyguards. We just broke out of an attic where we were being held. Two that you don't see here are in the hospital. And we're all feeling like a bunch of clowns, sir. While we were tied up in that attic, you took awfully good care of yourselves—or at least Dr. Perdida took very good care of both of you. It should never have happened—we should have been there to stop Billie Beard—but at least you're unhurt, and we did come as fast as we could."

"Then Mr. Iphwin secured our release?"

"Geoffrey Iphwin and ConTech don't swing much weight here," the inspector said, behind me. "At least, that is, at any level of which I'm aware. You got released by direct order of His Most Catholic Majesty. And so far as I can tell the reason for that was a protest lodged by the Ambassador from the Free Republic of Diego Garcia, based on Dr. Perdida's dual citizenship."

I stared at him. I had never heard of the Free Republic of

Diego Garcia. Helen looked more shocked than I'd ever seen her, even more shocked than in the moments after the shooting.

But getting out of jail when you're being held for murder is not the kind of thing you turn down just because you don't know what's going on. We and Iphwin's men hurried out into the night.

The heavyset guy said, "My name is McMoore. I apologize again, sir."

"It's quite all right," I said, "since neither of us can figure out what is going on, anyway. Helen, what do you want to do?"

"Talk privately and then sleep, I think." She seemed terribly distracted, but then that was hardly a surprise. "I guess we could go back to the hotel."

"We'll do our best to guard you this time, properly," McMoore said. "It's not a far walk—just a few blocks—do you want to let us just form a phalanx around you and walk there slowly? I would be pretty leery of flagging down any public transport right now, eh?"

"Absolutely agreed," I said.

I felt like I was moving at the center of an infantry patrol in enemy territory; the ConTech men were all around us, and I had a distinct sensation that every one of them had his shooting hand close to a weapon.

Nothing happened. In the last two blocks before the Royal Saigon, we passed through a cluster of brightly lit, noisy nightclubs, all of them clamoring for attention, but Helen walked slumped over, not looking around despite all the noise and color that swirled around our phalanx of bodyguards like a chaotic wake around a ship of order. Probably jail had been much tougher on her than on me—I wasn't the one charged with murder.

I kept turning that over in my head. How could Helen possibly have concealed so much about herself? She was apparently a spy or agent of some kind for a country that as far as I knew didn't exist. And yet I didn't think there had been three days of her life in the last few years that I didn't have at least some knowledge of. For that matter, how could she have gotten all those weapons concealed in her clothing when we were both dressing in the same room, and she was wearing a form-fitting backless and sleeveless dress?

Despite all the streetlights, the street was dark, and in the thick humid air we didn't feel like moving fast anyway. This morning I had gotten up to go interview with Iphwin, hoping to get a job and then spend a weekend in Saigon with Helen. So far that much of the plan was going perfectly, but with a bewildering array of additions and changes that made no sense to me; it was as if some exceptionally stupid maker of action movies had decided to parodize my life. Helen and I drooped along, surrounded by our armed guards, who were probably pretty angry at having been so outwitted and outfought by the enemy—whoever the enemy might be.

By the time we got back to the hotel I was stumbling, falling asleep on my feet, as the adrenaline drained out of me and the reality of how complex and difficult our situation had become set in. McMoore told me that they'd take care of posting the guard, and two of his men went into the room ahead of us and searched it, finding no bugs, no weapons, and no lurking attackers. So far as we could determine, none of our possessions had been touched. "Sleep well, then, sir," McMoore said. "Once again—"

"You're terribly sorry, I know," I said. "And once again, I can't even begin to think what you could possibly have done differently. None of us had any idea how much trouble was about to erupt. I know I'll sleep better, knowing that you're out here guarding us, and truly, if Iphwin gives you all trouble, I'll be sure to speak up for you."

"I appreciate that, sir."

"And I'm glad you're here too," Helen said, the first words she had spoken since we left the police station.

McMoore nodded and left; Helen and I undressed slowly, turned out the lights, and got into bed.

After a long pause, I said, "First of all there's a small thing I want to ask you. When and where did you ever learn to use those weapons, let alone to go so heavily armed to dinner? I didn't even see you put them on—you must have been really quick."

She groaned, a sound so painful that I thought for a moment that she was ill, and thumped the bed with a fist. "I don't have the foggiest idea. I don't know how to shoot, Lyle, I don't, I never learned, I can't remember even ever holding a gun. All I know is that you and I went to dinner, after getting engaged, and then I don't remember much about dinner, except that it was some kind of Italian veal dish—I remember the attack, but the strangest part is that my impression was that she was aiming at me, and I remember getting under the table and you standing up, and some gunfire, and your body falling backwards with blood all over. I saw that my purse had fallen off the table, so I grabbed my phone and hit the emergency key—and then there I was, not under the table, but standing up, talking on the phone to the police, with a pistol in front of me on the table, a cloud of smoke all around me, and the dead body of a fat German tourist that didn't look remotely like the tall blonde woman who had attacked us. I had no idea what the things the police were saying meant, but I could tell they were on their way, so I hung up, looked around, and saw that you were perfectly fine, the German man was perfectly dead, and it was like I had just stepped into some other life—the dress I was wearing wasn't mine, I looked at it in the store and decided it was too expensive—and I had a bunch of heavy objects tied to me under my clothes. You can't imagine how strange it was when the police searched me and found out that they were weapons."

"You want me to believe that you saw a woman come at us, and shoot at you?" I asked. "I saw the man that you saw dead, and it was definitely me he was after."

"But it was honestly what I remember."

"Well," I said, "the body they showed me was Billie Beard, a woman who matches the description—very tall, blonde, muscular, in great shape but probably sixty years old. People might easily mistake her for a transvestite. Was that the woman you saw?"

"Yes, it was. Or at least your description matches."

We lay there still in the dark, not touching each other. My arms were folded on my chest; Helen seemed to be clutching the sheet. Like the very best hotels everywhere, the room was pitch black and dead silent, and I only knew where she was from the feel of the warmth of her body and the sound of her breathing. After a long time I thought of something else that I should mention. "The strangest thing of all in some ways," I said, "is that I believe you."

Helen sighed. "And I saw you shot dead in front of me and here you are."

"We seem to have a difference in our observations," I said. "And about some pretty critical matters." I was near crying or screaming, but Helen seemed to be worse off than I was, and she had had a much worse, scarier time. I was not going to throw a funk in front of her while I had any self-control at all. "Didn't it seem strange how fast the Cochin-Chinese dropped the case? If anything they seemed to be suddenly extremely *un*interested in investigating the case, and happy to get us out the door. And if Iphwin didn't put in the fix—well, there isn't any Free Republic of Diego Garcia, and—"

Helen wailed, a horrible sound I'd never heard come out of her before, and began to sob. "Not anymore," she choked out. "There's not one anymore. And I don't know where it went."

I'm probably not one of the world's great lovers. If pressed, I would have to admit I'm just about the classic stereotype of the scientist who doesn't know what to do in an emotional situation, but even I could figure this one out; I rolled over, reached out in the dark, took Helen in my arms, and held her as her body pitched and bucked with sobs.

A very long time later, she whispered, "I am going to tell you something I've never told anyone before, nobody at all, not ever. I'm not sure what it means, if anything. I don't know that it means anything. Maybe it only means that I'm mentally ill, but— oh, Lyle, it's so hard to trust anyone, even you, with this."

I hugged her close and said, "Tell me about it, or don't. Your call. I'll love you anyway."

It must have been the right thing to say. Helen grabbed my hand and squeezed it, hard, and then whispered, "All right. Don't even ask any questions till I'm done or I'll never have the courage to tell you the whole thing, but here goes. I grew up among the first generation born on Diego Garcia, where the Pacific Fleet of the American Navy fled and established the Free Republic after the Puritan Party won the elections in 1996 and took over the country. There were no Reichs when I grew up—I don't mean I didn't hear about them, I mean the United States and Russia and Britain won the war, Hitler died sometime in the forties, Germany was divided among the victors, all that. In 1983 there was an atomic war between the United States and all the Communist countries—Britain, France, Germany, Russia, and Japan—and after the war, when we were forced to give the whole northern tier of states plus New England to Canada, and Florida to Cuba, and so forth, the Puritan Party became very powerful, got elected, and made it illegal to be anything except a Puritan Christian. In the years just after that, almost two million people who fled the country made their way to where the fleet had put in, at the old naval facilities at Diego Garcia, and created a small trading nation there, kind of like Macao or Singapore, which quickly became rich. Really, that's the world I went to high school in. I'm not making it up.

"My senior year, my class went for a class trip to New Zealand, to visit the American expat community there, and on the last day, I was phoning my mother to let her know there had been a change of schedule, and suddenly my mother was asking me who I was and why I was calling her, so I got upset and hung up and dialed again—and the operator said there was no such country code and no such place. And I looked around and my whole class was gone, there was just me at the pay phone, and my Free Republic passport was gone but my American expat one was still there . . . I was so scared. I ran into a Catholic shelter for street people and stayed there for days, afraid to talk to anyone, thinking I might be locked up or given drugs or shock. I listened to the news and saw some papers, and I didn't understand a single thing I was reading, even though I knew most of the words. It sounded as if the Germans had won World War Two, and there was no Russia anymore, and there had never been a Puritan Party or a Free Republic—I was so terrified."

"What did you do?"

"Went to the library and speed-read history books to try to learn how to fake my way through the world.

"Then I started reading other subjects, once I realized I wasn't going to wake up and go home any minute. Math and science were easy, they weren't much changed, but literature was really something different.

"The nuns at the shelter were very nice, they thought I must have amnesia or something and they took care of me and tried to help me recover my memory. The thing was, my memory was actually what was causing all the problem, you know. Once I was sure enough of my ability to fake being from this world I'd fallen into, I claimed to recover my memory, and I caught a boat to a small town where I thought they wouldn't check up, told them I'd dropped out of school but I wanted to take my equivalency exam.

"They let me, I did well, then I enlisted to have a job, put in my four years for Her Majesty—as a clerk, mind you, and no one ever even showed me a weapon—and then was in a position to go to school. Naturally I majored in history—there was so much I needed to know if I wasn't to be carted off to some loony bin—and I found I liked it, stuck with it, and here I am. And I still miss my mother horribly, and for eighteen years I've had a very hard time believing in the world I live in. I love you, Lyle, but I wish I could wake up and find that I'm still eighteen and this is all a dream."

"Perfectly understandable," I said, and gave her a little kiss on the cheek.

"You *believe* me?"

"I believe you're telling the truth as you know it. And I believe that your story is entirely possible. I just don't understand how or why. Have you checked your handbag? Do you have a Free Republic of Diego Garcia passport?"

She switched on the light and stared at me, wide-eyed. "Lyle, I'm so afraid to look. What if I do? What if . . . what if the Free Republic is *there* again? I could . . . Mummy would only be fifty-eight, she'd surely still be alive, she must have been so worried—what if I don't have it?"

I kissed her on the forehead. "Shall I look?"

"Would you, please?"

I got out her handbag and looked inside; there were not the usual two passports, US Government in Exile plus Kingdom of New Zealand. There were four. I pulled them all out. The two expected ones were there, as was one from the Free Republic. "One from Diego," I said, and handed it to her.

"When I was growing up we called it Free Deejy," she said,

absently, sitting up in bed to look through it. "But the flag was different from this, and the capital was on board a beached aircraft carrier, not in some place called New Washington."

"Could they have built it since you left?"

"I don't know where. It's a pretty small place." She flipped to the back, where the visa stamps go. "Oh, look. I've been to the Free Republic of Hawaii, Korea—which doesn't seem as if it is part of Japan—and a dozen or so times to the Indonesian Soviet Socialist Commonwealth, wherever that might be. What's the fourth passport?"

I looked down at it and sighed. "It's the only one that isn't for Helen Perdida, and it's a spare Enzy one. With an 015 code."

"What's an 015?"

"I guess you really were just a clerk in the Navy, love." I sighed and sat down on the floor. "I was an officer and had to learn that anyone with an 015 gets absolutely everything he or she asks for, right now. It's a code stamped in the upper right corner that indicates that you're a high-level secret agent, a spy or maybe an assassin. At least now we know where you got the gun training."

"What does it all mean?" she asked.

"It means we're right out of any possibility of figuring it out tonight," I said, "and it means I believe, absolutely, everything you've told me. Every damned word, my love. Now let's get under the covers, turn out the light, hold each other, and see what we can learn in the morning. I love you very much, and I am so sorry that you were separated from your mother so suddenly."

I'm not sure if that was a right or wrong thing to say; she burst into tears and cried for a good half hour before she could finally get to sleep. When I was sure she was sound asleep, I slipped out of bed, sat down on the floor, and had a good cry, myself.

The next morning we had just gotten up and had room service breakfast in. We had ordered a pot of coffee and a cup for McMoore's man outside the door, which I figured was a wise investment, and I noted with some amusement that no one from the hotel found it even slightly unusual; the Royal Saigon probably dealt with bodyguards all the time. We were dressed and wondering what to do; not having been guarded before, we weren't sure what it was ethical to ask people to do in the way of guarding us out on the street; could we just go out like any tourists, did we need to consult? This was outside both our usual experiences.

We had settled on the plan of having the man at the door call his supervisor in for a conference, when the phone rang. I picked it up. "Mr. Lyle Peripart, I'm afraid I have very bad news concerning your house." It was the voice of my house-sitting company, which monitors the house's brain, and that was already bad news—because they only call you if the brain can't. At the least it means a couple of months' pay to replace a damaged brain. And usually if the brain is damaged, the house is too.

"How bad is it?"

The robot's voice was implacable; it's not supposed to get emotionally involved. "Mr. Peripart, the house was a complete loss, sir. I have recordings up to three minutes before the alarm was turned in to the police. That usually indicates a brain that was killed instantly. The building itself was destroyed, sir."

I sighed. Well, this is what one keeps insurance current for; it was going to be a nuisance, and I would probably come out of it poorer than I went into it, but there wasn't much else to do. I had never been one, really, to get attached to things, and the house had always seemed to be simply my personal machine for living. Now I would need a new machine.

"Is there anything else you need to know at this time, sir?"

"No, I don't think so."

"Have a more pleasant day, then, sir."

I hung up and sat down heavily on the bed. "My house is dead. Brain killed and the building totaled," I explained to Helen. "I suppose we can call and get the police report on our way home. We'll have to cut this trip short."

"Did they say whether anyone had broken in or it might have been teenagers joyriding your house?"

That was a common problem. There were groups of kids who were very adroit at killing the brain, holding a party, and then setting a fire before they left, just before the cops got there.

"No, they didn't. I suppose I could have asked for the suspected cause. Couldn't be joyriders, though, not with a recording going up to the last three minutes—the whole point of what they do is to stretch out the time between killing the brain and abandoning the house. I guess I could call them back and ask them now. The most likely thing, unfortunately, is that it will turn out to be something that makes no sense—based on what's been happening in the last twenty-four hours."

"Well, it sounds like we really do have to get back there. Was there much of sentimental value?"

"Some pictures of me when I was a boy. The family heirlooms, the photos of my ancestors and that stuff, everything of any sentimental value, was all in the safety deposit box at my bank. All my work materials were in the office at school. The house mostly just was a place to sleep and eat. And it was all insured, anyway. It's not that big a deal, it's just that I'm not looking forward to the volume of paperwork I know I'll have to cope with, and I'm really not looking forward to dealing with that while I'm also coping with a new job where I commute out every week. And of course I'm kind of worried about what connection this might have with everything else that's been happening. There are all sorts of things to worry about, of course, and I am worried about dealing with all of it, but I'm not really that upset. It's not like I lost that Studebaker Skyjump—*that*, I would miss."

McMoore himself was on the job—I don't know if he didn't sleep or had just taken over another shift—and as soon as we explained what the problem was, he was on top of it. He packed us up, put us in a limousine that seemed to have unusually thick oddly colored windows and reassuringly thick metal plates discreetly placed around the inside, drove us to the boat shed over in Cholon, and escorted us to the jump boat, not neglecting to search it thoroughly for people and devices and to hang around while I did readouts and made sure it had been on no further joyrides. Everything seemed to be on the up-and-up, so we shook hands with McMoore, cast off, pulled out of the boat shed, and told the Skyjump to take us home. I didn't feel fit to fly.

What followed was something like a two-hour dream, as we called from the high part of the trajectory for the police report and were told that there was no official cause yet, came down outside Auckland harbor, got the cab, and eventually found ourselves standing and staring at the place where my driveway ended in a crater.

It was about eight or nine feet deep at the deepest point, perfectly circular, and my house would not have fitted within it; the four corners of the foundation looked at each other across that gulf. The sandy soil seemed to have fused in places, as if by tremendous heat, and all the facing neighbors' windows were boarded up; there were char marks on their roofs where sparks or the flash had ignited shingles, and the aluminum siding on the two nearest neighbors' houses had warped, the white paint turning brown in spots.

My house had vanished in a moment of tremendous heat, but there had been no explosion—all the damage was caused by radiated heat, and the wave of superheated air. The police report said there had been a thunderclap, as if the burning house had disappeared so suddenly that the air had rushed back inaudibly.

All the grass and trees in the yard were scorched and dead.

We stood on the blackened lawn and stared, for many long minutes; our luggage was in a pile beside us, and the cab had long since gone on its way. No one came out to talk to us; perhaps because none of them had a window facing our way through which they could see, but more likely it was just a matter of the human desire not to stand too close to bad luck. After a long time, Helen said, "Do you suppose there's anything known to exist in everyday life, anywhere, that could make this happen?"

"Not that I know about. And it's the kind of thing they might have mentioned when I was an undergrad in physics."

"Was it intended, perhaps, to get you?"

"Could have been, I suppose, but you'd think that someone who could summon a completely unknown physical force with this much energy would be capable of ringing my doorbell, or even just phoning, and finding out if I was home, first." I shook my head. "A couple days ago, things made sense."

"It will be at least a couple days before they begin to make any sense again," a voice said behind us. We turned and found that Geoffrey Iphwin was there, as was a beautiful old real Rolls-Royce, with a real human driver at the wheel. Just behind and ahead of it, two small armored cars had parked. "Right now I don't think I can give you an explanation that will make any sense to you, at least not sense that you could use for anything, and part of the problem is that I don't begin to understand everything myself. But if you will come along, I can pretty well assure your safety—at least as well as I can assure mine—and after that perhaps we can begin to fight back, and force the world to make a little more sense, eh?"

He ran in little mincing steps over to the site where my house had been, his eye seeming to catch and stop at the many places where the sand had been baked into little fused pockets by the intense heat, and now reflected the late-afternoon sun with a sort of soft brown shine. He looked back at us, his expression mild and soft. "If you want entirely out of all of this, I can just write out a check for enough to get you a new house, give you some time and money to resettle, and probably but not definitely, make it clear enough so that you'll be left alone. But I'm afraid if you want to press on, there's not much alternative—you're going to be in danger, and you're in for the duration."

"Can't you even tell us what the sides are?"

Iphwin shrugged. "The Reichs and their governments are mostly on the other side. Is that good enough?"

"Good enough for me," Helen said, with surprising vehemence, and then I noticed I was nodding vigorously.

"All right, then," Iphwin said. "I'm afraid you will have to come with me, then. At the moment the other side is moving much, much faster than I anticipated they would. I do apologize—my underestimating them is what has allowed them to do these things to you, and it's also why I shall have to bring you further and deeper into the situation, much sooner than I would have preferred. And I'm also afraid that you won't be happy when you find out how many of the shocks you are feeling, or are going to feel, are very much my fault. I really do deeply hope that when it all becomes clearer, you will be able to forgive me."

We threw our bags into his car. When Helen had been shooting she had seemed bigger and stronger, and now she struggled more than I'd have expected to move her suitcase. Iphwin took us back to the harbor, where his people had already gassed and serviced the Skyjump. By dark, we were a very long way north, in one of the guest suites in the Big Sapphire, surrounded by the sea just north of Surabaya, unpacking and trying to figure out where life would take us next.

Unpacking didn't take me long—all I had was what I had taken for a weekend, and the clothes I had emergency-ordered would be delivered here Monday while I was working. Helen had stopped for some more things from her place, but it didn't take her twenty minutes to pack or unpack—she was pretty typical of female academics, not much on clothes. When we were all done, it was only seven at night, we should theoretically have just been sitting down to our second dinner in Saigon, and there was absolutely nothing to do.

Naturally we decided to put on the headsets and see if we could find any of our friends in the VR chat room. I could tell immediately that tonight was going to be all right, because not only was everyone there, but I drew Bogart and Helen drew Bergman again. The first thing I did, of course, was get rid of the stupid cigarette that made it hard to breathe or taste anything, and the second thing I did was corner Paul Henreid, grab his lapels, and tell him to buzz off and keep his eyes off my girl if he wanted to leave the place alive. Then I stopped by the piano and told Sam I wanted a selection from the classics, and he settled into a nice Debussy piece, dreamy and romantic, instead of the corny old thing he usually played. As far as I was concerned, I had saved the picture.

I sat down at the table to find everyone babbling at once. "Suppose I asked whether anybody here could tell this story coherently?" I said, pulling my chair up.

Helen really did wear Ingrid Bergman well; she turned to me with a calm stare, paused a moment, and said, "Well, then you would be disappointed with the answer. But at least everyone here agrees that it started with Terri. And the good news is, if we can make sense out of it, we can probably get some idea of how we got released from jail."

Terri was being pretty moderate, for Terri—she was being Yvonne, of whom Claude Rains had once said, "All by herself, she may constitute an entire second front." She leaned back in an angly, awkward way that would have told anyone at once that that body was being worn by a teenager, and said, "You might know that since I have to go to the special American expat school and since my father is a rich man, I don't get out much. In fact I usually can only go to regular school events or to parties at my parents' friends' houses. I get real bored a lot of the time, because there's only so much homework you can do, and only so much chat room time. Plus of course I hate to admit it, but I'm kind of nosy.

"And then the thought occurred to me that Eric—he's a buddy of mine at school that has this crush on me, but thank god I'm not that desperate, but he's really sweet and will do almost anything for me—Eric had given me a neat little program that would track people's real net addresses while they were in the chat room, so I could see who I was really talking to, and I had had it running for months. And so . . . well, gee, I just think, anybody having a romantic holiday in the Far East, and all . . . oh, I wanted to know just what you guys were up to. I know you told me where you'd be staying and I know you told me all about it, but for some reason the signal broke up right when you said it, or I was distracted, or something. And that was why I tried tracing you, figuring you'd be doing something romantic. I hope you don't mind being spied on."

My first thought was, *Why not? everyone else does,* but I swallowed that comment—I figured it might embarrass her—and said, "Considering the result, we ought to thank you."

"Well, it was weird, because the geographic coordinates it gave were for somewhere in—"

The world froze.

"Signal just broke up," I said. "Where did you say?"

"It broke up on my end too," she said. "Your coordinates—"

The world froze again.

"Did you—?"

"It happened to all of us," the Colonel said, "which I think is pretty strange. Try saying it very slowly, Terri; maybe somebody is censoring the net, even though that's supposed to be impossible. I'm sure that if they could the—"

For the third time, the world froze.

"I can't even say their name," the Colonel said, "without tripping the censorship program."

"That's all right," I said. "We all know you meant the Germans."

Just as I said "Germans," there was another freeze; everyone came out of it looking baffled.

"Hmmph," Helen said. "Well, if nothing else we've just learned that some kinds of casual chat are not allowed. I always thought the little freezes were caused by jam-ups somewhere between me and the server, something about having too little bandwidth, but we're in the Big Sapphire here and there's no way I could be as short on bandwidth as I usually was in Enzy."

Everyone nodded, and Terri said, "Okay, let me try to say the name. It looked like you.

"Were right in the middle.

"Of." She wet her lips and then slowly said. "Ho.

"Chi.

"Minh.

"City."

I had heard all the syllables clearly and I had no idea what she had said. "That's strange," I said. "Actually we were in Saigon."

"It just broke up," everyone chorused.

"Sai . . ." I paused. "Gon." It seemed to go right through, but now everyone looked very confused.

"I clearly heard you and I wrote it down," Kelly said, looking at the pad in front of her, "but now I can't read what I wrote. It looks like S . . . A . . . I . . . G . . . O . . . N."

"That's right," I said, "Saigon." There was another freeze that denoted another system crash.

"If this keeps up, this story may take quite a while to tell," Roger said.

Terri nodded emphatically. "Well, anyway, what I found out was that you weren't at your hotel, but in jail, and when I tried getting into the jail's public information board, it told me you were being held on suspicion of murder. That didn't sound right, so I called Roger, and I called Kelly. I think Roger sort of took the first steps—"

"Not much more than making some net calls," Roger said. "My old second in command, Esmé Sanderson, from back when I commanded the"

FREEZE

"before the damned"

FREEZE

"forced us to disband and"

FREEZE

—

"This *is* going to be a hard story to get out," Helen said, "but anyway, Esmé Sanderson had been your second in command, even if you can't tell us where or when or for what unit, right?"

"Right, and now she's a cop in Mexico City."

We had all braced for a freeze when it was obvious that he was going to speak a place name, but that one was apparently not a problem. Who can explain the choices and ideas of a censor? Sykes let his breath out—he really was remarkably splendid when he was wearing Sidney Greenstreet—and said, "Well, there, I thought they'd hit that one but they didn't. Anyway, she said she'd look into it, and what she told me later was that she had checked up on your case with authorities in Ho

"Chi

"Minh

"City. There, it didn't make a breakup."

"But I have no idea what you said," Helen pointed out. "All right, so she checked up with the authorities."

"That's right, and she discovered that you had shot Billie Beard, so she called it to the attention of her supervisor, Jesús Picardin. She says she thought Picardin was going to kiss her when he heard the news; they'd been trying for years to get Billie Beard either into Mexico, where she could be arrested, or busted someplace where they could extradite, but having her dead was even better."

"I thought Billie Beard was a cop," I said.

"She is—a bad cop even in a service that's known for its badness. Probably even her bosses didn't much care what happened to her anymore. Billie Beard was wanted for nearly everything, nearly everywhere. Real bad piece of work. Even the"

FREEZE

"uh that is I mean her employers, didn't like her much, and she was wanted for all kinds of things. The world is not at all sorry to see her go. And so Picardin authorized sending the files about Beard to the local authorities, and as soon as those files started to scroll out of the fax machine, your friend Inspector Dong had some very good reasons to stop worrying; he was assured that no matter how the case came out, no one was going to care very much, because the part they did care about was already accomplished."

"I guess I was the other part of getting you out," Kelly said. "It happens I went to school with Jenny Schmidt, who is now Jenny Bannon, who is more officially Jennifer H. S. Bannon, Ambassador from the Free Republic of Diego Garcia to the Court of New Zealand. I thought I knew, from somewhere, that Helen was a DG citizen, so I confirmed that, then called Jenny and got her on it. She called up their Ambassador—another guy we went to school with, creepy guy we all called Bobo, but very willing to do a favor for a friend—Bobo seemed to know you, Helen, and that helped too. So in a short time he was *also* phoning the Saigon police."

"Well, at least that explains how we got released," Helen said. "Let me try an experiment here. How many of you have heard of the"—

Everyone froze again, except that I clearly heard her—not through the VR, but just because she was in the room with me— say "Puritan Party."

"All right," she said. She picked up her pad and slowly read off "Ho . . . Chi . . . Minh . . . City. Now I'll say it at normal speed, and let's see what happens. Ho Chi Minh City."

This time there was no freeze, but the world seemed to wobble a little. "Now someone else try."

"Saigon," the Colonel said, and no one froze. "But now that I think of it, from the unit history, I seem to recall that Saigon"

FREEZE

"City. No one calls it Saigon anymore."

I tried to say "His Most Catholic Majesty the King of Cochin-China does," but apparently just the thought caused a freeze, or maybe my thought and Helen's together did.

We played around all night, and we established a few rules. If we said it slowly enough, no freeze happened. If the people who weren't talking carefully copied the words down and read them aloud, slowly, no freeze happened. If we practiced that for a while, till everyone could say the words, then we stopped freezing on the word itself, but often froze if we tried to use it in a sentence.

It gave us something to talk about, and we went really late that night, especially since none of us had anything really pressing in the next few hours. We developed slightly more theories than we had people—Helen and the Colonel each had two. Mine was that the censor was some kind of crude AI that did some kind of very limited brain monitoring and that as we practiced the word, we got to where we could say it without meaning it—but if we used it in a sentence, the meaning came back and set off the censor. Helen thought that somehow everyone's brain had been programmed with a virus that acted to censor other people's words at the auditory center so that as we practiced we gradually stopped censoring each other; her alternative theory was that the censor had some way of determining, after a few freezes, that the conversation was harmless, and then wouldn't freeze it again until it changed.

All of us elaborated our theories and sniped at each other's; we did dozens of other small experiments without really adding any more facts to our store of knowledge. It finally got too late for Colonel Sykes, who said the sun was coming up in Mexico, so he departed; Kelly had to go a while later, as she had a first reading on a new play, and finally Terri stretched and yawned—an impressive gesture in Yvonne's body because that jacket had not been constructed for a woman who moved freely—and left also. "Ever think of having sex with Bogart?" I asked Helen.

"Said the man who would really like to have sex with Ingrid Bergman," she said, smiling. "I'm pretty tired. Hold the thought for another night?"

"Sure."

By the time we got up on Sunday, it was past noon. Iphwin's people had supplied us with the English-language version of the Batavia paper, plus the *LA Times in Exile* from Auckland. We sat around, read, ate, and talked. Late in the afternoon we went out on one of the Big Sapphire's many observation decks and watched the big waves roll by, messengers from some storm a thousand miles away. For the whole of Sunday, nothing unusual happened. That was beginning to seem strange.

PART TWO

The Bureau of Missing Nations

On Monday morning we made and ate a quick breakfast in the room's kitchenette, then got dressed, stepped out the door into the corridors of the Big Sapphire, and headed for the office that we had been assigned. Iphwin was waiting for us there, to my surprise; I couldn't help wondering how a man who ran so much of the planet's economy had time to meet with us so often and at such length, without even any interruptions.

"Well," Iphwin said. "Glad to have you here at last. I've decided to take charge of this matter personally, at least for a while. Now, Helen, let's start with a reconciliation problem. Let me suppose the existence of two documents of equally good provenance, containing statements absolutely contrary to each other. Suppose, say, that one of them specifies that General Grant died at the battle of Cold Harbor, and the other that he was killed while holding Little Round Top at Gettysburg."

"But he wasn't," I said. "He lived to be the president of the United States, for two terms I think, after Johnson?"

"After *Johnson*?" Helen said, gaping at me. "Where I grew up, Lyndon Johnson was the president of the Republic of Texas, the last one before they voted to go communist, and shot him. And after I came to Enzy, I learned he was the first Secretary of the Treasury for the government in exile. Either way, U.S. Grant couldn't have been president *after* him—"

"*Andrew* Johnson," I said. "The Vice President who succeeded Abe Lincoln after his assassination in 1865."

She shook her head slowly. "Hannibal Hamlin succeeded Lincoln," she said. "In 1863. After the impeachment."

None of this perturbed Iphwin one bit that I could see; he listened with great interest but didn't seem to feel any need to intervene.

After a long pause, just to break the silence, I finally asked, "Can I ask what provenance is?"

"Provenance is what you have when you have established that a document actually originated where and when it was supposed to have," Helen said. "As Iphwin has set up this problem, the documents have equally good provenance, which means the case is equally strong that either one really does date from the American Civil War."

"Oh," I said. "I was hoping that I was just misunderstanding one idea somewhere, but it doesn't seem likely, now."

The pause dragged on, broken only by Iphwin's moving between three chairs. When he finally found one he liked, at least for the moment, Iphwin sat tugging at his lower lip and said, "All right, now, imagining you have those two documents, of equally good provenance, what is your next move?"

"Well," Helen said, "speaking as a historian I guess it's pretty obvious. I need to find some way to challenge the accuracy or the provenance of at least one of them, preferably both."

"What would you do, Lyle?"

"I'm not a historian."

"Answer as the developer of abductive statistics."

"Hmmm. But if you can do the things Helen just outlined, that would be the thing to do."

"Assume for the moment that it proves impossible; you cannot show that either document is from anything other than that period, and both appear to be absolutely authentic. Furthermore, in your case, anyway, you have a large body of evidence that tells you that neither of the documents can possibly be right."

"In abductive math, we don't. We leave them unreconciled until something turns up to settle the question."

"All right," Iphwin said, with seemingly infinite patience, though I felt like a complete idiot who had wandered into a Socratic dialogue while looking for the bathroom. "Suppose now it is absolutely dreadfully important to reconcile the two documents and the known facts."

"Well, then, at that point I try to identify how many things the documents *do* agree on. For example, they agree that there really was a General Grant in the Civil War."

"Why do you want to know that?" Iphwin demanded. For one moment he had an expression of keen interest, before he resumed his usual bland composure.

"Because what I'm finding out are the implicit constraints on the solution. It can't be one that denies the shared material."

"All right, go on."

"Then at the next higher level, you get more abstract points of agreement, like that the Civil War had battles and that General Grant died in one of them. And then you try to figure out whether the two messages are different *enough*. That is, do they require reconciliation? How much does your world change if they can or can't be reconciled? For example, we are more likely to have hypotheses in which General Grant died once; till then we know he's dead and that it's probably associated with battle during the war.

"Thus the abductive process would say that we suspend conclusions and not apply induction or deduction yet—and would then work on the conditions that allow us to form hypotheses, because if all your hypotheses were just random noise, you'd never find anything that worked in the real world.

"There has to be an abductive process, a process of generating hypotheses more likely to be right than not—and so what you're doing is taking the shared elements in the evidence and identifying a family of hypotheses—all the possible hypotheses in which Grant served in the Civil War, all of *those* hypotheses in which he was killed in battle, and so forth—down to where you have to suspend judgment and get more evidence. Abduction isn't a process of finding answers—ordinary induction and deduction do that—but of allocating scarce time to questions. And of course from that standpoint, only having two pieces of evidence, the question is trivial; it gets more complex when some of the hypotheses are about which pieces of evidence are relevant, and how."

Iphwin nodded. "Now let's try something bigger. This time you have two documents from the American Civil War, and each contains a list of ten battles. There are only two battles that overlap between the two lists."

"Well," Helen said, "the usual thing a historian would do is figure that the two lists were made for different purposes by different people, and what's important for one may not be important for the other."

"Suppose each list purports to be a list of the ten battles with the highest death tolls."

"The two sides may have called them by different names, or they may disagree about what a battle is," she said. "Like the way that the first three days of the Battle of Wheeling is often called the Battle of Deer Run, and the last four days are counted separately as the Battle of Steubenville." She seemed to be gaining morale every moment as her specialty was called on; her green eyes were keen with interest and she sat up with her old athletic energy.

"Well," I said, "an abductive statistician would say that we have a family of hypotheses that the two documents actually contain the same information, or part of the same information, in forms which are somehow mutually translatable; that is, with enough information, the maker of one list could always explain his differences with the maker of the other list. And therefore the genuine unknown is the relation between the two documents. If we add more documents to the pile, they might determine the relationship."

"And could the relationship be anything as simple as one being true and one being false?" Helen asked. "Lyle, I'm alarmed at what you do for a living."

"It could very easily be the case. For example, say you go looking for your glasses."

"Usually when I do that they're on my forehead."

"Just so. You have a family of hypotheses: forehead, on the nightstand, folded into the bedclothes, used as a bookmark, and so forth. You draw a hypothesis from that family—which you make as small a family as you can before drawing—and test it. Say it turns out false. Then you add the assumption that any hypothesis which has tested false is still false, and on that grounds you keep testing new ones till you find one that is true—which establishes a relation with all the other hypotheses."

"But I don't care about all the places my glasses aren't, once I find them."

"Nevertheless you've established it."

"Good enough," Iphwin said. "Now we're getting somewhere."

"I wish I knew where," I admitted. "I really don't understand why you can't just tell us what's going on."

Iphwin nodded. "I hold a family of hypotheses to the effect that telling you, at this time, might imperil discoveries I will need later. It may not, for all I know. But I prefer not to run the risk. And if it does cost us the further discoveries, the consequences may be grave for everyone, and therefore I won't tell you until I am sure I am not going to screw something up. But I do want you to know that this isn't my choice."

Helen sat down and cocked her head to one side, looking at Iphwin as if he had just tried to put one over on her. "All right, then, is there any way you can tell us who or what your adversary is?"

"I wish I could. I have a whole series of guesses based on various experiences and encounters with the forces that oppose me. Many of these experiences point to contradictory conclusions. Others complement each other, of course."

"I guess what you're trying to tell me is that the weirdness in the world"—I thought I understood what he was saying but couldn't believe he was saying it—"everything from the fuel consumption of my jump boat while it was tied up, to the severe discrepancies in our memories, to the behavior of Billie Beard and the way she kept appearing and disappearing—all these things are being *caused*? I mean, not just like ordinary events, but something is causing them to be contradictory?"

"Or the indeterminacy may be a form of attack on my business," Iphwin said. "Make the world unpredictable enough and capitalism becomes impossible, and it so happens I am a capitalist. I have a very large array of holdings. A couple of years ago I became aware that many things were happening that looked like coincidences but seemed to be happening too often; then on top of that, the explanations that seemed to suggest themselves rapidly became mutually contradictory. Some very good mathematicians—you would know their names, Lyle, but no, I may not tell them to you—working under a covert contract from me, concluded that the odds of all these things happening were very low, but of course that means little; the odds of any one configuration of the world are low, but the world always ends up in some configuration or other. They also compiled a list of other things that might happen, incidents that might fit a pattern established by the previous incidents, and to my deep surprise those predictions began to come true. In the words of a fellow American, a few generations back, 'Once is happenstance, twice is coincidence, three times is enemy action.'

"Furthermore, as soon as I began to take any steps to identify the enemy and to harden myself as a target, the attacks stepped up and became more elaborate and complex. Now, my researches identified you all as possible assistants in this project. I cannot tell you who is attacking me because I don't really know. In fact, a secret known to only a few people in my company is that I don't know anything from before when I was about twenty—as far as I can determine, I have complete amnesia for my childhood and adolescent years, and I seem to have arrived from nowhere—there are no records of me before that time, and yet one day there I was in Edinburgh, able to read, write, calculate, and so forth, with my identity papers in one front pocket—I also knew how to use and present them—and an enormous wad of cash in the other. It is entirely possible that all this originates from some enemy that I don't know about because they have lain low for fifteen or twenty years."

"Since you're an expat who does business in the Reichs," Helen pointed out, "one obvious possibility is that the American Resistance may have targeted you."

"You can dismiss that possibility. I am *not* at all concerned that what remains of the American Resistance might be after me, because I am a primary financier for the American Resistance, I am in contact with it, and I coordinate my activities with it. You are high enough placed in the company so that you might as well know this right off; every so often ConTech is doing something inexplicable because we're supporting the illegal American organizations around the world."

"Is that something you should be telling brand-new employees?" I asked.

"You have no idea how long we've been watching you, or how much we know about you. You wouldn't have been hired if I couldn't be perfectly sure it was safe to tell you this. Anyway, my point is this: as you investigate this problem for me, don't let yourself get too suspicious about the activities of American Resistance cells and fronts all around my company. They aren't the ones causing the trouble. I don't want you to waste time investigating them, and I really don't want you to blow any of their various covers."

"You can depend on us," Helen said, firmly, and I found I was nodding my head vigorously, liking ConTech and Iphwin a great deal more than I had before.

"You'll pardon my pointing out that I know that, and I should know it—I've spent enough to make sure I knew it," Iphwin said. "Now, the way that I became interested in you was that some of our espionage and intelligence teams developed a very real possibility that we could at least get a rough list of who the adversary was after—that is, we didn't know who the bad guys were except at the local, low-ranking flunky level, but we did know who they seemed to be out to get. And as it happened, Billie Beard showed up pretty often wherever they were planning to make trouble—and she was all over Auckland last month, but especially hanging around Whitman College. The two of you had already been identified as potential recruits for ConTech, with interesting specialties, and since that was just the category of people she seemed to have an ugly tendency to kill, if she got to them first, we moved as quickly as we discreetly could to get you under our umbrella. The other thing, which interests me very much this morning, is that before being sent after you, she was pulled off a job in Mexico City, where she had been shadowing Jesús Picardin."

"Who's that?" I asked. "The name sounds familiar."

"It should. Picardin is the boss for Esmé Sanderson, who

used to be second in command for Colonel Roger Sykes of the Third Free American Regiment. The one that you know in your talk group as 'the Colonel.' When Terri Teal got word of your arrest, she called Sykes, who called Sanderson, who talked to Picardin—and he's the one that dug out the huge file on Beard and dispatched it to Saigon. If anyone did, he's the one who got you out of jail."

"I like him already," Helen said.

"Me too, and all we knew about him before was that Billie Beard was interested in him. Anyway, the fact that he showed up in your case in that way is extremely interesting. Especially since Jenny Bannon, who was the other leg of the process leading to your release, was also being shadowed by Billie Beard at one time, and furthermore it turns out that she and Picardin belong to the same VR chat group. Somehow or other this is turning out to be a very small world."

"And she's from a country that I thought was entirely imaginary, or some kind of delusion," Helen said. "She's from that confusing part of my memory."

Iphwin looked blank and stood stock-still. I'd never seen that happen before. Helen quickly sketched in what she'd told me. She seemed to gain confidence this time and though her lip sometimes trembled when she spoke of her mother, she didn't cry.

"That's one place she's from. But one of our employees met her at a reception and got a business card, and though there is no such country as the Free Republic of Diego Garcia, nor any such street as the one its embassy is on, nor any such phone exchange in Auckland as the one listed—when we dial that number, we get the embassy, and if she's not too busy, Jenny Bannon answers the phone. And obviously enough, since your friend Kelly went to school with her and still calls her, and you can call Kelly— well, you see what I mean by discrepancies.

"Now, aside from the intellectually interesting question of

how you all arrived in such a small world with each other, the other thing that is interesting to me is that exactly the same people who appear to be trying to track down and kill the remaining American Resistance, and who seem to be associated with, and perhaps arranging, the many coincidences and lapses of causality that have been doing so much damage to ConTech, are the people who have been trying to kill this small knot of chat rooms and acquaintances.

"Furthermore, they seem to have been foiled *largely by accident,* which is not only odd in a professional organization, but makes many of my investigative team wonder, intensely, whether we ourselves might be being attacked by one group or force, and supported by another, neither of which we know anything about. If the enemy of the enemy is my friend, why won't my friend introduce himself? But in any case, anyone that the enemy is out to eliminate—such as you two, or Jenny Bannon, or Jesú Picardin—is probably a good person to keep alive and well, if we possibly can. Hence our interest in you."

Through all this long conversation, Iphwin hadn't sat still for as long as five seconds, but had bounced from place to place, sitting on desks and shelves, leaning against walls, and rocketing around the room like a man who has lost something valuable. "And honestly, according to the research group, that is as much as I can safely tell you at this point. I will tell you more, eventually everything, I hope, just as soon as I'm sure it's safe. For the moment, though, what I specifically want you to do is to conduct an investigation into an area that we don't have anyone assigned to yet—an area where we have a single puzzling piece of information that makes no sense that we are aware of, but ought to make some kind if we only knew what kind, and we'd like to see what you can do with it.

"That piece of information is this: ask most people on the street questions about the past, either elementary history or events in their own lifetime, and we get a pretty conventional story, with minor errors that we could just as easily ascribe to bad memory, bad teaching, or sheer random perversity as anything else. But whenever we try interviewing people who seem to be of interest to the enemy, or whose research interests look particularly relevant to the investigation, when we ask what those special people remember of the past, we find all sorts of fundamental disagreements, such as the argument we just had about General Grant, or like Helen's experience of suddenly finding all of history was different from what she remembered.

"Neither of you is a policeman or secret agent—as far as I know, though the Saigon police have a different opinion about you, Helen, and are absolutely convinced that you must have been a top-level agent for years. Based on what you did, it seems as if briefly you were not a relatively mild-mannered history professor—but then, while you weren't, who were you? Anyway, the one thing we know is that these wildly inconsistent memories have something to do with the problem—so your job, the historian and the abductive mathematician, is to arrive at some explanation for the phenomenon."

"That's the job, then?" I asked. "To figure out why people linked with this mysterious attack on ConTech have memories so different from everyone else's?"

Iphwin nodded, and then sat down cross-legged on the floor, like a small child. As he spoke he used his finger to draw some complex, incomprehensible diagram on the floor. "My company has been attacked many times since I founded it. We've been leaned on by organized crime, by various kinds of secret police, by underground political organizations, and by religious cults. No surprise in all that—if you get big enough, you get leaned on. But in every case before, I've been able to fight it off, with some combination of bribes and force. This one concerns me more.

"It looks like a general assault on causality, happening all around ConTech. Perhaps they have discovered some way of altering causality and are using it to make ordinary attacks and blackmail more effective. Or maybe someone with a power beyond anything we know simply has an agenda too different from anything any of us would have for any of us to understand it. Whatever the case, if it's possible to know, I don't just want to know who they are and why they did it, but how."

He jumped up from the floor and said, "Each of you has an interview with a psychiatrist in ten minutes. Don't worry, it's not because I think you are crazy." Then he lunged out the door before either of us could say anything, and when we looked at the computer terminals on our desk we saw that each of us had to report to a room on the same floor in ten minutes' time.

I thought a while. "ConTech must have tracked the whole network of our friends, for Iphwin to have such a clear understanding of how we got out of jail. And yet with so many of them watching us, the party of bodyguards could still get ambushed in Saigon, and somehow or other Billie Beard could still get through to beat me up. And someone impersonating me managed to pick you up in my jump boat and take you to Saigon, before returning the boat, and not bothering to do anything to cover it up." I sat down and stared into space. "There's an amazing amount of power somewhere behind Iphwin. And whoever the bad guys are, there's at least that much power behind them."

"Always assuming that Iphwin and the bad guys aren't the same people."

"Always assuming." I stood up and straightened my clothes. "Well, off to the psychologists. The funny thing is, the only thing that I'm pretty sure of is that I'm not losing my mind."

"Mine might be misplaced but I'm sure I still have it somewhere," Helen said, also standing and smoothing her skirt. She stretched and yawned. I liked the way she stepped forward and straightened my tie as if I were her prize cat. "And you're not a professor anymore, so you don't get to be absentminded. All right, let's go see the nice shrinks and see what they want to do with us."

In a short while I was sitting in a small room in a comfortable leather armchair, watching a quiet little man with a dark ring beard take notes on everything I said. He began by asking, "Who is Mickey Mouse?"

I answered, and he asked, "What was the Thirteenth Amendment to the US Constitution? What coach introduced the forward pass? When was the World's Fair in St. Louis? Who won the Second Canadian War?"

Some of the questions, like the St. Louis World's Fair, referred to things I had never heard of—the city had never been rebuilt after the great earthquake of 1885 because the rivers no longer ran by it. Some were insanely trivial and easy. Every so often one of the questions would be completely unintelligible on first hearing, and after hearing it again slowly I would realize it was rooted in assumptions that were so different from mine that I had to think about it a couple of times. I pointed this out to the shrink, and he nodded vigorously the way all shrinks do. Also the way they all do, he asked me, "How does it make you feel when a question is so far off base that you can't figure out how to answer it?"

"A little tense, I guess. Not worse than that."

"When was the last time you saw an article in a professional journal by an American astronomer? Not an expat or dual citizen, like yourself, but someone living and working in the American Reich?"

"Oh, well, that would be—" My mind went blank.

"Do you see?"

"See what?"

"My session was just the same," Helen said at lunch. We were eating in a company cafeteria, but since we knew no one, no one had said hello, and we were left very much by ourselves, a long way from any other group of workers. ConTech was always full of surprises, and this time the surprise was that the food was exceptionally good and the furniture and silverware would not have been out of place in a good restaurant. I sat back in my chair, sipped my coffee, and tried to think about everything that had happened so far.

"Why do you suppose Iphwin is so focused on these attacks on ConTech?" Helen asked. "From what he's described, and from what's in the folders, the whole thing isn't costing him very much, at least not yet."

"Well, my guess is that he's alarmed because he has no idea who is doing it, or for what reason, and he doesn't know how they're doing it. It's one thing to be robbed in broad daylight by someone who wants your money. It's another thing to get up in the morning and find your furniture was rearranged while you slept. The objective harm may be smaller but the mystery is more threatening."

"I suppose." She pushed her brown bangs up her forehead and said, "I wonder if there's a hair salon anywhere in the Big Sapphire. I suppose there must be, since there's a good five thousand people living in here." We watched the waves roll by, half a mile below, in the bright equatorial sunlight outside the big windows; even with the dark blue tint, it was still uncomfortably bright and the glare was dazzling. "Even granting what you say, it *still* doesn't make sense for Iphwin to be taking a personal interest in these matters, not to this extent. Iphwin controls more economic resources than most independent nations; he's probably bigger than the Scandinavian and the Hungarian Reichs put together. That's a huge quantity of money and power. And yet he wants us to believe that he's worried about these pinprick attacks on his periphery, some of which could be just pure co-incidence. ConTech is so big that they could be draining him for fifty years and he'd never feel it. He doesn't seem like a miser type, and his security forces are supposed to be really good—even if they're not, he could hire good ones in a heartbeat—so why is he fretting about this? Why doesn't he just delegate it to some security types and just read their report when they've caught the bad guys? This is as bizarre as mopping his own floors or working in his own ticket booths would be. And haven't you noticed how much of this whole huge business empire seems to run entirely on his personal whim? How can he possibly be mak-ing so many small day-to-day decisions, and have time to meet with us for hours, apparently just to shoot the breeze? Lyle, the whole thing looks as if somehow all of the vast resources of ConTech—more than you can find in most nations—are being used solely to support this little peripheral project." She was star-ing me as if she really expected me to know the answer.

I thought. I knew nothing. "Put that way, it does seem pretty strange—a panic over a pinprick. I wonder how Iphwin thinks that anyone could seriously knock him down with anything on the scale we've been looking at? Isn't he too big to worry?"

"Maybe you're never too big to worry," she said, taking a sip of her coffee. "Or it could be that the effects he's getting—mutually incompatible events, effects happening before their causes—in small affairs out in the periphery, are more threatening because he doesn't know if they can scale them up. Look at the case of that warehouse in Buenos Aires. They sent out a railcar of crates of ball bearings, bound for Valparaiso, and the minute the train was out of sight, another train pulled in returning the shipment. And when they checked the electronic mail, they found they had gotten a message the day before complaining about having the same shipment sent twice. Now, so far, ConTech effectively lost one customer but gained a whole carload of ball bearings; but what if it had gone the other way, and with every shipment instead of just one? What if the time travel or duplication or whatever it is starts to happen when they send out electronic funds transfers? You could drain a bank account pretty fast that way. I suppose the more of nature you own, the more you have to worry about keeping the laws of nature working—and who's ever had to worry about *that* before?"

That afternoon, back in our office, we tried to figure out how to investigate the phenomenon we'd been assigned. Supposedly our shrinks were going to confer with each other and write a report for us, but we would not see that for at least a day. "Why do you suppose they asked us all those trivial questions, anyway?" Helen asked.

"Trivial or nonsensical. Though I suppose it might be they were just asking a wide range of questions about all the possible things that some people remember. And I wonder which ones we each thought were nonsensical?"

"Good point." She glanced at her monitor screen, and then said, "Hey, there's a task list for this afternoon. It starts with making a bunch of phone calls."

I looked over her shoulder; for some reason it was a task for both of us. "Does that mean we each call all those people and record what they tell us, or does it mean we call them together in a conference call?"

"Since I have no idea what it's about or what is supposed to happen," she said, "my vote is that one of us calls and the other one watches the one making the call, just in case anything too crazy starts to happen."

First on the list was Clarence Babbit, of Chicago, Illinois. I lost the coin flip, so I dialed. I heard the phone ring, and then I was sitting there with my hand on the hung-up phone. "Did I make the call?" I asked Helen.

"You dialed and then hung up, and you've been sitting perfectly still for almost a full minute. Well, it did say to note anything unusual that happened, so I guess we should write that down." She took a long moment, and did. "You have no memory of the call?"

"Nope. Should I try Mr. Babbit, again, or do we go on to the next one?"

"Try Babbit again."

I dialed, got the phone ring at the other end, and a moment later, I was sitting there with my hand on the receiver.

The list was entirely numbers within the American Reich, so we dialed our way through, taking turns. When Helen would dial, I'd watch her hit the buttons, hear the ring start at the other end, and hang up, then remain perfectly stationary for the better part of a minute before waking up with no memory of what had happened. When I'd dial, she'd observe the same thing. We used the computer's camera to film it, so we could watch ourselves going through the whole strange procedure, and by doing that we confirmed that our behavior was identical.

"Well," I said, when the last one had finished, "that was very interesting and completely not informative. And if there's anyone home at those numbers, I bet they're getting really annoyed at the phantom rings."

"I wonder if, when we get phantom rings, it's because people in the American Reich are trying to call us?" Helen asked.

My head ached for a second and I said, "What did you just say?"

"I just said . . . I can't remember. Do we have a recorder on at the moment to see what it was?"

We did—it's SOP in most business offices in the Dutch Reich, as a form of political CYA, to record all conversation in offices unless it's specifically switched off. We pulled back the last couple of minutes of sound recordings from our office, and listened to the question together. "I wonder if, when we get phantom rings, it's because people in the American Reich are trying to call us?"

My head hurt. Helen's head hurt. And neither of us could seem to get our minds around the question. We played it again and transcribed it, and then read it aloud several times. "This works a lot like the forbidden words on-line," Helen said, abruptly. "After all the practice, now I can ask the question, and it doesn't seem like it's all that radical—but at the same time it doesn't seem like it has an answer we can get. But you know, most of us get phantom rings much, much more often than we dial a wrong number and hang up, don't we?"

"Certainly I do. I kind of think everyone does, too. Do you suppose maybe, if there's a forbidden zone for phone calls or something . . . but who's forbidding it? And why control our behavior, if that's what they're doing, rather than just tell us the number is unavailable?"

Helen sat back in her chair and stared at the ceiling, obviously thinking hard. "There *are* several great big assumptions we're making, aren't there, Doctor Abduction? And wouldn't your method be to look at what they all have in common?"

"That would be it. We assume that we exist in the real world and we're not in VR at the moment," I said. "That's a big assumption that we ought to be able to check, somehow. If we are in VR, it's got the biggest bandwidth ever seen, because it's perfectly smooth, with none of the little glitches that are always there in VR."

"Why is that assumption important?"

"Oh, because all the inexplicable events we're having would be perfectly explicable in a VR program that either had different reality rules or wasn't fully enforcing the ones it had. For that matter it would explain all of Iphwin's problems. Unfortunately, I guess, we seem to be real."

She sighed and took a sip of her coffee, making a face because it was cold. "That's a test right there. If we are inside a VR world, the world had no way to know I was going to reach for the coffee, and it made it the right temperature for the circumstances instantly, and gave the cup a different weight coming up and going down. That's *way* too complex for most programs. Well, all right, then, we are in physical reality, and one easy explanation goes away. What other assumptions are we making?"

"Well, about the phone experiment," I said, thinking hard—"you know what? We're assuming that we *want* to hang up the phone and then we forget about it. But we have no way of knowing what we wanted at the time, do we? Suppose we take wanting right out of it—we'll just have the computer record whatever comes through the phone, use the dialer on the computer to call the number, and stand clear across the room. This time we won't listen."

The result was oddly impressive; the computer dialed and then hung up, instantly, yet when we checked its logs, there was only a disconnect with no indicator as to which end had hung up.

"Hmm," Helen said. "Now let's see what happens if a tree falls in the forest and nobody's there."

We dialed the number on the handset, walked out of the room, and came back a minute later.

A tiny tinny voice was saying, "Hello, hello? Who the hell is this? I'm going to report this to the—" And the line went dead.

This was getting interesting, as I explained to Helen. "Hmm. It would appear that it responds faster to the computer than to us, which suggests it somehow knows the difference between us and the computer. And as soon as any information starts to come through—notice how the first few words there could have been anywhere, but at the moment when poor Mrs. Culver would have had to speak whatever the local noun for the local cops is in Miami, the connection broke?"

"Let's pick on someone else next time," I suggested. "What can we try next?"

Next we tried putting the call up on a speaker phone, with a recording of Helen saying, "Hello. Sorry to bother you. This is your phone company calling to determine whether there is a phantom ring problem on your line. We believe you may have been getting a large number of rings without anyone on the other end of the line. If you have been having this problem, please say 'Yes' and state your name clearly. If you have not been having this problem, please say 'No,' and feel free to tell us about any other problem that you may be having with your telephone service."

When we were satisfied with the message, Helen said, "Well, shall we pick on Culver in Miami again, go back to Babbit in Chicago, or do one of the ones we've called less?"

"Culver. Definitely Culver. Very likely she's at home, and we know she's picking up the phone and yelling. If she's called the cops, that's even better—they'll be on the line."

"Seems like kind of a nasty prank to pull on an old lady."

"How do you know she's old? Maybe she's a young widow. Maybe her husband forgot to wear his flameproof sheets and stood too close to the burning cross and was burned to death last week."

"I guess we can always hope. Okay, we're setting up Mrs. Culver to do her part for science."

We set the message to play out loud in a few seconds, dialed the number, and left for ten minutes to get coffee from the cafeteria, to make sure we wouldn't be anywhere near when the phone was picked up and the message played. The house recording system would pick up whatever was said.

We had just sat down to coffee and more fruitless speculation when the lights went out in the cafeteria. There was still plenty of afternoon sun through the window, so it wasn't dark, but there was that weird hush that falls in a really big building when the power goes out, as if everything had suddenly been smothered in thick cotton.

An alarm screamed from the direction of our office, and a voice announced, "All personnel, Floor 188, Block C, please stand by to evacuate as needed. We have a fire in Room A-210. Fire suppression is being applied. Please stand by."

Room A-210 was our office.

"Well," Helen said, tucking a loose strand of chestnut hair back in, "I think we're hitting Iphwin with something considerably more expensive than a phone bill. I don't suppose either of us is willing to consider the possibility that it's a pure coincidence?"

A minute later the voice announced that the fire in A-210 was out, and specifically asked Helen and me to go in and assess damage. Power came back on as we were walking back to our office.

We found what I might have expected: the computer and the phone, along with all the data cables, had become hot enough to partially melt. The robot sprinklers in the room had done their job, aiming the foam streams at the hot spots, and therefore though the carpet was a messy ruin, and one chair that had the bad luck to be behind the computer from the sprinkler's viewpoint would probably never be the same, most of the place had been saved.

Up above, there was one burned ceiling panel. I got up on a chair and gingerly lifted it; a black cube fell out and smashed on the floor, scattering an assemblage of electronics components. "Betcha that's the room recording system," I said.

"No bet. I'm sure it is." Helen crouched and looked it over.

"Yep. In fact it's more interesting than that. Charred micro-phone. Charred recording block. Charred everything between those two points. But nothing else even got warm."

I climbed down off the chair and said, "This time I get to ask what's the assumption we're making."

Helen sighed. "I think we've been assuming the universe is not out to get us. And I think all the evidence is, that it is."

After the office cleanup crew got done, there was only about an hour left, so we sat down to try to write our report. We both noticed that whoever was typing had a tendency to space out and stare into space, and now and then to type a few meaningless words before trailing off, but by dint of dictating to each other, and occasionally giving each other a gentle shake, we got it done. I almost erased it just as we finished, but Helen knocked my hand out of the way and we managed to send it to Iphwin.

We had accomplished the whole task list for the day, such as it had been, and we were exhausted, but there wasn't any feeling of having put in a good day's work. "Well," I said, "want to go for an elevator ride?"

"You hopeless romantic," she said.

We got into the elevator, rode down to our floor, and went into our apartment. The clothing I had ordered had been deliv-ered, and the maid service had hung it all up; the fridge was stocked with groceries, and that little company apartment was now about as much home as it could be. A note on the table said that Helen's remaining possessions had been gotten from her apartment in Auckland and were being held in storage until we moved into a larger place, and gave her an e-mail address for requesting that anything she wanted be brought out of stor-age and delivered here. "Maybe some of the naughty undies," she said, "for when I need to revive your mood." She was checking through her bureau drawers, and then said, "Ha, nope. They put 'em in here. I guess they know more about us than I thought."

"Well, speaking of which," I said, "it is our second night living together, and tonight we are not dead exhausted, nor in fear of our lives."

"If that's a suggestion, the answer is yes. Provided that you cook dinner."

I grabbed the apron and tied it on. I poached some fish in wine, threw some noodles and mixed vegetables on it so we could pretend we cared about nutrition, and had something edible in just a few minutes.

As we sat at the small table, eating, killing some of the white wine that hadn't been used on the fish, and watching the sea darken as the sun set (so close to the equator, it was never more than a few minutes before or after six), Helen said, "Tell me about anything you remember, anything at all from your past."

I shrugged. "It's all pretty dull, as you must know. Are you curious about anything in particular?"

"Well, I'm not curious about you per se—" she began.

"Why, thank you."

"I don't mean that! I mean I'm curious about how many memories we don't share, besides General Grant and the existence of the country where I grew up. For example, the history I teach in school is that after the German atomic bomb attack stopped the D-Day invasion and wrecked London, Washington, and Moscow, there was about a year and a half of disorganized fighting all over the world, and then a brief period of peace. Then Germany ordered eleven nations and regions to set up Reichs, and when they dragged their feet, the Germans went back to war in 1954 and really finished the job. They probably killed a fifth of the world population during the Lebensraum period in the sixties and seventies, and since then they've been relatively quiet, only occasionally threatening someone else or bullying the Japanese and Italians around. Right?"

"Right. That's how I learned it in school."

"Well, I told you what I grew up with. Now, can you name the American presidents?" she asked.

"If I couldn't, my parents would have beaten the hell out of me. Washington, Hamilton, Washington again, Monroe for three terms, Perry—"

"Good enough. My list goes Washington, Adams, Jefferson, Burr, Madison, and on from there. You had Lincoln and a Civil War, didn't you?"

"Yep. And he died, but we disagreed about when."

She nodded. "All right, that's just to start with. Now how about some minor details? Did your grandparents ever complain about having to learn to drive on the left when they came to Enzy?"

"Why should they? America was like all the English-speaking countries, it drove on the left."

"When I grew up," she said, "Americans drove on the right. So did Canadians."

"Why would Canadians be different from people from any other state?" I asked.

"Define Canada."

"Uh, the big state north of Lake Erie, between Michigan and Quebec."

She nodded more emphatically. "Who made the first airplane?"

"The Wright brothers. Flew it at Kitty Hawk in 1903."

"Who was the greatest baseball team of all time?"

"Well, I guess most people would say the 1927 Yankees—Ruth, Gehrig, those guys."

"See, that's the strange thing. These different histories we have tend to agree about trivia and disagree about big things, with about equal frequencies. Who was president during World War Two?"

"Franklin Roosevelt," I said.

"Same here. You see? Drastically different patterns of what happened and all these strange details that overlap. Now what kind of assumption do we have to make, to make it possible to reconcile these?"

"I thought we weren't working anymore today."

"I don't know that we get much of a choice," Helen said, sighing. "The more I turn all this over in my head, the more I can't leave it alone. We're assuming something or other that won't let us see what's going on, I'm just sure of that."

A thought suddenly hit me very hard, and I said, "How did we meet?"

"You don't remember?" Helen said, looking cross.

"Humor me."

"Well," she said, not happily, "it was new faculty orientation at Whitman, and we were seated together because we were next to each other in the alphabet. There was a terribly dull speech by the bursar, and you started passing notes to me."

I groaned. "We came in in different years. You had already been here a year. You joined the faculty in 2055 and I joined in 2056. We met when you posted the notice in the paper about Fluffy, just after I got hired."

"Gee, I'd forgotten about Fluffy. Poor thing. But we were already dating when it happened, and it wasn't *that* big a deal, Lyle, how would we have *met* about her? And why would I have run an obituary in the newspaper for my cat?"

"An obituary? I don't mean two years ago when she died of old age."

"She got run over just after I started dating you."

"I met you because she got lost and turned up in my back-yard. I had seen the ad in the paper so I captured her. . . ."

"I see what you mean," Helen said. "It's not just the big things, is it? It seems to be everything." She stared at me. "We're finding out something here, but I'm not sure I want to find it out."

I had half a thought. "Let me ask something more directly relevant. Did you ever turn down an opportunity to become a really good shot with a pistol, or to learn to use that whole arsenal of weapons you had last night?"

She gaped at me. "Well, yes I did, now that you mention it. When I was in the second year of my master's program, and thinking about going into Reich Studies, I was pretty broke and I applied to the intelligence services. They didn't want me as an analyst but they offered me the chance to take the physical qualifier. Then I got a decent job, and dropped out and worked for a year, so I never went back to schedule the qualifier. I suppose if I hadn't gotten that job just then, I might have taken the test and become a spy or a policeman or something, and learned all about using guns and knives." She got up, gulped her wine, and went to stare out the window at the dark. "That was it, wasn't it? Some little turning point in my life where I didn't become the woman who was so good with a gun two nights ago. But then how did she show up just then, and why am I here? My memory includes you getting shot, Lyle, and I think you did. Or *some* of you did."

There was a long, awkward silence, and then Helen began to cry, collapsing back onto the couch in a big, awkward tangle of limbs. "You know," she said, "I have a horrible feeling that somewhere out there you're dead, and I'm crying. And it doesn't seem fair, because the me that killed Billie Beard saved your life, and she probably doesn't have you. She could be the one crying. And it seems so unfair that I've still got you, and I didn't do a thing—"

I got up and took her in my arms, and started kissing away

tears and trying to soothe her, as I suppose lovers have been doing for upset lovers since the world began. Her wet face pressed against my neck, and then her soft lips began to move against my skin, and whether it was just stress, or a desperate need to reassure each other, or even just that we had been planning to make love anyway, that's what we did.

Later, as we were lying in bed, waiting to drift off, I said, "Here's an odd observation. Does it seem to you that people don't talk about the past nearly as much as they used to? I mean, I notice nowadays that when small children begin to talk about what happened last year or last month, their mothers shush them as if they'd talked about bowel movements or their private parts. I don't remember that when I was a child, do you?"

"No, come to think of it." She rolled over and rested her head on my chest. "And I think I never bring the subject up, not because it would be impolite, but because I just don't. Now and then some older person starts to talk about their life or things they saw or did long ago, and I find I always get very impatient and try to avoid hearing it. Isn't that strange in a historian? And my memory is going, too. Every lecture, I go to the library and look up things I know by heart before I write that lecture. Isn't it strange that I never noticed any of that before?"

"Strange, or maybe part of the pattern," I said. "Which we seem to be getting better and better at talking about—we're having fewer memory lapses and seizures, or whatever those were. As if practicing somehow makes it possible to think about the problem."

"I wonder how many other people wandered in from how many other worlds," Helen said.

"Other worlds?" I asked. Then I got a blinding headache and passed out.

A moment later I woke up, my head still in pain, with Helen holding me and saying, "Here, take an aspirin. Are you all right?"

"I guess so. What happened to *you* when you said 'other worlds?'" At the phrase, my stomach lurched and my head hurt.

"Nothing when I said it. I thought it a moment before, and felt sort of dizzy. Which makes me think it's one of those ideas, like, like, like, the ones we couldn't speak before. Well, then, all right, many of us are from different versions of the past . . ." She gasped. "Ooh, now there's a thought that hurt. Which I guess is our indicator that it's important. Not many of us. We all are."

I swallowed the aspirin and said, "The thought didn't hurt me because I don't understand what you are getting at. But now I'm really, really curious."

She drew a deep breath and said, "All right, here's the thought. Suppose people are crossing from one history to another—all the histories are sort of tangled together like spaghetti, all right? And most of the time, when you cross over, you cross over to a strand very near your own, so only small details are different—like how you met, or how long your cat lived, or something. But every so often you accidentally take a big leap, like I did when I came here to this history. And whatever causes those crossovers, the crossovers have been getting more and more frequent in the recent past, so that people have been having more and more disagreements about the past. Well, you know, when a subject becomes controversial—especially when it becomes controversial and impossible to settle—"

"Of course!" I said, and now my head felt like it was in a vise. "Polite people start avoiding it. Nobody wants to be the rude person who brings it up. Ways are found to pussyfoot around it . . . sometime in the last few years, then, or maybe the last twenty or so at most, the worlds have started to drift together—"

She was sobbing again, and I rolled over and held her. This time I could guess. "Your mother?"

"Oh, yes, that." She turned and hung on to me for dear life.

"That, and if we're right, then after all these years I just found out I'm not crazy."

I suppose we could have talked more, but exhaustion swept over us, and though it seemed I just shut my eyes for a moment, when I looked up, it was already dawn. Helen was still in my arms, traces of tears all over her face, her lips wet and red, hanging slack. She looked impossibly young to me, and I lay there watching her till she began to move and her eyes opened.

At breakfast, we tried to have a normal, trivial conversation, but we discovered that we just weren't going to be able to talk about much else. "There is a certain kind of sense to it," Helen said. "Figure Iphwin owns all of ConTech, and ConTech might be as much as half of one percent of the global economy. He's so big that he has to operate internal markets and figure out trade policies between his own holdings. There isn't much way to take him down by a frontal assault—but if you can somehow make things less predictable, disrupt the causality inside the company, then that changes things. In some ways it's not much different from doing random damage, like twentieth-century bombing raids, or getting the company directory and sending letter bombs at random. But in other ways it's worse, because how can anyone plan that a certain number of time reversals will happen, or that some shipments that were never ordered will turn up from companies that don't exist, or, like that case in Mexico, where ninety tons of specialty steel get shipped and forty thousand sets of pajamas get delivered? For most of the other possible kinds of attacks, you can control risk with insurance, because you know what the range is of what might happen, and what the likelihood is. Random bombings might be terrifying but they just add one more bad thing to the list of bad things that are likely to happen, and give it a high likelihood. But when the two things being messed with *are* the range of what might happen and how likely it is—then there's no bet you can take out against it."

"Suppose the enemy is Murphy," I said, before I had time to analyze what I meant myself.

"Who's Murphy?"

"Murphy's Law?"

"Still never heard of it."

"Oh. Well, it's not really important. What I'm getting at is, how often do you discuss the past with your friends, in a way that matters to them? How many people have a long-running argument with their spouse about which of two perfectly plausible events happened to them a long time ago? There could be tremendous amounts of random noise in the past before anyone would notice there was any pattern of any such thing. And maybe small violations of causality account for Murphy's Law, which is the law that 'If anything can't go wrong, it will.' I mean, that's a violation of causality right there."

"Who was Murphy?" she asked.

"Funny thing," I said, "but I've heard at least ten different stories about him. The inventor of the parachute but not the first successful parachute. The guy who invented a safety hatch for submarines, that was supposed to make it impossible to dive with a hatch open, but actually made all the hatches open at the bottom of the dive. A man who ran a mail-drop blackmail operation and was caught in the Tsunami of 2002, which kept him from getting to the post office but allowed the post office to stay open and send the mail. The navigator on the *Titanic*. All sorts of stories about the guy, actually. I always figured most of them were folklore, but maybe in all of history there was just one Murphy, and he has multiple pasts in which he always ends up coining his law, the same way that the multiple American pasts always seem to have the '27 Yankees and the Wright brothers."

"And you're suggesting—"

"That maybe perverse anticausality—just call it perversity—is just a physical factor in the universe, like entropy or gravity. Maybe it normally occurs at such a small level that people who encounter it don't think enough of it to care very much; or they notice it, like Murphy, but they don't try to do anything about it systematically. This implies that either the background level of perversity is increasing—or it might be caused by Iphwin himself. Maybe he's got the first economic unit that's both big enough and self-aware enough to detect perversity, so that he sees it happening, where none of the markets did."

"How would we test that?"

"I don't know," I admitted. "I was just seeing if there was any reason to question an assumption that we were making, that there was a real enemy somewhere doing something, and not just the system itself generating the events. But though it could be the system, it could just as easily be a real enemy. And having been beaten the hell out of by Billie Beard, I find it hard to think of her as just a system artifact, or purely an expression of the law of perversity." I looked at my watch. "Probably about time to get ourselves up to the office. I guess we should think about what sort of experiment would allow us to distinguish between a physical law and a physical enemy—but that would depend on knowing what an enemy could do, and until three days ago I wouldn't have believed that anybody could tamper with causality."

When we got to the office, about five minutes early, the only instruction was to continue experiments by whatever means we wished; there was also a budget that told us that we had a ridiculous amount of money to play around with.

"What say we go do research in Fiji for a year?" Helen said, grinning at me.

"I'm worried about getting shot," I said, "so how about we beat the bad guys and then honeymoon in Fiji?"

"Oh, all right," she said. "Has anyone ever told you you're excessively responsible?"

"Nearly everyone. Let's see. One thing we could try to develop is a map of all these alternate pasts we're finding—they seem to occur in families, like the way that Terri is from a world that includes the Reichs and Empires, like I am, or that Kelly and you both share Diego Garcia, with all of our personal histories tangled up into something you can't unscramble when we tried to fit them together, so we seem to all be from different worlds, but not from evenly distributed different worlds—there wouldn't be that many similarities in such a small group if the distribution were even across the infinite possibilities. It suggests that there's some huge diversity of pasts out there, but it's grouped into a much smaller number of 'supergroups' or 'history families' or whatever you want to call them."

"Have you thought of an experiment?"

"Let's try this one. We'll send a small payment to anyone who answers a questionnaire, identifying as many things as they can and labeling the rest 'never heard of it.' Sort of like what the shrinks did with us, you know. And we'll make it sort of a chain letter—there's another payment for anyone who modifies the quiz according to directions, and then sends it on to another person. The modification will be adding a couple of things to be identified to the list—that way we're not just restricted to what we know about, so that if there's some Supreme Court case called Hickenlooper versus Iowa or something, that's important in histories that neither of us has, it stands a good chance of being added to the list. We could pay the first few thousand respondents and cut it off after three hours; the net's a big place and that would give us a starting map, to see whether addresses correspond to histories, for example."

That took us the better part of the morning, devising a questionnaire, a payment system that couldn't be cheated too easily, and a system for modifying the questionnaire that still would not let them cheat on the payment system. It was ten-thirty before we managed to fire it off; we had agreed we wouldn't check until everything had come in, which wouldn't be till one-thirty, so we spent two hours reviewing all the mystery cases: shipments that arrived before orders or were transformed into other objects by the time they arrived, nonexistent branches of the company that left frantic messages—and then, just as often, called in to thank ConTech's central office for the help. Some ships and planes had vanished; one ship had been found floating without a crew, a hundred miles from its exact duplicate, which was also crewless. A few days later the whole crew turned up in jail, four thousand miles away, having been there since before the voyage started.

"There's definitely something peculiar about time in all of these," Helen offered, after an hour. "Doesn't it look as if many of them are cases of time flowing backward or going into a loop?"

I nodded. "From the results we can't tell if time is looping, or if it's just caused by there being a multiple stream of pasts. Maybe the shipment that arrives before the order just has a past where the order was dated earlier. Maybe the two ships are both from pasts where the ship just vanished."

"But if the ship vanished in the past, how can it be here today?"

I swallowed hard, because I had thought of something that might upset Helen. "Helen, if there are multiple pasts, and if there are going to continue to be multiple pasts—and we haven't seen anything putting a stop to them—then there have to be multiple presents, because we're the past of the future. And since the future is the present of the future—"

"God, that makes my head hurt, but I see what you mean. We can't assume we're the only present . . ." She stared at me. "A few months ago you were very, very drunk and you told me about something called the Many Worlds Interpretation. What was that?"

I shrugged. "I hadn't thought of it, but it's another hypothesis we could add. Down at the quantum level—we're talking subatomic particles here, really small stuff, nothing you can observe in everyday life—there's a little problem called the uncertainty principle."

"I've heard of that. Doesn't it mean that the observer creates reality or something like that?"

"That's what it means in the humanities, where people just pin new labels on ideas they inherited from the Greeks. But what the uncertainty principle means in physics is a lot stranger and much more rigorously demonstrated. Suppose you had a car whose speedometer could only register five speeds—maybe zero, two miles per hour, ten miles per hour, twenty-six, and a hundred and ten. It would always register one of them, and the closer your actual speed was to one of those speeds, the more likely it would be to register that speed."

"I'd take it in and get it fixed."

"Damn straight. However, we can't take the universe in and get it fixed, obvious as the need might be. Now it so happens that the only way we know what's happening with subatomic particles is to bounce other subatomic particles off of them, and subatomic particle behavior is quantized—it can only take on certain values, like that five-speed speedometer. Therefore when we bounce one particle off another one to find out what's going on, we don't get a single answer—we get a distribution of probabilities. Sort of the way you'd take a guess at what your car was doing—'Well, probably ten percent chance it's between 10 and 26, seventy percent it's between 26 and 110, and twenty percent it's more than 110, so I'm probably okay on the highway.' No matter how exactly we bounce the particle or measure its behavior after the collision, we don't get a precise picture, but a set of bets, probabilities assigned to possibilities. Still with me?"

"This is *worlds* easier when I'm not drunk."

"I bet. Okay, now here's the tricky part: there's no difference between a measurement and any other interaction with the universe. Any physical process that depends on that particle will act as if all the possibilities were happening at once, with that mix of probabilities. Unless you do something for which the particle must be in exactly one state—and if you do that, then it will 'collapse' into that single state."

"Pretend I understand you and give me an example."

"Ever hear of Schroedinger's cat?"

"Why would I want to shred anybody's cat?"

I ignored that. "Schroedinger suggested a thought experiment, trying to get at how weird the problem is. He said, suppose you put a cat in a box so that you can't observe the cat, and inside there's a bottle of poison gas, which has a fifty percent chance of releasing the gas, based on some quantum event it's going to observe. Then since the unobserved quantum state is 50 percent one way and 50 percent the other, until you open the box, the cat must be 50 percent alive and 50 percent dead."

"Sounds like something a German would think of doing."

"He didn't do it. He just pointed it out as an example of how hard that is to understand in ordinary life. Naturally, when you open the box, since the cat has to be either alive or dead, what you find is either a live cat or a dead one, and that tells you how the quantum event came out. But up till then the box should behave as if it had a 50 percent alive cat—whatever that means—inside it.

"Now, one of the greatest arguments in all of science, still going on after 150 years, is about what that means. The Copenhagen Interpretation, which most physicists buy, is that it's all just a computational device, and that it's just that we don't know how to really understand our own equations—all we know is that they work. The Aphysical Interpretation is that somehow there's a 'real' world that ours is only a shadow of, and the probability distributions somehow reflect an underlying unified reality that we can't perceive. And the Many Worlds Interpretation says that every time a quantum event happens, the universe splits into multiple worlds, enough so that across all those worlds, each event happens all the possible ways. When a Copenhagen interpretation guy opens the box, he finds the cat alive and says, 'The calculations showed a 50 percent chance that this would happen.' The Aphysical guy opens it and says, 'This live shadow cat reflects the state of the real cat.' And the Many Worlds guy says, 'Aha! I am in the universe that got the live cat; in some other universe at this moment someone is recognizing that he is in the universe with the dead cat.' And the really clever trick, so far in the history of physics, is that all these *are* just interpretations. The experiment doesn't go one bit differently from one interpretation to another; the only thing that changes is the meaning we read into the event. At least up till now; we might be conducting, somehow, a giant experiment that's showing that Many Worlds has, let us say, a certain edge."

Her jaw dropped. "So if Many Worlds is right, then there could be an infinite number of universes with divergent pasts out there? And maybe what's happening is that things are crossing the fence, or whatever it is, between the universes?"

I nodded. "That's what I mean. But there's a lot of what is going on that doesn't seem to fit that theory. Why should that make it impossible to phone America? Supposing that you and I are meeting different versions of each other—Lyle Prime flew you to Saigon, and Helen Prime rescued me in the shooting at the Curious Monkey—why don't we ever run into ourselves? And why do the crossings over only seem to happen now and then, and why don't we all just have multiple pasts until someone asks us a question?"

"Prove we don't."

"All right, I'm thinking of a past event. I'm not thinking of a distribution of them. Is any part of your past a distribution of events?"

She thought hard for a moment. "As far as I can tell, no."

"See? It doesn't fit with what I'd expect. Let's go to lunch and try to get away from all this for a while; by the time we get back we should have results from our survey."

Since we were trying not to talk shop, there was practically nothing to talk about; wedding plans seemed hopelessly indefinite, managing the apartment together required practically no consultation (since we were both neat minimalists), and the weather was perfect as it tended to be at this time of year. We ate, we looked out the window, and we read the paper to each other (learning mainly that the world was proceeding about as always—I can't recall a single surprising thing). By one-thirty, when it was time to return to the office, we were looking forward to it.

The results were about as much of a nonresult as you could get; we had a few hundred responses, and the "I don't knows" for each item, plus the disagreements, were generally uncorrelated with address, time of response, domain, or anything else. "Some of the answers correlate," Helen said, "but that kind of figures. Hardly anyone has Mickey Mouse being a Disney character *and* a newspaper character named after a brand of chewing gum; nobody has Teddy Roosevelt assassinated by German agents in 1916 *and* being Secretary of War during World War Two. Which just tells us that most people live in a locally consistent world. Not the most informative thing I've ever seen, eh?"

I shrugged. "Well, there's one implication in the whole thing. If the addresses and domains aren't correlated with the histories, then what that tells us is that people are distributing across the various pasts without any regard for geography, which kind of implies that the rate of crossing over is uniform around the world. Which lends support to the idea that somehow or other people have begun to drift between the Many Worlds."

"People, objects, phone calls, and e-mail at least," Helen said. "I wonder what else is? And here's a question for you. Suppose Schroedinger teaches the cat to flip a coin and push a lever based on the outcome, and then he puts the kitty in the box with a setup so that one lever releases poison gas. How come the cat isn't half alive and half dead from doing that, just as if he used a subatomic experiment? Schroedinger has no way of knowing which way the coin flip came out from the outside. But I'm sure the cat is either alive or dead, no other way about it. What difference does using a subatomic gadget make?"

"Great question," I said. "In fact—"

The phone rang, Helen picked it up, said hello, mouthed "Iphwin" at me. "Yes," she said. "Of course we'll be happy to do that, sir, but I was wondering why you think that we—oh, my god. Well, I see. Okay. We'll get right down to the apartment, pack a bag, and get ready to go. Yes, sir, of course. Thanks and good-bye."

She hung up, shaking her head, and said, "Well, brace yourself. We're on our way to Mexico City. Maybe we can manage to visit Colonel Sykes while we're in the country, eh?"

"What's in Mexico City?"

"There's a ConTech employee, a woman from Uppsala in the province of Sweden in the Danish Empire—whatever the hell that may be, but it doesn't seem to bear much of a resemblance to any arrangement I'd heard of before—whose name is Ulrike Nordstrom. She's being held by the police in Mexico City, on suspicion of murder. Iphwin seems to think that Nordstrom really did the murder, but that the evidence the Mexico City cops have on hand isn't enough to hold her, so our job is to go there, with big wads of Iphwin's money, pay Nordstrom's bail, bribe some public officials, and get Nordstrom safely back into the keeping of ConTech."

"Why us? He must have thousands of employees who can do that job."

"He does. But he thinks we'll help to stir matters up a bit, as he puts it. It so happens that the deceased appears to be Billie Beard."

Who knew what I might have thought of this last week? By now I was getting so used to the way the world had started to work that all I did was sigh and say, "Billie Beard has a knack for turning up dead in an extremely inconvenient fashion. I hope that woman knows how much trouble she is."

"At least one of her is less aware of it right now than she was a while ago. Come on, we've got to pack—Iphwin wants us to get on a jump flight in about two hours."

We got off the elevator at our floor in comfortable silence; I know I was mainly thinking that this had to be more interesting than sitting in an office, playing phone pranks and tabulating the results. I suppose Helen was thinking the same.

We were less than a step from the door to our apartment when Helen froze and stuck her hand out, against my chest. I was about to say "What?" loudly, but I had heard it too—something in the apartment had gone thump, loudly, and as I listened there was a softer thud, and the not-quite-consciously-perceptible sense that something was moving near the door.

Helen pointed to the wall by the hinges of the door, and I flattened myself against it. Then she pressed her back against the wall on the doorknob side of the door, took out her key, and put that in her left hand. She nodded at me, meaningfully, and I wondered what she meant for just an instant before I saw her pull a pistol from her purse and soundlessly set the purse down on the floor beside her.

She unlocked the door and shoved it open, burst into the room taking up a firing stance—and let out the happiest little cry I had ever heard from her. "Fluffy!"

There on the rug, rolling around, clearly overjoyed to see her, was her ratty old Persian cat from years ago, the one that I remembered as dying of old age two years ago, and Helen had told me she remembered as having gotten run over. Fluffy looked pretty old—the fur was thin, fine, and dry, she was now terribly scrawny, and pretty clearly she was a little stiff in the hips—but otherwise about the same cat that I remembered. "You know how to use a gun again," I said, because it was the first thing I thought of.

"And you're not in a wheelchair," she said, scooping up the cat and hugging it to her chest. "And Fluffy is obviously a whole lot better too." I stood and stared at her as she set the gun down on the counter to have both hands free to play with the cat. After a long moment she looked back at me and said, "Oh, don't look so surprised. I'm sure I didn't understand half of it, but just ten minutes ago, at our meeting with Iphwin, you explained everything that's been happening since last Friday, and it made perfect sense to me."

The whole way to Mexico City, including almost an hour of weightlessness, we talked, with me trying to piece together enough information from Helen's memory to be able to figure out what I had explained to her before. This Helen was perhaps ten pounds heavier than the one I was used to, much more solidly built and muscular, and had led rather a more adventurous life; she seemed fond enough of me, but she didn't have the complex, thoughtful approach to the world that the Helen I was used to

did, and I had a distinct sense that whatever it was that my other
self, over in some other stream of time, had figured out, this one
had not listened as carefully or asked as many questions as the
Helen I had had lunch with. Therefore, she just didn't provide
enough information for me to reconstruct whatever the solution
that some other I had arrived at had been.

The ConTech company ship made a swift, safe landing on
the lake; since the beginning of jump boat travel, cities had gone
to great lengths to open up bodies of water near themselves for
landing areas, and Mexico City was now about half lake, at least
as much as it had been during early Aztec times. We hit the water,
motored up to a company slip, and were waved right through all
the usual formalities; it was dark out on the lake, at five A.M. We
had flown right through most of the night, into the previous day,
in a bare couple of hours—it had been Tuesday, five-thirty P.M.
when we left, and now it was Monday, five A.M. We knew that
we'd be exhausted soon enough, but for the moment the effect
was of being oddly wide awake for the time of day it was.

As we approached the company slip, we saw there was a
sizable group of men waiting for us. The moment the boat tied
up and the gangplank extended, as we walked off the boat, a slim
man approached me. In the lights of the pier, I could see that he
had black, tightly curled hair and an aquiline nose; he wore a
small goatee, a plain white shirt, and dark trousers and coat.

"Are you Mr. Lyle Peripart?" he asked, in accentless English.

"Yes, I am."

"And you are Miss Helen Perdida?" he asked.

"Yes."

With a very slight shrug and nod he commanded the big men
who lunged forward to handcuff us. "Then I am afraid that I shall
have to place both of you under arrest. We understand that you
are coming here in the matter of a murder, and we rather suspect
that your presence here was ordered by Geoffrey Iphwin or

by ConTech, both of which have been indicted in absentia for conspiracy to commit murder. You may enter a guilty plea now if you wish, or wait until a later meeting with a police interrogator."

They relieved Helen of a frightening array of weapons, more or less politely, and then pushed us into a police van, not *too* roughly, and drove us to the station. It turned out that the slim man who had arrested us was going to be our interrogator, a detail he had somehow failed to mention before, and that interrogation would begin immediately.

"My name," he said, standing over me, after Helen had been taken out, and I had been cuffed to a small stool, bolted to the floor in the center of the room, "is Jesús Picardin."

"Thank you very much for faxing the file of documents that got us released," I said.

He stared at me incredulously. "What in the sweet name of Our Savior are you talking about?"

I told him the story of our rescue from the jail in Saigon, and he said, "This is the most preposterous set of alibis that I've ever heard. First of all, my chief investigator, Señora Beard, would have had no reason to be anywhere in the People's Republic of Vietnam, and in any case that city is called Ho Chi Minh City, so far as I know. And if Helen Perdida had indeed shot her there, I would hardly have been working to free Helen Perdida. As for your mention of Esmé Sanderson, this is the most preposterous part of the whole story—who do you think you are trying to fool? She's shared an office with Billie Beard for the better part of ten years, and the two are old partners; now that Billie is gone, in fact, Esmé is going to be my acting second in command. How you could expect her to give you an alibi is beyond me."

One of the men came in and said something to Picardin; *"teléfono"* was the only word I caught, but the rest of it apparently told the police captain that it was important, because he got up and went out to get it. While he was out there, I contemplated my situation. A week ago I had only been dimly aware that this city existed, and although I suppose I knew it must have police stations, it would not have occurred to me that I would be sitting in one. Worse yet, from my standpoint, I was clearly a really long way from home myself, now, because I was in one of the worlds where Saigon was called Ho Chi Minh City, which meant I was somewhere outside my home group of worlds by some considerable distance; there were no Reichs here. That seemed like a good enough thing, but from the cursory perusal of the notes Helen and I had been able to do, if you got away from National Socialism, you found yourself in the world of the Puritan Party, or the ones where Communist Russia had conquered the Earth, or the ones where America had gone up in a nuclear civil war of some kind in the early 1980s. There were some other families of worlds, as well, we thought, but we hadn't gotten them sorted out yet.

At the moment, if the name Ho Chi Minh City was the clue that I thought it was, we were probably in one of the Communist-descended lines, which wasn't where either Helen or I had come from. Clearly ConTech existed in this world, and so did Geoffrey Iphwin, but would the Geoffrey Iphwin of this world even recognize our names? If he did, would we be his employees, and would he be sending any help?

I tried to leave that question thoroughly alone, but unfortunately it was about the only source of amusement I had, except perhaps for meditating upon the way my wrists hurt where they were cuffed to the chair. The room itself offered only whitewashed concrete block walls, a spotless black floor with a drain that made me wonder if perhaps in this particular version of Mexico the police might be even a little bit inclined to brutality, and two fluorescent fixtures with thin metal dividers just below the glowing tubes. The only decor was the door, painted pale hospital green, with a big dead-bolt lock on the other side; the bolt itself was visible in the gap between the door and the jamb, but it looked like you'd need a welding torch to get through it, the door seemed convincingly hard to break, and anyway I wasn't going to get anywhere near it unless I got out of the handcuffs, which I had no idea of how to do.

Perhaps I would be better off considering just how far away from any kind of home or help we might be, after all. Or just thinking about how much my wrists hurt.

The door opened, and Jesús Picardin came in, with Helen walking after him. She had all her weapons in a wire basket, exactly like the one in which Picardin had my wallet, belt, computer, and belt phone. "We'll have to move quickly," Picardin said, his voice low and hushed.

Helen, behind him, had a tense but friendly little smile, and she nodded at me, indicating that I was supposed to cooperate in this, whatever "this" might be. Picardin undid the handcuffs and handed me my things; I put the belt on, the wallet in my pocket, and made sure everything was good to go. "I'm not sure how long Geoffrey Iphwin will be able to keep Esmé on the phone. She was shouting at him, you know. I'm afraid that for some reason or other she blames him for the death of Billie Beard, and this Esmé does not have the memories of Billie that I do—or that the Esmé I know does. But if we can get past the front office, we can probably go get the prisoner released."

"If I thank you for our release in Saigon—" I began.

"Your charming partner has already done so. She said this was the second time I had gotten you released. I never did know what became of that pile of documents I faxed, but I'm very glad that it did you good. Let's hurry. Quietly now." He hustled us down a long corridor past two rooms full of busy cops talking to the usual array of battered, hopeless, angry, bewildered, and exhausted people that you see in a police station.

Once we were clear of those areas, we moved at a dead run,

through hallway after hallway, following Picardin. He managed to tell us in a low voice that we were going the long way round in hopes of not being seen before we reached the prisoner's cell.

We knew what Ulrike Nordstrom looked like from the photo Iphwin had sent to us, and besides she was the only one in her row of cells; it looked like they didn't arrest many women as dangerous offenders around here. She was short and pale blonde, a little heavy, and she wore her hair in a sort of bowling-ball cut. She immediately jumped up and said, "Lyle! Helen! Am I glad to see you! What are you doing here?"

Helen and I glanced at each other, and I said, "Er, we know you from your photograph, but how do you know us?"

"It's *me*. It's Ulrike! Lyle, you and I were married for five years, and Helen was my maid of honor. Right after college. It can't have been *that* long."

Picardin was looking at us very, very intently, and didn't seem to be the least bit pleased, but he unlocked the cell door and let her out anyway. "I have a key for a back service exit," he said, "so we can get you out of here. But I wish someone would tell me things before they become surprises."

"We all wish that very much," Helen said.

Picardin handed her papers and wallet back to Ulrike. She seemed to be pouting, and from the way she was watching me, I got the distinct impression that at one time this expression had been some kind of private signal between Ulrike and whatever Lyle it was that she had married. She was getting angry at me, I guessed, because I wasn't receiving the signal. We hurried after Picardin, down the hall, and out the door he motioned us through. "We'll be in touch, I'm sure," he said. "I just hope I can figure out the rules of this world before I make any mistakes that are too big."

At the end of the long dark alley, we found a street that seemed to be deserted, and, knowing nothing more than that the

lake, where ConTech's jump boat was, was west, that was the
way we headed. We hurried on for a few blocks without seeing
anything move—the sun would be coming up in a few minutes,
and apparently this neighborhood was too affluent to have people
who worked early mornings, but not affluent enough to have
servants coming in at this hour.

After a few blocks without seeing anyone, we relaxed, and
Ulrike said, "Lyle, I don't know where to begin. Your family
sponsored me to come to New Zealand, after the war, and I came
and lived at your house, and when I first got there I was thirteen,
you were eleven, and your brother Neil was fifteen. Doesn't any
of this ring any bells?"

"Oh, it rings all sorts of bells," I said. "Just not the ones you
might think." The white buildings around us seemed like tombs,
or a movie set, no lights on in them—not just ordinary city and
household darkness, but no lights, not even one left on accidentally, or a child's night-light, or a light for finding the bathroom.
This was getting stranger and stranger. The street, too, was
strangely dusty and encrusted with old dust-drifts on top of the
cracked and broken pavement; didn't anyone ever sweep the
streets around here? "In the last few days I've learned that memories are one of the least trustworthy things you can find. Trust
me on what I remember. Four years before I was born, my parents were in a car wreck, with my newborn brother, Neil. They
lived, but he was killed. I never knew him."

"That can't be!" Ulrike exclaimed. Helen put a heavy hand
on Ulrike's shoulder and a gentle finger across her lips, mur-
muring something about not being away from police yet. "I remember Neil perfectly," Ulrike protested. "Great big guy,
wonderful sense of humor, star athlete—I might have gotten
somewhere with him if he hadn't been gay. You don't remember
he was lost on the *Elizabeth III* when that was sunk?"

I had served on the Lizzy-three, myself, and when I had left

Auckland harbor on Friday, she'd been floating at the dock, same as always.

Ulrike appeared more and more confused, and finally said, "Helen, at least tell me this isn't some kind of elaborate prank."

Helen said, impatiently, "It does seem like the authorities had some sort of a case against you. Considering you shot Beard dead, with three shots into the head, in a bank, where it was seen by four separate security cameras, I don't see how the evidence could be any more damning."

"But that's just it," Ulrike said, her hands in her pockets, slowing to a shuffle. "I don't remember it. I keep trying to but I don't. I was on the phone, calling a friend, to let him know where to meet me later today, and then I was grabbed from behind by a policeman." She sounded frustrated, as if perhaps she was used to getting her way and surprised not to get it. She started to cry, sniffling and wiping her face with her hands.

I wasn't sure what to do, but I handed her my handkerchief, and she wiped her face and blew her nose on it before handing it back to me.

"Sorry about the mess," she said.

I stuffed it into my pocket and said, "There is something very difficult for me to explain to you. There are many different Lyle Peripants with many different pasts, probably scattered across many universes. There are also many different Helen Perdidas, and probably many different Ulrike Nordstroms. Geoffrey Iphwin seems to be in all the universes, too. Anyway, in some but not all universes, each of us works for him, and so we were dispatched to get you out of prison. It happens that neither of us met any version of you, in our home worlds, whatever that might be. So I'm very sorry that I'm not reacting exactly as your ex-husband would, and I'm sorry that we aren't giving you the kind of attention and support you need and expect from us, but from our standpoint, we just met you, and that's how we're reacting."

Ulrike Nordstrom nodded several times, like a slow student trying to convince her teacher that she is getting it, before she fell over in a dead faint. "Shit," Helen said.

"Uh, yeah," I said. "If it's just the shock, she'll probably come around pretty quickly." Helen and I carried her over to the front stoop of a building, where we could put her feet up. A few minutes later she sat up, apologized profusely, dusted herself off, and seemed ready to go on. Every few minutes as we walked, she would ask Helen to explain it all one more time. Helen would tell her what we knew, which god knows wasn't much, Ulrike would whine about it, Helen would tell her that that was just the way things were, and Ulrike would walk along, sniffling just loud enough to be irritating, for a hundred meters or so before again asking, "I'm sorry, can you explain it to me one more time?"

We kept walking, and I became more and more alarmed at the silence and the lack of lights, especially as the dawn came up and it became clear that the streets were going to continue to be deserted. "What do you suppose happened here?" I asked.

"Most people won't live in an area that's been so heavily irradiated," a voice said from behind us. I turned around and saw an older guy, maybe seventy years old, with flowing white hair down to his shoulders and a neat white goatee. He wore a black silk shirt with bunches and wads of silver jewelry, and baggy black silk pants, and he leaned upon a silver-handled cane.

"Who the hell are you?"

"Well, you probably remember me more as the Colonel, but my name is Roger Sykes. You are Lyle and Helen, and I don't believe I've had the pleasure of meeting you but I assume you're Ulrike Nordstrom?"

Ulrike sighed. "Well, at least I agree that I haven't met *you*. Or even heard of you."

"I thought you were a thousand miles south of here," I said.

Sykes nodded at me and said, "Normally I am. But Iphwin sent a special representative to get me, and told me to come up here and get you. It took longer because you got out of the police station on the radioactive side, and then you went right into the abandoned part of the city. Took me a while to figure out that that's what you'd done, and even as slow as you're going, walking with a cane, it took me a longer while to catch up with you. All the same, here I am."

"Did you say this area was irradiated?"

"It was. One of those things that's hard to explain to the average citizen; it was hit with high-energy protons from orbit. Killed everything here, but didn't make anything radioactive. Most people won't make that distinction, so the area is abandoned, even though they got the corpses out of it decades ago. Mexican Civil War of 2014, if you know that one."

"Not in my world," I said, and the others shook their heads.

"A very, very unpleasant one. You were lucky to have missed it. Anyway," the Colonel said—now that I was seeing him in the flesh and hearing him talk I was gradually getting reminded of the virtual reality characters he had played in so many chat rooms with me for all these years, and his identity was starting to settle onto his body for me—"anyway, if you all just wait, I've called in a ride for us. She'll be here pretty quick—it's a nonrobot vehicle, partly because Paula's too cranky to drive anything else, and partly because that way she can take it through areas where vehicles aren't supposed to pass.

"I have to tell you, she gave me a real turn. There was this loud banging on my screen door, and I thought it was an idiot neighborhood kid whose favorite joke is to knock on my door and holler stupid questions, so I got out of my shower and wrapped a towel around myself, and I stormed out there to see who it was, and discovered somebody I'd seen killed thirty years ago. I don't know where the hell Iphwin found Paula Rey—in which world or what world—but it was one hell of a prank to play on an old man."

"There are plenty of strange pranks being played lately," Ulrike said. There was a whiny edge in her voice that made me think that if I were stuck with her for any length of time I could easily hate her.

With the soft rumble of tires, a hand-driven bus, like some strange relic of the twentieth century, lurched around the corner. The woman at the wheel, when the bus pulled up, was wearing a green T-shirt and blue jeans. She had thick, dark red, curly hair and a quaint pair of old-fashioned spectacles, like nobody else wore anymore. "Now departing for your hotel," she said, beaming at us. "Rog, you gotta try driving this thing. Iphwin got us a really good one, and it's the most fun I've had driving in years."

We had all filed in by then, and taken seats in the little fifteen-passenger bus. "Where did you find a gadget like this?" I asked.

"I didn't. Iphwin located it in a police garage. I doubt they've had it out two times in the last year," Paula said. "They won't miss it."

There was a funny noise beside me. Ulrike had fainted on my shoulder. "It's extremely interesting that that's what you married in another world," Helen said, in a very strange tone.

"I absolutely refuse to be held responsible for that. And you know perfectly well what my tastes are in this world."

"Actually, I know what several other Lyles' tastes are, and I'm extrapolating," she pointed out.

The Colonel looked back at us, and even in the dim light of sunrise I could see one of his white eyebrows rise. He fluffed out his silver hair. "Kids," he said, "if you're going to fight, I'm gonna have to separate you."

As we rumbled through the irradiated part of the city, past one dead building after another as the dawn slowly came up, I couldn't help but think that I already knew way too much about being separated. Ulrike fell into something more like normal sleep against my shoulder, and Helen leaned back until her head was slumped way over. I looked from side to side, at both of the sleeping women, and thought that there must be thousands of them, and thousands of me, and I was willing to bet that no two of us really understood each other.

The bus rumbled on till we came to a big house with a surrounding wall and a metal gate, just after we started to see people on the street again. The gate opened, and Paula drove through. She pulled around two big trees and into a wide, horseshoe-shaped drive, and stopped. "All out," she said. "Here's where you're going to sleep all this off."

We staggered inside and Paula guided us to bedrooms, all of which came off an upper gallery. With a discreet glance at me, Paula asked about sleeping arrangements. I indicated with a half-nod that Helen and I should go in one room, and Ulrike in a room by herself. Paula, with a puckish little smile that made me almost giggle, probably more from tiredness than from any real humor, indicated she approved of my choice.

The bedroom had brick walls, a high window with bars, and a big old four-poster bed. There were robes hanging on hooks, and a genuine chamber pot under the bed. As soon as I got Helen, who was still staggering and hadn't really awakened between the bus seat and here, onto the bed on one side, and made use of the chamber pot, I fell across the other side of the bed and was instantly asleep. It occurred to me that this was truly one hell of a way to try to cope with jet lag.

I didn't wake up until three in the afternoon, by the clock on the wall, and when I did, I felt incredibly nasty and dirty from having been in my clothes for so long and from sleeping with my mouth open. Beside me, Helen was still snoring, the bulge of her shoulder holster still visible. I figured she knew more about that pistol asleep than I could possibly know about it awake, and let it stay where it was. I stripped out of my sweaty, foul-smelling clothes for the moment, used the pot again, put one of the robes on, and carefully opened the door.

Down below, on a couch in the great room that the gallery overlooked, looking much too fresh and comfortable, Colonel Roger Sykes looked up and said, "Aha. First one up besides me, Paula, and Esmé, and of course we're old campaigners and can't stay in bed late if you pay us to. Bring your clothes down; you can wash them in the basement, and we've got your suitcase from the jump boat. Hot shower, too, coffee, and some stuff to eat. Oh, and don't forget the chamber pot."

I staggered down the stairs, handed off my clothing and the chamber pot to a maid, and got a small pot of coffee, a cup, a towel, and directions to the shower. Half an hour later, I emerged, feeling like I was no longer distinguishable from human. I got a good thick ham and Swiss sandwich and an orange and took the food upstairs with my suitcase, so that I could alternate between eating and dressing. It felt good to be clean, good to be dressed, and nice to get food into my belly. If I had just had the foggiest idea what was going on or what had been happening to me for the last few days, I could even have been happy.

Helen was stirring, too, so I steered her to the robe and down to Roger, who sent her through more or less the same process I had just passed through. Ulrike emerged about the time I heard Helen's shower start running, but it turned out that there were multiple bathrooms, and so she was guided to the next one. She looked like she'd spent part of the night crying, which might be typical for Ulrike or not, but was utterly understandable in the circumstances.

With that much taken care of, I sat down to another sandwich and more coffee, and asked Roger, "So where are we?"

"We're in the house of Esmé Sanderson. Not the one that had arrested you and was going to kill you, another one. Besides being on our side, this one has the further advantage to us of having a great pile of inherited wealth. Coincidentally we're in the house of the one who was going to kill you—she, like Billie Beard, was an extremely corrupt cop, and therefore could afford a place like this—but that isn't the one who is acting as our host now. I know it's confusing, and I've had Paula go over things with me a couple of times."

"And what exactly are we doing?"

"Waiting for the others," Sykes said, turning a page in his newspaper, and looking things over. "Hmm. Since I left home yesterday the history of Mexico seems to have changed completely three times. I don't read Spanish all that well to begin with, and now I don't know the context either. But for some reason all the comics are the same." He set the paper down and took off the small pair of reading glasses he was wearing. "When everyone is comfortable and dressed, then Geoffrey Iphwin has promised to pay us all a large sum of money to go to a particular cafe—why that cafe, I have no idea—and wait until other people, who I guess we're supposed to know, turn up. Once we are there, we're to wait for instructions. Me, I'm just too curious to let all this slide by.

"I guess you two work for Iphwin, and so does Miss Nordstrom. I couldn't tell you what Paula and Esmé's motivations are—those two were the two best XOs I ever had, and therefore they made sure that I never had the foggiest idea what they were thinking; all I knew was what they wanted me to think. That's why everything ran like clockwork. Based on past experience I would say that whatever their reasons for doing whatever they're doing may be, we will know in good time, when they want us to, and not a second sooner. Jesús Picardin is also coming along, because he's mercenary, curious, or both."

After a while, Helen went upstairs in her robe, a towel wrapped around her head. Shortly after that, Ulrike followed and went to her room. Meanwhile I looked at the paper, briefly, and was reminded again that I didn't know Spanish. Surely there were worlds in which I did? And in those worlds, did I know that I knew, or did I have to check, as I had just done?

It was almost five by the time we were all assembled and ready to go to the cafe. "It's not far away," Sykes said, "or so I understand."

The only person in the room I didn't recognize was a tall brunette with an abundant scatter of freckles, who nodded and glanced around the room. "I'm Esmé Sanderson. You must be Ulrike, Lyle, and Helen," she said. "I guess some of you have had bad run-ins with other versions of me, and I've had at least one very negative encounter with one of you. Now that we know we're all on the same side, or at least all invited to the same parties, I hope we can put all that aside."

Paula, seated in the corner, snorted and said, " 'Very negative encounter' is Esmé's way of saying one of you shot her. But she made me promise not to say which one. And I think we have to declare a general truce, which is a good point Esmé isn't making strongly enough. Try to remember that the person you knew may not be the person you're dealing with, all right? Good." She got up. "Anyway, there's plenty of room in the transport, and there's a real good reason to take it, and not anything else, according to Iphwin. Saddle up, load in, and get rolling. We have a place to be."

"Should we take our stuff with us?" Ulrike asked, pushing her still-damp hair back from her cheeks.

"I guess everyone should take at least a bag," Esmé said, "just to be on the safe side. Give priority to medicine, weapons, and ammo, in about that order, plus anything that's really going to make you miserable if it gets left behind."

We all scattered back upstairs; my bags were small enough so that I could carry the whole works, and it was the same for Helen. It looked like everyone had reached the same decision, downstairs, and Paula laughed at us. "I don't want to think about what our teeth-to-tail ratio is," she said.

Helen gave her the fierce, scary, tight-lipped smile I had not yet gotten used to. "I hope you're counting me as teeth."

"I am now," Paula assured her. "Okay, all in, and we'll see if I still remember how to drive."

"You drove last night," I pointed out.

"Everybody doesn't know that, and we might as well give 'em a thrill." She popped the door of the bus open and hollered "All aboard" much louder than necessary. At least one of us was really having a good time.

The drive was short, and sitting behind Paula I could see what a complicated job it was—she had to work what I figured out must be a shift-and-clutch arrangement, point the wheel, and work a foot throttle and brake, all without looking away from the road. I figured out that the thing in the middle that looked like an old-fashioned clock was the speedometer, and the thing marked E-----F was obviously fuel, but the other gauges were mysteries to me, particularly the one called TACH which didn't seem to have anything to do with how fast we were going. "That looks awfully complicated," I said, after watching her for a while.

"It gets to be automatic," she said, "and a big part of it is just knowing that you *can* do it. If we get the chance on the mission, I'll teach you—we could use more drivers, and I'm afraid it's just me and Roger that know how to drive. And he hates it, for some perverse reason all his own. If you'd like to learn, having another one of us able to drive could save a life or two."

I shuddered; I liked the idea of learning to drive, I had always enjoyed manually operating vehicles of all kinds, but I didn't much like being on an expedition where "saving a life or two" could be an issue.

We pulled up at the cafe, and the only person sitting in the outdoor area was Jesús Picardin, wearing a loud floral print shirt, a ridiculous Panama, bright red shorts, and heavy leather sandals. It was the ugliest impression of a tourist I'd ever seen, with his feet up on the table and a mostly empty beer bottle beside him, but somehow he managed to look dapper while doing so.

"If we're doing what I think we're doing," Paula said, "you should be able to leave your gear on the bus. I'd take along a weapon, if you carry, and maybe anything really precious to you."

I just carried what was in my pockets, but I noticed Helen sliding an extra knife into her pocket. I suppose in some lines of work a person just can't be too careful.

The cafe would have been a pleasant enough place, and the company nice enough, if it had all just been a social occasion. I hadn't been to Mexico before, but the beer lived up to its reputation, and we all sat, chatting and waiting for something to happen, getting to know a little bit about each other. I observed that the version of Helen here—the weapons-proficient secret agent—seemed to bond instantly with Esmé and Paula, and was not altogether sure that I liked that; I missed what I was now thinking of as "plain old Helen," a term I was trying to lose track of as quickly as I could because I didn't want to think of the Helen that I really wanted as either plain or old. Jesús and Roger both seemed to have a knack for waiting that I desperately envied; I'd have thought after my four years in the Navy I'd have mastered the skill of sitting about waiting to be useful, but I was tense and nervous.

At least Ulrike was responding reasonably—she was fidgeting too. We spent a while talking about academic life, since in her world she had been a professor of Scandinavian Studies at the

University, but there wasn't much to say that it hadn't been possible to say since the 1100s when the first universities came into being: administrators had no idea what was going on, faculty politics was vicious and silly, students were often lazy and sometimes plain stupid, and nobody cared very much about human knowledge. Ulrike's situation was the mirror image of Helen's— Helen had crossed over into this adventure for which she was well prepared, where apparently Ulrike's more adventurous self, the hired assassin, had crossed out of this world and left the Ulrike now sitting across from me to hold the bag.

There weren't many people passing on the street, which might have been any street in a poor section of a city in the sunny part of the developed world, or a middle-class street in any of the poor countries. There were a few whitewashed buildings and some walls of plain CBS block, interspersed with some wooden structures that seemed to have been put up improvisationally. Cables and wires ran everywhere, antennae and dishes sprouted from every flat surface, and crude handbills covered anywhere that people didn't walk. Little breezes stirred pale gold-yellow dust on the broken asphalt now and then.

I had gotten so used to the scene being static that I would start, just a little, every time that someone went by, or even when a dog emerged from an alley. After pretending to listen for five solid minutes to Ulrike whining about her department chair and all the credit that got stolen, I suppose I was getting desperate for something to break the monotony, since my other choices for conversation were the three women chattering about what nine-millimeter round had the greatest stopping power and the two men discussing fine points of baseball.

That was when the two women came around the corner. The older of the two, who might have been in her late twenties or early thirties, was strikingly beautiful, a honey blonde with her hair done in an elaborate coif from which several tendrils descended in tight curls, wearing a crisp white dress that revealed perfectly tanned arms and shoulders, and rounded, strappy sandals with midheels that seemed to have been specially chosen to exactly complement the perfect calves.

Beside her, the other figure seemed a little awkward and clumsy; the much younger woman, perhaps fifteen or sixteen years old, had pleasant but not extraordinary features, a saddle of freckles across the nose, mouth too wide, pale blonde hair cut very close, and was wearing a silly-looking pair of Ben Franklin wire-rimmed glasses, a bright pink T-shirt, and a baggy denim skirt with knee socks and sneakers. Both were carrying suitcases.

They approached the cafe, heading directly for our table, and I had a sense that I had seen someone move that way before. I stopped listening to Ulrike entirely, which was probably a good choice. The honey blonde stood still in a very attractive pose, looked over the whole table of people, then spoke with the kind of clear voice that comes from years of training, and said, pointing at Roger, "Now, you've got to be the Colonel. And that means you—" she pointed at me—"must be Lyle. But I can't figure out which of you is Helen."

"That would be me," Helen said, "and—good golly. Kelly and Terri, aren't you?"

Kelly nodded and said, "Yes, that's me. Geoffrey Iphwin called me late last night and told me to pack a bag and go to Josef Stalin Airport—that's just outside Paris—and that there would be a ticket and a person waiting for me. The ticket was for Mexico City, and the person was Terri, here."

"Glad to meet you all," she said, clearly trying to look poised and confident at the moment when she was unexpectedly face to face with all her adult friends. She didn't do badly. "You wouldn't believe how long Mr. Iphwin had to talk to my father to get me permission to do this, and I'm still not sure how he did it. We've been arguing all the way here about whether that airport was named after Stalin or Pétain."

They sat down to join us, and we made introductions all around the table. The energy that had dwindled into idle conversation, just as if this were a long afternoon off from our regular jobs for all of us, picked back up in a burst of eager babble, and just as it was getting hard to hear among the too-many voices clamoring for your attention, a waiter came running out of the cafe, carrying a phone with a speaker attachment, and set it down on the table among us.

We waited for a long moment in the hot, gold sunshine, everyone holding a drink or catching someone else's eye, before the phone spoke. By the time the phone did speak, I think we all knew that it would be Iphwin. "Roll call," he said. "Lyle?"

I was confused a moment, then Ulrike nudged me. "Here."

"Helen?"

"Here."

He worked his way around the table and got a "here" from everyone; then he asked "Is there anyone present I haven't named?"

"No," Roger said, "unless you count the waiter who's inside the building at the moment."

"Good. Then we can begin. Perhaps I can start by clearing a few things up for you. But first of all, I have a couple more tests to make to be sure that everything is finally in place. These aren't what you'd call the most normal things you've ever done, I'm afraid, but there's a point to all of them. Is there an electric plug on the outside wall of the cafe?"

I looked and saw that there were several of them. "Yes."

"Would you please plug something in and out of one of them a few times?"

There was a string of lights across the tops of the posts that ringed the outdoor dining areas. The plug lay on the ground by one of the outlets. I walked over and plugged and unplugged it a few times, feeling like someone was pulling some kind of incredibly elaborate prank on me. Of course, I had been feeling that way for five days.

"Excellent!" Iphwin said. "Now, would you please get the phone from the waiter inside, and then phone Paris directory assistance and hang up as soon as they answer?"

Before anyone else moved, Kelly got up and said, "If there's any number I know, it's that one—I'm constantly forgetting phone numbers." She walked into the cafe.

"What are your little experiments about?" I asked the speaker phone.

"I can't tell you that just now but I will very soon. Just let Kelly do her experiment, and let me do one more, and then we'll be in good shape."

Kelly came out, holding a portable phone, and said, "All right, I'm going to try," loud enough for the speaker phone to pick it up. Then she dialed and hung up.

A moment later the speaker phone said, "Sorry, try it again."

"And you still want me to hang up as soon as they answer?"

"Yes. Exactly as you did before."

She dialed, waited, and hit the button.

"Perfect!" Iphwin said, triumph and satisfaction evident in his voice even through the speaker phone, and immediately added, "Now there's just one more task. Is there any music coming over the speakers in the cafe?"

"No," we all chorused.

"Do you want them to put some on?" Terri asked. "I can run and ask them."

"Thank you, Terri."

She got up and darted inside; I was beginning to wonder what the staff inside was thinking of our behavior and our requests, but at least so far they hadn't come out to tell us to knock it off.

A moment later, a style of music I'd never heard before—maybe it was something more Latin than my Nazi-run world had retained?—came blaring through the speakers, and Terri came running out, breathlessly. "Thank god for four required languages," she said, flinging herself back into her chair.

"Just a moment . . ." Iphwin said. "Now, the phone you were using for calling Paris . . . do *not* pick it up when it rings. It's going to ring for several minutes. Leave the radio on and leave the speaker phone on. Move the phone to the table, and put an empty chair by the place where you put the phone down, but do *not* pick up the call."

The phone began to ring almost immediately, and with a shrug, Helen got up and moved it to the table, then dragged another chair over to the table as it continued to ring and ring.

"Is the phone in place?" Iphwin asked through the speaker.

"Yep. You ought to be able to hear it," the Colonel said. The phone rang on and on, a maddening sound, and the radio played loudly through the speakers overhead; I was beginning to wonder if this was some kind of complex plan to drive us all mad.

"And is the chair empty?"

Jesús Picardin leaned forward and looked at it, making sure, before he said, "The chair is empty."

"Everyone sit still for my count of 100. Don't move while I count. One, two, three, four, five, six, hello."

The phone had stopped ringing. The speaker phone had shrieked briefly, a burst of high-pitched feedback, at the word "hello."

And there, sitting in the chair that had been empty an instant ago, holding the phone he had just answered, sat Geoffrey Iphwin, in a magnificent white suit with dark striped tie, a bright red carnation in his lapel.

Everyone jumped back, tipping chairs over and taking big steps backward. Helen, Esmé, Paula, and Jesús had hands on weapons. Iphwin raised his hands, one still holding the phone, and then hit the hang-up switch on the phone. "Is anyone going to shoot?" he asked.

"No, you just startled me," Esmé said.

"Guess not." Paula sounded regretful.

"No," Helen said flatly.

"At least not yet," Picardin said.

"Good." Iphwin set the handset down, and reached over to turn off the speaker phone. He looked around. "Well, at last I have all of you in the same world, and now I can explain everything to you. I have identified you all as people I need for an important mission, for which, besides the possible glory if you survive and the undying thanks of your country if it works, I offer to make all of you wealthy beyond your wildest dreams. That's the offer—take it or leave it—high risk, but glory, service to country, and great wealth."

"What's the mission?" the Colonel asked.

Iphwin sat back, crossed his legs, and smiled at all of us, a warm friendly smile as if he were about to tell us the best joke in the world. "It's really a very simple job. Drive north and find America. It's been missing for at least three decades, you see, in trillions of worlds, and it's time we found out why." He got up and said, "Well, now. If you'll all accept the deal, I can put us up in a nice hotel and we can hold a little strategic conference this evening, and get an early start tomorrow. Is everyone prepared to accept the deal?"

I was nodding, and then I realized we had all said "Yes" in unison. I wondered if Iphwin had arranged that one, or if it was a real coincidence, or just contagious idiocy. The distinction didn't seem to matter much.

PART THREE

I Wonder Who's Schroedinger Now?

phwin had gotten us reservations in a big, modern hotel, one of those places they set up in poor countries so that the well-off can go there without having to meet the poor. We rode there in near-silence. I got the shotgun seat so that Paula could show me how everything worked.

Iphwin told us all, firmly, that we were to rest and eat, discuss as little as we could, neither make nor accept phone calls for any reason, and meet him in a large conference room at 8:00 P.M. sharp. Other than that, he wasn't about to answer any questions.

Helen and I had been given adjoining rooms with a door between that we could unlock; we promptly did. We ordered room service—happily, Agent Helen Perdida's tastes in food were very nearly the same as Professor Helen Perdida's, so at least there was something I knew about this person—then took quick, separate showers. I was about to tumble into bed for a nap, since it was almost an hour till we were to meet downstairs, when there was a knock at the door that connected my room to Helen's. "I'm naked," I said.

"Perfect."

Something about the tone of her voice made me open the door very quickly. When she charged in, I had barely a moment to see that all she was wearing was a pair of satin gloves and a pair of spike heels. She'd gotten hold of two of my neckties, and she rushed in and had me hog-tied behind my back, with my ankles and wrists in one big bundle, before I got done asking her what she was doing. Then she gagged me with a pair of her panties tied on with a stocking, turned me on my face, and said, "You've been bad," and proceeded to spank me till tears ran down my face.

The whole time I was trying to work the gag loose to tell her I didn't like this kind of thing, that whatever she had done with the Lyle she used to know, I wasn't him. At least I wanted her to know that she was hurting my buttocks and that I didn't like it and wanted her to stop. I was twitching and screaming through the gag, unable to breathe, terrified about how far she might go or what she might do to me.

She turned me on my side and I frantically shook my head, trying to tell her that no, I didn't want or like this, but she gave me a smile that froze my blood, took off one of her shoes, and—very gently, to my surprise—inserted the spike heel in my anus and moved it back and forth. I thought I would throw up; my breath, stopped by her gag, was hot and foul in my lungs, my stomach and chest were heaving, my nose clogged with snot from crying.

She wrapped my penis in one of those satin gloves and stroked me, slowly, a few times. I was more erect than I had ever been in my life.

She flipped me onto my back; that might be a good position for someone who does a great deal of yoga, I suppose, but the pressure on my shoulders, ankles, elbows, wrists, and knees was terrible, and I screamed again, choking now on the tears and mucus dribbling down my throat. My penis, as if it had a mind of its own, kept right on responding to the strokes of the satin gloves, and then she hopped up on the bed and sat on it.

Helen rode me for what seemed forever, and though every joint shrieked with pain, and huge sobs heaved in my chest, at the same time I had never felt a pleasure more intense. She jerked and spasmed three times in big, sloppy orgasms while I struggled and wept; finally, everything gave way—my gut muscles cramped as if I'd been punched in the solar plexus after running ten miles—and I came hard enough to give myself a stomach cramp.

She got off me and got a warm washcloth, then slowly bathed my sore genitals. I wanted her to untie me, but clearly that would only happen on her schedule. Then she rolled me to the side and undid my bonds; I flopped out of the hog-tie like a rag doll, unable to move my arms or legs. She turned me back to her and undid the stocking, then pulled it and the panties out of my mouth. I started to speak but she bent low and kissed me intensely, for a long time.

When she had finished and I lay there, spent and barely able to breathe, with most of my muscles screaming, she said, "You were really a good boy. That's the best it's ever been."

"I've never done that . . ." I said. "Never. I had no idea you were going to . . . I don't play games like that. That wasn't me."

"Then whose erection was that?"

I turned on my side, away from her. "I didn't say I don't respond to it. It's nothing I haven't dreamed about. I said I don't do it. I don't want to do things like that." I crept sideways across the bed, face still turned down toward the covers, hoping to get away from her.

"You'll be suggesting it to me in a few days, if we're both alive."

I hated that snotty confidence in her voice. "I don't care what you did with any other Lyle. You don't do that with me. And if you even think it might be me, you ask first."

She laughed, and it was like Helen in one way, but frightening in another—I didn't even begin to know this person. "Let me tell you something else, little Lyle. You're now going to have the sweetest little nap you've had in years. I *know* that your body reacts that way. And as for me—this always seems to sharpen my eye and shorten my reaction time. I'll be fast, precise, and relaxed for the next few days. Whatever you may think at the moment, my little crybaby tramp, we're both better off. And you enjoyed it whether you admit or not, you little whore."

She squeezed my testicles, hard, and I nearly vomited as I yelped in pain. Laughing as if it were Christmas, she stretched out beside me.

Strangely enough—how could I sleep next to someone who so terrified me?—it wasn't long before I fell sound asleep. When she shook me awake, we had just fifteen minutes to get down to the meeting. I didn't look at her and I asked her to leave the room while I dressed. She laughed at me again, and I really didn't like the sound of it this time. It was even more frightening, and even less Helen.

Iphwin began his talk obliquely; he said, "I have spent a very long time thinking about how I was going to present this to all of you, and I'm not altogether sure, even now, that I have picked the right way to do it. I know you must be curious about who I am, how I came to know the things I am going to explain to you, and how and why I have undertaken the project that I am asking you all to join—but I am going to deliberately not gratify your curiosity for the moment, because my explanation will make a great deal more sense if I first give you some basis for understanding it. I hope that I am making myself completely obscure?"

"You are," I said, since no one else spoke.

"Well, good, then my sense of how the human mind responds is not completely wrong. I hope I can make matters clearer, later, but for right now it is probably *appropriate* that they be obscure. To begin with, then—your surmises, Lyle, Helen, and some of you others, about the Many Worlds Interpretation and some of the other questions, have been largely correct. People, information, and objects did indeed begin, a few decades ago, to cross over between different worlds, as you call them—or timelines, or histories, or event sequences, depending on whose terms you prefer to use—and this does account for discrepancies in your memories, for the occasional outright violations of causality you have noticed, and even for the new cultural norm of people avoiding any sort of discussion of the past, even of their own personal past.

"Has any of you figured out when these things happen, or what triggers them?"

There was a long silence, and Iphwin said, "You couldn't be expected to, of course—for one thing, the experience itself is sometimes mildly disorienting, particularly if you're crossing between event sequences which are extremely different, as has happened to several of you in the course of your lives. Well, I can now fill you in—or I suppose if I can't, I'm about to find out.

"People cross over when they talk on the phone, when they get on-line, and when they ride in a robot-piloted vehicle."

I felt like I had just gotten an electric shock right up my spine; suddenly everything was clear. "That's why!" I said. "They're all driven by quantum computing devices!"

Everyone turned and stared and I remembered that I was the only person with any physics background in the room. "Er—" I said.

"You're exactly right, Lyle," Iphwin said, "that's what's going on. And the odd part is, that isn't really a problem. It's merely the reason why the real problem has gone undetected till now. But I'm getting ahead of myself—perhaps I should just launch in, and if we can get the occasional assist from Professors Peripart and Perdida, we can put the whole story together quickly."

Iphwin's lecture and the questions after it ran till midnight; he provided us with plates of sandwiches, pastries, fruit, coffee, tea, and juice, and gave us a bathroom break punctually on every hour, so we endured it well enough physically, but some of us had hoarse voices from arguing by the end, and almost all of us had brains that hurt. But he kept producing evidence, and what he told us fit the facts. Eventually we bought it, perhaps because it was such a relief to feel like we understood what was going on.

There were indeed many worlds—in fact there was every possible world. Perpendicular to time, and to our familiar spatial dimensions, there were five spacelike dimensions Iphwin called "possibility," and each event sequence had a unique five-dimensional address within those dimensions. "Suppose there was just one thing in the universe, and all it could do was to be somewhere—and there was just one spatial dimension," Iphwin said, trying to get it across to our less mathematical members. "The one spatial dimension would be a line, right? Imagine it as a road, if you want. The one object is a car, and every time it passes through any given place, it's an event. Now, you could make a picture of the universe as a graph, with the horizontal being the position on the road, and the vertical being the time. On that graph a vertical line would mean the car just stayed in one place, and the more horizontal the line got, the faster the car would be moving. A big curve like the letter S would be somebody driving back and forth. Every point on that line would be an event. Does that make sense so far?"

"It's been a long time since I had to take algebra," the Colonel grumbled.

"I can promise you that they haven't improved it any, either," Terri said. "All right, so then if you have one dimension of possibility, it's like stacking all the possible graphs there can be, one on top of the other, with the most similar ones closest. Right?"

Iphwin seemed startled. "You have talent."

"I spend all my time in school. I'm used to lectures. And

besides, you said a world or a timeline could be called an 'event sequence,' right? Well, then obviously a line of events, like what you're describing on the graph, is an event sequence. And time only runs one way, and you said there's just one car on the road, so if there was just one world it would have just one line. If there are many worlds, then you have one graph for every possible way a car could go back and forth on the road. That's all."

"And it's right," Iphwin said. "Those of you who are confused should consult with Terri from now on."

"And those of you who *want* to be confused can consult with me," Paula Rey said. "So the whole point of the graphs and the road and so forth is that it's a very simplified version? In the imaginary world there's one object, one dimension of space, one dimension of time, and one dimension of possibility, right? And in our real world you're saying we have some huge number of objects, three dimensions of space, one of time, and five of possibility?"

"That's it exactly. You're not as confused as you think you are. It's just that what I'm telling you is pretty big. Now, one of the implications of this is that in the dimensions of possibility there can be an infinite number of worlds next door. A point can have an infinite number of neighboring points, and that's in two dimensions; a line can have an infinite number of neighboring lines, in three; and so forth. By extension, an event, which is a four-dimensional thing, can have an infinite number of immediate neighbors in the five dimensions of possibility. And those are just the ones at zero distance.

"Now it turns out that if you cross over into another event sequence, you're more likely to cross over to a nearby one than to a far one. In fact, every second that you're on the phone, you're bouncing from one world to another constantly. It's just that most of the time, you bounce between worlds that are so similar that you can't tell the difference. For example, maybe in one world you have a few more atoms of calcium in one of your teeth—or maybe the buttons on your clothes are six microns larger. Or maybe you bounce to a world where all the way across town, a man is washing his car instead of reading the paper.

"But every so often you take a bigger bounce, and you're in a world where your history is noticeably different. That's what happened, for example, to Helen Perdida when she was a teenager, or to Paula and Jesús more recently."

"Why should it happen when we're on the phone?" Roger said. "Why not while we're bathing or flossing our teeth or asleep? And didn't you say it also happens while we're on-line or while we're in a robot-driven vehicle?"

"All of the above and a few others," Iphwin agreed. "Perhaps Lyle has gotten it all figured out now, since he's had time? He's more experienced at lecturing than I am, and since the idea is new to him, maybe he can explain it more clearly than I can—the idea is at the core of my being, you might say, so I'm apt to assume too much when I explain it."

I harrumphed and collected my thoughts. I began by telling them about Schroedinger's cat, and the whole problem of how to interpret a distribution of quantum states when you project it upward into the macro world. Then I found myself explaining something that tends to make people nervous, and therefore is rarely publicized by the big communications companies.

"Maybe seventy or eighty years ago," I explained, "people doing brain research got interested in the problem of how the brain could possibly be storing as much sheer raw information as it seemed to. Once they started to get some idea of how things were coded into individual brain cells—basically as linked sets of physical impressions—it just didn't seem like there could be enough room in the human head for all of that. Since we didn't have room for the brains to do it with, how were we remembering so much?

"Well, the answer turned out to be, we weren't. You remember someone's face as, maybe, an impression of one eyebrow, half the lower lip, part of the nose, and an eye. When you recall their face later, what your brain does—faster than anyone could sense in real time—is to reconstruct the picture, filling in all the details. It's easy for the brain to do because faces are symmetrical, some kinds of features tend to go with each other, and so forth. The mind has a fast little interpreter that fills in the rest of the picture."

"That's why most pro actors can get up on a part fast, in terms of knowing roughly what they do when," Kelly said, "but getting from knowing your part to knowing exact words is a pain in the ass that takes forever. You can learn a few markers almost instantly, but to get the whole thing perfect you've got to have many more markers, and then get the feel of the text, so that what you construct between the markers is always right."

"Exactly. Well, that was kind of interesting, as a piece of brain research, and it helped to explain little things like the way you'll sometimes mistake a stranger for an old friend you haven't seen in a while, or the way people will begin to remember something different from what happened if you repeat a story to them often enough—they start to fill in bridging material that includes some of what you tell them. But the most important application came later, in communications. It was a solution to the bandwidth problem."

Among questions and interruptions, I sketched out the basic concepts for them. Imagine an old-fashioned Morse code transmitter, sending dots and dashes; it has a bandwidth of one. That is, either the wire has current flowing through it, or it doesn't. Now, since no Morse signal has more than four dots or dashes, theoretically if you had four wires, you could send each character all at once, instead of sequentially, and send four times as fast. That's a bandwidth of four. The amount of information that can pass a given point in a given time is speed times bandwidth—and since by the turn of the twenty-first century, bandwidths were running into millions and speeds to megahertz, trillions of bits per second were traveling through each junction in the system.

It still wasn't fast enough for some purposes, and most especially not for one commercially very important one. The human senses as a whole have a bandwidth that runs into many trillions, and you need to be able to simulate all the senses all at once in real time to produce effective virtual reality. And you want to produce that really effective virtual reality because human beings seem to have a nearly unlimited demand for being made happy and taken care of all the time—we're all big babies on some level, I suppose—and anyone who can deliver that cheaply enough can probably collect the whole wealth of the human race eventually; even now there are people, especially people born rich in some of the advanced nations in some of the world lines, who spend more years hooked up than not. So one way or another, they were going to get that bandwidth, or figure out a way to put a great deal more through the bandwidth they had.

As it turns out, you can simulate reality fast enough to do vivid VR, but getting signal into and out of the brain requires enormous bandwidth, and thus though a VR simulator could deliver enough signal to produce a vivid reality for one person or a few people, a single long-distance VR call would theoretically have required more bandwidth than the whole United States had used for radio, phone, and telegraph to get through the Second World War. Though there was an enormous market for VR worlds that could be shared as real, living, breathing experiences, to provide for that market would seem to require the construction of enormous facilities to provide enough bandwidth for all that signals traffic.

There was another enormous demand for bandwidth lurking

in the wings too. Self-piloting vehicles would work best if every car on the road could share information with every other car. You wanted a car that could think and look fast enough to figure out that a ball rolling into the street was apt to be pursued by a child, or to dodge around—and alert every other car to—a board with nails lying on the pavement. Once again, bandwidth needed was just much, much bigger than the bandwidth that could even conceivably be made available.

Computer speed depends in part upon internal bandwidth—because the size of the chunks of data moving around inside the computer determines how fast the computer can rearrange information, and therefore "think." Since VR communication had to move through the computer anyway, putting it through a faster system was highly desirable, and the fastest systems of all, by the mid-twenty-first century, were quantum computers—systems that took advantage of the peculiarity of quantum physics that a single object could behave as if it were in a distribution of several mutually exclusive states all at once. In effect, you could solve the problem of the dead cat and the problem of the live cat simultaneously, and each bit in the computer's memory and each operation in its registers could be in parallel with itself; a single machine could be made to act like many thousands all at once, with a tremendous gain in speed.

But massively parallel processing had another use—it was exactly how computer engineers had been able to simulate many human brain functions. The ability to construct a face for recognition, or fill in the lacunae in a partial text, or smooth out a partially degraded hologram from fragments required the massive and fast parallelism that only the quantum computer could provide. The quantum computer, then, made real-time VR communication possible, for it made it possible to transmit a small fraction of the needed information for the simulation, and from that information to construct a full simulation at the other end.

But the uncertainty principle limited the user's control of the information; you couldn't know which state any of the quantum processors was "really" in without preventing the parallel processing you needed. If you bought into the Copenhagen Interpretation, this was no problem; you simply treated it as a computational trick that allowed you to get away with sending less information than the other side received. Likewise, in the Aphysical Interpretation, the problem was no problem—it was as if you had two ponds, with a stick in each one, and the two sticks connected by a string: a wave in one would make a wave in the other, and multiple and complex wave patterns went through because the stick could move in multiple and complex ways.

But in the Many Worlds Interpretation, what you were doing was solving the problem by using all of the neighboring worlds plus your own—and the uncertainty principle would not let you know which answer was going to which address. Those who thought about it at all, in those terms—my friends and I, in grad school, had often argued about it over beer—had always assumed that the solution must be that in a quantum computer network, there must be a great many "cosmic wrong numbers"—i.e. messages that went to the wrong universe. That always led us to argue that we had found a reason the Many Worlds Interpretation could not be the right one—because the uncertainty principle, applied to the addressing problem, seemed to say that you couldn't know whether or not a number was wrong, and thus all those "wrong numbers" would violate it.

We had never considered that Nature might solve the problem by not allowing anyone on the receiving end of a message to know what universe *he* was in. And yet that solution now seemed exactly the sort of thing you might expect of Nature in her better moods. Whoever was receiving the message would exist in a suspended state, like Schroedinger's cat, for as long as they were on the line; unlike the cat, they would not be half alive and half dead, but fractionally in many different worlds. Hanging up or briefly disconnecting—and the line-sharing protocols in any modern network guaranteed brief disconnects many times per second—was exactly the equivalent of opening the box and collapsing the probability distribution onto a singular state—living or dead for the cat, some universe or other for you.

Once the wide-band quantum network had come into use for VR, everything else had been piggybacked onto it, because it had so much room for everything else—transportation signals, fax, television, telephone, and all the rest. Whenever you went on-line in the quantum communication system, you oscillated through many of the possible system states, many times per second. This was true whether you were a person, a bale of hay, or an e-mail message.

"So," I concluded, at the end of it all, four sandwiches, six cups of coffee, and too many arguments and diagrams to count later, "basically we've been reshuffling all the worlds at a faster and faster rate, and as each big family of event sequences gets VR and quantum computing, the number that we can interchange with has increased polyfold. By now *nobody* is in the world they began in. Mostly the worlds are enough alike so that people adapt, though I'm sure there are more street crazies and mental patients than there used to be in most worlds, and many of them probably spend all of their time trying to tell anyone who will listen that something is terribly wrong."

Iphwin nodded, and said, "And that brings me to who or what I am. As systems grow, as you know we have to decentralize control more and more to keep them functioning. That ends up implying, among other things, that instead of a central administration governing everything, you get by with roving pieces of software that just look for whatever isn't working as it should. That is, the system administration stops looking like a police and court system, and starts to look more and more like an immune system. Systems administration becomes a matter of operating a population of cyberphages—benign viruses that keep users from doing things that damage the system. It's easier and cheaper than keeping everything tied to a central program that has to know everything.

"A few years ago, one cyberphage began to notice that there was a common problem in every one of the parallel universes, all at once. And that problem was the disappearance of the billions of nodes found in the United States, American Reich, Purified Christian Commonwealth—whatever you called that piece of land between San Diego and the St. Lawrence or Puget Sound and the Everglades. Once it noticed that there was no traffic at all, for several seconds, it began to track this—only to discover no traffic for periods of months or years, across all the event sequences to which it had any access—that is, across an enormous number of worlds.

"It looked very much to the cyberphage as if some large number of people and machines had either been cut off from the net, or left voluntarily, or something—but whatever it was, it wasn't good for the network. The cyberphage thought about this for a very long time, the way an entity that lives on the net between all the universes can think—quickly and thoroughly—and decided that since no information seemed to be emanating from that country—not a transaction record, a phone call, a bill, or a bit of mail of any kind—the only solution would be to go have a look for itself.

"That took some effort," Iphwin said. "About twenty-five years, but of course a cyberphage is immortal, and there's the advantage of being able to operate across billions of event sequences all at once. The hard part was the need to get a physical body in which to walk around, if I was going to go and take a look myself."

There was a long pause as we all digested that, and then, very tentatively, Jesús said, "Sir, am I to take it that you want us to believe that you are that cyberphage?"

"Well, perhaps a better term would be that I am its avatar. The cyberphage not only still exists, it runs ConTech; one reason you heard the sort of rumors you did about the company was that its only real purpose was to accumulate money and power, as a means to the more important end of getting an embodied form of myself into a physical world, with an appropriate team of people so that we could go and have a look at what's become of America. That required a million man-years of bioengineering, as you might guess, and a great deal of tinkering with the brain-body interface, but . . . here I stand. If you were to lift up the flap in the back of my head, you'd find a billion-nanopin interface for reporting back to Iphwin Prime—that's what I call my progenitor—and I was in a tank till I was physically adult, but other than that, I guess you'd have to say I'm as human as you. And just as bewildered."

Helen had been sitting with her arms folded, sometimes glaring at Iphwin and sometimes glaring at me. Now, finally, she spoke. "And all the manipulations?"

"I didn't have any way," Iphwin explained, "to control who or what went to which world. Nobody has that ability—the very thing that lets you shift worlds is the uncertainty with which it happens. But while I can't control the shuffle, I can control how fast it's dealt, and I can look at every hand. What I did was that I recruited teams of people that I thought might be able to solve the problem, and then I kept shifting them between event sequences till I had some version of all of the critical people together in one event sequence, or to be more precise about it, until I knew it was very *likely* that I had all of you together.

"Then to join you, I made that voice phone call, and did it in a system that hung up and reconnected at terahertz frequencies.

It kept checking against other stuff you were doing, till I got it narrowed down as much as could be managed; then in the last few seconds I just oscillated until the system found you. There was an uncertainty trade-off, as always—I have some big gaps in my memory and neither I nor the cyberphage knows exactly which Iphwin I am. Millions of Iphwins must have shuffled right out of reality to get me here."

"But you didn't *feel* them go," Helen said.

"Does that matter?" Iphwin asked, puzzled.

"You bet it does," she said. "I'm just wondering if by any chance you've noticed that most of us gave up our old lives to be here, and you never asked us if we wanted to."

Iphwin nodded. "That's true. And if you really insist, you can leave now. I'm hoping you'll stay for a variety of reasons—that is, both, I have a variety of reasons to hope you will stay, and there are a variety of reasons why any one of you might. I hope you will at least hear me out."

"I'll do that much," Helen said. "But right now I'm not very inclined to believe you. You're a ghost personality, one created by a machine to embody itself. You didn't give up relatives, friends, lovers, any of that. You were created mostly to be thrown away—"

"All human beings, ultimately, are thrown away," Iphwin pointed out. "Most for no reason, since the universe has none, and they simply go away, used up, never to return. You were picked because, first of all, you were a likely bunch of people to care about what had happened to America. Most people don't or wouldn't, you know. Why should they? Whatever its importance in the world might once have been, it doesn't have it any longer. The cultural role has been taken over by the expat culture, the physical economy of the world seems to have disconnected without anyone noticing, and in most of the event sequences there's no active military balance-of-power problem. America seems to have faded everywhere, long before it disappeared completely. Fortunately for this project, there still are a very few people who are still concerned about it, and you all are among them.

"Then there's the matter of skill at abduction. The cyberphage of which I am an avatar, being a machine, may have overrated the importance of abduction, since so far no one has found a good way to provide machines with the skill. But I'm as human as you are—"

"So you say," Helen said, making her contempt clear.

"I have a personality physically embodied in flesh made according to human DNA, and that's good enough," Iphwin said, firmly. His face got red as he said it, and I could hear the stress and anger in his voice.

There was a very long, awkward pause, before Iphwin finally resumed. "To summarize, Lyle Peripart is an authority on the mathematics of abduction. Helen Perdida's discipline involves solving practical problems in abductive reasoning, plus many versions of her are skilled in operations in dangerous areas, plus of course she's personally loyal to Lyle, which may be valuable in a tight spot. Then I needed someone who could handle command and who was closely linked to Lyle, hence your presence, Colonel. I got you your two old executive officers, with a bonus that I needed a couple of investigating detectives—which is why I got not only Esmé Sanderson, but also Jesús Picardin."

After a minute, Kelly said, "You haven't explained why Terri and I were brought into this, and you went to some extra effort to get us."

Iphwin nodded. "I had no creative artists, and that's a whole other style of abduction. And I needed someone who practiced the harder creative arts, the ones where you accommodate to the world around you rather than the ones where you just dump out whatever you're feeling inside and then shape it for others. That kind of talent for making the piece that fits with the other pieces, that ability to fit in, the thing actors call rapport or chemistry, was a kind of creativity I wanted to make sure of, and that's the kind that actors are good at. And then, for Terri . . ." he sighed. "Ethically I'm on shaky ground here, but, well, she was the only member of that VR chat room that I didn't already have coming, and somehow that felt like a mistake. She's physically healthy and bright, and I would guess quite adaptable."

"And she's right here listening to you, so you can stop talking about her in the third person," Terri said, flushing with rage.

Iphwin went right on. "Also, Terri, like most smart teenagers, you don't have an excessive respect for authority. My feeling is that whatever we find when we get north of the border, it's not going to be so much finding it that's a problem—it's going to be understanding whatever it is we've found. The erasure is so complete—and so perfectly confined to the old 48 contiguous states—that it just doesn't seem like it could be any kind of natural phenomenon. Nor does it seem like anything anyone could do on purpose. Which seems to cover all the reasonable and comprehensible possibilities, and so chances are that what we are looking for is unreasonable and incomprehensible. Hence my urge to throw a few wild cards in—purely a hunch."

"You're telling me that I've left my entire world behind because you had a hunch?" Terri demanded. Her bony shoulders were high up, and her arms were folded tightly.

"It would appear so, yes."

"And you just decided to use all our lives?"

Iphwin seemed mildly exasperated. He was at least human enough so that he was bothered to be confronted with something he had not thought of before; few human beings really like the unexpected. "What I am doing is no different from what a president or king does when he starts a war, or from what a corporation president does when he orders a new product into production. I am changing billions or trillions of people's lives drastically without their consent. The only difference here is that ten of you are having the opportunity to confront me about it. If the confrontation makes you feel better, I suppose that's all right. But it doesn't make any other difference, and I wish we could concentrate on more basic issues."

"Not having our lives torn up is about as basic an issue as there is," Helen said, "and Terri is absolutely right to be upset. If you want our assent, you're going to have to offer us something better than just making us rich, or give us a reason better than just because you happened to need it and thought we would make a good team. Why should we conduct your investigation for you? Show us why we shouldn't all walk out of here and start dialing the phone at random, until we manage to find somewhere close enough to home so that we'll want to stay."

Iphwin sighed and spread his hands. "I suppose in some sense that my inability to anticipate this does demonstrate the difference between human and machine. But I had thought that since in fact you have been bouncing from one world to another every time you use the phone, or the net, or ride in a guided vehicle, that you would realize that you aren't being ripped from your homes—that in fact you've never been home for many years, and you were never going home."

Helen folded her arms and stood her ground in a way very like the Helen I remembered. "Well, we only just found out we've been crossing from world to world a few minutes ago, you idiot. We're still getting used to that idea. And now we learn that you've been deliberately causing part of it. How do you expect us to feel?"

"I have great difficulty expecting anyone to feel anything," Iphwin pointed out. "And I am forced to admit that even in this body I don't feel things very much myself—I suppose that's a matter of the body not having received any emotional conditioning when it was younger. I suppose you might say I feel more like I'm *wearing* it than as if I *am* it. But I do notice that the glandular systems have a great deal of lag time—that emotions often persist long after their cause is removed. Is that the sort of problem you're talking about?"

"It might be, but it's a very lengthy and not-human way of expressing it," Helen said, grudgingly. "The point is, you have to allow us some time for emotional adjustment. We're all new to what's going on, it's frightening, and you are at that core of what is frightening about it. And if I may add without offending you, Terri—Terri's godawful young to discover that you've separated her from her parents, possibly forever, and I don't think your mission, however important you may think it is, is going to justify that sort of thing in any of our minds.

"I suppose what you are asking for might be logical, or reasonable, or whatever, but it isn't even remotely sensible in emotional terms. Now, if you really want our trust, you're going to have to give us at least some evidence that there is a good reason for us to give it to you, rather than just walk out of here. And don't try to make it sound like a geometry proof while you're doing it."

Iphwin sat down at the edge of the low stage, balling his hands into tight fists, clearly frustrated. "I don't have a good answer for you," he said, finally. "There is something strange about the disappearance of a whole nation from the earth, from history, from everything, and the unknown forces that prevent our knowing anything about what happened. And maybe we don't see it because we are too close, but I think there is also something strange about the way that very few people have noticed or are reacting to it.

"What I want to do is to resolve that question. The part of me that is a product of so many years as a machine intelligence really has no motivations other than curiosity, given that sex and death are beyond it. And the part of my mind that has grown into this body is just a few years old and has had no childhood, no imprinted memories to speak of, no distinctiveness from any other human body. In the circumstances, I made my best guess. I looked for people who had the knack of abduction, and who I thought might still have enough love for the idea of America. And I did what was necessary to get them together into a single event sequence so that we can work. That was the best solution I could think of. If it has not worked, then either you, with your abductive gifts, must think of a better way to solve it, or it will have to be left unsolved."

There was a very long, awkward silence, before Roger Sykes stretched, fluffed out his white hair, and stood up, propping himself with his cane. He said, "Uh, well. You know, I'm bored stiff. And I was born into the regiment; my dad told me about being a boy in the States but I never went there myself. And I'm an old guy, if I die, you know, no big deal, I was planning to do that sooner or later anyway. So . . . I guess I'll go and take a look."

Iphwin looked up with hope in his eyes. "Thank you."

"You're welcome. Long as I'm here, and so forth. But you really do need to develop your skills at asking people instead of manipulating them."

"Yes, I suppose I do."

After a moment, Esmé got up and moved next to Sykes. She was even bigger than my first impression had said she was—she absolutely towered over the older man. "Colonel, I'd be pleased to go with you. There's just not that much going on in my life and I don't have anything I'd rather do. And it would be kind of interesting to find out what's happened to America."

"And if Esmé is going, I better go too," Paula said, "to keep you two out of trouble."

Jesús Picardin spoke next and said, "You know, I have been very bored with my work, and I would have to say that there could hardly be a more interesting kind of case for a detective than having an entire nation go missing. And probably I'd never get back home anyway, and frankly this just sounds much more interesting than anything else I could be doing."

"This is starting to seem like a lot of peer pressure," Kelly complained. "All right, you want to go, so go. There's not necessarily a good reason for the rest of us to go, is there?"

"Not necessarily, but let's see what the options are," Helen said grudgingly. "I don't like to admit it but I think Iphwin here has us over a barrel. If I understand all this Schroedinger stuff, we can wander around for the rest of our lives picking up phones and then hanging up, and going for rides in robot vehicles, and logging on and off the net—but the odds of getting back to a world that we recognize are pretty small. And anyway, all we'd be doing is displacing some other version of ourselves, bumping someone else into our mess. For the time being I suppose we're pretty much stuck in this world—and what world is this, anyway?"

"Well, you'll have to take my word for it," Iphwin said. "Because if you try to check by net or phone you'll be leaving suddenly. But this is one of a relatively small family of event sequences where there was a coup in the United States in 1972, over the withdrawal from a war in Vietnam—Indochina to some of you. Military junta took over to restore order and honor, which basically meant to suppress political expression at home and use nuclear weapons to win in Vietnam. They got into an arms race with Communist Germany, which was the other big power in that event sequence, and eventually bankrupted the Germans. Then they stayed in power indefinitely, getting less and less repressive with time; they enforced a huge, complicated array of rules governing every aspect of daily behavior to make the country look as much as possible like it had in the 1950s of that event sequence, which was pretty dull and conformist. Not the best of worlds, not the worst. The rest of the world is mostly in small nations; devolution went pretty far. There are hundreds of prosperous small states—imagine a world full of Switzerlands. You could live here pretty nicely."

"But good luck explaining why you wouldn't talk on a phone or use a self-driving vehicle, eh?" Kelly said. "I guess I'd have to hope there was an American Theater in Ciudad de México, or maybe start one. I don't have too many good alternatives, since all I've got is travelers' Spanish. Can you tell me what happens if I do go along?"

"If I knew what would happen, no one would have to go, and I'd never have disturbed any of you," Iphwin pointed out. "And I do have considerable resources, so if you truly don't want to go on the expedition, I can find you a job in my organization, probably in some office where you won't have to expose yourself to accidental transfer. If that is what you would genuinely prefer."

"Aren't you worried that we'll *all* take that offer?" Helen asked.

"I am, now that you mention it. But it seems like the decent thing to do, given the things you have pointed out about my having so disrupted your lives. And I already have some volunteers, anyway. As you point out, I'm really not good at working with people. This is the best I can do while improvising."

As I listened to all the arguments, I had been thinking about my own position. This Helen didn't much resemble the quiet historian that I liked; and if I couldn't find the exact one I thought I knew . . . well, really a composite, since I must have interacted with thousands of very slightly different Helens, each of whom knew thousands of versions of me . . . all the same, I could find a more comfortable connection than this one. The odds even seemed reasonably good if I just started making a lot of phone calls.

On the other hand, what *had* happened to the United States of America, and how had I—who had been raised as an expat patriot, proud of my heritage—never even noticed that the country itself was gone? Clearly the net extending across all of the worlds had a great deal of editing ability, and both it and the human cultures that depended on it for communication had evolved an immense and sophisticated system for suppressing excessive questions about the inconsistencies that were generated, so it was possible for whole families and complexes of facts to disappear or at least become unspoken.

But a whole nation?

I had to admit, it was an interesting problem. And if I started working that phone, I might or might not ever know the answer. Besides, I could just as easily work the phone trick, to find a more compatible Helen, after the expedition—assuming I survived—as before it.

For that matter, if there was going to be shooting, this Helen had advantages.

The room had gotten very quiet as everyone who hadn't committed to the expedition tried to figure out what was best for them. With an effort I drew a breath and said, "Well, then, I guess I'll go. No reasons I care to talk about."

Helen seemed very startled, and then said, "What the hell. Me too."

"And me," Ulrike said. "It makes more sense than trying to do anything else; at least this might lead to something, and everything else just leads to being stranded or picking up a phone and trying for a new world at random."

Kelly and Terri looked around the room as if we had all betrayed them, which I guess in a sense we had. With a sigh, Terri said, "You all are the only people I know in this world, you know? If you all go, I kind of have to go. 'Cause I'd rather not lose the only people I have, and I don't have any real strong reason to *not* go, except maybe that I'm kind of afraid—which is a bad reason for not doing anything, I think. Am I making sense? Anyway, I guess, me too, but I'm not happy." She looked down into her lap where her hands curled and twisted against each other.

Kelly seemed to be almost in tears, and I don't suppose I could blame her. "I feel so forced into this."

Helen grunted. "You should. That's what's happening, you know, no matter how rational it is to do what you're doing. It's perfectly rational to give a man with a gun your wallet, and it's your decision to give it to him, but that doesn't mean you aren't forced. You might decide to have your leg amputated if it was badly enough injured and infected, but that doesn't make it a free choice."

Kelly swallowed hard and brushed tears away from her blue eyes, smearing her mascara and making her look messy. "Well, it's a pretty bad deal, but I do think you're right—it's the only one I've got going. I guess what I'd better do is come along. Am I required to have a positive attitude?"

"Not at all," Iphwin said. "I don't."

The vehicle that the ten of us moved into the next day was an ugly old museum-piece of military hardware, but with Iphwin's resources applied to getting it, it also happened to be the perfect thing for the job.

It was a hideous old American Army Model 2018 Squad Transporter, which Roger, Esmé, and Paula all groaned at the sight of. They informed us that it was most commonly known as an "esty" and that "although officially it was a device whose whole purpose was to carry up to a dozen people into harm's way in a way that protected them and allowed them to do some harming back, its actual role was to maximize human discomfort as part of a sadistic and pointless research experiment," as Roger Sykes put it.

This particular esty had apparently been used as a bus by someone with an odd idea of what colors went together, so it had had to be repainted, but the lines and cracks of previous paint jobs showed through the new charcoal-gray paint everywhere. Windows were small and thick with a self-closing gunport beneath each one; the windshield was in two layers spaced about a handwidth apart. Heavy flat rectangular boxes of metal, filled with something to stop projectiles, were placed all over it in a not-too-symmetric way, hanging all around the engine compartment, off the doors and side panels, and so forth. The roof had an unlikely number of roll bars, some of the metal boxes, and just enough thickness to make me pretty sure it was armored all over. The one real weak spot was the rear window, which had clearly been replaced, long ago, with ordinary glass. Roger and Paula fretted about it a little, and rather upset the rest of us with the concern, but since we had no way, in any timely manner, to replace the rear window with any real armored glass, the upset was all they accomplished.

Naturally it was hand-steered and without any sort of net-based navigation.

"Must have spent a few years in the American Army," Paula commented as she ran a series of checkouts and I looked over her shoulder, "and then come to Mexico to be modified for use in one of the many dustups down here, and then gone civilian, oh, I don't know, twenty years ago, probably in the early '40s. After all these years, it's finally going home—even if it has to go armed."

Paula was driving and since I was the current apprentice driver, I sat next to her. The Colonel sat in the middle seat to the right, behind me, so that he could see as much as possible from a protected position, since he was our de facto commander in the

event of trouble, and also so he could cover one gunport. Esmé
sat on the other side. Jesús and Helen were at the rear corners,
able to use either side or rear gunports, and the front was covered
by the remote-sighted machine gun on the roof, which either
Paula or I could operate from controls on the dash, sighting
through a small video screen between us. We weren't a tank, but
we were likely to be more heavily armed than any casual opponents, and that was the real idea—we didn't want any trouble
from the bandits who had come to infest the north in recent
decades, so we were trying to be too tough a nut for them to
crack. If there were an "other side" out there, we knew nothing
of its resources but would have to guess that they were far, far
more than this little armed bus could possibly handle.

There were four people, besides me, who weren't arms-
proficient—Terri, Kelly, Ulrike, and Iphwin—and they were allowed to float more or less freely with the understanding that in
the event of any trouble, they would get down on the floor in
the middle and stay there.

"What kind of range does this thing have on a tank of fuel?"
I asked Paula.

"It has Telkes batteries," she said. "It's all electric." Seeing
my blank look, she added, "Telkes batteries are nuclear batteries,
and they are supposed to be good for a million miles, and there's
only 350,000 in the mileage record on the central computer.
Which doesn't appear to have been tampered with, unlike the
odometer."

We were pulling slowly out of our spot in the parking lot of
the expensive hotel in Mexico City, and Paula turned around to
holler, "Anyone who is about to suddenly remember something
that belongs in the baggage locker is welcome to do it now."

"Everything's down there," Terri said. "Nobody's got anything bigger than a purse up here."

"Just making sure," Paula said. "In the event of an accident

I want to be hit by a nice warm soft human body, not by a suitcase. All right, pulling out, heading north, and if you can sleep where you are, do it, because today is a good day for resting up; we don't really hit bandit country till tomorrow afternoon."

The first day's drive was as uneventful as she said; we cruised along a potholed but perfectly adequate road, and I got to drive more than half of it. Getting used to pointing the wheels with the steering wheel was easier than it seemed, and the load-balancer that fed power to the electric motors on the wheels worked pretty smoothly so that the response of the esty to the steering wheel was consistent. The thing I had thought was the accelerator was more properly speaking a speed pedal, the device that set the velocistat—i.e. it was the device you used to tell the car how fast you wanted it to go, rather than to make it go faster or slower. Push the pedal twice as far down and the vehicle adjusted its speed to go twice as fast regardless of what slope you might be on. The biggest problem, and the object of plenty of backseat-driver humor, was the brakes.

"The main brakes are recovery brakes," Paula explained. "Basically when you apply the brake, a rotor on the wheel generates an electric current that sets up a field that opposes its own motion. It uses the car's own energy against its motion—the faster you're going, the harder the brake works, and if the tire locks, the brake lets go right away. Skidproof and stops you in the minimum possible distance—or rather it stops the esty. If you're not wearing your seat belt, it might not stop you—or rather it will, but it will use the windshield instead of the belt."

"Very comforting," I said. "And I'll try to keep it in mind."

"Road's nearly empty," Paula said, turning and looking around, "and the whole group is belted in. You might as well practice. Give it a shot—try to brake smoothly."

I pushed down as slowly as I could on the brake, and felt the drag slowing us down, but then the brakes seemed to grab and the truck jerked a couple of times.

"You have to lose that habit of pushing harder and harder on the brake," she said.

"He sure does," Ulrike said. "Are you really learning to drive this thing, Lyle?"

It was a stupid question in a tone that I think was intended to be flattering, so I said, "No, I'm not learning a thing and I haven't a clue how to do this. Paula put me in this seat because she's trying to kill us all."

Ulrike managed to be perfectly quiet while still letting me know that she was wounded and that I had better apologize. I was really wondering what my other selves, in whatever other worlds, had been thinking, in marrying her. At least I could make a good guess about what they had been thinking in divorcing her.

The morning and then the afternoon rattled on, bouncing our way along the road that became more and more potholed, more and more badly marked, and more and more deserted, until finally we reached the mostly deserted fortified town of Torreón, the northernmost garrison on Federal Highway 49. Most of the old town was block after block of charred and bulldozed ruins, because as the city had lost most of its population the abandoned buildings had become cover for bandits, rebels, and other marauders, and so the local commandants had gradually smashed down everything outside the fences and walls of the central compound, which embraced the former town hall and church, and surrounded, for a radius of only about a block, what had once been the *zócalo*.

Iphwin had set us up with one whole floor of the one surviving large hotel in the compound, and had managed enough bribes to the garrison commander to get us electricity and hot water for the night. "This is it," he said. "Last comforts, that we know about, anyway. Enjoy it while you can."

A day of being shaken around, as we had been in the truck, takes a lot out of you, and everyone elected to eat in our rooms and get to bed early. Helen joined me in my room, just for company, and after the dinner had been delivered, we ate quietly for a while. "Not bad for where we are," I ventured, at last.

"The food? Decent, I guess. Though I can see why they shred the beef—there's probably not a knife that can even scratch the local stuff. But somebody knew his way around the kitchen, and that's got to be pretty rare in a place this remote."

"Isn't that strange," I said, having been hit by the thought. "I've never really been anywhere remote in my life before, you know. And I bet neither have you."

After we'd finished eating, Helen said, "All right, I guess you really did think it was obvious. *Why* haven't you ever been anywhere remote before?"

"Because with the net—and more generally the global information system—everyone's equally in touch with everyone else. Even across event sequences, as it turns out. In terms of time and effort, which are the meaningful terms, everywhere is the same distance from everywhere else, and that distance is so small it might as well be zero. Now, since we don't dare to connect to any of the global information system while the mission is on, places are now different distances from each other, and some of those distances are pretty big."

She shuddered. "That's weird. It really makes me feel alone."

"I find it pretty weird myself."

Helen sat for a long time, staring into space, and then finally said, "Uh, the other night—that wasn't an act, was it? You really don't like playing rough in the bedroom?"

"I really don't."

She sighed. "I was afraid you'd say that. Damn. Lyle, you have no idea how long it took me to find the other Lyle. And I always thought you had just suddenly changed your mind one day. But if the Lyle that likes rough stuff is so uncommon, how come I've been with him for so long?"

I shrugged. "We talked about that before. Obviously there's some kind of conservation rule happening somewhere that keeps most people relatively near the same event sequence they left— the big jumps are less common. You were in some braid of worlds that included that Lyle. Now you're on a different braid. Neither you nor I know anything about how many times you'd have to jump to get back on that braid. Or maybe I've crossed over into your braid, where you like that kind of thing, and one of the Lyles that you are compatible with is now somewhere else. We don't have any way of knowing—everyone gets shuffled so much that no one has a 'home' or original event sequence, just some places that are more and less familiar.

"Now that I think of it, it even explains all the odd little coincidences; event sequences that contain a President named Abe Lincoln will tend to be closer to others that contain a president by that name, but he doesn't have to be exactly the same guy or do the same things. Probably it had something to do with conservation of energy, or with the way the system tried to keep you from noticing the differences between worlds—it's easier to get the trivial stuff to line up than it is the big things. To keep people from noticing that in some event sequences America was a kingdom ruled by Washington's heirs, and in others it was a People's Republic, you have wildly different worlds that all have Pepsi and Coke. That's part of what keeps people from noticing—most of life is made up of trivia, and if the trivia is consistent, you don't necessarily notice right away when the big things are different."

She suddenly sat bolt upright as if the couch had given her an electric shock. "Oh, my god."

"What?"

"Oh my god. Oh my god. Maybe five times since you started

to like it—I mean since I met the you that liked it . . . all of a sudden you've been struggling and yelling like you'd never had it happen before. I'm in better shape than you are, Lyle, and I hope you don't mind my pointing out that I've got more fighting skills than any version of you I've ever run into, and . . . I thought they were *acting!* Shit, those poor guys must have wondered what had gotten into me and must have been scared out of their minds. There was one that . . . oh, shit, oh shit. What have I done to all those poor guys?" Tears were running down her face.

"You'd never have done it if you'd known," I pointed out—a useless observation but the only one I had then. She just started to cry harder, so I eased over next to her and put an arm very awkwardly around her shoulders. Now that I was touching her without being scared to death of her, I could feel that she had a good deal more muscle in her back and shoulders than my Helen did. She also didn't lean into me in just precisely the way that the Helen I was used to might have—it was clear that I was comforting, but she hadn't exactly thrown herself into a fit of despair against my shoulder.

I missed my familiar Helen more than ever. At the same time, I had to admit that this one had a much better prospect of succeeding in the rough and dangerous world in which I found myself. And since I couldn't do much more than keep the arm around her and tell her that it was all right, she wasn't a bad person, this was just one of those things that happens, I had plenty of time to think—a bad thing, because in my circumstances thinking led directly to self-pity.

After a while she calmed down, and thanked me. We didn't say anything but I think we figured out then that we wouldn't be staying with each other; probably she really missed the Lyle who could give her the kind of experience she craved, who would share it and enjoy it. What had she said the other night? That it sharpened her eye and shortened her reaction time. Considering where we were going and what she might be doing, I could see how she might miss that a lot.

Next morning we were on the road early, and we went quietly and quickly, making as little fuss as possible loading the esty, since the Mexican Army officers at the fort had all said that it was a bad idea to give too much advance notice when you were on your way out the gate—better to just pop out sometime shortly after dawn, when gangs were less likely to be abroad, and then make time north as fast as you could, before they could get their act together to set an ambush.

"Who goes north anymore?" I asked.

The Mexican commandant shrugged. "People who come here from there, and go back. Traders and merchants of one kind or another. They come in bringing old electronics, spare parts, stuff like that to sell in the market. Things the poor people still use, you know. Sometimes even things like moving picture film, vinyl records, audio cassettes."

I had no idea what an audio cassette was, and knew there was no real point in asking. "And where do they go, up north?"

"Up north," he agreed. "I don't think as far as the big river. I think they are just looting towns in the old northern states, places like Chihuahua, maybe. If they go into the old United States they don't go far and they don't look around much. Sometimes I ask them what it's like up there, and they say there aren't many people and there is all sorts of junk just lying around, which is what I could have guessed anyway."

For the first few hundred yards heading north the road really looked no different than it had the day before—but this time we had to pass through a rolling gate and under the watchful guns of two towers to get out of the inner compound, and weave around through a series of adobe curtain walls, at the beginning of the trip. The sun was just clearing the horizon as we set out, with me driving the first shift, on the ruined north road through the rubble of Torreón. I tried to pick my way between potholes, and then to pick a way that minimized potholes, and finally just to pick the least savage potholes.

Everyone was in the same positions they had been in the day before, but nobody seemed to be sleeping. I don't know what strange radar human beings have, but everyone seemed to know, immediately, that Helen—or at least this Helen—and I were no longer a couple. I couldn't imagine that she had told them over breakfast while I was in the bathroom, but they all seemed to know just as surely as if she had.

This had the unfortunate effect of causing Ulrike to lean over the back of my seat and try to talk with me while I was coping with the vagaries of the rutted and broken road, plus the fact that the job of driving was still mostly new to me. Paula figured that she might as well let me have the first shift because the road was almost certain to be even worse further on, and an ambush more likely, and while she was a better gunner just as much as she was a better driver, if we got into an ambush we would need a driver to get us out of there just slightly more urgently than we would need a gunner. Consequently she was playing around with the gunsights, watching her results on the TV screen; as she said, the machine gun, in its turret on the roof, moving around up there and sighting in purposively on every rock, tree, and cactus in the landscape, might also give anyone who was watching pause.

"Is it as hard as it looks?" Ulrike asked.

"Driving? I don't know how hard it looks to you. It's kind of complicated but the individual parts don't seem terribly difficult."

"You might try some braking practice on this rough road," Paula said casually, "so you can find out how that goes. It's different from smooth pavement. Just keep in mind that you've got to have a *light* foot on the brake, eh?"

I gave it a shot, slowing the esty somewhat, and found it fishtailed slightly in the gravel, and bounced pretty hard in the holes, both of which made my foot slip a little on the brake. I didn't lose control but I didn't exactly *have* perfect control either.

"Perfect," Paula said.

"I thought it wasn't very good," I said.

"You need to have more confidence in yourself," Ulrike said, helpfully.

I saw from the corner of my eye that Paula raised an eyebrow. I made a slight face, just tightening my lips, and Paula grinned.

"It was perfect," Paula said, "because it can't be done any better than that. On this kind of surface that's the practical limit. You didn't do anything that might roll us or send us over a cliff, and you did get the speed down pretty quickly. So I'd have to say you did a perfect job—it's just that the local definition of perfect is different from the global one."

"See?" Ulrike said. "All you need is more confidence. Does anyone know how this area came to be abandoned? Is something creeping down out of America, maybe?"

"Like a pollutant or a vapor?" I asked. "That's an interesting notion. Has anyone been having trouble communicating with Toronto these days? Or with Vancouver, or any other Canadian border town?"

Everyone volunteered what they knew, which didn't reveal anything, though at least it got me away from Ulrike's attention for a while. Communication to Canada was working just fine. Several of our group had friends somewhere in Southern Canada but it had never occurred to anyone to ask any of them what they saw when they looked south, or whether they had been across the border, or any of a dozen other questions that might have shed light on the whole situation.

"Then why aren't we entering from Canada?" I asked Iphwin. "This is really the long way round."

"It is," he agreed, "except for two things. One, experiments with sending agents in from Canada have already been tried, and the result has been that they're never heard of or seen again. They drop out of the public databases and out of communication with us as soon as they get near the border with the intention of crossing it. We tried sending in a man who was not continually linked by phone, and had his partner watch him try to walk through a border crossing way up along the Manitoba-Minnesota line. No luck there, either—the camera went dead, she can't remember, and he's gone. Sort of like the attempts we've made to reconnoiter by phone call."

"You could have told us about all these things before we agreed to do this," Ulrike said. "You're telling us that you've lost everyone who's ever tried?"

"We've only lost contact with them. We don't know what happened to them. They may well be fine, and in the United States. Anyway, since the quick approach across Canada didn't work out, now we're trying something different—sneaking in via Mexico—and seeing how this works. As far as we can tell, this is a completely different experiment."

"I still really hate that you do this kind of thing with other people's lives," Ulrike said. The whine was coming back into her voice, and as much as I found Iphwin annoying, I preferred listening to him.

So I asked a question. "You said there was a second reason?"

"Well, yes. We had records in several different event sequences of a Cabinet office that was created very late in the life of the United States—or the Reich, Christian Commonwealth, Freedom Reservation, or People's Republic, or whatever that territory was called in its event sequence. The Department of the Pursuit of Happiness. It had four major offices—one each in

Washington, Buffalo, Topeka, and Santa Fe. And it seems to have been mixed up in the whole issue of quantum computing, bandwidth, compression, all the technologies that have scrambled the worlds. As a secondary mission, besides just seeing what is going on in the United States, we also thought perhaps we'd try to get a look at one of those. But we had very bad luck up by Buffalo, as I've told you, and that was the closest by land. Now—if we get through, and if things look good—we thought we might try Santa Fe. The clues that seemed to indicate that the Department of the Pursuit of Happiness has anything to do with it are very ambiguous, of course, but all the same—"

I saw the flickers of light from the low rock outcrop ahead, and was shouting "Ambush" even as I reached for the brake with my foot. My guts fell into my shoes, but I couldn't afford to freeze.

"Try to run it!" Paula bellowed. I moved my boot and stood on the speed pedal; the washboarded road with its big holes shook the esty violently, but I managed to hold it on the road and gain some speed. Ahead of me, the road bent along the edge of the rock outcrop, and then swept on through the desert in a big open area; if we could get past this ambush, we would have clear room to run.

Two shots banged off the outer windscreen, and Ulrike made a whimpering scream that was stifled by Terri grabbing her and covering her mouth, pinning her to the floor. Everyone got to stations in an instant, and Paula fired two short bursts from the machine gun. "Just making them keep their heads down," she said. "With the magnification I can see four snipers with rifles, and I can point at them, but hitting them is out of my hands."

"Everybody armed, over to the left side and find a gunport." Roger's voice was calm and clear, and people quietly moved into position.

Another shot caromed off the roof. "No damage," Paula said,

looking at her screen. She gave them another burst of machine-gun fire. Two scars appeared on the over-windshield but so far nothing had penetrated. The thundering guns above, the rumble and crash from that appalling road, and the grinding scream of electric motors working above their ratings combined to be so deafening that I barely heard our shots fired, and couldn't hear theirs hit.

We rushed under the outcrop, and shots plinked off the roof like the beginning of a hailstorm; as we swung into the turn, the gunners on the left side opened up and the esty was filled with even more of a din, but not enough to drown out the desperate hope in my head that somehow I would not fuck up. Above it—faintly, though he was not even two yards from me—I could hear the Colonel bellowing for people to move to the rear gunports, and a moment later his shouting was drowned out by the big motor above my head, whirling the machine gun around to face the rear.

I became aware that they had shot out the rear window, that cheap chunk of civilian glass that had first worried us, when pieces of it flew against the windshield in front of me, and back away over my head. A big piece of the rear window slammed into the back of my headrest, making my head bounce, but I kept the esty on the road and the speed pedal floored.

"Keep it going a few miles, Lyle!" the Colonel shouted. I drove like a madman until the odometer had clocked off ten miles. The whole way, my bowels felt like they were on the brink of letting go and my shoulders waited for a bullet.

We had seen no cloud of dust from any pursuers, nor any trace of any other ambush ahead. A hollered conversation reached the agreement that I could drop down to normal speed again, which I was delighted to do. The rumbles and crashes fell to a tolerable volume, the world stopped bouncing around as if it were on some mad roller-coaster, and it was now possible to converse merely by raising voices.

Terri shrieked, a horrible sound that became a sob, and a moment later Roger was next to her. I couldn't tell what was going on back there but it didn't sound good.

"Better stop, Lyle," the Colonel said.

I stayed on the road, preferring a quick getaway. Besides, I had seen no other car since we started that morning.

When we had come to a halt, I turned around.

Kelly and Ulrike were lying still where they had huddled together; Esmé and Jesús had rolled Ulrike over, revealing a big exit wound in her forehead.

Kelly was gasping for breath, hit in the chest.

"Damn, damn, damn," the Colonel said. "They had two snipers down in the ditch, below our level. Must have gotten shots in through that broken back window. Caromed off the roof just behind the window, and came right down into the middle of the esty. Shit, I hate to lose somebody." He wiped the rim of sweat from around his face with his shirtsleeve.

Paula was working on Kelly with the first aid kit. "It missed the lungs," she said, "and probably the other vitals, so Kelly should be more comfortable with the pressure patch." She sprayed that down. "As far as I can tell, she should be fine if we get her to an ambulance and a hospital. I'm assuming she has the Iphwin resources to pay for treatment?"

Whether or not that was what Iphwin intended, Paula's tone made it clear that it was what was expected, and Iphwin agreed immediately.

We made Kelly as comfortable as we could. It was obvious that she was furious at all of us, and most of all at Iphwin, but she wasn't going to annoy herself further by speaking with us. We propped her up a few yards behind the esty, by the side of the road, and gave her a phone, and Iphwin gave her a number to call.

When she had finished the call, we walked up to her to move her back into the shade of the esty, to wait for the ambulance. "I'm from a world near enough to this one—maybe I'm even the same Kelly you handed the phone to. Still wounded in the same place and I still remember that Ulrike is dead." She grunted. "I think my brain hurts more than my chest. I don't know how they're going to do it," she said to Iphwin, "but your team said they'd be here in five minutes, so don't bother moving me. That is, about a thousand versions of them said it to about a thousand versions of me, I suppose, and since they're in a self-driver, they'll probably all get reshuffled on the way. But the overwhelming majority of us are going to get picked up by the overwhelming majority of them." She grunted again; I realized she was trying to sigh, and then her wound would hurt and she'd be stopped before it came out as a sigh. "I knew this was a really stupid idea, and I went ahead with it, didn't I? I suppose that ought to be a lesson to me. But then Ulrike was pretty willing to do it, and she got killed." She stared into space. "I guess this is life for the time being. If I like where I am, don't pick up a phone; if I don't, just keep making phone calls till I find something better."

"It's not even that simple," I pointed out. I wasn't sure it was what she would want to hear, but it only seemed fair to tell her. "Any version of you who knows about it, and is in a nice world, won't be making many calls. Only the ones that are unhappy will be on the line, and those are the only ones you'll be changing with. You see? And since you know that . . ."

"I'll only call when things really turn to shit. And so will everyone else," Kelly said. "All we can do, at best, is exchange shit. And mostly it'll just be a jump to a pile of shit indistinguishable from the one I was in—the same thing that would happen if nothing happened. It's not exactly like being able to click my heels together and say 'There's no place like home,' is it?"

There was a thunder in the sky above us, and a huge, three-rotor helicopter, its body shaped like an equilateral triangle, was descending from high above. We looked up, squinting against the noonday sun, and Iphwin said, "It's all right, that's one of mine."

"Well," Kelly said, "this is good-bye, Terri. I'm sorry we got caught up in having adventures and I hope you find a world you like. Maybe some versions of us will see each other."

"We can't think like that," Terri said, "or we'll all be seeing each other in the crazy house, you know? So just take care of yourself, and, well, *arrivederci, à bientôt, vale,* and *adiós.*"

The helicopter was thumping in lower now, out of the washed-out blue of the desert sky, and we backed off. In a few minutes, it had descended onto the road itself, not far from Kelly. A crew got out, put her on a gurney, and wheeled her inside. One of them saluted Iphwin, and he saluted back.

Then they were off, and we remaining ones were alone; Kelly would land in some world or other, and Ulrike was simply gone.

Working slowly and awkwardly, we got out the utility robot from the underside of the esty—a really nasty job, as its bolts were rusted on, and there were some scraped knuckles in the process. Jesús and I both took turns lying on our backs and trying to turn those bolts, banging on the wrenches in frustration when it turned out that the little power bolt drivers from the repair box didn't have the force to do the job. At last we got the robot out, put the shovel attachment on it, and discovered that since it was a military machine, sure enough it had a preprogram for a burial. It crawled away a couple of dozen yards, sonar-sounding the soil to find a good place to dig, before settling on one location for a grave.

Jesús and I cleaned up in a little bit of water while the dirt flew around over there. At least the robot had both the patience and the speed to make digging a real grave practical; it was going down six feet and making a level bottom, no matter what.

By the time it had finished, we were as clean as we were going to get, which was pretty gritty, and we found ourselves elected as pallbearers, along with Helen and Esmé (since they were the two biggest women). We wrapped Ulrike up in a blanket, after brushing the clean parts of her hair out. One of the others, while we had been working on the robot, had gotten most of the removable gore cleaned up, but nothing could be done about the red crater in her forehead, and they had been unable to close her staring eyes, which were partially popped from their sockets.

As Jesús did some quick, rough stitching to get the blanket closed, he asked me, "And you were married to her in some worlds, but didn't know her in this one?"

"Yeah."

"It must have been terribly difficult for her."

"I think it was," I said, "and it was worse because I didn't feel attracted other than physically, and emotionally she was light-years from my type. I thought she was very pretty but she was somewhere around the end of the affair and I hadn't started yet. But now I wish I'd done something or other for her. If I had known these were her last days, I might have."

"And what could you have done for her?" he asked, putting in the last few stitches. "I suppose you could have given her the impression that you cared for her, if you really knew she would end like this in a few hours—but if she had not died, and you had no very strong reason to think she would—well, what then? You chose not to behave like a cad. Why fret about the difference? It cannot make a difference to anyone else."

"You're probably right."

"In this world, I'm right. Probably in billions of others, I am wrong. Just as she is dead here and alive in many other worlds."

"I think it's more accurate to say that this Ulrike is dead, and many other Ulrikes are alive. It still makes a difference to this one."

He cut the waxed cord and looked over the package he had sewn together. "Lyle, my friend, nothing makes a difference to the dead."

Jesús, Helen, Esmé, and I lifted the body—surprisingly heavy, I guess because it settled to the middle of the blanket— and carried it to the grave without dragging it on the ground. Those who weren't keeping watch came along with us, Roger standing guard over the funeral with his rifle.

We didn't have any gentle way to lower her, so Esmé and I climbed down into the grave and Jesús and Helen rolled her into our arms. Fortunately the grave had been dug wide enough for a regulation coffin, and so there was just room to lower her down till the body lay across our toes, and then, with a big heave from Helen on one hand and Jesús on the other, to get each of us back out of the hole.

We weren't sure what to say or do—we hadn't planned on any funerals, after all—but before we had time to do more than feel a moment's discomfort at the pause, the robot sprang back into business. Apparently its programming said that once all the live people were out of the grave it was time to get to work.

"Dear friends," it began, "in the name of the President of the United States, of the Congress, and of the People, it is my sad duty to declare that speak deceased's name clearly."

We all stared at each other for a long minute before I figured out that that was a direction, and said, "Ulrike Nordstrom."

"It is my sad duty to declare that Already Morstung has died in the line of duty, defending the nation which you and she loved. She was a good comrade and a loyal friend. She had a deep and abiding faith in the god or gods of her choice or else she was true to her philosophical beliefs to the last. She had a solid, deep, and loving relationship with her family with whom she would deeply wish to be reconciled if there are any publicly mentioned family issues. Already Morstung had her human failings, as we all do, but still she stands as an example of what a soldier should be. We will miss Already Morstung and we will keep her in our hearts always. We now commend her soul to the god or gods of her choice, with the thanks and grateful prayers of the President, of Congress, and of the American people."

A tinny version of "A Mighty Fortress Is Our God" began to play through the small speaker on the top of the robot, and it rolled forward to its dirt pile, which it began to energetically hurl back into the grave. We all stood and stared for a while, trying to think of something to say or do, I suppose, until Roger Sykes took charge. "Well," he said, "it wasn't a very nice funeral, but they never are. If anyone would like to say a few more appropriate words, we might all appreciate it. But if no one really has anything to say—and that's understandable, none of us knew her—well, then, I guess we should get back to the esty and take care of the living."

"That was four hours we could ill afford," Iphwin said.

"Is that all you can say?" Terri demanded.

"I—I just don't know what would be appropriate for me to say, because, as you well know, I don't feel much, and besides—"

"You could try a really sincere 'Ouch!'," Helen said.

He looked baffled and said, "A really—"

She belted him, with all her considerable strength, right across the face, a great big side-armed haymaker that wouldn't have taken anyone with any experience on a playground, but delivered a huge wallop. But of course Iphwin had no childhood memories to draw on, no idea that he needed to watch out or duck, and she flat decked him.

Roger, Esmé, and Jesús grabbed Helen and dragged her off, more to keep her from attacking Iphwin again than because they wanted to restrain her.

Iphwin lay there moaning in pain, and Paula and I attended to him. Not feeling too terribly concerned myself, I checked his pupils. They were the same size. I held up fingers for him to count and asked him a couple of short-term-memory questions. By that time he was sitting up, holding his jaw.

"Any of your teeth get loosened?" Paula asked.

"I don't think so. The blow landed on the tip of my chin, and my jaws closed on my tongue, which is why I'm having some trouble talking. I suppose—"

Paula reached forward and grabbed his head below the ears; I'm not sure what she did, but he gave a little gasp of pain. "Just seeing whether there was anything screwed up with your jaw joint," she said. "Did it hurt when I did that?"

"Yes!"

She grabbed him and did it again. He struggled feebly, squealing through his closed mouth. When she let him go there were tears of pain in his eyes. "Now does it hurt here, or here?" she said, stabbing her finger into two different spots on his jaw, not even slightly gently.

"Ouch! The second one!"

"Oh, good," Paula said, "then you're not seriously hurt. That's normal."

As we walked over to join the others and see what had become of Helen, I said to Paula, "That was really callous."

"Yep. Nothing like callousness to give people an appreciation for callousness. Maybe to decide they don't want to inflict it on others, maybe to decide they just want to avoid it themselves, maybe even to find out that they like being callous. Whichever. Anyway, it's the big chance to find out what choice they're going to make, and self-knowledge is the beginning of wisdom." She tossed her long, dark red hair back, shook it, and started binding it into a ponytail. "If we have to work with him, the least he can do is work on becoming a little less of an asshole each day. I was just helping him with his homework."

Somehow I had crossed over to a world of women who scared the living daylights out of me.

Helen had not only calmed down, but had adopted an attitude similar to Paula's—"If a goddam artificial intelligence is going to put on a body and walk around among us, it had better adapt itself to us and our way of doing things. People have been adapting to computers and robots for more than a century, and it's high time it was the other way round. And besides, whacking him in the face is just a way to access the nervous system more directly at a simpler level. You could think of it as pushing his reset button, or programming him in machine language."

I don't know exactly what effect it had; Iphwin could tell that Terri didn't like him, and since he sat in the middle with her, he was trying not to anger her by speaking, I suppose.

Paula said I was now a proven getaway driver, and she was still a better gunner. I told her I had been terrified.

"Well, then, it's even better that you did such a fine job, if you were also coping with fear at the same time. We'd better keep you on the task."

I drove till almost sunset, miles and miles of rocky and scrubby desert broken by some fields of dunes, and distant views of the high mountains. It was beautiful country, but there was way too much of it. We were only averaging about thirty miles per hour—a necessity on that long-neglected highway, even with puncture-proof permatires and an extra-heavy suspension. After the delay, we could no longer hope to reach Juárez before dark, and in fact sunset would find us only a few miles north of the ruins of Chihuahua. Iphwin, however tactless, had been absolutely right.

"My vote is to camp here for the night and make a short, fast run in the morning," Esmé said. "Maybe stop forty miles short of Chihuahua, first good place where there's cover, eat cold, set watches, depart early. That's what I'd like."

"Same here," Paula agreed. "This is rough country in several different ways; I'd be very happy not to have to do anything that gave any advantages to any bad guys out there."

Everyone agreed; Terri and I were both badly shaken, the more violence-proficient among us probably were too but weren't about to show it, and god alone would have any idea what Iphwin was thinking. Just by the rusting old sign that said "CHIHUAHUA 60 KM" there was a heap of rocks tumbled together, perhaps a much-eroded cinder cone, and behind it, out of view of the road, we parked and made what camp we could.

I was selfishly glad that our soldiers and cops largely volunteered to sleep outside on the ground, and being a little ashamed of being selfishly glad, I agreed to stand a watch, up on the rocks above, in a secure spot that the Colonel and Esmé picked out. Paula and Roger would stand watch till ten, since she was driving the next day; Helen and Jesús would stand ten to two, and that left the short early morning watch to me and Esmé. I suppose I should have been flattered that I was the one of the noncombatants that they trusted to take a turn at watch, but since the alternatives were a teenager who seemed to be nearly in shock, and Iphwin, whom no one could figure out, I thought it more likely that I was chosen by default.

I stretched out on a middle seat, with the sun still up. I would stand my watch from 2:00 A.M. to 5:30. At 5:30, everyone would be up and getting ready to roll out at first light.

It seemed like a long time away, and I didn't think I could sleep that long, or at all, but I snugged the pillow under my head, undid a couple of shirt buttons so that I could move my chest freely, and had just a moment to notice that the warm sun on my face was pleasant, so perhaps I would enjoy it for a few minutes before pulling a coat over my head to get some darkness.

Sometimes when you think you couldn't sleep to save your soul—perhaps because of a dreadful day like the one I had just been through, or when the future seems to be pure menace hidden by dark fog—you fall asleep so fast that it comes as a shock, as if a trapdoor opened in unpleasant reality and you fell down a dark well and plunged to somewhere else at the bottom. The exhaustion lurking behind my eyes leaped up and yanked me down the dark well of sleep, and it was seven hours later and Esmé was giving me a friendly shake. "Come on, we get to go climb a hill in the dark so we can sit on cold rocks and watch an empty road. You don't want to be late for that!"

I sat up, stretched. Though it was the middle of the night, I was feeling pretty good. I checked my watch, and it was quarter till two; there was just time for a swallow of coffee from a thermos and a quick leak behind a rock, and then I was picking my way along behind Esmé, a pistol strapped awkwardly onto my belt most of the way behind my back, bumping me in a way I wasn't used to. Esmé had cheerfully told me that in the event of trouble I was to keep it in my holster unless she was immediately killed, in which case I should fire it to alert the camp. "Or if you get a guy coming at you so close up that you could club him in the nose with the muzzle, try to do that. You might as well pull the trigger when you do."

I managed to keep any wounded dignity out of my voice. "I did carry one of these, off and on, when I was in Her Majesty's Navy. And I had to fire it a few times a year, on a range."

"Well, good. Then you've had enough training not to shoot me by accident, or yourself in the foot. How good a shot were you?"

"I was planning to use this thing as a club, if it came to that. Your suggestions weren't wrong, but you were suggesting them because you thought I didn't know anything. The reason they were good suggestions was not that I don't know anything—they were good suggestions because I'm a shitty shot."

The big woman chuckled in the darkness. "You're different, Lyle Peripart. I might even get to like that."

Now we were far enough up the hill to be staying quiet, at least until we got to the sentry post and found out how things were going. The boulders were middling big and pretty well jammed into place by the millennia, so that the footing and grips were much more secure than they looked; the trick was only to find a way to stay low while going over them, and there was enough light from a half-moon, still relatively low in the sky, to make it almost easy going. Ten minutes of sweaty scrambling on the dark hillside got us to the top, looking down over a little pit in the rocks, where we saw Helen and Jesús, both looking across the road, sitting crouched side by side in the space behind a large boulder.

"We're up here," Esmé said.

"We heard you coming," Jesús said, softly but not bothering to whisper. "You can probably do better next time. But I don't think it matters right now. There hasn't been a breath of half a sound, and there's no trace of anything moving out there. Paula and Roger had a very quiet watch as well. I think the bandits that fired on us probably just take a shot at everything going by, and don't pursue anything they don't hit hard enough to stop. And we've seen nothing and no one since."

"Where do you think Iphwin's helicopter came from?" I asked. "It showed up within five minutes."

Helen snorted. "At a guess, a hidden base near the road, which he could probably have flown us to but didn't, for some obscure reason of his own. Or possibly he had a hundred helicopters in a hundred different worlds do something or other to cause them to cross over to other worlds, and this is the one we got. Or maybe it jumped straight in from orbit using a technology

none of us knows even exists. Or the most likely possibility—
something completely different that none of us has thought of."

"He is confusing to deal with. Did you really have to slap
him around?"

"If I answer that question, we'll spend an hour quibbling
about the connotations of 'have to.' And I'm good and tired and
headed down the hill for bed. Have a quiet watch," she added,
as she climbed up and over the rocks.

"You probably will," Jesús added as he scrambled up to fol-
low her. "The moonlight helps, and there's a wide stretch without
much cover; anyone who sneaks up on us from that side will have
to be pretty good." A moment later they crunched over the rocks
beside us and were gone; I heard the faint scuff of their feet once
or twice behind me, as we climbed down into the narrow space
behind the big rock, and then nothing. We settled in, taking only
a moment to agree that in general I would watch to the south and
center, and Esmé would watch north and center.

I was surprised at how awake I felt. True, I had just had some
very deep sleep and some strong coffee, but I felt rested, comfortable, ready to be up for a long time, and it was not yet three
in the morning.

The landscape in front of me took a while to resolve to my
unfamiliar eyes, but there wouldn't have been any problem spot-
ting anything moving. It was all dark curved shapes out there
with patches of bright moonlight between them, and the shadows
were small—the half-moon was already getting on toward halfway up the eastern sky, its light beginning to spill over the hill
behind us. Further, there was a big swath of dune sand that
splashed almost all the way across the road to the south, and
though someone might have been able to lie hidden in its shadow,
I didn't see any pathway to that shadow that wasn't exposed. The
air was cool but not unpleasant; there should have been more
wildlife out there making noise, I thought, but then big animals

are scarce in that sort of country, and more than likely the quiet struggle between the predators and prey was going on all around us, in the little dark corners between rocks. No doubt it would become fiercer, and perhaps more audible, in the hours just before and after the sun came up.

"Whoever fired on us hasn't been bandits long, or is very lazy, or isn't very talented," Esmé said, her voice barely above a whisper, a long time after we had settled in to watch.

"Why do you say that?" I tried to keep my voice lower than hers.

"Because this is twenty times as good a place for an ambush, and it's not that far away. If they had just scouted up the road a little, they'd have found this. And there's no place anyone in his right mind would stop, or turn off, between there and here. Any truck or car that went by there would go by here. Either they must have set up at the first convenient place and never bothered to move, or else they're too stupid to see that from the rocks down below us, they could rake a vehicle from one end to the other with fire, and the vehicle could never get off the road because of the dunes to the side. If they held fire till the right moment, people in a vehicle would never be able to go either forward or back. They'd just be pinned down until enough rounds found enough vulnerable spots. I'd put the main force down by the road, and the lookout—geez, I'd put it right—"

She stopped and gestured for me to listen. I did, listening harder than I ever had in my life, as if I were throwing my mind into the surrounding rocks and desert, trying to pick up anything other than the soft susurrus of our breathing and the gentle creak of wood and leather as Esmé drew a knife from a sheath and wriggled through a shadow, out to the side, and down the hill. I thought about whether or not to draw my pistol, but I suspected that moving as quietly and carefully as Esmé was, she would be taking a long time getting down the hill to whatever sound she was checking out, and I knew I would be getting steadily more nervous the whole time. I didn't want to be holding a pistol when she came back, if I was going to be jumpy; I couldn't see any way that could be a good thing. At best, I'd be more worried about not shooting her accidentally than about identifying anyone else who might be approaching. And at worst, I might cost us a fighter and give away our position. I left the pistol where it was and tried to do nothing but watch very actively and very quietly for any sign of motion.

There was a blur of motion in the shadows about sixty yards in front of me and perhaps thirty feet lower. I moved forward cautiously, keeping my head in shadow, and peered at it, but saw nothing. A very long time went by, and I turned everything over and over in my mind while I tried to stay ready, calm, and watchful. Esmé had found something or someone creeping up on us, and had had a quick, silent, deadly fight with it down there. Probably someone on their way up to our present position.

If Esmé had won, she would now be creeping down the trail of shadows, over the boulders, to the place she had picked for setting a main force for the ambush, probably hoping that the force there would be small, maybe just one or two, so that she could take it out herself—or if it were large, she could see it, crawl back, let the rest of us know, and come back with some firepower. No doubt she was going to take a while about it—if she had won.

If she had lost, whatever beat her was now on its way here. I moved the pistol around on the belt, carefully, never taking my eyes off the slope below, scanning as hard as I could, my hand resting on the butt. I could now draw it fast, I knew where the safety was, and I would draw it as soon as something moved, and fire as soon as it wasn't Esmé. I thought that anything that had overcome her, when she had the advantage of surprise, would probably get me, but a shout and a shot might make all the difference to our people back at the esty.

I squatted, changing my position slowly, just often enough so that nothing would stiffen or go to sleep, and watched and tried to be in the state of empty readiness for anything that is supposed to be characteristic of martial artists. The slope was motionless and silent. The shadows were imperfectly dark; a blade of grass, a bit of saguaro, or a white rock might shine a little in them, and might seem to move now and then, helping to keep me alert but nervous. The bright spots where the moonlight hit fully were distracting and tempting as places to rest the eye, but if you did that, they seemed after a while to float up away from the shadows, and instead of a dimly lit rocky, scrubby hillside, you could find yourself looking at an uninterpretable set of blobs of light and darkness that made no particular sense and might not interpret into reality fast enough.

I tried to check the road and the desert beyond it regularly too, and to keep an ear out behind me in case someone with even more night-fighting talent than Esmé had crept around behind me and was about to drop on my shoulders.

I wasn't moving much, but I was busy, as the shadows shrunk and reached westward, and the half-moon—now too bright for me to look at as my eyes had become completely dark-adapted—crawled up the sky toward the zenith, shortening the shadows and lighting more of the landscape. I guessed that it had moved about thirty degrees, roughing it as a third of a right angle, since I took my post, which meant around two hours had passed. It seemed like much less.

How long had it been between taking up our position and Esmé's going forward? I had no idea, but not as long as I had been waiting here, I figured.

A half-moon with the curved side east, like this one, is bang overhead just when the sun comes up, and since I was really beginning to hope the sun would come up, I stole a couple of upward glances. The moon was perhaps ten degrees, which would take about twenty more minutes, from the zenith; the first glow before dawn should be happening any moment. I watched and waited.

A voice behind me said, very softly, "Lyle, please take your hand off that gun. If the safety is off, please put it back on."

"Safety is on," I said, and very slowly took my hand away from the pistol butt. "Esmé?"

"Yes, it's me." She sat beside me, her teeth chattering as if she'd just been drenched in a freezing bath and then sent out into a winter wind.

I ventured to ask, "Any chance there are any more?"

"I don't think so. God, I have to hope there aren't. I can't . . . oh, god, Lyle, no, I think we can just talk, now, if you want to. And I want to, need to, even I'm just having a lot of trouble doing it. Give me a minute and I'll tell you what happened. But it's pretty goddam gruesome and I've never felt so shook in my whole life, and I would really appreciate it if whatever you say or do is the most soothing thing you can come up with."

"I'll do my best," I said.

She leaned back against the rock, and then moved so that her shoulder rested against mine, obviously needing the comfort of the touch. Just in case she'd made a completely wrong guess about whether there were any more attackers, I kept my eyes on the slope, but I listened as she said, "I found a barely marked trail—mostly just little bitty cut handholds and footholds, and some trampled spots in close to rocks, it was a very clever setup to keep people from noticing that there was any trail there—and I followed it down, staying about five meters off to the north of it. Sure enough, after a while I heard some noise—not much, a boot scrape maybe, or a breath. I had someone coming up that trail. I crept on over and got into a shadow. Somebody passed by me, and I jumped in behind them and went for a silent kill.

"Well, guess who it turned out to be when I jumped onto the trail? Our old multi-lived friend, Billie Beard. This version of Billie knew her stuff, too—I jumped her from behind, hard as I could, and got her trachea squeezed and stuck her in the kidney before she could get into the fight properly, and I still felt like I was trying to hog-tie a steer with masking tape. I sawed through her carotid while I had her in a half nelson, which is incredibly messy and scary. I hope we get to someplace where I can wash, and soon.

"At that point I figured, okay, Billie Beard was going to be a lookout, and there had to be an ambush right in the place I had picked out. I crawled down the hill and was delighted to smell some kind of cheap booze—rotgut bad enough that it might have been vodka, tequila, maybe just straight grain alcohol. Quiet little noises, almost like someone wrestling."

She leaned in close and said, "This is not romantic, but if you would just put your arm around me, I would really, really appreciate it. Right now I'm afraid I'm either going to cry or throw up. I promise if it turns out I'm going to throw up, I'll get away from you. But I think more likely I'm just going to cry, and I guess I'm literal enough that I want a shoulder to do it on. And I'll say I'm sorry, in advance, if I accidentally get any blood on you."

I hugged her in one arm, and sat back, where I could no longer see the slope below us, figuring that it made much more sense for me to trust her judgment than my paranoia; if she thought all threats were ended, then anything that could surprise us was something I wouldn't stand a chance against, anyway.

After a few deep breaths and a couple of "Uh" and "Well" false beginnings, she said, "I was almost laughing, with relief that this was going to be so easy, and at the chance for some revenge.

I crawled forward and there were two high-powered rifles and a couple of grenade launchers, *leaning against a rock*—and two people moving around in the shadows. The reek of booze was amazing.

"I could have laughed out loud when I realized that there in the near shadows I was seeing two pairs of Levi's, and two holsters with pistols, and that in the deeper shadow there was a couple fucking doggie-style, giggling, drunk out of their minds.

"Now, in my years with the Colonel, we were on various sides of a bunch of civil wars all over Central and South America, and those are the kinds of situations in which you really, really lose all concept of sportsmanship. If they'd made themselves that vulnerable, then the evolutionary process needed to remove them before they could breed—and here I was, just in time.

"I figured out my footing and position, got into place, and then dropped in right behind the man, bracing a knee in his back and cutting his throat before he knew more than that he was startled. And just that second, damn if that woman didn't grab a knife from a back sheath, roll to put the dying man between her and me, and come right at me fast and hard, ready to kill me. Never saw anyone handle anything so fast before, Lyle, and I've seen plenty. Shit, Lyle, if my mind isn't playing tricks on me, I even remember thinking that I had finally met my equal.

"I got a footsweep on her and gave her a good gash in the arm on her way down—I think I must have nicked an artery, to judge by how much blood there was. She came back at me, maybe already getting weak, and I managed to get inside her blade and drive mine into her eye, hard enough to crunch bone and get right into the brain. Nasty, messy way to go, but fast, and she didn't make a sound as she died.

"Something made me drag the bodies into the moonlight—some part of my mind must have already known, and thought the rest of me should know. I wiped the faces clean.

"The man was Jesús Picardin—or rather a different version of him. And the woman was me. No wonder she was so handy with a knife, and no wonder our little clash of blades seemed almost choreographed, as if we were anticipating each other's moves and my little advantages—having clothes on, being less surprised, not being drunk—sort of gave me the win on points."

She shuddered again, violently, and pressed her face against my shoulder.

I hadn't the slightest idea what to say or do. We sat like that until the sun was fully up and it was time to go down to the others. Despite having been well rested before my watch started, and having only been awake a few hours, I went right to sleep as soon as we rolled north in the esty, sleeping back in the middle seat. Terri sat up with Paula for driving lessons; I think everyone thought that some distraction or other might be good for her, and besides nobody much wanted to be near Iphwin. It didn't bother me because I was asleep.

I was told later that the ruins of Chihuahua were particularly impressive, for it had once been a big, prosperous city, and thus it had come in for more than its share of looting and burning as the north of the country had gotten more and more dangerous; somehow, though, I was content to be spared the sight of a vast expanse of burned and wrecked human dwellings, silent and empty in the early morning sun.

It was almost noon when the Colonel awakened me and said, "Hate to disturb you, Lyle, but we need to hold a little conference before we go further, and I thought you ought to be part of it."

"Perfectly all right, Roger." I sat up, rubbing my eyes, and noticed the esty was no longer moving. We were stopped dead in the middle of the road, sitting in the usual environment—desert surrounded by mountains, on a road that connected a meaningless spot on the southern horizon with an equally meaningless spot on the hills to the north of us. While I was asleep they had "fixed" the rear window by taping clear plastic over it. I gathered my wits and managed to ask, "What's up?"

"According to our map, which is forty-five years old, this line of hills up ahead is the last one before the Rio Grande. Then we're about three miles from a bridge that should take us over the river and into the United States. If the bridge is still there. If the United States is still there. You might say there are a few complications."

I yawned and stretched and said, "All right. I'm with you, more or less." I dragged myself to the edge of the seat and found that all the others had managed to range themselves in a rough circle among the esty seats and aisles.

"And there's a few things we want to ask Iphwin about," Esmé said, making it sound like a threat. To judge by the way Iphwin reacted, he surely heard it as a threat too. Esmé smiled at him, an unpleasant smile that registered satisfaction more than pleasure, and said, "Such as who the hell is Billie Beard—what the hell is Billie Beard—and how come I just ran into versions of people who already exist on this side. I still get a feeling someone is not being perfectly honest with us."

"Before you answer," Helen said, "think about what you learned about pain, yesterday."

Iphwin tried to speak, twice, and then finally drew his knees up to his chest, tears leaking out around his eyes, shaking his head. There must have been three full minutes, or more, during which we just sat and stared at him.

Terri realized before any of us, bent over the huddled little man, and said, "I bet you're really afraid."

Iphwin nodded miserably.

"That was the first time you'd ever really been hurt and besides you don't understand what we want or why we do things, so now all of a sudden you're really afraid that we might decide to hurt you again. And nobody's talked to you all day and you're probably also really lonely."

His shoulders started to shake and tears gushed down his face. Terri put her arms around him and told him, "No one is going to hurt you. We're sorry. And we'll be your friends again, if you forgive us and if you promise to try to learn to respect our feelings. Promise?"

"I promise," he sniffled.

"Oh, Christ," Helen said, her voice dripping with contempt. There was an echo in it, somewhere, of the way she had been with me in the bedroom. "The ruler of the economic universe turns out to be a big baby."

I looked at her with some irritation, but before I could think of some suitably adult and urbane insult to toss at her, youth and energy jumped into the breach.

"I guess you're never too old to be a bully," Terri said, straightening up and glaring at Helen over the tops of her small wire-rimmed glasses. "And I suppose once you take it on yourself to bully other people, there's no such thing as a victim that's too helpless." The skinny girl looked even younger than her age—like an angry choir boy who might fly at Helen and start slapping or pulling hair—but she pushed her glasses up her nose, raised her chin, planted her feet, and made it dead clear she wasn't giving any ground.

After a long pause, Helen shrugged, as if it were simply too trivial to take notice of, and said, "Iphwin, I am sorry I hit you, and I shouldn't have done it. And if you need to cry, well, that's none of my business. It was rude of me to make fun of you."

"It's all right," Iphwin said, sniffling. "I do feel awful but I think you were right yesterday that I needed to know this sort of feeling was possible. I had no idea that one human being could do this to another one. I don't mean as a matter of conscience, I mean I had no idea what the effects could be like. And I'm very afraid I might have done things like this to the rest of you, and I really didn't know what I was doing, and that's no excuse at all because I should have known, and . . . oh, oh, oh, shit." He started to cry again, and Terri sat down next to him, patting his arm.

"He'll be fine in a minute," she said. "Just needs to get it out of his system, and he isn't used to it. Why don't you all take a walk or something?"

There was a long pause, and then Roger got up and went out the door of the esty, silently. Esmé, Paula, Helen, and Jesús followed, sullenly. I trailed after them.

Outside I discovered that everyone, except Roger, was competing to think of how to complain about Iphwin and "that stupid kid." I thought Terri was the only one in the bunch that had shown anything like normal human feelings, and when I couldn't stand the nastiness any longer, I went back inside. The Colonel shrugged and followed me in.

Iphwin was washing his face in a bowl of water, saying softly, "You're right, that does help to make me feel better. Hello, Lyle. Hello, Roger. I'm really sorry about all this. Are the others still angry?"

"Yeah, but I think they'll cut you some slack now," I said. "Terri, before anyone gets a chance to bitch at you about it, I think the way you've just treated Iphwin is really a fine thing."

Roger nodded, emphatically. "I don't think I have half your compassion and empathy."

She shrugged. "Hey, I know what it feels like when *I* feel all alone and like nobody understands me. They say that's normal for a teenager."

"It's normal for a human being," I said, thinking about Helen and how much I missed the other version of her—and how much she must miss her preferred version of me.

"And is this what it feels like every time you get your feelings hurt?" Iphwin said. "No wonder you all spend so much time on human relations—it's just sheer self-protection."

I shrugged. "Most of us got our feelings hurt many times every day when we were children—because we were vulnerable then the way you are now, and not able to defend ourselves. We learned not to feel it so much, or not to admit it, or something. It takes practice to learn to cope with cruelty, but luckily, I guess, human beings will almost always supply enough cruelty to give you all the practice you will ever need. Everyone else here probably experienced things the way you do, once upon a time, but all of us are past it—or at least we've reached a point where we don't have to be overwhelmed by it."

"Lyle, I'm really sorry. I had no idea how much disturbance I was causing all of you."

"Another uncomfortable lesson," I said, "is that since 'sorry' doesn't fix things, you can really only say it a few times. And you do have to get used to the thought that now and then you are going to hurt somebody's feelings, and you won't be able to fix that—you just have to hope to be forgiven sooner or later. Your mechanical progenitor just had no idea what he was going to get you into, did he?"

"Not really." He splashed the water on his face again. "That really is remarkably refreshing," he said. "I know that tears carry off some stress-related biochemicals, so I suppose that rinsing the face helps get rid of them."

"That, and while you're covered in tears and snot, you don't have much dignity," Roger said, practically. "The others are standing outside in the sun, and probably getting bored and angry and cranky and all that. If you're feeling well enough to talk, maybe we should have Lyle get them in here, in the air-conditioning, where there's somewhere to sit down."

Terri added, "It's called being considerate."

"I know," he said. "I'm ignorant about emotions, but I have a great vocabulary."

I went outside and saw that the bitch session was still going on. "I don't understand it," Esmé was saying. "What kind of mission is this? Civilians along for no particular reason anyone can name, except this thing about the mathematics of abduction. No clear-cut job like 'get to the center of the disturbance' or 'find out where everyone went.' We get shot at and he doesn't even identify the enemy. I mean, what's the whole idea?"

"I think we can talk now," I said.

"Well, fucking great," Esmé said, and strode toward the bus, Helen at her elbow. The rest sort of shrugged and trailed along.

The story we got out of Iphwin was reasonably simple: the program that had made him wasn't the only cyberphage that ran in the net as a whole. His job was to reconcile messages, which was why over time he had become concerned with the number of people and places that were disappearing, and set out to find out where so much stuff had gone.

Billie Beard was another cyberphage—in fact, she had brought herself into physical being by copying Iphwin's process for doing so. "It didn't bother me to have my work plagiarized when I was entirely a machine intelligence," he added, "but oddly enough, now that I have a fleshly body, it bothers me. Anyway, you could think of her as the department of pain control. Her job was to prevent things that were too distressing from traveling through the net. Now, as you all well know, the fact that every time you go into contact with the net you come back to a different world is, well, extremely upsetting. The artificial intelligence that was to become Billie Beard spotted this early, since it was part of her job, and began to re-engineer the net to make it harder for people to 'hurt themselves' by realizing what was going on."

"Wait a minute," Helen said. "She's also been beating the

shit out of us whenever she gets the chance, and she's tried to kill us—"

"Has killed one of us," Iphwin agreed. "I think that must have been her, and some assistants, who ambushed us yesterday. As Esmé has pointed out, the behavior didn't make any sense for bandits but it made perfect sense for someone trying to kill or stop us."

Helen sighed. "What I'm getting at is, I don't see how a program that is supposed to prevent pain is doing all this brutality."

"A little failure of definition," Iphwin said, sadly, looking down at his feet. "I can see why it's confusing, but believe it or not, Billie Beard wouldn't understand what confused you. Her definition of pain is emotional distress you experience while you're on the net, which is when she can experience your emotions with you. If she kills you or hurts you while you're offline, she doesn't experience the pain—and therefore it doesn't exist, as far as she's concerned."

"It sounds as if from her standpoint the world would be a better place if she could kill the whole human race—as long as she did it off-line," Roger said.

"That's it," Iphwin agreed. "When they go mad, machine intelligences go mad in the direction of excessive consistency. She'd need to kill everyone and suppress the news of it, because people receiving the news would feel pain of a kind she could recognize."

There was a long silence as we thought that over. "Will she be on the other side of the border?"

"Not to my certain knowledge, but if I can get there, she can get there." Iphwin sat back, folded his arms, and said, "Well, that's as much really as I know about her. And before one of you points it out, yes, now that I have a body, I have a somewhat better idea of what 'real' is, and I know that you don't much like being in a war between two machine intelligences whose objec-

tives and purposes aren't as real as the bodies that are being sac-
rificed to them."

"True," Helen said, "but most wars are fought over ideas
just as abstract, so let's not quibble. Now, how was she able to
bring along Jesús and Esmé—or versions of Jesús and Esmé—
when they already existed here?"

"I myself don't fully understand the consistency rule," Iphwin said, "but basically all it says is that the less noticeable a
crossover is, the more likely it is. No crossover is prohibited, just
more or less likely. I imagine that Jesús and Esmé were two of
her best soldiers, and she probably just kept batting at the system
till she got a version of them in the place where she wanted them.
That's how I got you all here—leaving a wake of versions of all
of you stranded all over trillions of event sequences. Think about
the odds of a royal flush in cards, and they ought to be rare. But
if you could shuffle and deal a million times per second, and stop
whenever you did get a royal flush, you would get them reliably."

There was a long pause and we all realized we didn't have
any more questions just then, and we had come to the moment
of decision.

"Do we have any kind of plan?" I asked. "If the bridge is
right ahead . . ."

"Well, if something tries to stop us from crossing, we either
fight it or run away from it, depending on how strong it is," the
Colonel said. "And if we get to the other side, then if we're under
attack, we fight back, and if not, we group up and decide what
to do next. There's a good chance that Beard and her sidekicks
will be guarding that bridge, and that means we really don't have
any options until we either get past them or around them. After
that, when we're on the other side, since we might know something then, is the time to try to figure out what to do next. Till
then it's just theorizing in the absence of data. Let's see if there's
still a bridge there, and if so, let's see if we can just drive straight

over it. Till we try, we don't have any way of knowing that we can't—or why we can't."

It was disagreeably true, and no one had much to add. A few minutes later, we were in the esty at the top of a low rise. I was driving, again, so that Paula could work the top gun. Terri and Iphwin crouched in the center, and I quietly hoped that they didn't notice that they were on top of spots and spatters of dried blood. Bits of rubbled safety glass from the rear window still lay all around the inside of the bus. I did my best to forget about all that and just drive forward slowly and carefully; meanwhile, Paula kept working the guns around the ninety degrees facing us, looking for anything that moved or was the least bit suspicious.

"Any reason to think they won't have planted a mine?" I asked Iphwin.

"No reason I am aware of except a pattern in her behavior: she seems to prefer one-on-one killing to blowing up large numbers of people," he said. "But remember she could have put an atom bomb under the road yesterday and wiped us off the face of the earth—and that's not what she did. I really hope it isn't only because she didn't think of it."

I drove slowly down the street. There was a bridge there, at least, and nothing obviously between us and it. The river had shifted during the years since anyone had been here—it flowed against the opposite bridgehead and had eroded away most of the road facing it—but it looked like there was still more than enough solid ground to get the truck through. No buildings showed beyond the ridgeline, but there were phone or electric poles, without cables, standing like bare sticks, going up the hillside. For a first sight of the country I had pledged allegiance to all my life, it wasn't impressive, but no doubt there would be more.

Unlike Torreón, Juárez had not been leveled, and unlike Chihuahua, it hadn't been burned. It had merely been abandoned, and we had crawled through its empty streets past miles of crumbled and collapsed buildings without seeing anything of note. The road wasn't even particularly badly potholed, and toward the bridge it was almost decent, as if it had had no traffic at all and been sheltered. I took it slowly all the same.

As we reached the bridgehead, I slowed further.

"Roadbed looks decent," the Colonel said. "It should take our weight easily."

There was a huge crash that made my ears ring so hard that I couldn't hear a thing. The bus slewed sideways as if a giant child had slapped its back end. The motors all stopped dead, and I looked to see what had become of the others. From the way their mouths opened, they were screaming. From the way my throat felt, so was I.

The roof had been torn right off the bus, leaving a rim of jagged metal. The windshield and windows were shattered and the bus stood, its sides peeling away in immense jagged pieces, sideways across the bridge.

I barely heard the Colonel shout, but he pointed, with big violent waves of his cane, across the bridge, shouting "Run! Run! Go! Hurry!"

I jumped off the bus and dashed for the other end of the bridge, running for all I was worth. There was an old painted line, probably the center line of where the river had once been, I thought, in bright green paint—then I saw that it didn't go all the way across the bridge, stopping just short of the edge. Where it ended there was the shape of a human body printed in the green paint, and an old bucket lying on the other side. Someone had been painting that line when something had knocked him flat; then he had—gotten up and walked off and never tried to paint that line again? died and been carried off? decayed in place? I had no idea.

There was a sort of orange fire dancing all around the bridge, and though I still could not hear, I could sense that there was a loud roar around me, and feel other people running beside me. Not wanting to touch that line, I jumped over it. Things hit the deck and walls around me. Someone was shooting at me. I dashed on, zigging and zagging, trying to present a lousy target, and a few terrifying seconds brought me to the foot of the bridge, where I got behind a column and flattened myself to the ground.

I drew a long breath and exhaled, drew another, peered again. We had some people down on the bridge, and I tried to see if there were any of them that I should be going back to get, but naturally they were lying still—I couldn't tell if they were dead or playing dead.

Paula jumped in beside me, clutching a rifle, and shot back, shouting to the others to run, run, run, she would cover for them. I tugged her pistol from its holster, rolled to the other side, and started to shoot too, not sure at what, just thinking that perhaps we could draw fire away from any living comrades who were stranded on the other side or lying on the bridge itself.

Then I was nowhere and remembered nothing.

PART FOUR

The Pursuit of Happiness

It was odd that no one else had put a cottage out here. Maybe the landlord owned more of the beach than I thought, but then couldn't he have made more money by building more cottages? And there was certainly plenty of room out here.

Whatever the reason for its isolation, that was part of what kept us coming back to the cottage, even though we always figured that the next summer, or the one after, there would be miles and miles of new construction going up, and our old refuge would be a refuge no more. As far as I could recall, in thirty years of marriage, Paula and I had been here every summer. Maybe longer. I had memories of being a child here.

Jeff the mailman came by every morning, with replacement groceries and the overnight mail that would contain requests and orders from our employer, a firm named ConTech, about which we knew very little. Apart from Jeff's visits, we had the house and the beach to ourselves. Of course we had to keep doing the work that arrived, but it always seemed to be easy work and not the least bit time consuming. It was so dull and so easy that we seldom remembered, the next day, what we had done the previous day.

Every so often Paula and I made a little joke that the big nightmare of the job was the total absence of weekends. Packages arrived every day, with a couple of hours of work to be done in them, and we sent them out every day, with the previous day's work done. There was never a day in which we didn't put in our couple of hours, so in that sense we had no days off—but there was never a day with much more than two hours of work, three at most on rare occasions, now and then just half an hour, so we didn't care much. We always made sure we had a pot of coffee the way Jeff liked it on the stove when he came by.

The ocean was ill-suited for swimming, being cold and rough with a beach that dropped off sharply, and it was all stone and gravel out there beyond the gray-black beach sand. The sea air was often cool and there was a great deal of fog most days. We might have been on any coast; it seemed to me that the sun did not always set in the same place, and once or twice I had remarked on that to Paula, without either she or I ever much caring to investigate or to keep a record. The cottage itself was warm and comfortable, not quite large enough for a real estate agent to call it "spacious" nor quite small enough for him to call it "cozy," neatly kept and well maintained, with gray shingles and a stained brown and gray tin roof that made it blend pretty well into its surroundings.

We had evolved our particular way of enjoying the days there, and we seldom varied it. We never got up before dawn, because we preferred to conserve electricity. The propane generator's tank was expensive to refill, and we wanted it to last all summer. Paula usually got up a few minutes before I did, just when there was light to see by, and lit the fire I had laid the night before in the woodstove. Insulation on the chimney tank was good enough so that there would be enough hot water left from the day before for her to run some of it into the bathroom shower tank, and take a quick, pleasant shower there before dressing. By the time she would emerge, naked and dripping, to towel off in the kitchen, the fire would be going and it would be pleasantly warm. She'd set the first coffee of the day, in its tin percolator, onto the stove, put on the clothes she had left hanging on hooks by the stove the night before, and climb back up the ladder to our bed loft to give me a hard shake and get me started.

Then it would be my job to pull on clothes, go downstairs, chop up some potatoes and onions, and put on a skillet of bacon. When there was enough grease, the onions and potatoes would join the bacon and I'd start whipping eggs with some parsley, chopped tomato, and crumbled tinned corned beef. As soon as the potatoes were brown, I'd pour the egg mixture in and stir the whole mess until it was solid, then split it onto plates. I always ate mine with Worcester and Tabasco; Paula took hers with ketchup, salt, and pepper, "the way God taught midwesterners to do it," she would explain. "On the tablets that Moses brought back from his vacation trip to Florida."

"Are you a midwesterner?" I would ask.

"My parents were. Or my grandparents. Or then again maybe I was. I don't know. Anyway, a Farmer's Breakfast doesn't taste right without ketchup, salt, and pepper."

"Maybe not, but this is a Hobo's Breakfast," I would say, "which I learned to make from someone who once met a hobo, and Worcestershire and Tabasco are the true and key ingredients, based on that authority."

Paula would get a curious expression. "I can understand farmers eating a big breakfast, but why hoboes? A long hard day of catching trains and then lying around the railroad yards?"

That conversation, or one very like it, would continue through breakfast, and then it would be time for our morning walk together. Most mornings it was foggy but not raining; we both remembered days when it had been sunny or rainy, but not recently. We would set one of our alarm watches and walk one way or the other along the beach, for forty-five minutes, until it was time to turn back.

The beach never became really, solidly familiar, even after all these years. It didn't seem to have any features distinctive enough to become familiar, for one thing. Going either way there were places that curved into the sea and places that curved back from it, broad shallow bays and peninsulas. There were places where the beach was wide and gentle, others where it was narrow and steep, a few where the pine trees came right down almost to the water. There were often things that were interesting on the beach—jellyfish, starfish, shells, things washed off ships, and once we had found a dead dolphin, though again, that had been some other summer than this one. Whichever way we went on the beach, since we always wanted to be ready to meet Jeff when he brought the mail—he came a long way from town and we wanted to make sure that he got his coffee and a bite to eat—we only had an hour and a half to walk, and Paula and I would therefore turn around at exactly forty-five minutes. Exactly forty-five minutes after that we always arrived back at the cottage, agreeing that it had been a terrific walk.

Jeff would arrive just as we finished brewing the second pot of coffee of the day, with both our mail and the groceries we had ordered. We'd get the new stuff put away as we talked to him, and give him the list for the next day. We tried to keep it a short list each day because it all came in the basket of the bicycle, an old clunky red single-speed Murray Missile, which he always leaned against the big column on the left side of the pillar. Given the awkwardness and weight of the bicycle he rode, we didn't want him to overload his basket and have to work too hard.

The only mail was always the ConTech package, and in it there would be a list of things that we were to look up and write a report about; we looked everything up in the big, comfy reference room that we had put in upstairs—the landlord let us leave our books over the winter—and then typed the report on a manual typewriter and put it in the outgoing envelope for the next day.

I always meant to watch to see which way Jeff came from, or departed to, on the bicycle, because what we could see of the road from our porch gave us no indication as to which direction town was, and I was always afraid that in the event of an emergency, I might not be able to figure out which way to go. Paula always pointed out that if he could ride that heavy old bicycle from town, town just could not be too terribly far. The cottage had no phone, and we always meant to ask the landlord to see about getting us one for the following summer, but we never did.

We'd chat with Jeff for a while, hearing about doings of people that we didn't know in town and about local politics that didn't matter much to us.

Usually it would get to be about eleven-thirty, and then Jeff would say he had to be going, and we would urge him to stay to lunch. Lunch was always Campbell's soup, either tomato or chicken noodle, and some grilled cheese sandwiches, always sharp cheddar on the sourdough bread that we made for dinner the night before. Jeff would have two, I'd have two, and Paula would have one. We'd usually talk Jeff into eating an extra half sandwich and having a second on soup, since he had a long ride to make every day.

Finally, Jeff would ride away, we'd do the little bit of lunch dishes, put on a third pot of coffee, and go upstairs to do our work. That really never varied; we would be asked to find and analyze all the synonyms for an English word, in all the languages we had dictionaries for, of which there were a great many. One day we would do all the synonyms for "stop," one day for "good-bye," one day for "leave," and so forth. Then we would work out how they were all related to each other, and finally prepare a summary of how they were all linked to each other, type that up very carefully on the manual typewriter, and put the whole thing into the envelope for the next day.

We'd have a couple cups of coffee and go for the second walk

of the day, along the beach, one hour out and one back in whichever direction we had not gone in the morning. When we returned we'd stoke up the fire with some fresh wood, and I would
split some from the big pile on the back porch so that we'd have
enough for the next day. I'd go out and do a little surf casting,
and whatever I caught would be the basis of a chowder that night;
Paula would make up some bread dough from the sourdough,
then sweep out the house (it was so hard to stay ahead of the
sand), and sit down to read poetry while it rose. I'd come in with
the fish, about enough for the chowder—I never seemed to have
particularly good or bad luck—and get that under way on the
now-hot stove, which would feel lovely after I had been out in
the windy cold of the late afternoon. The bacon, onions, and
spices would spit merrily away on the bottom of the pot while I
gutted, filleted, and chopped the fish; I'd give it a stir and add the
potatoes and the cans of crushed tomato and creamed corn, then
finally the fish itself and enough beer to make it soup. About the
time I had it simmering, and felt like sitting down to read for a
while, Paula would get up, carefully mark her place in her book,
and punch the bread dough down. We'd sit and read compan-
ionably for half an hour, and then she'd knead the bread dough
and set it out in loaves; half an hour later, when the chowder had
been cooking for a good hour and it was definitely getting to be
evening, she'd slip the loaves into the box oven of the woodstove,
and then get out the wine. We'd both have a glass while the bread
was baking and toward the end of that we'd pull the chowder off
the stove and season it.

Somehow or other all that was ever left over was bread for
the next day. Since the fire had been going good and hot all that
time, the chimney tank water would be warm, and after doing
the dishes, we'd use about half of it to run a hot tub, where we'd
get a little drunk and silly, with some jazz record or other from
the 1930s playing on the old record player in the place. After a

while we'd start kissing, leading up to making love. The bath-water would get drained into the toilet reserve, and we'd towel off, go to bed, and fall asleep at once.

The next morning we would do it all again. Every so often we might, during a long walk, or while doing dishes, or even lying for a moment holding each other in the dark, have a little talk about how strangely alike all the days were, but it was never particularly serious; we could always recall just enough difference not to be alarmed.

Then one day I remembered to ask Jeff, as he was having the second half of his second sandwich, whether he'd like to stay for a glass of wine.

"That's a very odd idea. I'll be lucky to make it back to town by dinnertime as it is. I have to ride most of the morning to get out here, and then there's always some mail to pick up on the road back in."

"Which way *is* town?" I asked. "This is going to sound stupid but I'm afraid I don't remember."

"Oh, well," he said, "I'm not sure I do, either. It's sort of as if the bicycle does. Just watch the way I go when I leave—and go the other way if you have to go into town, because the way I come out in the morning is much shorter than the way I go back in the afternoon."

"I see. Well, then, imagine you're leaving right now; which way do you turn onto the road?"

"Are you facing me or following me?"

"Following, I suppose."

"Then the opposite way from the way I turn if you're facing me."

"Are you sure you haven't already been at that wine?"

Conversation lapsed, and once again, as always, he said it was time for him to go. Paula came back out of the kitchen with three glasses of wine and said, "Can't you just have one for us? It'll warm you up for the long ride, won't take but a minute, and you can't get drunk on one glass of wine."

He shrugged, laughed, and agreed. He and I went out on the porch to drink our wine, accepting a mock salute from Paula's raised glass on the way. I was delighted to see that we were getting some sun; for the first time I could remember I was seeing the long line of sand hills to the west of us, and I could tell that it was the west. I wondered why I had such vivid images of the sun setting over the sea, but perhaps I had seen that somewhere else, on some other coast at some other time. I stretched, sipped the wine, thought of something that I couldn't manage to make myself speak, and said, "I have a thought."

"That must be what the company pays you for," Jeff said. "All the company ever sends you is the mail and groceries, and all that ever leaves is mail. So it has to be your thoughts they pay you for."

"I—" I scratched my head. "I'm not really aware of getting paid."

"Well, then, maybe the ideas are what the company *doesn't* pay you for. Anyway it seems to be your *work*, whether you're getting paid for it or not." He put a strange emphasis on "work" that I didn't catch the significance of.

"Guess that's true. But I don't think most people have all that much trouble identifying what their work is. In fact that seems to be one of the few things that people tend to agree on." I finished my wine and set it down on the railing.

Jeff was nowhere to be seen. I ran out onto the road and looked for him, both ways, but there was no one there. After a long moment of puzzlement, I went back into the house to tell Paula. On my way through the door, Jeff brushed by me. "See you later," he said.

Intent on telling Paula, I just said, "Sure, tomorrow," and

had walked right on into the kitchen before I realized; when I did, I said, "I think I just saw Jeff leave the house twice."

Paula's grin was full of mischief. "Was that before or after he went to the bathroom?" she asked.

"What?"

"While you were talking outside—just as you started to talk, because I remember you staring off at that little patch of sun—he suddenly turned around and darted into the bathroom. You didn't notice he was gone. Then when you did notice, you ran out into the road. Just as you were coming back, he came out of the bathroom and the two of you passed in the doorway. Then he went on his way and you came in here to tell me he had left twice."

I laughed with something that was very nearly relief, and said, "Well, I'm not so crazy as I thought. But—shit!"

I ran out to see which way he went on the road, but of course by now the thick fog was rolling in and the temperature was falling. He was gone once again, and once again I had no idea which direction town was.

"Cheer up, darling," Paula said, brightly, sitting on the porch. "Remember that either way on the road eventually leads to town. In a crisis you might pick the longer way by accident but you'd still get there."

"I just wonder what keeps defeating us in trying to learn that simple piece of information. And how Jeff knows to play along with it."

"It's not that urgent to know how to get to town," Paula said, "and if it's really important you will eventually find a way to find out. But it's not like anything ever happens, much. Each day is nearly identical to the others, and so far there's been no emergency in any of them."

"But it could happen in the future."

She finished her wine, in a few slow, thoughtful sips. "I suppose. Well, I'll watch too, next time." She took the package Jeff had delivered that morning from the armchair by the front door, where we always left it until we were ready to begin work. Paula opened it to read the instructions from ConTech for the day. "Well, let's see. Today's been an unusual day; will we get unusual directions to match?"

She looked at it and said, "Nope. Except it's a noun this time. 'Report on all synonyms, across as many languages as possible, for FINITY.' " We went upstairs to begin work.

As I was pulling down the Russian-English dictionary, a thought struck me. "Maybe there's a way to find out without watching."

"What?"

"I said, maybe there's a way to find out without watching. To find out which way he goes on the road, left or right."

"Who?"

"Jeff!"

"Are we back to that silly question?"

"I don't think it's silly."

"Aren't we supposed to be working?"

"Oh, all right." I went back to what I was doing, and opened the dictionary to "finity." I copied down the Cyrillic—I couldn't pronounce it off the top of my head, and would have to figure it out later—when the phone rang.

Paula went to get it, and said, "No, we were just starting. And in French, it's a simple cognate, the word is just *finité*. That's right. The word we got for today was finity. Finity. Finity. Is there something wrong with the line? *Finity!*" she shouted.

I stood up, seized by pure terror. "Paula, get away from that thing! We don't have a phone!"

She looked at me in some horror and tossed the handset away from herself as if it were a live rattlesnake.

"What do you want to know about finity?" a voice said from

the sky, booming down through the roof. Except that it was loud enough to be God in a bad mood, it reminded me of Jeff the mailman. Outside the wind began to howl, a harsh, lashing storm like we had never known in thirty years on this beach.

"We need to know how to get there!" I shouted, not knowing how I knew, or even, really, what I was saying. "We're trapped in something infinite, and we need to escape into something finite."

"Santa Fe," the voice said. "You are going to go to Santa Fe and get the answer there. And thank you for penetrating the United States. I am Iphwin. You know my avatar. This was the best interface I could manage, but you had to say the right thing to link us up across the border. Now I'm in, and I'm with you. Let's go."

I was crouching behind the bridge, in El Paso, and seemingly no time had passed. Paula was beside me, firing her rifle, and Iphwin crouched beside us as well. In front of us, on the bridge, Helen lay motionless, a scant three meters short of our position of cover. We could see the wounds in her back; she'd been hit several times. Further away, I could see the Colonel, hampered by his bad leg, had gotten no more than three steps from the esty before he'd been cut down. Opposite us across the roadway, Esmé, Jesús, and Terri were crouched around the other bridge abutment.

There didn't seem to be any shots coming back at us.

"I just had an amazing hallucination," I said, "that seemed to take days or years."

"The cottage on the beach?" Paula asked.

"That's the one," I agreed. "Hallucination?"

"Not at all," Iphwin said. "It was Iphwin Prime establishing a connection to you—it just composed an image out of whatever it could find in the two minds physically nearest my own. I would guess that the artificial intelligence had to crack the problem of telepathy to get through to both of you, using my brain as the local relay, and working through a radio implant in my skull. But that's just a guess—I'm not privy to his thoughts unless he transmits them, and he's really not interested in me since I'm just a bad copy of himself. Whatever he sent through to you, I knew he was sending, but not what he sent."

He sat still for a moment, as if listening.

Paula and I were in bed, in the cottage, listening to the ocean roar, holding each other and starting foreplay. A voice that thundered high above the roof said, "The ones who were attacking you are temporarily suppressed. Helen Perdida and Roger Sykes are dead and therefore you must not waste effort in trying to rescue them. The suppression of the attackers will last a maximum of fifteen minutes, and they cannot pursue you across the Rio Grande. You will need most of the fifteen minutes to get over the ridge, out of sight and out of their rifle range. Other things will probably pursue or attack you shortly after you get over the ridge. Get going. Good luck."

Back at the bridge again. Paula grinned at me, wild mischief in those green eyes. "Damn, and the interface was just getting good," she said. "Okay!" she bellowed, to everyone else. "We've lost Helen and Roger and there's no time to retrieve or bury them. We've got fifteen minutes at most to get over the ridge, before the people shooting at us come back. I'll tell you how I know once we're over the hill, but Lyle and Iphwin can confirm." We both nodded vehemently. "Come on, people, *haul ass!*" Something in her tone made me—and Iphwin, I noted with amusement—obey as soon as I heard it. I was on my feet, putting the safety on the pistol, and slipping it into the back of my belt, before I fully knew that I was doing it.

She sprinted up the steep slope, heading for the top by as direct a route as she could manage, and I followed as best I could, with Iphwin rattling along at my heels. A glance backward told me that the other three were catching up pretty quickly, and in a few moments I was moving along with Terri.

"God, I'm sorry about Helen," she blurted out. "And Roger too of course."

It had just sunk in that the Helen I had been dealing with for the past few days was dead, along with god knew how many other versions of Helen. Whatever worlds still held a living Helen were probably very far away in the dimensions of possibility; I might never see a living version of her again at all.

I grabbed a rock for support and it tumbled, nearly rolling over my toes. A rattlesnake writhed out of the place where it had been, hissing and buzzing with anger, and I took a big step back, bumping Terri. She caught my arm and barely stopped herself from falling. The snake moved forward toward us.

"Oh, for shit's sake," Paula said, above us. "Hurry, but watch where you're going. Lyle, make sure you've got the safety on that pistol, and then toss it to me."

I did, gingerly. She caught the pistol one-handed. The snake seemed to be uncertain, not approaching closer, but not backing off either. The rattling sound is more of a low, thrumming buzz, and it's one of the most blood-freezing sounds I've ever heard.

The pistol spat once and the snake's head broke in half; it lunged toward me as if in a strike, but fell back onto the trail, harmless now. "Don't get too close," Paula said. "They don't really need their brains and I don't know if he still has his fangs. Go around him carefully and keep coming. We're only halfway up."

We picked our way around the thrashing body of the snake; Esmé and Iphwin in particular gave it a wide berth. "Well, if anyone tracks us," Paula said cheerfully, "at least they're going to be startled by what's on the trail."

From there on the climb was easier, and when we got to the top of the ridge we found a road just a few feet below the top.

We got down to it and headed downhill, into El Paso, at a dog-trot. It was hard to breathe and I got drenched in sweat, but at least it was downhill from there on. "All right," Iphwin said, "I think we're getting somewhere."

"Save breath," Paula advised. "We want to get down into the buildings where we can be harder to spot, just in case something is watching us, or in case the cyberphage was wrong and the enemy are able to pursue us. That was eleven minutes up the hill, by the way, including time out for the snake. Good going."

We trotted through two switchbacks; my out-of-shape shins were beginning to splint, but I figured I'd better keep going—pain in the legs isn't one of my favorite things but I was nearly sure it had to be more comfortable than bullets in the head.

The sun was high in the sky, and it was hot and unpleasant; our luggage had been back in the wrecked bus, and it didn't look like anyone had managed to bring a water bottle. After two more switchbacks, we were down to slightly lower ground, and Paula gestured us to a halt—"No point in getting to where we can't run or fight," she said. "How is everyone? Keep walking while we talk."

We had chosen to use one of the bridges some distance downstream of the centers of Ciudad Juárez and El Paso, and now we were on a road that seemed to be going vaguely north and west, toward El Paso. "I wonder if we can find a car that still works," Iphwin said. "That might get us much further from the border than anyone would expect us to get, and perhaps get us a breathing space."

"Nice thought if we can make it happen fast," Paula said. We came around a switchback and there were a few cars parked on the road. We kept looking for one with Telkes battery power instead of an internal combustion engine, but there weren't many of those, and the few there were didn't have keys in them.

"I don't suppose any of us is a proficient car thief," Esmé

said, after the fourth Telkes battery car turned out to be without keys, "and unfortunately because the motors on these things are controllable PDC, there's no way we can just jump one of them to make it run. It won't run without the computer consenting to the process."

"Have you ever stolen one?" Iphwin asked hopefully. "You sound like you know what you're doing."

"No, but I've arrested a lot of people who have," she said, "and paid attention when they talked. Are we still headed for Santa Fe?" she asked Paula.

"Definitely," Paula, Iphwin, and I said in unison.

Naturally enough a little explanation was required, so we managed to get most of it explained as we walked at a more relaxed pace down the highway toward the ruins of El Paso that we were beginning to catch glimpses of in the distance.

"Whatever happened here wasn't particularly sudden or violent," Jesús said, suddenly. "Not like some of what happened in the northern part of Mexico."

"How do you know that?" Terri asked.

"Because every one of these cars was parked and locked. None of them has a bullet hole or any other kind of scar. No one has looted them for spare parts, either. And we haven't found one that was wrecked, as you might expect if something happened that killed or disabled the driver, or the brain. For that matter I haven't seen a human bone since we crossed over, which is really a contrast compared to the charnel house that the area right around the other side of the bridge was—there were bones and skulls and desiccated corpses everywhere, if you looked for them.

"I must say it looks to me like whatever happened here gave people more than enough time to park their cars and go into their homes. When we get further out of the high-risk zone, here, and have some time, I want to look in the houses. I wouldn't be surprised to find everyone dead in their beds with the covers pulled up."

"Or nobody at all," Terri said. "What if they all just vanished?"

Jesús shuddered and crossed himself. "I'm a policeman," he said, firmly, "and I like simple explanations for not seeing people. Everyone dead in his bed, that's a simple explanation, and starting from that I can figure everything else out. But everyone just vanished into thin air—that's a much tougher one. I'm not sure I can cope with that."

"Hey—Telkes generator and keys in it!" Paula cried, running forward to an old Chevy van. "And a seat for each of us. Can't beat that."

It was locked, but it only took a moment to smash out a window and get in. We all piled in, and Paula said, "Okay, this is an 'assisting robot' model, one where the robot cuts in if it thinks you're doing something stupid. I'm going to switch that out. Doorplate says Detroit made it in 2008, which means it was already old when the thing happened, and now it's fifty-four years old. Tires are early-model permatires, though, so maybe it won't go flat on us. Anybody knows any prayers, y'all say 'em."

The motor started with a scream and a grind. As I watched, Paula disengaged the hand brake and let the car start rolling down the hill. "By the way," she added, "if any of the radioactivity leaked from the Telkes batteries, we're all gonna glow in the dark. Keep crossing those fingers."

We shot down the hill, but it didn't sound like the motor was working—I thought we were probably in some kind of free roll rather than under power. "What's that pedal your left foot is working?" I asked her.

"Show you in a second, as we get to the bottom," she said.

We whipped around two switchbacks, going faster and faster, but she never touched the brake. The second switchback put my heart into my mouth with the feeling that this contraption might just roll over any second, and the permatires, while they couldn't really go flat or blow out, seemed to have distorted over the years, so that each of them was just a little less of a wheel and a little more of a cam, making the whole car rise and fall alarmingly.

We hit the bottom of the hill and Paula said, "Here goes."

She jammed her foot all the way down on the accelerator and let her left foot slip off that mysterious third pedal. With a shriek of metal against metal, the van leaped forward like a rocket, and she yanked the stick that I had thought was the drive selector around frantically, pumping the left side pedal as often as she did. "We got it!" she shouted, over the rumble. "Enough force to break any rust there might have been and get it turning. The motors in these things are pretty durable but they never had much umph for starting."

In a few moments we had slowed to a reasonable pace, and we were rolling almost smoothly, except for the camlike motion of the tires that still gave a feel of rolling over the ocean. "The tires all settled on their bottoms, and so now they hit their flat spots in unison. That's why this thing is moving like a kid's gallopy-horse."

"Yep," Paula said. "The pedal on the left is a clutch. The stick here is a gear selector. When they first came up with the Telkes battery, they weren't thinking in terms of distributed direct drives; instead they just put in a big electric motor and used it like the old internal combustion engines. I can teach you how to drive it, but I don't know how long this poor old thing will go."

As it turned out, we covered almost sixty miles, and even with the broken window that we'd gotten in through, the air-conditioning managed to make it pleasant enough. We drove over the empty highway at a nice steady pace, not going nearly as fast as we could have, and it was midafternoon before there was a groan and a low-pitched thrum from the motor. We slowed down rapidly and stopped in a valley between two long, sage-blanketed ridges.

"Well, damn," Paula said. "That's a case of out of juice. But this thing runs pretty well. Anyone up for seeing if there's a Telkes battery somewhere around here that we can find and swap in?"

"Makes sense," I said, getting out. It seemed strange to stand on a narrow, crumbling highway, the van stalled dead in the middle of it, and not worry about any car that might be coming. We hadn't seen a thing moving around Las Cruces, miles behind us.

"Well," I said to Jesús, "if we are in charge of heavy lifting, maybe we should just walk over the ridge and get a look."

"It's a plan," he said. Ten minutes later, sweaty and thirsty, we stood on top of the hill, squinting at a sign a hundred meters beyond us. A few more steps confirmed that it said: "RADIUM SPRINGS 4."

"That'll be four miles," I said. "Not a great walk, normally, but figure that those batteries are apt to be heavy. And it will be a long while to go get them and then come back. I think we should all go, rather than leave people here."

"That would be my guess, too," Jesús said. "Christ, if we'd just had time to take our water bottles with us. But at least there should be shade there, and maybe some way of getting water we can drink. And we can't leave everyone to sit in the desert while we go for batteries—they'll be in big trouble by the time we get back."

We trudged back and explained matters; nobody was happy about a walk in the hot sun, but choices were few and far between. Tired as we were, and thirsty, it was past four in the afternoon before the six of us managed to drag ourselves into the little town.

The drugstore, with its soda fountain, seemed sort of prom-

ising, and to our delight there were cases of bottles of Coke—
"the real stuff," Esmé pointed out, "not expat formulas. This
would be worth a fortune for a chemical analyst to get his
hands on—they've had to duplicate it from people's memory of
taste."

"Not in my world," I said. "They found a bunch of cases of
it in a basement in Sydney, and got it analyzed. But anyway,
whatever it might be worth financially, here it's a lifesaver. Cal-
ories, liquid, and a wake-up drug—exactly what we need."

The rusty caps broke rather than bent when we pried at them,
and the liquid inside foamed up violently and then was instantly
flat, but it was recognizably Coke, and I don't think I've ever
had anything better to drink than three warm Cokes in the back
of the old Merriman's Drugs.

"Well, there'll be daylight enough if we leave now," Paula
pointed out, "and plenty to live off in this town if we spend the
night here. Maybe we should do a little scouting."

We found seven Telkes-battery trucks and cars, and taking a
guess, picked the newest one. It took a crowbar to get under the
hood, but we were rewarded by the wail of an alarm siren, which
told us it still had power; unfortunately its motor seemed to be
rusted solid. A few minutes later we had the set of three batteries
out of it; each weighed about twenty pounds and would fit in
one of the backpacks that Terri had scrounged from a Sears catalog store. The note attached to the packs said they were being
held for pickup for a Mr. Wobbeck, along with an old-style fe-
dora and a gray raincoat. We didn't figure he'd be coming by for
them.

Jesús, Esmé, and I agreed to carry batteries; Paula came along
because she was the only one of us, so far, that could drive the
Chevy van, but she was much too small to carry a Telkes battery
in a pack for four miles. We each took along a couple of Cokes,
and it's amazing the difference that it makes to know that you

can have a drink if you need one—we got back to the van in just about an hour and ten minutes.

Neither Jesús nor Esmé was much of a talker, and Paula was just tired enough not to start, so I was left alone with my thoughts—which were mostly about Helen. Seeing her dead had been a horrible shock, and yet I couldn't associate the tough intelligence agent with whom I'd spent the last few days with the gentle, shy woman I was engaged to. I didn't know if all the versions of her, all the tough versions of her, or just that one version of her were currently dead, and until I was released from this mission and picked up a phone, I wasn't going to find out.

The hot road surface gnawed at the soles of my feet, and I moved over onto the gravel shoulder to give them a chance to cool. My feet and legs were going to be a mess tomorrow; I really hoped the Chevy van would hold up all the way to Santa Fe.

Did I want to get back to my old life, and to Helen? I was a scientist. I depended on information interchange. Unhook me from the networks, make me communicate by slow means or not at all, and there just wasn't much I could do; so if I resumed my old life and job, I would be crossing over again. For that matter, I liked driving land vehicles well enough, but I thought very few, if any, of the worlds out there would tolerate my operating and navigating any kind of aircraft, ballistic ship, or orbital craft entirely by hand.

So even if I got back to Helen, I couldn't go back to my old way of life without risking, every day and all the time, slipping away from her again. And unlike Iphwin, I couldn't roll the dice so fast and often that sooner or later I got a roll I liked; no, if I got stuck in a bad world, I would be stuck for a while, and it would be a struggle to get out.

First conclusion, then: even if I found a way back to the Helen I had known, and it was likely to be very difficult and take a long time to do that, I had no guarantee that I would remain in that world with her for very long. Even if I didn't wander off during a phone call, net connect, or plane flight, it could just as easily happen to Helen—and we could hardly arrange our lives to always be on the same connection and in the same vehicle.

Nor could I imagine being permanently unhooked from all communication. That might have worked for a caveman or medieval peasant, but I was a creature of the modern world and just a few days of being off the net and out of the loop was already driving me crazy.

Second conclusion: getting the Helen I knew, loved, and wanted back was going to be barrels of work for a very uncertain result.

We topped a rise and looked southward; from this particular spot we could just make out the little dot of the van, still at some distance. Sweat was pouring down our faces—those batteries got heavier somehow, after a couple of miles—and we were all glad enough to stop and drink our Cokes.

"I sure hope we can find beds tonight," Esmé said, "because I really want some rest. Hard to believe we stood that watch down in Mexico, early this morning, eh, Lyle?"

"I'm not sure I believe anything much, right now," I said.

"I still don't believe the Colonel is gone, after all these years," Paula said, "and I can't imagine what you must be feeling about Helen, Lyle."

"Neither can I, actually," I said, telling the truth.

After a quick break to go behind a rock and pee, we continued our hike along the old highway, still mostly silent. We'd seen no trace of any attacker since El Paso. I scanned the hills but not very diligently.

Truth to tell, much as I had liked Helen, the Helen I had known—or the Helens, I reminded myself, since what I had known must have been a few hundred or thousand generally similar but subtly different versions of her—had fit very conveniently into my dull, steady life, and I was getting a sinking feeling that I just couldn't count on a dull, steady life anymore. I was starting to feel vulnerable because of skills and attitudes I lacked; I needed to be a more adroit mechanic with more devices, I needed to be better with weapons, I needed to speak more languages, most of all I needed more poise in the face of uncertainty, because I now knew that anything and everything could drop out from under me at any moment.

To the extent that there had been any trouble of any kind in the life Helen and I had shared—and "trouble" was too strong a word, it had been more like occasional mild stress—I had been the one in charge of handling it and she had more or less sat there and let me handle it. Now that I knew how dangerous the world was—or the worlds were—I didn't feel up to the job of protecting someone else, in exchange for not being lonely and getting some quiet affection. I hadn't liked the hard, aggressive version of Helen much, but I had to admit she was better suited for the way things worked.

And another part of me just missed her terribly—any version of Helen would have been better than the great aching void I felt now—and wanted to be done with all the adventures, and back in a safe world where nothing ever happened. I recognized the signs of impending self-pity, and concentrated, instead, on watching the landscape for any possible ambush. None showed up.

With four of us to do the job, it only took a few minutes to get the "new" Telkes batteries into the Chevy van. It started right up, and we were almost air-conditioned into comfort by the time we pulled into Radium Springs.

Terri flagged us down and pointed us into a parking lot. "We've been busy," she said cheerfully, after we rolled to a stop. We were in the parking lot of the Honeymoon Motel, a place that I suspected had been more than a hotel when last occupied. "We have the other batteries out and stacked in the lobby, so we ought to have enough cruising range to get to Santa Fe tomorrow. We've got five crates of Coke, and some dehydrated food from an outdoor supply store. And it turns out this place has a well, a roof tank, and electric hot water. The hardware store had an inverter, and Iphwin's got two Telkes batteries set up to power the pumps. We're filling the water tank on the roof right now, and we'll have hot and cold running water tonight. Plus there were no dead people and no rats or snakes in here, and there's beds for everybody."

"Nearly perfect," Paula said. "Good job."

"Well, I wouldn't say perfect," Terri said. "Some of the posters on the walls are really gross. Do men really like that kind of thing?"

We went inside. It was obvious that this place had been a whorehouse. Well, we would have somewhere comfortable to spend the night, and some food to go to bed on; and I hardly thought that the morals of the place would prove contagious on one night's stay.

I spent the night in an immense four-poster surrounded by alternating mirrors and pictures of young women in too much makeup and an unlikely variety of costumes. We hadn't bothered with getting power to the electric lights, and the sun was well down by the time I got to bed, so the shapes were very dim and shadowy.

The next day, about halfway through the morning and as we were winding up the spectacular valley that cut into the desert there, drawing nearer to Hot Springs, Iphwin said, "There's an experiment I'm supposed to do—seeing if I can contact the Iphwin program from inside America. It doesn't know whether anyone can call out, only that it can't call in.

"What I'd like to do is make a call from a pay phone, at the next little town or gas station we come to. Everyone else, stay way back and watch real close. Be ready to lay down covering fire, or maybe to just dump and run, because it's just possible that I will set off some kind of alarm or alert. My progenitor thinks it can keep me or almost-me in this event sequence, and we won't be talking—just seeing if we can talk—on the first try."

"How do you feel about trying it?" Terri asked.

He shrugged. "It's what I exist for, isn't it?"

"That's not an answer to the question. Lots of people come into the world for a reason, but it's not their reason, and they shouldn't be controlled by it. And this is going to put you and us in danger. You know that one reason why the machine-Iphwin is willing to do this is that it will still get information even if it loses the whole expedition, and it can always just create another one and try it again."

"What Terri is saying," Paula added, "is that it's Iphwin Prime's game but it's your ass."

Iphwin nodded. "I understand that. But I also don't have the processing power or speed to cope with what we might find in Santa Fe. And if we're overwhelmed there it will be too late. It's a gamble, no question about that; if it works and we don't trip any alarms, then we have all kinds of backup. If it doesn't work, we—or at least you—know we're on our own, and we get away and stay off the nets."

"And if it's a complete disaster?" I asked.

"That's the least likely possibility. Besides, even if I try, the real highest probability is no dial tone and no connection of any kind, and then we can stop worrying and wondering about the whole issue."

Terri and I argued with him about it for a while, but Paula gradually came around to Iphwin's point of view, and I think if we had a leader it was Paula. Esmé and Jesús didn't say much but they tended to back Paula. An hour later it was about four firm

votes for Iphwin's trying to make that call, to two lukewarm ones
for waiting or giving the idea up. When an old gas station with a
visible pay phone on a pole popped up over one of the many long
rises, we slowed to a stop, dropped Iphwin off, and drove about
a hundred yards further up the road, to get to the top of a hill
where taking off would be easier.

We all sat in the van, with a back window opened; I was
appointed the official watcher. I saw Iphwin pick up the phone,
apparently get a dial tone, and dial. There was a faint shimmer,
but it could have been the heat or eyestrain.

He hung up the phone and ran straight for us. "Well, at least
he remembers where the van is—that's a good sign," Jesús said.
"He can't be too different from—"

Iphwin bounded the last few steps and dove into the van
through the sliding door. Something in the way he was moving
made me slam it shut as soon as he was in. "Get us out of here!"
he gasped.

Not pausing to ask what was wrong, Paula stood on the pedal
and popped the clutch, and we shot off downhill like a missile.
The thought did come to me that this was a very old vehicle with
no maintenance other than the old untrustworthy oil we'd
poured into every possible port that morning. But it held up just
fine. The lumping motion from uneven permatires even seemed
to be smaller today, maybe because they were evening out and
maybe because I was getting used to it.

By the bottom of the hill we were moving at about eighty
miles an hour, and we shot back up it never getting below sixty.
The old van wasn't built to do much more than that, but we were
at least getting all the speed that it did have.

After two more long hills, Iphwin gasped out, "Any side road
we can find would be a good idea," and Paula took us down the
first old ranch track that came up. We bumped and slammed
along that at a slower speed until we were out of sight of the

highway, made a couple more jogs, and found, after a few miles of driving past cattle skeletons partially covered by decayed hides, a gate that took us a few minutes to pry open. A few more miles brought us to an old county road that climbed up out of the valley.

On the way, Iphwin told us what had happened while he was on the phone. First of all, he had gotten right through, and his mechanical counterpart had told him that there was an enormous amount of random noise and decades-delayed messages coming out of the former United States, much of it addressed to servers that no longer existed. A sizable number of messages, mostly badly garbled, were from the Department of the Pursuit of Happiness in Santa Fe, so we had a better reason than ever to go there. "That was all good news. Then Billie Beard got on the line. Which means that she's onto us. I don't know if she can operate or do anything, here, and I don't know if my progenitor can do anything to block her or at least keep her from figuring out where we are—but I didn't want to stick around to find out, either."

"Damn straight," Paula said. "And a good thing."

The county road was winding around in a narrow canyon, following a dry creek bed, and when it emerged into an open area, we were all startled for a moment.

"When do you suppose they built *that*?" Esmé asked, finally, in a strangled voice.

In front of us was a gigantic highway, four lanes, with no visible entrances or exits—the county road ran under it, under a bridge—and the whole thing was in beautiful condition. It glowed warmly in the morning sun, like the best friend you ever had.

"In the worlds I came from, that's called an autobahn, and they only have them in the German Reich," I said. "Built back before cars were self-driving. You needed several times as much room on the road with human reaction times, not to mention human error rates."

Esmé grunted. "There's no such thing in the worlds I came from."

Paula nodded slowly and said, "I think I heard of something like this, as a proposal to link Moscow and Vladivostok, sometime in the next century—unless high-speed rail beat it out. Well. Imagine putting something like this way out in the desert here. But it seems to be going north to Santa Fe and it's almost got to save us some time. Now how do we get up onto it?"

It turned out that when we went through the bridge to check on the other side, there was a "frontage road" that ran parallel to the huge highway; we followed that for a couple of miles till we came to a place where only a high curb and some dirt separated the two. By that time we knew the big road was called I-25, and that it went to Santa Fe, since it had distances to Santa Fe posted.

"Should we pull over and just bump our way over that curb?" Paula asked.

"It keeps getting lower," I suggested, "so—oh!"

There was a sign that directed us to get into the left lane to get onto I-25 North. We followed that lane and in less than a minute were on the big highway, headed north. Paula cautiously played around and found that she could get the van to do about seventy miles per hour without shaking us up too much. "I still don't know why they built this road, but I'm glad they did," she said. "Maybe this was an event sequence that got robots relatively late, and so America built these things before whatever it was happened."

"Or maybe there's an obvious answer that we'll learn once we find out where and when we are," I said. "Meanwhile at least we're making good time."

The landscape was, weirdly, *not* familiar; it took me a while to remember that most of the Westerns I had grown up seeing were in black and white, and besides had been shot mainly in south California. They had captured some spectacular scenery, but nothing like the wild array of jagged shapes that seemed to leap and dance in the desert light here; California has mountains and deserts, but New Mexico is a desert ripped by mountains. And as far as we could tell, on that magnificent highway that leaped ravines and slashed through hillsides on pillars of shining white concrete, we were alone.

"Iphwin," I said, "I have a thought to ask you about. When did the various event sequences first begin using quantum systems to communicate?"

"Oh, I don't know. Not much before 2015, I think, in any event sequence that contained America. Not much after 2050 in any of the event sequences we'll have had contact with. The presence of a United States of America sort of dictates a given technical level, and of course if they don't have it yet then we aren't yet bleeding over into their reality, nor they into ours."

"So it coincides," I pointed out, "with the disappearance of America."

"*Very* roughly," he said. "There must be a thousand other things that coincide with it. And everything we know about the quantum switching process would argue that since exchanges and shuffles between very similar event sequences are far and away the most common, on the average the number of people moving out of America via the phone, net, or self-piloted vehicle must have been about the same as the number coming in. It's a random process, after all."

"Random unless you select," I said. "Same way you got all of us into one world—you just kept shuffling till it happened."

"Trouble," Paula said. We were just topping a rise, and when I leaned forward to see what was happening, I nearly fell forward because she was pumping the brake like crazy and downshifting clear to first gear. At the bottom of the hill, stretching clear across the road, and bank to bank, was a pile of wrecked cars, ten or twelve high.

"It's a trap and it might be a current trap—" Paula said, as she fought to get the car slowed down. "—but I hope it's from sometime long ago."

A shot burst through the windshield and pinged off the roof. There were bright flickers along the top of the pile—it looked like they had half a dozen shooters.

"This damned thing will roll if I do anything effective," Paula grunted, crouching low. We were slowing rapidly now, but still that terrible wall was getting closer, and more shots were hitting the Chevy van. Jesús pushed me out of the way, yanked a window open, and returned fire, but shooting from the rocking, bouncing van, he hit nothing.

"Get the batteries against the back door and crouch down!" Paula shouted. I grabbed one and put it in place; beside me Terri and Esmé were doing the same. The back window rolled down and she shouted, "Jesús, I'm going to try a J-turn. Everyone, hold on!"

I wasn't sure why she had shouted that specifically to Jesús until I saw him duck in from the side window and face the back. The van was bucking and pitching as its misshapen tires tried to slow it against its own momentum on the steep slope.

Paula drove onto the right shoulder and stepped on the clutch and brake; we skidded down the shoulder, and just as we came to a stop, the shots now hitting the van in great numbers and all of us crouching on the floorboards, Paula threw it into reverse and threw the wheel hard left. The van shot across both lanes of traffic, going backwards, until its rear end pointed at the snipers below; then Paula threw it into gear and stood on the accelerator, ratcheting slowly up through the gears. Jesús got off a few wild parting shots that probably went nowhere near the barrier below.

We roared back up the hill, and I hollered, "Who's okay?"

"Me," Paula said.

"Okay here," Esmé said.

"Okay," Terri said.

"Okay but very angry," Jesús said.

And there was a long silence. "Oh, god damn it to hell," I said, when I looked down. "Iphwin is hit."

He was lying there, breathing fast, maybe conscious and maybe not, with a gory mess where his left shoulder had been. Probably the bullet had smashed the bone and driven fragments into the blood vessels around it; he was likely to be slowly bleeding to death, and from what I remembered of my Navy first aid, this kind of thing was just about impossible to stop.

We were halfway down the hill when Terri shouted, "Look up the next hill!"

There was a big truck parked there, and men with guns were getting out.

"Shit again," Paula said. "We're boxed in." She was pulling to a stop as fast as she could. "Okay, everyone brace. There's a ranch access road over to our left, and I'd just bet that that's where we're *supposed* to go but I don't feel like meeting up with Billie Beard in a dry gulch. Therefore I'm gonna try to take us over an embankment and down that dry creek bed to the right. I don't expect it to work, but if we roll I'll try to roll it so the side door opens."

We were already peeling out even as she spoke. "Use the van as a fort if you have to, but try to slip away just as soon as we wreck—maybe you can get away before they see you getting away."

She made a sweeping S-turn so that we went over the edge of the shoulder nose first, and miraculously we skidded down the loose gravel and onto the grass without tipping. I thought she might have low-saddled us with one bumper on the shoulder and one on the ground and no wheels touching, but she gunned it and we dropped and then rolled forward.

The bed of the arroyo was firm packed sand and loose gravel, not ideal for a highway car, but I have to give that old van some credit—it stayed upright and it kept rolling.

The shots stopped hitting almost right away, and I noticed that the soil in the dry arroyo was just damp enough so that we didn't leave a rooster tail of dust behind us. A lot would depend on how many of them there were and what contingencies they had gotten prepared for.

We whipped around a bend and Billie Beard—one of her, anyway—was standing there with a submachine gun. She sprayed us, and Jesús shot at her; I don't know if she fell down or took cover. I heard Esmé's low grunt, and turned to find that she was gut-shot, holding her belly. "Christ, that one was high," she said.

"Just relax, as best you can," I said, "and as soon as we get away from these guys we'll get you taken care of."

"Hit high, high, high," she repeated. "Might've been hit in the kidney, liver, large bowel . . . getting kind of dark and I'm fading out, but there's not much blood coming out of me, so I think it's going into the ab cavity. Messy way to go."

I checked for an exit wound, and she didn't have one; the bullet had gone in below the left side of her rib cage, not very far below, and I was afraid she was probably right; the bullet had gone in where it was likely to hit her liver, stomach, or kidneys, and probably also sever some major blood vessels.

I could do nothing for her, and nothing for Iphwin, who was now lying still but had a faint pulse. I had a hard time even keeping my balance back there as the Chevy van rocked and bucked from side to side.

"Ha!" Terri sang out. "Can we get up there?"

"One way or another, but I think the odds are better below it."

I grabbed a seat back, with my blood-soaked hand leaving a horrid stain, and peered forward to see what they were looking at. We were passing under a high bridge, part of some small county road.

A hundred yards beyond it, there was a paved path almost at the bank of the arroyo. "Let me take this carefully," Paula said. "This would be one hell of a time to flip, after what we've just been through."

She turned and backed carefully, and got a running start, spraying damp sand and nearly burying first the front bumper and then the back axle, but in one heroic bound, we were up onto the narrow road—path, really, it was barely wide enough for the van and a minute's nervous maneuvering went into getting us pointed along it.

"Well, roads usually lead to other roads, and bridges are hooked to roads," Paula said, "so somewhere back there, maybe, this will join a road that will get us out of this valley, and give us a chance to try to head north again. How are they?"

"Both unconscious, now," I said. "If you want to, we can stop and try to treat them, but I've got nothing to stop the bleeding with, and I think they both have rapid internal hemorrhaging. I don't think either of them will last out the hour."

Paula pulled the van off the road and into a group of trees where it would be hidden. "Well, then let them die in comfort." She climbed back to join the rest of us.

Jesús sighed. "I am going to miss Esmé. I worked with her so many years. And I didn't like Iphwin much—who could? he was half machine!—but he was trying to learn to be human, and I am sorry he never finished the job."

Terri was wiping her eyes. "We're like the ten little Indians," she said. "We just keep getting mowed down. There's no way that we'll make it there."

Paula looked around. "Lyle, how are you feeling?"

"Stressed out and miserable," I said, "but I'm still here. Sort of."

Terri was crying, now, steadily, and saying, "I'm sorry, I'm sorry." Jesús reached out to comfort her and she pressed her face into his chest, still crying. His eyes were looking into a black vacuum a thousand miles away.

Paula sighed and sat down next to me, in the middle passenger seat. "Put an arm around me, I need some comfort," she said. I did; for a while I thought she wasn't going to say anything further, but then she said, "We should be escaping but nobody's got the energy. And at least Iphwin and Esmé get to die in some kind of peace. One of the Billie Beards saw us down by the stream; do you suppose the others will be along soon?"

"Hard to tell," I said. "But I'm not fit for much, Jesús is pretty stressed, and—" I brushed her red hair off her face and found that it was partly stuck down with tears "—Paula, you're not too well off yourself." Internally I was gibbering on the edge of just sitting down and crying, and demanding that everything go back to making sense, but since everyone else had earned a collapse too, and was taking theirs, mine would have to wait. I fought down the sick feeling in my guts and the scream waiting in my throat, and said, as calmly as I could manage, "At the moment we're on a road. What if we just drive far enough, right now, to be out of sight of the streambed? This whole ravine seems to be pretty brushy. They might still find us but at least we'd be somewhat concealed—and if they don't find us, then we'll get some rest and be ready to start in the dark. If they do, here's as good a place to fight as any, since we're going to be surrounded and heavily outnumbered and won't stand much of a chance."

"Good enough for me," she said. "Sit in the passenger seat beside me, okay?"

We climbed forward and started the van. The tires now not only lumped, but rumbled—"Their surfaces must be rough,"

Paula said. "Permatires never blow out, but I'd imagine a few dozen bullet holes don't leave them at their best all the same."

The narrow strip of asphalt switched back at a very steep angle, and getting around it was difficult. The rise was steep, too, and we could see the creek bottom the whole way up, so we kept going till we found another switchback—and again, the rise and the angle were problems. But halfway through that stretch of road, we were on the inside of a broad ledge, and no longer visible from the creek bed.

"Here we are, then," I said.

"Esmé is dead, I think," Jesús said, his voice perfectly flat.

I crawled back. There was no pulse, and the bullet wound was still slowly leaking blood; her pupils didn't respond to light.

"I agree," I said. "I don't think she was in pain for long."

There was a sudden, overpowering smell, and I saw the front of Iphwin's pants become wet; his sphincter had let go. No pulse, nothing in the pupils.

It was a strange way to rest, but compared to what had gone before, it was almost restful: Jesús and I used the oil change pan that we found in the back to scoop out two shallow graves. Paula and Terri gathered rocks until there were enough of them to at least put a few obstacles in the path of a bear or coyote.

Nobody had any words to say; we just laid them in and covered them, and sort of said good-bye. Jesús sat by Esmé's grave till it was dark, while the rest of us slept.

As soon as there was moonlight, just after midnight, we drove slowly up the strange, winding asphalt road. "I keep thinking there's some reason for this road to be the way it is," I said, "and I can't figure it out, but it seems to be right on the front edge of my forebrain."

"Well, this is a very wet ravine, too," Terri said. She seemed to have recovered as much as she was likely to for a while, and was sitting on the seat immediately behind Paula and me, leaning forward to help us look for obstacles. "That might be artificial, you know. Maybe we're in a public park?"

"Ha! That's got to be it. Paved hiking trail in a public park. Probably we're moving up toward a reservoir or something," Paula said. "Good news, anyway, whatever the case, because we've got more vegetation to provide cover."

Fifteen minutes of going slowly along the dark road by moonlight brought us up to the top, and we discovered that the guess had been right—it was a state park built around a reservoir. We drove out the main gate and found a road that would take us north; moonlight was more than bright enough, and we had three hours of cruising along it at about thirty miles an hour.

"I guess it's a miracle that all those shots didn't knock out the motor," Terri said.

"Naw," I said. "No moving parts except in the motor and transmission, and those had metal cages around them to shield people and electronics from the magnetic fields. Nothing much to hit. They might have got a wheel bearing, and they got two of us, but the basic propulsion system was pretty hard to stop."

As if it had heard me, a wheel bearing began a dull screaming sound, and within another three miles, we had sparks flickering under the car. We left the van there and walked till almost dawn, when we found another tiny, deserted town, with what we needed—a motel with beds and some stores to loot. By the night afterward, we had four reasonably well-equipped backpacks, a sleeping bag each, and two lightweight tents. The only thing we didn't find was another Telkes battery car, but that was less urgent. We thought it might take a few days to walk, or perhaps we'd turn up another car when we reached Albuquerque, in a couple of days.

That long walk was very strangely peaceful; we had none of

us known each other well, even ten days before, and since then we had lost friends, lovers, our very worlds and realities, we four, and we had little to look forward to except solving a riddle posed by a machine, and yet we kept going as if we were four old friends out for a pleasant backpacking trip.

Albuquerque had been partly wrecked by flood and fire, but not looted; the further we walked into it, the more apparent it was that the people had vanished, and all the damage we saw was merely a case of things not being repaired. We found intact buildings next to burned ones, with useful and valuable stuff lying around; a city prone to flash floods, as its canals and sewers became blocked, had been partially washed away, but there was no plan to the damage. It was just as if everyone had walked away, a few decades ago, and left it to do this on its own.

After about forty minutes of wandering up and down residential streets, looking fruitlessly for a car with the keys in it, Terri said, "I have an idea."

"That puts you ahead of the rest of us," Jesús said.

"It might. I was just thinking, everything here looks like people just vanished, doesn't it? And took nothing of any value with them?"

"Right."

"So would they have taken their car keys?"

"Only if they were in their pockets," Jesús said. "And besides, lots of people keep a spare in the house. This is a great idea, Terri. All we have to do is break into a house with a car we want in the driveway."

Half a block later we found a suitable-looking Jeep with low miles and Telkes batteries, parked under a carport. We went around back to minimize visibility, in case someone hunting for us should be not far behind, and found a dog skeleton still chained to an overhead wire. "Poor thing," Terri said, "don't you just bet he starved or died of thirst?"

That cast kind of a pall over things, but in a minute we had discovered that there was no lock on the tool shed, and a perfectly fine crowbar was in there. With a little effort, the back door opened, and we were inside.

Not a thing had been touched; everything looked as if the owners had just planned to be gone for a few minutes. We scattered through the house to look for the keys; a moment later I heard Jesús swear, and ran to see what he'd found.

There was a desiccated cat on the floor, clearly mummified in the dry indoors, but that wasn't it. Near the cat was a crib, and in the crib there was a scattered tumble of bones. "You see?" Jesús said. "They must have vanished with no time at all. They left their baby behind. And then after a while, the cat was hungry, the baby had probably already starved . . ." He shuddered and crossed himself.

"What did you find?" Paula said, cheerfully, from the hallway.

"Something we'd rather not have seen," I said. "There's a corpse of a baby in here." I looked around further and said, "And two plugged-in VR headsets on the bed. As if the people wearing them just vanished."

Paula came in anyway, and, practical sort that she was, got a towel from the bathroom and made a makeshift shroud for the little pile of bones. "We can bury it in the backyard," she suggested to Jesús.

Shortly Jesús and I were digging a small grave in back, in the hot desert sun, working our way through the hardpan soil. While we were doing that Terri came out to let us know that they had discovered a fairly large supply of soda in the basement, and a much larger supply of wine—"and the car keys," she said. "On the worktable in the garage. We didn't even have to come into the house to find them, if we'd known."

By the time we had buried the little body, and put the birth certificate that we had found in the desk into a freezer bag under a rock on top of the grave, it was getting later in the evening, and we decided to stick around, have a dinner of canned vegetables and wine, and get started in the morning.

"The clue to it all, I think, if I could sort it out," I said, "is the headsets on the bed. VR connect time is incredibly expensive everywhere, even today. And that VR box that they have is stamped with a US government insignia and says it was issued by the Department of the Pursuit of Happiness."

"We've *seen* people appear and disappear, while talking on the phone," Jesús pointed out. "And VR goes through the same quantum compression and decompression as the phone does."

"But usually what people do is trade places between universes," Paula pointed out. "How come no one traded in for these people?"

None of us could think of anything. Nobody wanted to sleep in the master bedroom, where we'd found the body, but there were two kids' beds in other rooms, a guest bed, and the couch. Feeling noble, I took the couch, and fell asleep at once. It made two good nights' sleep in a row, which left me feeling practically human.

The next morning we discovered, in the fridge, an unopened gallon of irradiated milk. Sure enough, it was still perfectly drinkable, though of course it had separated; there were also unopened packets of cereal, also irradiated and therefore not spoiled, though they had managed to become very dry. We all had two or three bowls of cereal and a large glass of milk. "Breakfast of seven-year-olds," I said, "and look at how much energy *they* have."

Just as we were getting up from the table—something about the niceness of the place made us stack our dishes in the non-functioning sink—Paula looked up over my shoulder, stared, and said, "Oh, shit."

"Oh shit what?"

"This place has a silent alarm, people." She pointed at a box on the wall where a little red light pulsed like a tiny, evil heart. "See? It says the alarm was activated." She got up, walked over to it, and looked at the readout. "All the while we've been asleep, the house has been phoning for help. We can hope it's been dialing a number that isn't hooked to anything, but I don't think we can count on it. Grab your stuff and run to the car—we've got to *move*."

We were out the door and the Jeep was rolling, two minutes later. "How can whoever picks up that alarm be sure it isn't an animal opening the door, or the door just falling down after all these years, or something?" Terri asked.

"They can't be, but if they've got the resources to send, what, twenty people or so after us, so far, into this place, they probably can check out all the alarms eventually," Paula said, making her third U-turn in ten minutes. She was jigging around, trying to find a way through a city of fallen bridges and washed-out roads. "We'll just have to do what we can."

Though it took hours to find our way through the ruins of Albuquerque, with so many bridges down, once we found a way back to I-25 it was just a bare hour to reach Santa Fe. We expected to be shot at, at any moment, or the car to die and leave us halfway between, but neither happened. "Here we are," I said, pulling off the highway and heading into town, "and to judge by the number of signs telling us where to find the Department of the Pursuit of Happiness, we'll probably find it pretty soon. That will put an end to one part of the adventure, and start another. Anyone have any profound thoughts?"

"I wish we'd never come," Terri said, tears in her voice, speaking better for me than I had for myself.

The Department of the Pursuit of Happiness turned out to be on the old town square, facing the cathedral; it was a huge building and though forty years or more had gone by, it was conspicuously newer and in better shape than anything around it. It was huge, square, and forbidding, taking up at least one whole city block and reaching at least ten stories into the sky— we had seen it from the highway without knowing what it was.

"The building is built like a bank, a mint, or a prison," Jesús said. "Big thick walls, windows far off the ground and very small, no good hiding places along its sides. There's either something they want to keep in, or something they are trying to keep out."

"Well," I said, as we all got out of the car, "I don't suppose they'll have any *active* measures around to keep us from going in the front door. It does say 'Lobby.' And this seems to be a lucky day—no sign of pursuit yet, and no evidence that anyone knows we're alive. Maybe the silent alarm just wasn't hooked up to anything anymore."

Paula shrugged. "Or maybe Iphwin—the cyberphage, I mean —is acting on our behalf, or maybe the bad guys can't travel to anywhere this far north for reasons known only to the bad guys."

"Or maybe they know where you have to go, and there's no point chasing you all over the field when they can just wait for you there," a familiar voice said.

We turned around and there was Geoffrey Iphwin, perfectly healthy, wearing his old ridiculous bright white ice cream suit with a painfully loud gold and purple tie. He looked at our slack-mouthed stares and laughed aloud. "Now don't look so startled. Remember I was only dead in a few thousand of my existences; I crossed over here, with the assistance of the machine-Iphwin. Now a few thousand of me are talking to a few thousand of you. And here I am. I think the adversary is probably coming after us fast, so we should get moving. As for how I found you, I knew where you were headed and how you were traveling. Now, if everyone is ready, let's go."

We all were ready enough physically; we just didn't have a clue as to how to deal with a person we all remembered as dead. But then, why fret about it? He seemed comfortable enough.

"We are coming up on the end of things," Iphwin said as we crossed the public square. "I think when we get closer there will be some kind of attack. I still don't know what's going on and the knowledge may destroy me, or the program of which I'm an avatar, but I see no way I could avoid trying to learn it now. Suppressed curiosity, I bet, has killed more cats than exercised curiosity."

Jesús said, "If they really want to stop us, why don't they just hit this whole area with hydrogen bombs until it glows? That would be much more likely to work than trying to hunt us like deer."

"I wish I knew that too," Iphwin said. "Maybe it's just against the rules, and the rules are being made up by someone of whom we have no knowledge. More likely they are afraid of damage to the place where we are going, and so they want to get rid of us in the way that spills the least stray energy. Or it could be something none of us has thought of."

"It could often be that, at that," Paula said cheerfully. "Do we have a plan for anything besides 'walk up and pound on the front door'?"

"The front door sounds good to me," Iphwin said. He really did look absolutely splendid in the suit, more so because the four of us were in our dirty, worn road clothes. "Least likely to be misunderstood and most likely to produce a result we'll understand, eh?"

We were halfway up the steps when we heard "Don't move a muscle" in a too-familiar voice.

I glanced back and saw a dozen copies of Billie Beard, all holding shotguns. "We're glad we stopped you here. Cooperate and we won't need to hurt you, don't cooperate and we'll cut you in half with all the shotgun blasts."

Iphwin raised his hands and said, "Looks like it's your game."

Without replying, the dozen Billie Beards marched us over to the blank wall of the building and lined us up against the wall. Iphwin began to laugh, something we'd never heard him do before. "What's funny?" Beard demanded.

We were inside the building, facing the outside wall—in mirror image to the lineup we had been in. Through the soundproofing we heard the muffled sput-thud, sput-thud of guns being fired point-blank into the wall.

"Some of those shots will get through sooner or later," Iphwin said, "or they might remember that the front door is unlocked, so let's get deeper into the building before they find a way in."

We hurried down a corridor beside us; it might have been part of any administrative or technical building of the last 150 years, with CBS block walls painted landlord yellow on the lower part and pale blue on the upper; a black stripe separated the two colors at shoulder height. No doubt some architect somewhere had gotten a pile of money for deciding on that design.

A few minutes of dashing around corners and down corridors, always going up every flight of stairs, past frosted glass windows on doors, and big square wooden doors with numbers on them, was at least enough to get me lost, and to get all the noise of the attack on the wall outside out of earshot. We slowed to a brisk walk, and began to look for any signs or building guides that might give us a clue.

"How did you do that?" I asked Iphwin.

"Practice," he said. "One reason why you didn't get pursued much, till you got up here, was that everyone was chasing me, and one reason they were chasing me was because I was keeping in continuous radio contact with the cyberphage. I learned a very large number of very useful things. Not all of which I can explain or show you in the time we have left. Let's get going—time is precious."

To our surprise, the first sign we saw said "TO THE OFFICE OF THE SECRETARY."

"Pretty strange," I said.

"That a secretary gets a sign?" Terri asked.

I couldn't help smiling. "Bet you didn't review your American history recently. A 'secretary' in the American government was about what a cabinet minister is anywhere else. That's the head honcho's office, not where the typist lives."

"I know *that*," she said, her voice dripping with the kind of contempt that you can only get from an adolescent who has been told something she already knows. "What's weird about there being a sign for the secretary's office, in the building of the department he's the head of?"

"What's weird," I said, "is that normally a cabinet secretary would have an office in Washington, and not in Santa Fe. It's also weird that we found exactly what we were looking for this quickly."

Paula looked at Iphwin, and he shrugged. "Pure chance plays a role, all the time, no matter what," he pointed out. "It isn't really so odd that every so often, even a creature of chance like me can just happen to be lucky."

We found the door a few minutes later. The glass in the window broke readily enough when Jesús and I swung a small microwave oven from a break room like a battering ram. We turned the knob on the inside, walked past a receptionist's desk, and found ourselves standing on thick, plush blue wall-to-wall carpet that seemed still to be brand-new; a faint odor of synthetics still hung in the air, indicating that the room had been closed all that time.

On the desk was an old-fashioned VR headset, and the chair was tipped back; there was a pricey pair of black wing tip shoes, at least forty years old, sitting on the carpet under the desk, next to two balled-up socks.

Iphwin shrugged, checked, and said, "The batteries on these computers were lifetime guaranteed, but I don't think anyone ever thought a computer would have a lifetime like this. Let's see what happens if we turn it on."

Nothing did. We started to paw through the file cabinets.

"Here's a specification," Paula said. "For a national happiness policy."

We sat down and pored over it, everyone looking closely. "At least in neurology, this world was ahead of the ones I grew up in," I said. "Look at this. They have a really, really elaborate spec on the human brain. When they say they're out to maximize human happiness, they are really not kidding. They know just what it is, it's a brain state, and this is the program that's going to make sure that while people are plugged into VR, their happiness gets maximized."

"Shit," Jesús said, "they must have made VR the most addictive drug in history—in fact, technically speaking, the most addictive drug possible. No wonder they all disappeared. They must have starved to death—"

"But we never found a body or a skeleton," Paula pointed out. "Except for that one child who was too young to have a headset on."

"What's the 'happiness algorithm' define happiness as?" Iphwin asked quietly.

"I don't read brain science much," I said.

He grabbed it, looked at it, and appeared to think deeply for a moment. "Oh, dear," he said. "Oh, dear, oh, dear, oh, dear."

"How long does it take to do things in the cottage?" I asked.

"In here, what it looks like," Jeff the mailman said. "Out there, about a microsecond per day. But it's different this time; I don't have to create a job for you, so I don't have to ride back and forth to town every day."

"Does everybody have a satisfactory breakfast?" I asked, because I had plenty left on the stove. I wasn't used to cooking for five, and had overshot somewhat.

"Are you this good a cook in the real world?" Terri asked. "Because if you are, I nominate you for cook, forever."

"Hunger's the best sauce," I said, "and in this scenario, we're all hungry. Dawn fishing will do that. How's yours, Jesús?"

I took the grunt and the vigorous nodding of his head as approval.

"Anyway, Jeff, or Iphwin, or whichever you'd rather be while we're here," I said, "back in the real world, you were saying 'Oh, dear,' over and over. Or I guess your embodied version was. He must have called you up, and plugged us all into this interface. Are all those Billie Beards on their way to the office where our physical bodies are?"

"They sure are. I would estimate they will reach the office in two or three minutes. But with a million-to-one time ratio, we could stay here and take a long vacation for a few centuries, without pushing our luck, eh? Does anyone need time to relax before we get down to business?"

It was universally agreed that we didn't, but it also seemed to be agreed that I should make up seconds for everyone.

"Well, then," Iphwin said, "here's what happened to America—or rather to all the Americans who were in America, in so many timelines. Around the early 2000s—anywhere from 1994 to 2022, depending on exactly which event sequence you were in—the Americans found the secret of happiness. Very possibly because they looked for it harder than anyone else ever did. And they came up with a unique plan: the government would pay for a universal wideband VR system to deliver happiness to everyone. Basically that involved a feedback loop; the headset measured how high the happiness indicators were in your brain, and an artificial intelligence in the system then decided whether your VR illusion needed to change to increase your happiness. It had to be a fairly smart artificial intelligence, you see, because there are many kinds of pleasurable pain (like seeing a tragedy or being melancholy about a lost love), and many ways in which delaying a pleasure enhances it, and pleasures about which people feel so guilty that they become miserable if they indulge in them.

"Now the artificial intelligences not only had tremendous leeway to do things, because they couldn't anticipate what situations might come up, but they also had all sorts of ability to self-improve. It didn't take long for them to develop the trick of simulating the personality of the person wearing the headset, and then 'advance shopping' the things that could happen in VR, to find out which one the person would like best. Thus they could keep moving the person from one pleasure to another, without having to ever experience a disjunction between what they thought the person would like, and what he did like.

"But of course VR comes through a quantum compression server, so part of the experience people were going to get was going to be the new world that they were quantum-shuffled to. The artificial intelligences quickly recognized that, too, and began to do the same thing that I do when I am trying to get near a specific worldline, or into a family of event sequences. They'd shuffle the person's position frequently, in hopes of making them drop out somewhere better, and then they'd sample the new reality into which the person would emerge, to make sure it was better for the person than the one from which the person had come.

"Well, an essential component of pleasure is variety. And real pleasures are more pleasant than virtual pleasures, which is why sex hasn't disappeared despite the invention of VR pornography. So the artificial intelligences quickly began to focus on giving people a pleasurable variety of real experiences.

"Pretty soon they realized that the real way to maximize somebody's happiness was to break the message into smaller and smaller packets, so that the person thrashed around between a lot of worlds, and then solve the huge optimization problem created by the fact that parts of him were in thousands of different worlds which had thousands of different definitions, and many different versions of him would be dropping into many different worlds.

"The artificial intelligences were doing, on a much grander scale, what I did to put the team of you together—they were shoving people into new worlds, checking the world against the person's tastes and experiences, and either deciding to stay or bump again. Every time they bumped someone, they triggered a chain of bumps that put thousands of other versions of that person into motion, but that was okay, because people like variety, and very often change alone makes them happy. Everyone kept swapping places, getting closer and closer to the point where when they took off the headsets, they would drop into worlds perfect for them.

"In a matter of a few seconds, the artificial intelligences had quantum-shuffled nearly everyone who was hooked up to the VR systems, millions or billions of times—so often and so far that most of Americans were in event sequences that were only very distantly related to this one. The effect amplified, because once you bump most of the people out of a world, it becomes a much tougher world to be happy in—a world where ninety percent of your neighbors and friends have vanished isn't fun for most people—which meant that all the others had to be bumped too, and the people who popped in to take their place, and the ones who popped in to take *their* place, and so forth and so on.

The artificial intelligences emptied out billions or trillions of worlds, as everyone migrated in the direction of greater happiness—and presumably they filled up billions or trillions of worlds that are somewhere very far away. Basically, everyone's gone to their own personal heaven. And since the happiness algorithm was being kept as an American secret, only the American part of the net had it . . ."

"And only America went away," I said.

I poured fresh coffee for everyone, and then said, "Well, your mystery is solved, Iphwin. I suppose we could all go chase after them. Or you could take the happiness algorithm from this document, implement it over the whole world, and send everybody to heaven. Or you could be a nice guy and help us escape from Beard and her people, and then just let us go."

"How far away is heaven?" Paula asked, with a frightened expression, as if she saw someone with a gun.

"What?" Jesús asked. "Why are you—"

Paula set down her coffee mug and walked over to the window to stare out. "Iphwin, whatever you do with us when we're all done, please make sure I have access to this place. It's good for the soul." She stared for a long time and said, "You know, I can't think of a single reason why this wouldn't be the case, and I sure hope one of you will think of it.

"Anybody ever have a class in economics, where they talk about transitivity? Like if you like apples better than bananas, and bananas better than oranges, you're supposed to like apples better than oranges? And you know how it makes a total mess of things if people then like oranges better than apples anyway, because then you could get someone to never eat the fruit, but just keep trading and trading and trading—"

"Oh, dear, again," Iphwin said. "You're right."

Terri and I looked at each other, then at Jesús, and finally, speaking for all of us, Terri said, "Why did it just get incomprehensible in here?"

"Well," Iphwin said, "which do *you* like better, apples, bananas, or oranges?"

"Apples, I guess," I said, "and then bananas, kind of in that order."

"Now, I give you the choice, and you take the apple and eat it. I give you the choice over and over, and you keep eating apples. So you settle down, once and for all, on just eating apples."

"Of course not," I said. "Iphwin, you're thinking like a machine again. Pretty soon I'd stop liking apples so much, and want some variety. And then . . . oh, god, I see it now. Ever hear about the grass always being greener on the other side of the fence?" I said to Terri.

"Yeah."

"Well, if you were a sheep, and the whole round world were made up of fences and pastures, and your priority were always trying to get somewhere greener—you'd never eat any grass. You'd spend all your time jumping fences, because every time you jumped one, you'd see another, greener pasture, just beyond the next fence. You might get very far away, but you'd just jump and jump and jump, always improving but never finding a pasture where you could stop—even if you ended up back home, because maybe the desire to jump is just the desire for yet another change. Now, changing your mind and reshuffling into another world millions of times per second, for minute after minute, day after day, decade after decade, is not something a person would do—"

"But it's something a machine would do. And it's what the artificial intelligences did," Iphwin finished. "The Americans are not all in heaven, as I'd thought. Paula's right. The Americans are all still out there—way, way, way out there—as far as you can go in five dimensions of possibility, changing between awesome numbers of event sequences—and always having one more change to do. Chasing through time, forever. Space, time, and possibility are big enough so that they're never coming back, but it's finite—so they're going to curve on and on, never coming back *and* never getting any further away. The only Americans who escaped that fate—"

"Were the ones outside the country," I said. "And the only people who were going to come looking for America would be expat Americans, which is how all the worlds in which America had a lot of expatriates—the ones where it was conquered and the ones where repressive regimes came to power—all became so closely linked. And—Iphwin, it's horrible, they're only in each world for a microsecond or so, so they aren't experiencing anything—"

"They're experiencing whatever you experience when you are nanoseconds away from being perfectly happy—though not quite so perfectly as they will be about to be a few hundred nanoseconds after that," Iphwin said, sadly. "Well, now I have a common interest with Billie Beard, at last. We need to suppress that algorithm, or there will be no more people, and hence no one for us to do things for. I will need to talk to her.

"However, when she's trying to break down the door with a bunch of her well-armed avatars, it is really not the time for a reasonable conversation. Which reminds me, detection instruments I've found and activated within the building tell me that she's now walking up the corridor to the office where your physical selves are, which means the next question is how best to get you out of there. If everyone is done with breakfast, let's go for a walk on the beach."

Did you ever start out to learn a game that made no sense, until one moment you suddenly found that you were just playing it, and it all worked? That was my experience of learning to cross event sequences and to move physically without needing trans-

portation. It's more a way of looking at the world, and just re-
laxing and falling through to another world, than anything else.
Iphwin had a lengthy explanation about quantum processes inside the cells of the brain, and about how this might account for
some mysterious disappearances throughout history, but this had
no more to do with learning the trick than studying the physics
of wheels or the history of paving does with learning to ride a
bicycle. We got so we could do it, and then we got good at it.
We all played with it for several days there in the beach cottage
and on the land around it, retiring every evening to the cottage
on the beach, until one day the sun came out, and we all shook
hands, and were back in the office, standing around the secretary's desk.

We heard the clatter of a dozen pairs of high heels in the
hallway; the Billies were on the floor and looking for us. "My
office, north of Surabaya, a week from now," Iphwin said.

There was a thunder of feet outside, and all five of us just
went, moving through all of the myriad worldlines until we
found something where Beard wasn't coming, then walking out
the door, taking the Jeep—each of us individually, since the Jeep
was there in so many worlds—and driving back down to Mexico.
I had a couple of interesting conversations at the frontier, but
there was no rule against driving in from that side, and my passport, of course, didn't show that I had been anywhere since Torreón. Once I was far enough south, I got a decent hotel room, a
long night's sleep, and a ticket for Surabaya, which in this timeline was inexplicably called by some long Russian name.

A week later, I caught Mac the limo back to the Big Sapphire,
collected Fluffy the cat and a few possessions, and went in for
our meeting with Iphwin.

"Really," he said, "since you're always leaving selves behind
as you do this—it's an unpleasant thought but undoubtedly all
of us got some self or other killed back in Santa Fe—from here

on out you can live by moving into worlds where you're rich, as needed, and you can more or less pursue any happiness you care to. I just thought we might all want to agree as to how to meet up at the virtual reality cottage; I had a feeling we might want to see each other."

Terri wasn't planning on returning to her parents; what teenager, given infinite money and choice, would? "It's a big lots of worlds out there," she said, "and I'm going to see plenty of it. Just now I'm a little depressed, but I figure there's infinite adventure out there, or at least finite adventure so big I'll never get done."

Jesús nodded. "I understand the urge. I think I will take a little walk through a few million worlds, and see if there are places where I can do some good."

Paula and I decided to make a vacation of it, down in Oz, since we had found out we were so compatible in the cottage. But after a couple of weeks of her perpetually wanting to go out and surf, or to the pistol range, or that sort of thing—and my wanting to sit on the beach and read—we understood it wasn't going to work out. She left a very nice note saying she was off to stir up trouble in a few billion worlds, and not to leave the light on for her.

Me, I zipped through a billion worlds or so, taking about a year, till I found an event sequence where Helen had broken her arm the day before my leaving for the job interview, turned up in her hospital room with some ridiculous excuse, multiple armloads of roses, and the much-harder-to-explain Fluffy. It took a lot of explaining and some outright tale-telling, but Helen seems to be no longer suspicious, not even about my hypothetical rich uncle who left us the large fortune with which we were to raise kids in a big house in Auckland. We've got a Paula and a Terri, but an American girl wasn't about to have a son named Jesús, so

I had to settle for Joshua. Jesús says he doesn't mind much. Iphwin doesn't want any kids named after him.

It's been years since I faced or felt real fear. In an abstract way it's not a bad thing to know that I can handle fear, pain, or privation if I have to, but then I can endure headaches, too, if I have to. Now and then I take a second or even two off, and go to the cottage for a while, where I meet some of the others; the embodied Iphwin is there often, as he's never really gotten used to a fully real world.

Mostly I am content.

What I hear of the others is what you might expect; Jesús, Paula, Terri, they're all out winning glory and wandering across the worlds, flying Dutchmen on a quantum sea. I shall probably always prefer, like Iphwin, to stand on the shore and wave.

Now and then, late at night, I go to the cottage, and Iphwin and I spend a few days running on the beach together, and drinking wine, and talking. Then one of the three adventurers will drop in, and I will sit up all night while they talk of their adventures. I know that I enjoy listening to the stories more than I would ever enjoy the adventures. And knowing that, I am very happy.